THE
WRIT 212

B. Riddick

VMH Publishing
Atlanta

Copyright © 2019 by Brittany Riddick

VMH Publishing
3355 Lenox Rd.NE Ste 750 Atlanta, GA 30326
www.vmhpublishing.com

All rights reserved.

This book may not be reproduced in whole or in part, in any form or by means, electronic or mechanical, including photocopying, recording, or by any information storage and retrieval system now known or hereafter invented, without permission from the publisher.

Bulk Ordering Information:

Quantity sales. Special discounts are available on quantity purchases by corporations, associations, and others. For details, contact the publisher at the address above or via email at: info@vmhpublishing.com

Book Cover Design: VMH Publishing
Cover Image: Shutterstock
Interior Layout: VMH Publishing
Editor: Sara Prescott

Library of Congress Control Number: 2020900071
Hardback ISBN: 978-1-947928-34-3
Paperback ISBN: 978-1-947928-35-0

Made in United States of America

10 9 8 7 6 5 4 3 2 1

The more knowledge, the more power; but the knowledge and power never stopped. The YSW processed everything, and it began to mean nothing.

THE
WRIT 212

Contents

Chapter

1.	Connected	9
2.	Vision of the End	13
3.	Solomon's Flashback: EAD	19
4.	The End of the Second World	33
5.	Waking in the New Age	35
6.	Foreshadowing - Warnings from the Writ	57
7.	Community Begins	59
8.	Sophos Warns of the Ambers	65
9.	Building Community - Potentiam Libertas	69
10.	Taming the Beasts	77
11.	Vision	83
12.	Governess Writes	93
13.	Guidance	97
14.	Flaky Feelings	105
15.	The Test	115
16.	Governess' Vision	125
17.	All Mixed Up	129
18.	Torn	139
19.	Led Astray	143
20.	The News Goes Viral	149
21.	Growing Up as Theiler	159
22.	Athirst Watches the Union	163
23.	The Butterfly	171
24.	The Butterflies Unite	195
25.	A New Era Begins	201
26.	A Mark in Time	215
27.	New Age - The Second Era	217
28.	Ugo and Cadmael	221
29.	New Knowledge	225
30.	Ugo's Test	229
31.	Unnatural	233
32.	Sparring	237
33.	The Storm	243
34.	Red Rain	249
35.	The Word Spreads	255
36.	Jabari's Walk	261
37.	Serpent's Tongue	265

38.	The River	269
39.	Like a Wildfire	273
40.	The Amber Glow	293
41.	Stop	297
42.	One Year of Peace (Athirst and Cearney)	301
43.	One Year of Peace (Ugo)	315
44.	Stultus Displays Her Light	323
45.	Colors	329
46.	Exodus	333
47.	The Feast of New Freedom	337
48.	The Signs	341
49.	The Third Sign	349
50.	The Battle Begins	357

1.
Connected

By the time the world was near its end, the majority of the Youth of the Second World (YSW) who could afford to implant digital information into their cranium, did. It was their third eye. The third eye became a symbol of fashion for the YSW. It was created with Lithorium technology, which allowed the device to recharge itself off the natural energy emitted from the human body. With the human body being its energy source, there was no longer a disconnect from information because there was no need to put the device down in order to recharge it. Lithorium was a relatively new element discovered in the 2100's. The discovery of the element was a breakthrough in science because information technology required so much energy. Lithorium created a mutualistic symbiotic relationship. The device fed off human energy and, in exchange, humans received all the information they could ever ask for.

The first design of such a device was hidden behind the ear because engineers thought most people would want it to be discreet, but the YSW were vain. They embellished them with diamonds, gold, and silver so the device would be more noticeable. When the developers saw this, the second design placed the device in the center of their foreheads and came adorned with jewels that sparkled and shined. This status symbol separated the haves from the have-nots because only the wealthiest people could afford to have their device permanently attached to them. Others who couldn't afford it, did unthinkable things to acquire the Third Eye. The YSW wore their cranium centerpiece with pride and mocked those who could not afford such luxuries.

Not having a third eye did not mean that others were not connected. Eighty-five percent of the world's population had the implanted piece on their forehead and ten percent carried a handheld or tangible device. Most were in the form of a timepiece that was strapped to the wrist. There were only a few who were too poor or had no interest in the technology. These people were outcasts of society and mocked for not being enlightened; many of the Elders found themselves in this position.

To the YSW, the humming and low murmur of constant information was intoxicating. It all seemed innocent at first, nothing more than wanting to be in the know. They needed to know what their friends and family were doing, and they wanted to know what was happening all around the world. To them, knowledge was power. The more knowledge, the more power; but the knowledge and power never stopped. The YSW processed everything and it began to mean nothing. All news, no matter how significant, was eventually dismissed as daily chatter and slowly, people became numb to those things that were once compelling and momentous.

For those who had implanted the chip, they could move to the next news story or get new information by blinking. Others who held onto devices would swipe away the news of impending doom as if they were swatting at a fly. Unnatural amounts of information were always there.

History books wrote of the initial cell phone that was created in 1973, but no one realized that the word 'cell' in 'cellphone' meant that eventually information would take over every cell in the human body. So, by the 2100s, humans had become addicted to devices since information had been running through their cells for hundreds of years.

Once people attached themselves to their devices, they were left with no choice but to gorge on every morsel of news or knowledge until they were full of everything; however, it all meant nothing.

Everyone and everything had a voice. Every platform, every feeling, and every agenda was important; every cause was worth fighting for to the YSW and yet, as things were happening, those watching from the outside became indifferent. It was a paradox of emotions. They viciously fought or protested no matter the issue's relevance. Everyone had answers, but no one knew the answer. Discord and harmony were one and the same. The lines were so blurred, but to the YSW it seemed so clear, for they had the knowledge of good and evil implanted and attached to them at all times. The YSW were all so well-educated and yet so stupid. They were all searching for answers, but so far removed from the original truth -- the Writ.

For they thought they were awake and found themselves wise in their own sight, but they were blind (Writ 212:29).

2.
Vision of the End

Solomon woke in the middle of the night with beads of sweat on his forehead. He had another dream, the final dream. Solomon went to his bathroom sink, splashed water on his face, and wiped the water off with a white cloth, which had a blue embroidered letter "K". Kristen died of cancer about four years ago, but something about seeing that "K" made things feel normal. He stood still and examined the lines in his face. *Sheesh, I am getting old*, Solomon thought to himself. "Would you like for me to add a filter? It will make you look 20 years younger," The voice from the mirror asked before scrolling through a series of filters that erased Solomon's age right before his eyes. *Stupid piece of crap*. Solomon dared not say the words aloud. He tried to find ways to override the feature or disconnect it somehow, but it seemed impossible. Every feature of his apartment had a question, an option, or a voice since the upgrade to his building about nine years ago.

It felt unfair that everything else could have a voice but him. His room was lit by the digital advertisements that continually scrolled on the billboards directly outside his window. Solomon had grown used to the constant dull hue that filled his space even when the lights were off. A small, piercing blue light from a drone hovering outside his window caught his eye. It was foreign; a new image cast against a familiar background. He had not gotten used to the intrusive surveillance. He knew Big Brother was watching, but this was more than he imagined. Solomon remembered reading George Orwell's 1984 in school. It was required reading for him when he was in the 10th grade. His teacher assigned him and his classmates the task of comparing their current society to a text that was written nearly 200 years ago. He thought Orwell was brilliant in his description of a totalitarian world constantly being watched by Big Brother. He just didn't think all of this might become real someday. No one would have ever thought that the Golden Rule Department (GRD) would begin arrests immediately after the silence ban law was put into action, or that seemingly innocent activities would be so closely monitored.

Solomon was frustrated and wished he could just hang large black blankets over the windows. Covenants prevented him from altering the window coverings. As he closed the blinds, the blue light of the drone zoomed off to peak into the window of some other unsuspecting home. Solomon knew he was safe because he was alone. He had no one and nothing left. His apartment had been empty for years. Just a few pictures on the walls of a family he once knew. He feared for the other families who wanted to communicate with each other, if families still communicated with each other nowadays. Maybe the silence ban would have the reverse effect? Solomon thought. Maybe that was the point, to get everyone to remember the days before devices took over and people actually had genuine conversations and real relationships. Maybe not.

Solomon remembered when the conflict between him and the YSW changed from quiet tension to full outrage. It all happened shortly after his wife Kristen's passing. She died unnecessarily. She died because she wanted to eat healthy, but their family could not afford to buy natural products anymore. Natural products were extremely rare and were so expensive that only the wealthiest YSW could afford them. Kristen was one of the few whose body could not properly digest engineered foods. And unfortunately, the cancer was aggressive and progressed at a rapid rate. It was only a few months between her diagnosis and her death. Solomon's two sons Knox and Kyle were upset at their mother's diagnosis, but Karina, his daughter was devastated. It was Solomon's idea to purchase a gaming system. Kristen was adamant about not allowing those "things" in her house, but when she got sick, Solomon thought, *What harm could it cause?*

The games did exactly what Solomon wanted them to do, which was to provide his children with a distraction from the sadness that consumed them.

The day of the funeral, Solomon remembered walking through his apartment, trying his best to put a smile on for the family members and coworkers that came to visit. He walked into his children's room to see them entranced by the world of virtual reality.

"I think you should come into the living room and speak to your family. They've come a long way to support us right now."

"Dang, hold on Dad! We're flying right now, about to save the prisoners," Knox replied.

"Turn it off now!" Solomon said sternly.

Kyle turned off the virtual reality simulator and walked out of the room. Karina rolled her eyes and brushed past her father as she walked out the door. Later that evening, Karina came to him and gave him some news that he would never forget.

"Dad, I'll be going off to school soon. I know that you and mom wanted to protect me. You wanted to keep me from being part of the YSW because you wanted me to get into school without their support. But let's face it, you can't afford to send me off to school on your own, and the YSW have tons of scholarships that I qualify for. They have the best programs with the best technology and, if I get in with them, I'm literally guaranteed a job working for the DEAD company," Karina told her father.

"Is this what you really want to do? Do you see what's going on with the YSW? What I have to put up with? They don't have a heart for people anymore. Most of them are depressed, committing suicide, and causing the world to descend into turmoil. Is this what you want?" Solomon was furious.

"No! What I want is to be free from this, dad. What is this? I have done everything that you and mom wanted me to do in hopes that my efforts to be 'noble' would pay off, but now that mom is gone and you're stuck with her hospital bills, you can't even afford to send me off to school. And I don't want to be stuck wallowing in misery when I can move forward and create my own future."

Solomon knew she was right, in a way. And he didn't want his daughter to feel trapped or obligated to stay just for him. He didn't want her to remain sad. "Well, if that's what you want, go ahead; do whatever it is that you want to do. But just remember...sometimes it's better to stand alone and live with dignity than to have everything and lose yourself."

"Okay, whatever," Karina responded, rolling her eyes. She headed back to her room.

Solomon knew after that day that there was no convincing her. She was now part of the YSW.

Shortly after, Solomon was looking through his mail. Nearly everyone he knew received digital mail; he was the only one in his building that still received paper mail. In his stack was a check from the Department of Artificial Vegetation. He knew that the president of the department was a young 30-something who was part of the YSW. Settlement checks were sent to families who lost a loved one, like Solomon. He held the envelope in his hands and hoped that it would amount to what he needed to help Karina pay for school. Maybe he could get her back. So, when he opened the envelope and saw the check for $130.00, Solomon was pissed. *That was what she was worth to them? One-hundred thirty dollars?*

The next envelope he opened did not have a return address or stamp. Someone must have slipped it in his mailbox. The words inside weren't typed out. It was a handwritten message that said:

We know your loss. You are not alone. Location: 444 5th Ave. Date: 2/12 Time: 7:00 PM. Use the code, 'Do you have a newspaper?' We hope to see you soon.

Sincerely,
EAD

EAD, Solomon thought, *what or who is the EAD?* He was curious and decided he would take a chance and go visit. He had nothing to lose.

He remembered how uncomfortable it was the first time he met the members of the Elders Against Devices (EAD), and how he had to force himself to go to the next meeting. But it didn't take long for meetings in that grungy, tucked-away room with people who understood how he felt to become the highlight of his week.

Solomon valued the relationships that he was building with the members of the EAD. They all shared their stories, and helped each other like they were family. He learned that a woman named Quantas had lost her husband in the same way that he lost his wife. Solomon remembered how he felt with everyone in the group, and thought it was safe for him to share his prediction about the silence ban.

3.
Solomon's Flashback: EAD

The EAD used an old convenience store as a cover for meeting locations. Quantas ran the place. She was an ornery woman who complained about everything. She complained so much that it became comical to the other members. They tried to push her buttons as often as they could in order to get a rise out of her.

It was no surprise to Solomon that when he first had the dream about the passing of the silence ban, no one believed him. He told the EAD about a new group of activists that were making headway.

"They're called the 'peacemakers.' They're a small subset of the YSW. But they're gaining in popularity," Solomon explained to the group. This was the first dream that Solomon shared with others. Up to this point, he had many other dreams, but he kept them to himself. He thought that if he could ignore them, they would go away, but he had no such luck. Sharing the dream of the silence ban would give him credibility so people would believe him when all of the other things started happening.

"Another activist group? I'm sure they won't be any different than any of the other groups we have seen come and go in the past," said Mediana. Mediana was one of the women who became part of the EAD a few months ago. She was a large woman with a hearty laugh. Solomon thought she was unattractive, but her cooking made up for what she lacked in physical appearance.

"This one is actually going to make an impact and we need to be prepared because it will affect us, our relationships, and our ability to speak to one another," Solomon warned.

"How is this going to be any different from any of the other crap going on in the world right now? It's all going to hell anyway," Quantas grumped.

Solomon shared the details of his vision to the EAD. He explained that this group of peacemakers was writing a bill that would become federal law within the next few months. People would not be able to talk for 18 hours of the day. Talking "time zones" would allow for brief periods of conversation but might be eliminated if individuals abused their talking privilege.

"You're already seeing evidence of the peacemakers now. When you walk the streets this afternoon, look around. The signs are everywhere -- 'If you can't say anything nice, don't speak at all.' We all know that social media, propaganda, and news media is affecting people like never before. Pay attention to what's going on around you. We don't have long," Solomon said worriedly.

"Well, I don't know about you, but this may actually be a platform that I can stand behind. I would love to not hear any of you speak again. Ha!" Quantas made herself laugh.

"I know things are bad right now, but do you seriously think the YSW would implement a silence ban? They love to hear themselves talk too much," Mediana pointed out.

"I know they will, and I really think we need to do something about it," Solomon pleaded.

"What? You want us --" Quantas said as she pointed to the members of the EAD, "-- to help you go up against the YSW because you had a dream that some Golden Rule Society will have enough power to force us all to stop speaking?" Quantas mocked. "Well, count me out! I have enough to do around here than create more tension with one of the many impassioned groups of the YSW."

Soon after Solomon shared his dream the law was put into effect. This premonition was followed by many others Solomon had in his sleep. And time after time, each one came true. Those that used to dismiss his dreams as crazy soon began to listen to him.

"So, what do you want to do about it?" Quantas asked one day. She would never admit that he was right, but her decision to help was gratifying enough.

"I think we should organize a protest," Solomon responded.

"Everything is so terrible. So which issue are we protesting, exactly?" Quantas inquired mockingly.

"Let's just start with one issue at a time. Let's get our voice back," Solomon responded.

"I wouldn't mind doing that. I participated in a few of those in my younger days," Mediana chimed in. "Maybe we should wait until our quiet hours and march down 5th Street."

"Yes, waiting until quiet hours is perfect." Solomon was elated.

Solomon remembered how they all stayed up late plotting their protest. That triumphant feeling was quickly lost when they got in trouble with authorities, who tazed and locked them in jail for going against the peacemakers of the YSW.

Solomon stayed in jail for ten days since he admitted that it was all his idea. Mediana and Quantas only served five, but they were all placed on monitoring surveillance for three months. It explained why that tiny blue light seemed to appear in Solomon's window so often.

Solomon's flashbacks were interrupted by the sound of a drop of water, which seemed to erupt at the bottom of a basin, crashing through the silence. His mind returned to the reason why he woke up, and his dream of the end. He pushed ear buds in his ears before putting on the rest of his clothes. He grabbed his brown trench coat and ascot cap before heading to his door. He clicked through the two-deadbolt locks and removed the chain from the door. As Solomon stepped out, he looked down the long hallway. He couldn't figure out why he felt the need to make sure the halls were clear. Not seeing anyone gave him some sense of privacy, despite there being cameras everywhere. He stepped out of his apartment lobby and into the darkness of the early morning.

As soon as he hit the streets, the noise began. The sound of advertisements filled the air. Even the sidewalks spoke to him. This was another brilliant idea to get people to purchase items or get them hooked on the next device. The concrete sidewalks were replaced a few years ago. Now, digital screens covered the ground. They could connect to your personal device to determine what you had been looking at most recently. Then the screens on the sidewalk would direct you to the store or street corner that could satisfy your desires or needs. If they could not connect with your personal device, the sidewalk would make suggestions for you based on your physical appearance. Solomon learned to hide as much as he could. As he began walking, the electronic sidewalk called Solomon by name. "Solomon, how can we serve you today? It looks like you will need a coat soon. May we suggest Vintage Coats on Twelfth Avenue?" the sidewalk said. As it made the suggestion, the sidewalk began to light the path to Vintage Coats with a series of bright orange, illuminated arrows. Solomon headed in the opposite direction.

"I am sorry Solomon, did we not satisfy your desires?" the sidewalk asked.

Solomon faintly heard the sidewalk's feminine voice through his earbuds. He jammed them deeper into his ear canal to block the sound, put his head down, and kept walking. The upper class YSW were boisterously roaming the streets. It appeared as if they were coming from a night of partying. They were allowed to talk. They were all wealthy enough to afford the fee associated with extending their speaking hours. Solomon found it ironic that the group of individuals, who caused the most harm with their words, were able to live above the law. He worked to dismiss his frustration with the YSW before he grew too angry.

He made it to the convenience store and took his ear buds out. He whispered to Quantas, "Do you have a newspaper?"

"I still think that is the stupidest password to use. If anyone were to come into this dump, they would know exactly what was going on. No one reads newspapers anymore. No one reads anything anymore unless it's on a device," Quantas responded in a poor attempt to whisper back.

"Just open the door. No one wants to hear you go on and on," Solomon responded. He looked around to see any sign of the blue light from a drone.

"You have nothing to worry about. No one comes around here. Besides, you have 15 minutes before speaking hours begin. I think you'll be just fine."

Quantas opened the door and Solomon went into the room labeled "Cleaning Supplies." He walked down the stairs to the lower level of the store. It smelled damp and musty. A leaky pipe above made a constant dripping sound. The smell and the sound added to the disheveled ambiance of the EAD's makeshift meeting location.

"I swear this has to be the only place that still has books." Solomon lifted a book labeled The Writ and took in a deep whiff. He loved the smell of leather. He allowed his fingers to thumb through its pages. Solomon took the book with him and sat at a high-top table near the kitchen. Mediana was in there trying to make a snack from the minimal ingredients in the cabinets. Several other members were there, some playing chess, others reading -- typical activities for the older members of the group.

One of the newest members was named Deiderick. He was also sitting at the table. Solomon always had his reservations about Deiderick because he felt that Deiderick dabbled in two worlds. Deiderick was not like the rest of the EAD. The common thread of the EAD members was they all had a story of suffering or loss due to devices. Deiderick was extremely well-off. Solomon knew him as the president of DEAD (Device Engineering &

Advancement Design), which was the largest device design and engineering company of the 22nd century. Deiderick had a seemingly supportive wife and extremely beautiful, successful, intelligent children who were being groomed to take over Deiderick's billion-dollar company. And yet, for some reason, Deiderick was here sitting with the rest of the EAD. Solomon didn't trust him and he wasn't the only one who found Deiderick's presence in the group strange. All of the members found themselves guarded when Deiderick was around. They wondered how a man who was in control of design plans for most of the world's technology swore off personal use of devices. Deiderick had only been a member for about a month and in that month, no one really spoke to him; Deiderick rarely spoke to anyone unless it was a greeting.

After Solomon's dream last night, he realized it was time to introduce himself.

"So, are you working on a new project?" Solomon pulled up a wooden stool to the table where Deiderick was sitting.

"We are. We are indeed." A long pause filled the air before Deiderick began speaking again. "You understand that you are the first person to ever speak to me in this place. I was beginning to feel like no one wanted me here."

"Well, I can't lie, I am a little confused as to why someone like you would want to be here with the rest of the commoners," Solomon chuckled looking around.

"Hey, speak for yourself," Quantas interjected. She was sitting near the top of the stairs so she could quickly go back to the convenience store if someone were to come by.

"Well you know that he's not like the rest of us. So, compared to him, we are commoners," Solomon said, hoping to get an answer from Deiderick this time.

"To be honest, this place reminds me so much of what the world was like before devices took over," Deiderick explained.

Solomon was astonished. "I can't believe you would feel that way. You are one of the reasons why we're in the position we are now." He felt good being able to get that off his chest. He was even more shocked when it appeared that Deiderick did not take offense.

"You have no idea how this all works. It is not that simple. I am one man on a board of 12 others who also make decisions. My wife and my children are on that board and constantly vote against me. It feels like I don't have a voice anymore. The technology is all moving so fast that I can't even keep up with everything anymore." Deiderick placed his head in his hands and then continued, "This new project. I just ...I just don't ...I can't support it, but I don't know what to do."

When Solomon heard this, he knew exactly what project he was talking about and all the images of his dream began to make sense. Solomon started whispering so that the others could not hear.

"This latest project -- does it have anything to do with Emojis?"

"How did you know?" Deiderick asked.

"Remember when I told everyone here about the silence ban? I have these dreams. They're all coming true."

"Yes, the latest project is going to be the biggest thing to ever be released in the twenty-second century. But what did your dream show you?" Deiderick's expression was a mix of curiosity and concern.

"Well, your company has already begun to advertise the release of the most authentic Emoji to ever exist, but the YSW don't know just how real it will become. The design your company created will essentially provide the actual feeling behind the Emoji icon. So, for example, if you send the Emoji blowing a kiss, or the heart Emoji, the device will release a feeling of love to someone. Or, if you send a sad face, then the person receiving it will feel sadness. But how do you plan to do this? I can't quite figure out how it all works exactly."

"Wow, you're pretty good. Your dream is extremely accurate." Deiderick was impressed. He looked around before continuing. "I don't know if you quite understand the level at which everyone is connected to their device," Deiderick responded in a very low tone, "but for many it's like their life line. Nearly eighty-five percent of the world's population has a device connected to their cranium. We literally control people's minds."

"I can't imagine having that much control," Solomon said.

"The pressure is unbelievable, and I don't know if I want any of it anymore. This new project, the Emojis... it scares me," Deiderick said.

"What makes this one so different?"

"The Emoji project involves attaching different chemical hormones to the Emojis' pictures. For example, serotonin and dopamine, the hormones associated with being happy or feeling joy, are embedded into the Emojis with hearts and smiles. The hormone is released to the receiver of the icon when they open their message. Pheromones, the hormones responsible for a feeling of euphoria, are released when someone receives an Emoji with some sort of sexual connotation. And because everyone has these devices connected to their brain, we can literally send the hormone directly to the limbic system, the part of the brain that controls emotions. The scary thing is that not only can we send chemicals to the brain, but we have the ability to remove chemicals from the brain as well. If a person receives an Emoji that is unhappy, instead of providing serotonin to the brain, we are actually physically removing a small bit of it. At first, the project seemed amazing, but now I'm fearful. This was never how any of this was supposed to happen."

"I'm pretty sure that you're not supposed to give me this much detail. So why are you telling me all of this?" Solomon asked.

"I don't know ...I ...I guess I needed to feel heard. It is ridiculous to be the head of a company and have no one listen to me. My wife, my children -- they know that this will make billions of dollars, so they couldn't care less what I think. It doesn't seem to matter that we've crossed the line. I thought if I came here, people would listen to me. I thought I would find someone who feels the same way I do, but no one has really spoken to me until today." Deiderick sighed.

"The dream I had tells me that your project will ultimately lead to the end of the world."

"How?"

"Let me ask this first -- are you all planning a worldwide release of this phenomenon in a few months?"

"That's what we are discussing now."

"And you have no idea what something like this would do on a global level?"

"I can only imagine," Deiderick responded with angst. "I have got to stop it from getting out there, but I don't know how."

Solomon could see the desperation in his eyes. "No matter what you do, it cannot be stopped. This is all part of a much bigger plan. So many nights I have been plagued with these dreams about the end of the world. I have spent so much time trying to fight the inevitable, but I want to let it all go now. I suggest that you do the same."

"Seriously? That is your answer? Just give up?" Deiderick slammed his hand on the high-top table. "You can actually sit there, and tell me that the end of the world is coming? It's all because of my company's project and you don't want me to do anything about it? This is ridiculous!"

"I have my reasons; besides, it is not going to make a difference. Jah is more powerful than all of us. Everything is in

His control. I suggest that you read the Writ and make peace with Jah."

"You are not the man I thought you were. I have watched you come here for weeks and tell everyone about your dreams and your visions of the future. You seemed so concerned about the future state of the world, but you're just all talk. I just shared my company's secret with you, and all you can do is tell me to let it happen? You are NOT Jah; you are NOT our Creator! If you don't help me, the death of an entire civilization will be on your hands. I couldn't live with myself knowing that I could have done something. I thought you would feel the same. What reason do you have to allow the destruction of the world?"

"You don't know me. You don't get to speak to me like this." Solomon was about to get up from the table. Deiderick pulled him back down.

"You are correct. I don't know you and the only thing you know about me is what the media says. But this is me. I am a man who has made mistakes, but I am also a man who would like to fix them. And I need your help to do that," Deiderick begged.

"It's not that I don't want to help. Look, I guess I will see what I can do. But my story is so different from yours. Unlike you, I lost my wife to cancer and all three of my children because of the YSW. I did stand up against the YSW. And, so did they." Solomon pointed to Quantas and Mediana. "We were put in jail for several days and were threatened to never rise up against them again."

"A few days in jail and you were scared off?" Deiderick scoffed.

"That's not all." Solomon never told Quantas and Mediana about his other ventures. He didn't want them to feel obligated to follow his lead. He also wasn't sure if they were able to keep a secret; So Solomon made sure to keep his voice low. "I felt so terrible about what happened to Quantas and Mediana. I couldn't bring them along again because my next plan was personal -- to get my kids back. Both of my sons ended up at the digital detox centers and it was all my fault. I thought the center would make things better but I hated the way they were run. How were my sons supposed to get clean if they were keeping them on technology? So I stopped the detox centers from keeping my sons doped up.

"What did you do?" Deiderick was curious.

"I caused a blackout. I set the electrical box on fire and it shut down the power over an entire city block."

"That was you? I remember hearing about that. My god, I thought they would have never released the person responsible for doing that. That incident was one of the reasons why my company began researching Lithorium more." Deiderick was astonished.

"They put me in the back of the hovercraft, and we were flying toward the prison. I could hear the officers talking about how long I would be locked up. I began to pray, and Jah answered. The same power outage I created was what caused the hovercraft to crash. There was not enough external electrical force to keep it in the air. The two officers were injured badly but I was able to get away. When the officers woke up, they couldn't remember the details of what happened. Somehow, the outage also caused interference with the droids' surveillance footage. No one could retrieve the video of the mysterious man who caused the blackout. So I was free, but I laid low for a while."

"For a while," Deiderick repeated. "So what made you come out of hiding?"

"My daughter found herself in this prestigious group of YSW her freshman year. She wanted so desperately to impress them. So she played--" Solomon's voice broke. He tried to hold in his tears, but they continued to flow. "--She played digital dare. She had to do whatever they asked in order to get "likes" from people on campus. The more popular the member of the YSW, the more likes she would get. She didn't realize that the more popular members made the most sinister requests. The YSW sent me the images of my daughter. They were surrounding her, laughing, and using the phone taser app to tourture her when she asked if she could stop. 'Just two more minutes,' one of them responded. I could hear one of them say, 'I bet daddy will be shocked to see his little girl like this.' She begged them not to send it to me. When I received the video, I tried to reach out to her. Even visit her in school, but nothing. I didn't know what had happened to her, if she was alive or dead. I wanted someone to help me. I wanted to go through the proper channels, but once they found out I participated in the silence ban protest, the YSW threatened to hurt my boys. They only let me know that she is still alive, and I believe that she is, but I can't risk it. I can't risk them discovering I was the one behind the blackout. I would lose everything."

"If the world is ending, you're going to lose everything anyway. I need your help."

Solomon sat there quietly. He didn't know what to do. Solomon realized he had misjudged Deiderick. This man was coming to him for help, but he was afraid to make any promises. The moment of silence was too long for Deiderick.

"Well, thanks for nothing," Deiderick said. He abruptly got up and left.

Deiderick didn't make it out of the doorway before Quantas made it over to Solomon. "Wow, that was tense. You sure know how to make someone feel welcome."

Quantas and Mediana started to laugh. Other members of the EAD appeared to be clueless. They stayed in dark corners of the room and continued to read or play chess.

"So, are you going to help him?" Mediana asked.

"Help him do what? How much did you hear?" Solomon inquired.

"All I know is that he kept asking you for help. A man like that doesn't come into a place like this unless he is desperate," Mediana replied.

"I wish I could give you advice on whether to help him or not, but you were whispering. How am I supposed to eavesdrop if you whisper?" Quantas made herself chuckle again.

"I swear, you are the most irritating woman!" Solomon replied incredulously.

"It's all part of my charm." Quantas took a towel and snapped it at Solomon's leg playfully.

"I'll see the both of you later. I need to go home and clear my head." Solomon put his coat back on and jabbed the earbuds back in his ears.

The last encounter Solomon had with Deiderick in the secret room of the convenience store was two days before the vanishing. The men did not speak to each other. Deiderick resumed his previous disposition, took a seat in the same dark corner of the room, and just observed. Solomon debated whether he should go over and break the tension but decided against it. Very few members of the EAD spoke to each other that evening. Most of them sat quietly in the basement of the convenience store with the Writ in their hand, trying to make peace with Jah. They prepared for the end.

4.
The End of the Second World

Jah looked upon the world and watched as chaos ensued. Billions around the world connected via devices. They connected despite their location and despite the hour so that they were all together at the same time. No matter the type of device -- third eye or handheld -- they connected. On this night, they were drawn to their devices and the attraction was stronger than anything they had ever felt before. The YSW took to their glowing screens and began sending messages that released unnatural amounts of synthetic hormone into their brains. Each time one of the YSW opened a message, an immediate emotion was felt and instantly the YSW became obsessed with the gratifying feeling that was released.

The YSW started off sending feelings of joy, love, and happiness, but their curiosity about the other Emojis began to take over and they started exploring Emojis that instilled fear and sadness. As they did this, necessary chemicals were slowly being removed from their brain, but they didn't stop. Their fingers began moving faster, their thoughts were growing more depressed, and their eyes were full of tears, but they did not disengage. They did not acknowledge the impact this had on them. They were losing the ability to do that. And so, in the last minute of the Second World, all of the YSW pressed the Emoji of a skull. It released chemical compounds in such high quantities that it resulted in neurotoxicity and apoptosis. The YSW died and Jah vanished them from the Second World.

After the YSW were eliminated, only a few, very special individuals remained. The survivors consisted of the Elders that Jah's heart bled for and the unexposed (infants who had not yet seen technology). The Elders were not perfect, and many times they grumbled against Jah for the world they lived in, but Jah could see their heart and He considered them to be honorable and just. Like the First World that was destroyed with flood waters because mankind displeased Him, the people of the Second World had to be destroyed because they grew too vain, too perverse, and filled their minds with false wisdom. Jah could only save Elders of that world because they had promised to never grow dependent on the technological advances that the Youth of the Second World loved.

It was written in the first 66 Books of the Writ, that man shall not live past 120 years, so Jah had to choose the right time to preserve the Elders and destroy the YSW. The Elders were at least 60 years old and had very little use for technology, only using it for their jobs. The YSW ranged from Youth of early exposure to 59 years of age and were individuals who depended on technology. So, anyone who placed their hands on a device and used it to connect for personal reasons, was destroyed. Anyone who had a cranium piece implanted was extinguished. Infants older than 11 months, and who were exposed to technology, were also eliminated.

The Elders who did not use technology, along with the unexposed infants, were placed into a deep sleep immediately after the vanishing. When the Elders awoke, they automatically knew the Second World had ended because Jah told them in a dream, which depicted the end and informed them of their role in the New World. Each Elder rose from their slumber knowing exactly what to do. They were to find the infant that Jah assigned to them and raise them in the Third World (The New Age). Most Elders were assigned one infant, but Elders who had the kindest hearts were assigned two. The Elders were then given specific instructions on how to raise the unexposed Youth so that they stayed in the will of Jah. Their instruction was written in a book called The Writ.

5.
Waking in the New Age

All of the Elders saved from the vanishing looked around, exploring the place that kept them protected from receiving the signal that had lured the Youth of the Second World just hours before the vanishing. A beam of light illuminated items in the room. A decrepit, wooden bar stool sat at the bottom of a set of stairs. The stairs were broken in a few places, but the Elders carefully navigated their way to the top. When they arrived at the top of the stairs, a sign that read "Cleaning Supplies" was posted on the door. The Elders realized that Jah must have sent them to the convenience store right before the vanishing. The convenience store kept them safe while Jah prepared the Third World for their arrival. The store was dark, but a small slither of light peaked its way through a crack under the front door. As they walked toward the light, it grew larger and eventually, all of the rescued Elders found their way to the Third World. Jah illuminated their path and led the Elders outside, where the soft buzz of insects filled the air and birds sang cheerful songs, dancing in circles to their own melody and showing off their beautiful, iridescent colors. The Elders watched as little ground creatures scurried about, running through grassy mounds that, upon closer inspection, appeared to be metal boxes that had powered entire city blocks in the Second World. Handheld devices scattered about were camouflaged by rainbow-colored leaves and other exotic, vibrant flowers. The smell of lavender, heather, crossandra orange, and rose with a mix of morning dew filled the air.

Solomon took in a deep breath. The air was so crisp it stung the inside of his nose; different than the smog-infused air of the Second World. Solomon appeared to be taking the lead in the exploration of the New World and Deiderick, Mediana, and

Quantas found themselves following him on the same path. A woman named Veronica also joined them. Veronica was an Elder that the others did not know from the Second World, but Jah gave her direction to head the same way as the other Elders. She quickly befriended the former members of the EAD. Veronica was timid -- her personality was in stark contrast to that of the other female Elders, who were extremely outspoken. But despite their obvious differences, Veronica enjoyed being part of the group.

"Well, I see that we've been placed together again," Solomon said.

"It does appear that way," Deiderick agreed.

Veronica, excited to be accepted by the group, smiled and said, "Yes, well...I'm actually happy to be walking with people I have some connection to. It's comforting to see someone from the Second World. I wasn't sure how many of us Jah would actually find worthy enough to save."

Mediana was about to chime into the conversation but was cut off by Quantas.

"I sure hope we find a stopping place soon. My body can't take much more of this. We're either put to sleep for many years or woken up and forced to walk for what feels like an eternity. Either way, we're relentlessly searching, and it seems like we're not getting anywhere. I can't wait until our search for the Youth is over and we can finally get to some sense of normalcy," Quantas complained.

The noise of the busy streets had gone. There were no more people looking down at their devices and running into each other on the sidewalks or blinking incessantly to change the news story that was being fed to them by their Third Eye. There were no more police sirens. The blaring alarms of the fire trucks and emergency response vehicles that were once part of their daily routine no longer filled the air. The gray haze of the sky was gone, and the brilliant yellow-orange sun shined through a soft blue blanket that met what appeared to be an endless sea of green grass.

The clouds that once held an ominous red hue in the Second Wor were now soft, white puffs that danced in the sky.

The leaves on the trees looked like a kaleidoscope of every shade of green imaginable, and they glinted in the sunlight whenever a breeze would ripple through the air. Fruits and flowers ranged in colors from the palest pinks to the most vibrant purples, and the cool air was filled with the smell of the sweet nectar of fruit trees and berry bushes. The tall limbs from branches and other vegetation broke through the paved streets of the world before, crumbling and cracking the once smooth pavement into fine pebbles. Vines bearing succulent delicacies covered old buildings of the Second World as if they were reclaiming their former place on the Earth. As the Elders took in all of the beauty of the Second World, Quantas stopped dead in her tracks.

"What the heck is that?" Quantas was shaking. She pointed up, her fingers trembling.

The entire group stopped to look in the direction Quantas was pointing. "It couldn't be. I thought they were all extinct," Veronica whispered.

"I thought so too," Sophos replied.

The Elders thought that Grizzly bears had all been killed, but one was just a few feet away, mulling about aimlessly and sniffing the air. When the bear saw them, he turned around and started walking toward the group.

"I guess Jah replenished everything," Solomon said breathlessly.

Hearing Solomon's whisper, the bear slowly walked over to him, its leathery nose just inches from Solomon's face. Solomon could feel the moist heat when the bear exhaled. All he could think to do was not move.

"We can't possibly stand like this forever," Deiderick whispered. The bear returned his whisper with a roar that shook the surrounding trees. You could see each one of his teeth. Saliva cascaded down the bear's fangs and he stood on two feet. Birds started squawking and the women started screaming. Solomon did his best to stand firm but could feel his legs begin to tremble. Deiderick quickly made his way over to Solomon in an attempt to grab him but ran back when the bear gave another massive roar. Mediana screamed and began putting her hands out, one hand reaching forward as if to halt the bear, and the other shielding her head. When the bear saw this, he stopped growling and got down on all fours.

Deiderick fainted. Veronica rushed over to fan him.

"Did you all see what just happened? What did you do?" Solomon continued to whisper.

"I don't know," Mediana replied.

"Do it again!" Solomon said curiously.

Mediana's hand was still trembling, but she slowly approached the bear and motioned for him to sit on his bottom. The bear sat down with a large thump.

"How are you doing that?" Quantas inquired.

"I don't know. You try."

"Have you lost your mind? I am not about to potentially undo whatever spell you have that bear under. Let's go!"

The Elders looked around to make sure they hadn't dropped anything in all of the chaos. The bear remained in place. Mediana then shooed the bear out of their path and he left. The Elders continued on their journey, but this time, they were a little more aware of their surroundings.

"I think that was the scariest thing that I've ever seen," Quantas said.

"Hands down the most terrifying experience of my life," Veronica agreed.

"You men are awfully quiet," Quantas observed.

"What is there to say? I was almost eaten by a bear." Solomon had no shame in admitting he was scared. "So Mediana, what were you thinking to make the bear stop?"

"I don't know. I was scared as crap. I was screaming internally, but all I could think was for the bear to stop. I didn't even realize that my hands were motioning for the bear to halt until he did. Then when you all asked me to do the same thing again, I just kept thinking, sit. Sit and let us pass."

"Hmm, so was it what you were thinking that got the bear to stop, the hand motion, or both?" Solomon wondered aloud.

"I don't know; what were you guys thinking?" Mediana asked.

"This couldn't be the way that I die. It didn't make sense to me that I would be saved from the vanishing to be mauled by a bear." Solomon chuckled.

"I was too panic-stricken to think," Deiderick said.

"What about you Quantas, what did you think?" Solomon asked.

"I don't remember my first few thoughts, but I remember my last thought."

"Well. What was it?"

"Better him than me!"

All of the Elders erupted with laughter. The Elders continued to walk, being guided the entire way by some intrinsic compass that let them know they were headed in the right direction.

After what seemed like another two hours of walking, they finally came to a large concrete structure that was covered with vines, moss, and other vegetation. It looked like it may have been one of the Catholic hospitals in the Second World. The architecture of the building was elaborate. Through the vegetation you could see stained glass on the lower level, but more commercial windows on the upper levels of the building. The entrance was marked by two massive wooden doors that had images carved on them. Outside the two doors were a pair of gray wolves. They paced back and forth, acting as guards. It seemed they were protecting what was inside.

"Crap, not this again!" Quantas was the first to say what everyone else was thinking.

"I don't think I can take much more of this," Veronica said.

The Elders stood still and just watched the wolves. The wolves didn't seem to recognize they had company.

"So what should we do?" Veronica asked.

"Mediana, you said that you thought about what you wanted the bear to do and then you motioned with your hands?" Deiderick asked.

"Yes, but I don't know if this is going to work for every scenario."

"We don't have a choice. We need to get into that building. I'm sure that's where the infants are located." Deiderick stated.

"He's right, we don't have a choice," Solomon agreed.

Quantas and Veronica huddled behind him. Mediana, feeling like she could contribute, stayed up front with the men and they all began walking toward the large wooden doors. They remained unnoticed until a twig snapped under the pressure of Solomon's feet. The wolves turned their heads in that direction. The Elders could see the wolves' bright hazel eyes narrow. They snarled as the Elders approached.

"We've got to give it a try," Deiderick said optimistically.

"Safety in numbers, right? Each of you, hold out your hands and think about commands that will subdue the wolves," Solomon instructed. "One...two...three!"

On the count of three, all of the Elders held out their hands. Quantas and Veronica, still cowering behind the others, eventually held out their hands as well. Each of them began making mental commands toward the wolves. At first the wolves were cautious and barred their teeth, the fur on their backs raised, but the snarling subsided, and the wolves sat down, leaving a clear path to the entry of the building.

"I can't believe it. It actually worked." Quantas was astonished.

"That is simply extraordinary," Veronica whispered.

"Let's see what else we can get them to do!"

"Come on, let's not continue to take chances. Let's just do what we came here to do!" Mediana said.

"What do you have to worry about? You were the first to discover that we have the ability to control these beasts!" Solomon said. He then made a bowing motion and the wolves stretched out their front two legs and lowered their heads. Deiderick joined in and motioned for the wolves to move away from the doors. The wolves got up and moved away from the wooden doorway, allowing the Elders to pass.

A tiny electrical box sat in the upper right-hand corner of the door, presumably used to automatically open the doors in the Second World. However, its light was out and the massive doors remained still. It took two of the Elders to manually push them aside.

"I guess Jah really didn't want to make things easy for us," Quantas commented.

They all stepped inside.

"Looks like a greenhouse doesn't it?"

"It sure feels like one. It's so humid in here."

"This place is huge. How are we ever going to find them in here? Look at all of the rooms. Do you think we should split up and search?" Mediana asked.

"Let's stick together," Veronica replied.

"Agreed, we'll figure this out," Deiderick reassured. He then walked over to an elevator and pressed one of the buttons, hoping that his previous assumption was incorrect. "I guess we'll have to use the stairs."

They continued to search the main floor. Mice quickly ran in the opposite direction of the approaching noise. Mediana shrieked. She swatted at a long vine that hung from the ceiling.

"Let's all keep our cool guys," Solomon said in a dismissive tone.

"Words of wisdom from the man who thought he was going to be mauled by a bear," Quantas said under his breath.

Deiderick snorted. Solomon looked back at Deiderick, trying to recall if he ever heard him laugh before. "Hey, I think I see a staircase." Solomon pointed to the left side of the building. The staircase was dark. Solomon led the way. Deiderick was right behind him and Veronica's fingers gripped the back of his shirt. Quantas and Mediana walked arm-in-arm behind the rest of the gang, tiptoeing up the stairs. The Elders went from room to room in search of their precious gifts.

"Room 212," Solomon observed, scanning the plaques posted near each door. He pushed the door open to find five infants wrapped in wool blankets, sound asleep.

"Look...there they are." Veronica pointed.
"How do we know which infant is ours?" Quantas asked.

"I want this one." Mediana pointed to a little girl with straight brown hair that slightly spiked at her crown. She had peachy-toned skin and round, full cheeks.

"I don't think that's how this works," Solomon responded. "In my vision last night, I got the feeling like there would be a note or some sort of sign to let us know which one is ours." Solomon began looking around the clear incubators that acted as a home for the infants.

The other Elders joined him.

"Oh, they look so sweet, I just want to hold one." Veronica opened the incubator. She picked up a little girl with a round face and dirty blonde curls and held her. The baby wiggled in her arms but did not wake up.

"Look!" Quantas said. "Look what's pinned to her blanket." It was a little piece of paper that said:

First Name: Nia

Mother: Veronica
Date of Birth: 3/17/2105
Weight: 7 lbs, 8 oz.

"Well, I'll be!" Quantas was in awe. "I wonder how it got there?"

Each Elder picked opened the metal fastener on the incubator and grabbed an infant. They each read the paper that was pinned on the back of the blanket.

"Well, I think this one is yours, Mediana." Solomon struggled to hand over the massive bundle to her.

"Well this can't be." Mediana said as she grabbed the wool sack that felt as if it were instead a pile of bricks. "Are you sure this is my infant?" She struggled to turn the baby over to find her name on the line that said mother.

"My god, he looks like a toddler."

"Well," Solomon responded, "his birthday is only a few days before my infant, Athirst," Solomon said like a proud papa.

Mediana opened the wool blanket and took a look at her baby. "He certainly is a big boy. But he's awfully cute! Look at him." The infant, still sleep, squirmed and grabbed onto her finger. Mediana immediately fell in love. "When you wake up, I bet you'll be hungry. Don't worry little one, I will make sure to take care of..." Mediana turned over the child once more and got another look at the paper secured to the back of his blanket. "...Jabari, yes, I will take good care of you, Jabari."

"This is amazing!" Solomon glanced at all of the infants now being held by their new parents. "They haven't aged at all! We must have been asleep for years, but it's as if He preserved them."

The infants squirmed in their hands, but the Elders made every effort to comfort them. They used the blankets to create a sack that could hold the infants close to their body. Mediana made sure to add an extra layer of security. She ripped the bottom of her skirt and used it as a harness to carry her youngster.

"Are you sure you don't want me to help you with him?" Solomon asked.

"No, Jah gave him to me. I will take care of him." Mediana gave him a kiss on the forehead before hoisting him into her harness.

The Elders made it out of the building and continued to head away from the remnants of their former city overgrown with plant life in search of a water source. They agreed that it was best to begin life near water, especially since they no longer had the ability to use technological advancements anymore.

"I can't take it anymore! I need to rest," Quantas said.

"I agree. It's been a long day and it's going to be dark soon," Solomon said.

"I hear water trickling nearby. We need to head toward the water," Deiderick said. "I think we should keep going."

"You can keep going. I need a break." Mediana's forehead was dripping with sweat. She quickly began unstrapping her large bundle. Solomon rushed to assist when he noticed the weight of baby Jabari was going to topple her over.

"It's getting a little cooler. Do you think they'll be okay?" Veronica asked.

"Here, let me get 'em while you and Deiderick find a way to make us a fire." Quantas grabbed baby Athirst from Solomon and motioned for Mediana to grab little Theiler from Deiderick.

"You think this is cold? You must not have lived in the 212 area code for long before the vanishing. It used to be bitter. Looks like Jah has already made it more bearable for us, or at least I hope so. I can't imagine living in a house with no heat during the winters we used to have," Quantas said to Veronica as she wrestled to find a resting place for the two babies she was holding.

"I'm actually excited about our new adventure. It's like we're living in the primitive days. I read about this when I was a girl in school and always wondered what it would be like to live in a time like this," Mediana replied.

"Speak for yourself. I appreciate Jah saving me, but living without some of the modern conveniences, I am not so sure about. I sure would've liked to have some type of technology to zap that bear today." Quantas chuckled.

"Yeah, I don't even want to think about that anymore." Veronica shook her head.

After finding a place to lay the babies down, the women started searching for food. They kept their eye on their precious cargo the entire time. It wasn't long before the men had a fire going when the women brought back a sack full of succulent fruits and vegetables.

Solomon bit into a sweet, fuzzy nectarine. He was weary and dehydrated from traveling all day. It was perfectly ripe, and its juice was refreshing to him.

"I need one of those as well," Quantas said as she plopped down next to him. The other Elders joined them and gazed into the fire. They were tired from the long journey, but thankful to Jah for saving them. Deiderick, seeing that the fire was dying down, picked up a twig that had fallen from a nearby hardwood tree and stirred the fire. The flames bolted into the air, casting a flickering light on the infants that were gathered together on the soft grass nearby. The Elders glanced at the innocence of the Youths' sweet, peaceful faces and thanked Jah for entrusting them with such great responsibility.

"So," Mediana began, "How much do you think they need to know?" Her eyes looked back over at the infants.

The other Elders looked around, trying to read each other's expressions. The glow of the fire seemed to exaggerate the wrinkles in their skin. The contrast of light and dark created an almost eerie atmosphere in the seemingly serene setting. The Elders knew they could not protect the unexposed from knowing about the Second World for long. In fact, part of their mission was to make sure that the infants grew up understanding that it was the actions of their parents, the YSW, that led to the vanishing. They'd make sure the children would not repeat the same mistakes by teaching them the dangers of becoming obsessed with technology.

Solomon interrupted the awkward silence. "The spirit of Jah will tell us what we should and should not let them know."

Deiderick nodded his head in agreement.

"Well, I must be right if I got a head nod from you. Don't think I didn't notice you run over to me when the bear tried to attack. I was so touched. It's like we're best friends now," Solomon joked and stretched his arms out, signaling that he wanted a hug, but Deiderick kept his stagnant demeanor.

"Leave him alone," Quantas fussed. "You are just upset that he commands the same amount of attention and displays the same amount of wisdom as you do with much less effort."

"Thank you Quantas," Solomon quipped.

"For what?"

Solomon laughed. "Even in your efforts to try to humiliate me, you admit that I am in fact wise."

Quantas huffed, upset that Solomon managed to find the silver lining in her underhanded comment.

"Can you imagine the world that these precious infants would've grown up in? What their fate would be? We're so blessed that they can now live under different circumstances." Mediana, along with the other Elders, glanced over at the infants again. While the infants slept, the Elders reminisced. They remembered the world before the government ban, before the digital regulations and policed words, and before the headlines and constant news feeds.

"I'm happy that we're able to speak again," Solomon said. "Do you all remember the silence ban?"

"Yes," Mediana said. "I remember it all. It was terrifying not being able to say a word and being watched constantly. I remember all the cameras and drones that would fly around looking through windows to see if any of our lips were moving."

"I felt like I had to monitor my own thoughts. I remember waking up in the middle of the night to that tiny blue light that was tracking my every movement," Veronica chimed in.

"It was so strange to be banned from speaking and yet hear so much noise. All the propaganda, the news, the headlines, and stories. The last night before the vanishing..." Quantas' voice quivered and trailed off.

"I remember how crazy everything felt right before it all ended," Veronica said in an effort to distract Quantas from her sadness.

"I do too. I didn't have a device feeding me information, but it didn't matter because news was practically shoved in my face anyway," Mediana replied.

Solomon looked at the Elders sitting by the fire. His breathing grew heavy. "The headlines that were playing -- I wrote them down," he said. Then Solomon began to frantically search his pants.

"You can't possibly think you would still have them. We've been asleep for decades. Who knows what possessions were destroyed by now!" Quantas said.

Solomon continued to search his pockets. "I know it's got to be here somewhere. Jah told me to write them down and keep them. He wanted me to remember what He saved us from."

The anxious search stopped as Solomon reached into his back-left pocket. He pulled out a tightly folded sheet of paper. As he unfolded it, it began to tear along the creases.

"Well I'll be." Mediana was astonished.

"Be careful with it!" Quantas snapped. "Do you need me to do it? You may rip it to shreds."

Solomon continued to open the paper carefully. As he sat by the warmth of the fire, the eyes of the other Elders watching him, he had a flashback to the night he wrote the headlines. He remembered sitting in his apartment at his desk. A picture of his wife and children sat in the corner. He picked up the picture and kissed the images of the people in the photo. He knew he would never get the chance to see them again.

"I can't remember the exact date, but it was about a month or so after Deiderick and I had our first encounter at the store."

"I remember that. Deiderick was really upset. I remember him asking you for help." Mediana said. "Did you ever follow through?"

"Yes, he did." Deiderick glanced at Solomon.

"You helped him? You didn't tell us!" Quantas said looking at Solomon.

"Nothing worth telling," Deiderick replied. "Go ahead Solomon, please, finish." Solomon cast him a grateful look.

"Jah sent me another dream. I thought I was wrong, because in this dream, he wanted me to turn on a device. He showed me a pencil and paper and I started swiping through stories and writing down as much as I could. Jah kept showing me the minute-hand on a clock that stayed on the number six. That signified that I was only given thirty minutes. When I woke up from the dream, I grabbed a sheet of paper and started writing."

"Are you telling me the sheet that you have is that same paper? Quantas said in disbelief. "Read it then. What does it say?"

The Elders scooted up closer to Solomon. They were hanging on his every word. Solomon tilted the paper to cast some light on the words he had written before the vanishing.

"Well, aren't you going to read it?" Quantas asked.

Solomon tilted the paper toward the light so he could see the words. He nervously read the crumpled sheet of paper out loud for everyone to hear.

Former leaders of all nations celebrated as they elected Yusef Aesis as the One World leader. All nations of the world will now fall under the leadership of President Yusef Aesis, who promises to bring an end to the division amongst the countries. He plans to unify them by creating a One World Religion. President Yusef Aesis says that it will bring peace to those countries that have been warring for thousands of years and promises that anyone who rises up against this will be severely punished.

-   SWIPE

The oxygen gardens that were created to remedy the need for cleaner air are no longer effective. These robotically-engineered trees that seemed like the solution to our air pollution problems can no longer separate the carbon dioxide from the oxygen. The number of individuals who have died from poor air quality has risen to 1.2 million in the last five years.

-   SWIPE

It is now against One World law to be seen using personal transportation. All citizens must use the air railway for travel. If you desire to walk, you must obtain a pedestrian pass…

-   SWIPE

In an effort to create one race, the ISOR (International Society for One Race) is having their 3rd annual mixer conference located at the Flaura Hotel in downtown Manhattan. We will now turn to Michael Spencer, president of the ISOR: "It has been a goal of the International Society of One Race to eliminate racism in this country for hundreds of years. The only way that can be done is if we learn to unite and blend with each other. We have created over 260,000 children of mixed race who cannot be labeled or defined by the color of their skin. We are gaining a lot of support. Tonight, we anticipate nearly 13,000 people attending and engaging in our desire to become One Race."

-   SWIPE

57 more bodies were found in Bronx County. The cause of death is contaminated water due to the…

-   SWIPE

"We are here in 212 Midtown, celebrating the first marriage of robot to human. The excitement in the crowd cannot be described. Many here are cheering and celebrating as we

witness a momentous occasion. Saul created his robot partner Abigail after experiencing several failed human relationships..."
-   SWIPE

Legislators have determined that social currency and your number of likes and followers on social media can officially be exchanged for One World Dollars. Less popular citizens, those with less than 10,000 followers, can now use One World Dollars to purchase more follower numbers and likes.
-   SWIPE

20 more children have been rushed to the digital detox centers located in the 212 area code district. These children are in critical condition after being overexposed to digital media technology. If you see your child expressing symptoms of anger and rage, aggression, vomiting, or eyes rolling in the back of their head, call the digital detox hotline at 212-914-5000; however, if they are already in a coma, please call 911.
-   SWIPE

A string of battles in the Western Hemisphere leaves nearly 4,700 dead in less than 48 hours...
-   SWIPE

The World mourns as global suicides have been orchestrated. These global suicides are becoming more common as depression rates increase. Despite their connection with friends and family through devices, many of the individuals who participate in these mass suicides express extreme loneliness and a desire to have authentic, physical connection in the afterlife...
-   SWIPE

The Device Engineering & Advancement Design company, or DEAD, has created the most revolutionary advancement of the 22nd century. Emojis which simulate real human emotions will be released at midnight to all digital platforms. The DEAD company is providing 30 minutes of free sample time to everyone who has a device. The icon will appear on your device or be released to your cranium piece for exactly 30 minutes before fees are applied.

The spokesperson for Emojis, Janice Dollard, the wife of Deiderick Dollard, has released a statement: "We are so fortunate to have found a way for people to truly feel exactly what is sent in messages. I think this will bring people much closer together." Pandemonium has occurred as people who were once using hand-held devices rush to get cranium implants. The DEAD company suggests using the Third Eye piece for maximum sensory effect. The Third Eye piece, also developed by the DEAD company, is currently selling for $666.66 and is located in stores everywhere.

After Solomon read the last headline, he looked at Deiderick, who looked solemn. Deiderick ran a hand through his hair and sighed. His eyes were glassy.

"It's okay, brother; we're all here now," Solomon assured him, seeing the regret in his eyes. "As long as you don't mind me making a few jabs at you, we'll call it even." Solomon patted Deiderick on the back and Deiderick cracked a smile.

"Let's get some rest tonight. We have a long road ahead of us," Solomon said.

Each of the Elders made their way towards their assigned Youth. They unfolded blankets and cradled the infants in their arms to keep them warm. Solomon nuzzled his head next to a brown-haired, olive-skinned little boy. Athirst reminded him of his own sons. He was absolutely perfect. Deiderick gazed at the golden locks and slightly rosy cheeks of Theiler, who cracked open his blue-green eyes for a moment before falling back asleep. Deiderick reached his index finger into the blanket to feel the infant's hands. Theiler wrapped his tiny hand around Deiderick's finger. "A strong boy you are, a strong boy indeed."

Before they went to sleep, Solomon called out to the other Elders. "Tonight, you'll all receive a vision. Jah will reveal to you your new identity. It may feel strange but try to remember every detail. When we wake up, we will no longer be able to use the names previously given to us in the Second World. Jah will also send us vision of where to find the Writ."

"What are you? Jah's right-hand man? You sound like a know-it-all," Quantas said.

"I don't know it all Quantas, I just happen to know more than you," Solomon replied. "Now, let's all get some rest."

The bright yellow sun peeked over the horizon. The Elders rose from their sleep, and the infants began to squirm around. They picked fruit off the trees and allowed the infants to drink the juice. This quieted them down, save for their satisfied little grunts and burps. Solomon couldn't wait to see if the others received their vision.

"So," Solomon said. "Who do I have the pleasure of speaking with?" Solomon grinned ear-to-ear and held his hand out to Quantas.

"I am Querulous now." Quantas looked dismayed.

"Ha! That's perfect! You quarrel so much! Jah is truly all-seeing and all-knowing!" Solomon could not contain himself.

"If you think that's so funny, what's your name, then?"

"I was given the name 'Sophos,'" Solomon responded rather boastfully. He puffed out his chest.

Deiderick joined in the conversation. "I am Discernmos."

Mediana chimed in, "Good morning, and let me introduce you to Mediorocris." She took a dramatic bow. Quantas snorted.

"And you, Veronica, what is your new name?" Solomon asked.

"My new name is Vera."

"From this day forward, we are no longer able to refer to each other using our Second World names. Jah gave us a fresh start in the new world. He gave us a new mind, a new tongue, and a new way to live," Sophos told the other Elders.

"And I received a vision of where many of the books are located as well," Discernmos offered. "I think that should be what we do first -- find the collection of books, The Writ. They contain our history and our instruction for our lives in the New Age."

"I see that you are quick to live out your new name by using discernment to guide us." Sophos felt a little insecure, like someone was encroaching on his territory. "So, where are these books located?" Sophos asked.

"That way."

"That way, he says," Sophos mumbled under his breath.

Noticing that Sophos seemed irritated, Discernmos asked, "Am I mistaken? I'm sure you received vision as well, so if I'm somehow wrong, then by all means lead the way."

A hush fell over the other Elders who, up to this point, had followed Sophos' every move.

"Looks like there's a new boss in town," Querulous whispered to Mediorocris. Both women began giggling under their breath.

"No, you're not mistaken, just thought you would give a little more detail than 'that way'." Sophos picked up baby Athirst and strapped him to his chest. The other Elders grabbed their little ones, secured them to their body, and followed Discernmos, who had taken the lead. The Elders walked for about an hour through the woods. The ground underneath their feet was lumpy, making it difficult to maintain their balance.

"Do you think we're walking over bodies?" Mediorocris asked as she struggled to keep up. Jabari, her infant, was awake. He moved around in her harness, knocking her about.

Vera began looking down at the ground. "It's creepy to think that we may be walking over skeletons of bodies hidden in all of this foliage. But maybe we're walking on all of the devices the YSW left, instead? I mean, the YSW vanished right? So, Jah wouldn't leave them here."

"I think you're right Vera." Sophos comforted her.

"The books are located over there." Discernmos pointed.

"Why would it have to be over there?" Querulous said, eyeing the particularly ominous-looking cave looming in the distance. "Give me a break, we have to hold on to the Youth while we navigate through there? Jah sure knows how to make us feel welcome in this New World. He couldn't have made it more difficult for us to follow His will."

"Querulous is right, I don't think it would be in there," Mediorocris agreed.

"Discernmos' vision is accurate, unfortunately. The sacred book, The Writ, is in this exact cave," Solomon declared.

As the Elders walked through the brush, twigs popped, and leaves crunched. Birds who were resting on tree limbs began squawking as if announcing that they had visitors. As the birds made their call, black winged bugs began to appear from all directions.

"What is happening?" Mediorocris asked with dread. "Are you sure we're supposed to be here? Why are all of these bugs surrounding us?"

"I'm not sure," Solomon responded as he swatted at them.

"We barely made this journey without tripping over all the devices buried in the ground, and now we're supposed to go into a dark cave while we swat at bugs? I don't intend to sacrifice our infants for some book," Querulous said.

"It is not just some book. It is the book; The Writ will give us instructions on exactly what we're to do in the New World. We must retrieve it. I'm sure we can figure this out." Sophos resumed swatting at bugs that flitted to and fro. "Don't mind the bugs. They don't seem to be biting. We just need to figure out how to create enough light to see in this cave," Solomon said.

As if on cue, one by one, the bugs began to glow and soon, every bug was emanating a radiant light.

"Well that was easy," Querulous said, laughing.

The Elders turned in slow circles, in awe of their surroundings. "So, they're fireflies. I remember them from when I was little. I haven't seen them in over 60 years." Mediorocris stuck her finger out to touch one. The firefly dodged her and headed in the direction of the cave.

All of the fireflies made their way inside the cave. "It's like they want us to follow them," Vera said, smiling.

The Elders followed them apprehensively, the bugs lighting the way.

As they entered the cave, the light from the fireflies began radiating off its cavernous walls. "This could be the most beautiful thing I have ever seen." Solomon touched what almost looked like an icicle. It was illuminated by the fireflies and appeared to be glowing as well. All of the Elders looked around the cave to see long, hanging crystals.

"Stalactites," Discernmos said. "Mineral deposits that form from dripping water. They make these beautiful shapes. I went on a field trip with my children when they were about five years old." Discernmos abruptly ended his story, as if speaking about his family was too painful.

The fireflies continued to lead them through the cave. "Look, Governess!" Querulous took her baby out of the wool blanket she had strapped to her and held her baby in her arms, gently swaying to give the tiny, brown-haired little girl the opportunity to see everything inside the cave. "Look at all of the beautiful -- what did you call those things again?" Querulous shouted to Discernmos. Her voice echoed in the cave.

"Stalactites!" He shouted back.

Sophos was the first to notice the fireflies stop and hover over what appeared to be a large hole in the floor of the cave. As he approached, he noticed that the hole was filled with books. The Writ was burned into the leather cover of each book. Each copy was thick and heavy since they had been added to after the vanishing. Initially, the Writ contained 66 books but as time went on, the book evolved.

"Here it is, everyone." Solomon held one up proudly. He was elated that he was the one to put his hands on a book first. In some way, he felt that it redeemed his role as leader of the group. He picked it up and read the inside the cover:

We are thankful to Jah, who has saved us to fulfill a special purpose by adding to the first 66 books. We have been given the job of a Scriptor, assigned by our creator Jah to write warnings, provide words of wisdom, and give instruction for inhabitants of the New Age.

The other Elders gathered around Sophos to catch a glimpse of the book they saw in the vision. Most of the text was familiar to all of them, because the first 66 books of the Writ were from the First and Second Worlds. Sophos quickly skimmed through everything that was familiar, trying to find a new addition to the text.

6.
Foreshadowing – Warnings from the Writ

Sophos began reading the new additions to the Writ aloud. The other Elders stopped looking around for books to listen.

"Free will is the gift Jah has given, yet man has turned it into their own hell -- falling away from the word to fulfill selfish desires and worldly freedoms only to find themselves entombed (Writ 212: 156-158)."

Sophos closed the book. "Well that seems obvious, but what do you think that means for us now?" Mediorcris inquired.

"It seems like a warning, but who knows," Querulous said.

"We have time to figure all this out. I'm sure that the spirit of Jah will help us understand what it all means, but for right now, we need to focus on collecting all the remaining books and finding where Jah wants us to set up our new community," Sophos responded, placing as many copies of the Writ in his wool sack as he could. The others made their last rounds looking for stray books, and then gathered together to resume their quest.

"Water. Finally," Discernmos observed as the group trudged up a hill that overlooked a long, winding river below.

Sophos looked around. "Looks like River Aesis."

Mediorocris plopped down, eager to take her massive bundle of joy off of her back. "We are...not...going any… further." She paused between each word, trying to catch her breath.

"Agreed," Querulous said. "Jah decided to save Elders for this? I am old and tired!" She said as she flopped down on a patch of lush grass.

"How long do you think we walked?" Vera asked. She took Nia, her infant, and removed her from the sack she created for the journey. Nia began to whimper.

"Hush now, my love. It will be okay." She started lightly bouncing her up and down and Nia got quiet.

"Well...let's see. I believe we woke up in the old store and now we appear to be near River Aesis. Look there-" Sophos pointed. "-Mount Boreal, so we may have walked twenty or thirty miles between yesterday and today," Sophos stated.

"Mount Boreal looks just as cold as it did in the Second World." Querulous said. "Won't be setting up camp there."

River Aesis started at the base of the mountain and ran for nearly 2000 miles. The once gray-brown, murky water that smelled of sulfur and caused a great deal of illness in the Second World was now crystal clear and teeming with life. You could look straight down to the bottom and see fish swimming.

The Elders ran toward the river and bent down to take sips from the fresh, flowing water, feeling their fatigued bodies being rejuvenated.

"I haven't felt this good since I was a child."

Sophos began doing jumping jacks. "Me either!"

"It's gone," Querulous said, amazed. "All my arthritis, all the aches and pains are gone." She continued to stretch her body and then looked up to the sky, "Oh Jah, please forgive me for doubting you."

Querulous ran over to her baby and picked her up and began dancing around with her. She felt a joy she hadn't felt in a long time.

Over nine-hundred thousand were saved from the vanishing and given the task of beginning a life in the New Age. They were all spread out and had set up villages all along River Aesis. The Elders from area code 212 started a village near the river and named it Eirene.

7.
Community Begins

Because there were few natural trees remaining in the Second World, the Elders used the presence of all the new, mature trees in the Third World as an indication that they had been put to sleep for at least 20 years, if not longer. As they passed River Aesis, the Elders couldn't help but look at their reflection. Although they hadn't aged during the time they were put to rest, many of them were still disappointed to see the same old face they saw in the mirror before the vanishing occurred. The Elders saw the same gray hair, wrinkles, and veins as they did before. It was another phenomenon they could not explain. They looked exactly the same but felt like they were in their 20s.

The Elders came together and named the new place Eirene, because it was a place of peace. And within a few years, the village of Eirene was established with houses that ran along the southwest side of River Aesis. Some of the houses were made of sticks and leather, others straw and clay, and others bricks and stones.

The Elders built a community kitchen and a large pit in the center of the village, where they would have fires and time for the community to come together. The Elders would strike flint and gather dry hardwood from the forest nearby to create a central, warm place to gather and rest. The crackling noises and illuminating glow of the fire provided the perfect backdrop for the Elders to sit down with the Youth and tell stories about the power that Jah placed in each of them. Each of the Elders had been given great vision and wisdom, and they constantly shared their knowledge with the Youth.

The Youth, now between the ages of five and six years old, would sit in the Elders' laps, soaking up every word that came out of their mouths. "Some of you will grow up to be great teachers, and one day you will shine like beautiful jade. Some of you will be wonderful peacemakers and you will glow with a gentle but powerful warmth. All you future leaders, you will shine like silver and will see the fruits of your governance and courage come to pass. You will all see your physical bodies begin to transform along with the renewing of your mind and heart."

"How so?" The Youth asked.

"You will no longer have a definite form. You will become a spirit, made of energy -- a loose figure, if you will, that cannot be contained in any shape," Sophos responded.

Sophos was one of the best interpreters of vision because of the affliction he endured in the Second World. But what seemed to be a burden in the Second World, was a gift in the Third. He used his dreams and discernment to not worry or be anxious, but to make plans and lead the other Elders. Sophos further refined his craft and spent much of his time in meditation and reading The Writ.

The Youth he claimed as his own was named Athirst. Sophos cared for him and he enjoyed teaching him the ways of Jah, but nonetheless he enjoyed spending time with any of the Youth who were willing to listen. You could see the fire reflected in each of the Youth's eyes as they listened to Sophos tell of things to come. They were full of curiosity, energy, and the desire to know what Jah had in store for them.

"So, we won't have arms and legs? How can we play? How can we eat?" The Elders loved the innocent and sometimes ridiculous questions that they came up with. It reminded the Elders of their childhood -- the childhood before devices existed.

The Youth would then pretend to not have arms and legs. They squirmed around, being silly like children were supposed to. The Elders relished in every question, giggle, and hug that came from them. Sophos was especially attached to them because he had lost all three of his children in the vanishing. Though he missed his real family, Sophos appreciated the fact that Jah did not take away his memories of them.

It was a strange feeling, because the memories were not always good; in fact, he remembered often being sad. He remembered losing his wife to cancer and doing what he could to take care of his children all alone. He remembered when devices were first introduced to him; how he was the one to purchase the first gaming system for his children, thinking that it would serve as a distraction from the loss of their mother. He remembered the laughs they shared before the cancer, before the devices. He remembered family trips -- those trips to the ocean before the waters became too polluted. He was thankful that he was left with all of those memories. Even though he had to re-hash the bad ones, he found joy in knowing that he got to experience all the good ones as well and was grateful that Jah left all of them intact. All the Elders had the memories of their family and reminisced over the times they had with them.

Many of the Elders were depressed in the Second World because they lacked the relationship, they desperately desired to have with their children. So, when the Elders heard the children laughing, it filled their hearts with joy.

They enjoyed seeing the Youth dance around the fire. They smiled when they played pretend and made jokes and whispered secrets, because these moments of interaction did not exist in the Second World. Sophos glanced over to see the young Athirst with a puzzled look on his face. "What's going on in that head of yours?"

"I guess I'm confused. I can't see me not having a real body. How is this possible?" Athirst looked up at Sophos with big brown eyes. The reflection of the flame caused them to flicker.

"Much of it you may not understand, but I'll see if I can explain the best way I know how. You see, each of you possesses a light inside of you. You all have gifts and talents that will need to be nurtured and developed. The more you work to develop them, the more your talents will shine. Eventually, you will shine so bright, we won't even see your body."

"Whoa, that is so cool." Athirst stood in amazement, looking at his arms and legs and wondering what it would feel like for them to shine.

Sophos picked up the Writ and read the following script: "For we are not just bodies of flesh and blood, but light and spirit that lives inside a vessel. Those who are truly connected to Jah will exist beyond the physical constraints of their earthly bodies and beyond earthly limits of space and time. (Writ 212: 17-18)"

"What does that mean?" Athirst asked again.

"You've got a big job ahead of you." Querulous patted Sophos on the back. "He is quite the curious one. Glad my Governess seems to get it, or at least doesn't ask me as many questions as your boy. She stays to herself. She can be a little indecisive; she changes her mind about what she wants for dinner at least three times, but she's a sweet girl. Much rather have that than having to answer all of those questions."

"No worries, Querulous, I have a story for that," Sophos boasted.

"I bet you do. I better get comfortable for this one." Querulous sat next to her Youth and cradled Governess' head against her shoulder.

"When I was a boy, I used to pretend that I was like the great beings trapped in the sky. You know, when we look at the stars, we're looking at mighty warriors. They had powers that were far beyond humans since they were half human, half spirit. My friends and I would jump, play, and pretend we were them. I wanted my children to grow up and do the same thing, but devices seemed to take away all of their creativity and imagination…" Sophos drifted off.

"Do you think it's real? Do you really think the stars are mighty warriors?" Athirst asked again.

"That would be amazing." Theiler, Discernmos' Youth, loved Sophos' stories. His Elder was very wise but didn't tell stories with much excitement.

"I want to be a warrior like ones Sophos talks about." Theiler said.

"Me too, that would be awesome."

"Oh, you all will be. You will be some of the greatest warriors the world has ever seen."

Jabari was another Youth who was sitting around the fire. It was clear why Jabari was assigned to Mediorocris. By the age of five, Jabari was nearly five feet tall and the width of two children put together. It took a lot of food to support a child of his size, but Mediorocris was up for the challenge. She was hands-down one of the best cooks in the village; she was no small woman herself. But unlike Mediorocris, who appeared to be mostly fat, it was evident, even at a young age, that Jabari was all muscle. Mediorocris was quite a burly woman. She had a raspy, croaking voice that sounded as if she'd been smoking all her life. But despite her hard exterior, she possessed a kind heart and sensitivity that the other Elders lacked.

Mediorocris would often meet with Sophos after receiving vision to gain clarity. She struggled in interpreting vision and this frustrated her. Today, Mediorocris watched as the Youth listened to Sophos with curiosity and admiration. She kept a close eye on Jabari, who seemed to take a liking to Sophos. In some ways, she felt a little envious of Sophos' ability to interpret vision and captivate an audience; she grew even more envious when Jabari seemed to be fascinated with the other Elders of the village more than he was with her. She loved Jabari like he was her natural-born child, and she felt like she understood him better than any of the other Elders because she knew what it felt like to be gentle on the inside, but have such a large, rough exterior. In some way, she was hoping that Jah would have softened her physical appearance, but she had no such luck.

Mediorocris battled with these conflicting thoughts. She respected Sophos and would often ask him for help interpreting vision, but she also could not remove the feeling of jealousy that seemed to plague her from time to time. Mediorocris decided to step away from the group and meditate, hoping that it would allow that feeling of envy to disappear.

8.
Sophos Warns of the Ambers

The other Elders were hesitant to even mention the Ambers, but Sophos knew that without knowledge of the Ambers their entire purpose would be compromised.

The light of the fire reflected in Sophos' eyes, giving them an orange glow. "You all are wonderful and good, but there are some who use their light for evil. They will glow brighter than all the other colors because they desire to trick people into believing they're right. They will be the color of Amber." Sophos remembered how detrimental their false teachings were. He decided it best to warn the Youth of them. He picked up the Writ and read:

"Many not truly connected to Jah will connect to the spirit of the World and release the powers of the Earth. These spirits are self-seeking and will confuse those who are drawn to their light, for their light will shine with the brilliance greater than that of the most precious stone and they will glow Amber. They will draw upon the powers locked within the Earth, where all those who sinned and perished in the First and Second Worlds are contained, and unknowingly turn away from the riches promised to them by Jah. (Writ 212:38-41)"

"Why does there have to be evil?" Athirst asked with concern.

"Jah must know that you are able to follow him despite the brightness and allure of the Amber light. The bright Amber light exists to challenge you in your discipline. Just stay focused on your own light and you will have nothing to worry about," Sophos assured.

"I'll never be blinded by Amber's glow! I'm going to make sure I'll only glow for Jah. Jah is the one who saved us from the vanishing of the Second World. I can never forget that and I will make sure my future does not forget that!" Athirst exclaimed with innocent excitement.

The other Elders, overhearing Sophos, looked at him with apprehension. Although all of the Elders read from the Writ and meditated with Jah, some expressed concern and caution about exposing the Youth to teachings of bad spirits.

Mediorocris walked over to Sophos and whispered, "The other Elders are waiting for the proper time to discuss the Ambers with their Youth. They are so young, so impressionable. We want to preserve their innocence. Right now, is just not the time, Sophos."

"Mediorocris, I follow the visions of Jah. When he tells me it's time, then it's time, but I will change the subject if it makes you uncomfortable."

"It doesn't make me uncomfortable; I just don't want the Youth to be exposed to evil, and then they have the choice to potentially choose wrong. I don't want the same things to happen all over again." This sentiment left the Elders with an uneasy feeling. Sophos decided to change the atmosphere by speaking of the Gold One.

"There is one exception to the light of the Amber and it is the light of Gold. There is only one who will shine Gold. This one is so special and unique, and many will look toward the coming of their light. Many who are Amber will try to imitate Gold, and because the Amber light is so bright, there will be many who confuse the light of the Amber for Gold, but I want you to remember now, there can only be one."

"Why is there only one who will be Gold?" Theiler asked.

Theiler was an exemplary Youth. It seemed he had it all. He was extremely intelligent for his age and followed Athirst's example of being naturally curious.

"The Gold One has an assignment that Jah has given to him and him only. All I know is that the Gold One will possess the most powerful light of them all."

During the day, the Youth ran and played. The heat of the day didn't seem to matter to them. Even after their chores and all the fishing, hunting, meditating, and reading time, they still found time to play despite their exhaustion. Their energy did not run in short supply.

"I am the Gold One!" Theiler announced. "You will never beat me!"

"I can beat you! It doesn't matter if you are the Gold One. I am claiming Silver, and I am your leader. You have to do whatever I say," Athirst said, bossing the others around.

Soon many of the other Youth chased each other around the hills, hiding behind trees and pretending they already had full use of their traits.

The Elders enjoyed seeing the children's enthusiasm and excitement, and were glad the teachings of the Writ had such an influence over them.

9.
Building Community - Potentiam Libertas

As the Youth grew, they began to take on more responsibility.

"Wake up, Athirst." Sophos nudged his tall, lanky ten-year-old boy to get out of bed. "Wake up and get your clothes on. You're coming with me this morning."

"Really? I can finally come?" Athirst jumped out of bed and quickly put on clothes, grabbed a piece of leftover sweet bread that was sitting on the counter, and made his way outside where Sophos waited.

"Took you long enough. The sun will be up soon. I don't like hunting when the sun comes up."

"They're just devices. None of them work anymore anyway so why does it matter?"

"The best hunters go when it is least expected. Besides, very few people know this, but the moon seems to shine on the ground in a way that illuminates them. I can find all kinds of Second World batteries, timepieces, microchips, and phones under cover of moonlight." Sophos drifted off, already beginning to look around.

"Are we really going on foot? When I've seen you go hunting for devices, you take one of those." Athirst pointed to a large brown bear that was snoozing on their front porch.

"I don't think you're quite ready for him yet. You have to be able to control them. But I will give you a test. Let's see what you learn during lessons. I want you to think about something and see if he will comply," Sophos said.

"Alright, I will then." A determined Athirst squinted his eyes and concentrated.

The sleeping brown bear woke up and slowly started lumbering over to Athirst. It sniffed and circled around him.

"See Sophos, I can do it." Athirst said excitedly.

Just as he spoke those words, the bear lifted itself on its hind legs and let out a ferocious roar. Athirst quickly ran behind Sophos in fear.

"What are you trying to do, wake everyone up?" Sophos put his hands up, pointing to the bear, then lowered his hands to the ground. The bear returned to all fours. Sophos walked over to him and patted the bear on the head.

"That's not fair." Athirst pouted.

"You broke your concentration. Controlling a large animal requires a great deal of concentration. I think that is more your speed," Sophos said as he pointed to a wild hog.

"Seriously, you want me to hunt with that thing?"

"Yep." Sophos hopped on the bear who he affectionately named Cuddles and waited for Athirst to climb aboard his hog.

"Concentrate, Athirst. Make sure you concentrate. Even he will give you a hard time if you don't learn to control him."

Athirst slowly walked over to the horned beast. The hog looked at him apprehensively and started to back up. Athirst lunged toward the hog and the hog squealed and ran away.

"Ha ha ha." Sophos couldn't contain his laughter. "Okay... let's just do it the ole'-fashioned way. Now that you are ten, it may be time to teach you to control beasts, but for now, we need to fill our bags with as many devices as we can so we can sacrifice them tonight at the festival."

Athirst and Sophos hunted for devices until the sun was directly overhead. When they were finished, they brought back a large quantity of devices before Athirst ran off to join the other Youth.

Many Youth found they were skilled musicians. They used woodwind, string, and percussion instruments and played tunes that created a festive atmosphere for all to enjoy. The Elders spent time either cooking food in the community kitchen or cutting wood for the bonfire. The bonfire contributed to the most important part of the festival, as it acted to purge all the technologies of the Second World. In fact, the Potentiam Libertas festival was given its name because it meant freedom from influence.

"So, did you take Athirst for his first hunt today?" Querulous asked.

"Yes. He did pretty well, but he didn't beat me. I collected 37 devices to sacrifice," Sophos bragged.

Sophos seemed to always find himself in the community kitchen on the day of the festival. He was standing a bit too close to Mediorocris, snagging some of the potatoes and carrots she was cutting for the feast.

Eventually, Mediorocris took notice and swatted his hand away.

"Ouch! Okay...I'll stop." Sophos rubbed his hand.

The Elders were looking at all of the activity going on around them.

"Look at Theiler over there! He can make a hollow piece of wood sound so melodic and divine! And your boy, Athirst, is amazing on the drum." Mediorocris continued cutting vegetables for the feast.

"Yes, well, I'm sure if they were given the strength of Jabari, they too would be dragging some gigantic beast around for tonight's meal." Sophos pointed in the direction of the woods, where Jabari was seen dragging a calf toward the village. "That is some boy you have there. Jabari has the strength of ten men."

"He's a good boy too. I am truly blessed."

The Elders continued to watch and take it all in. Sophos had already forgotten his reprimand from Mediorocris and reached his fingers into the center of an apple pie that came fresh out of the oven. As he quickly stuffed a disheveled piece into his mouth, he burned his tongue and began fanning his mouth.

"Ha!" Mediorocris laughed. "That's what you get for sneaking one of my pies!"

When the full moon was directly overhead, the Potentiam Libertas officially began. The Youth and Elders gathered around the fire pit and began to throw in all of the technology remnants they collected in the 28-day cycle. As the devices hit the flames, beautiful colors sparked and popped. This act of devotion was pleasing to Jah.

After this ritual was over, the Elders would begin to tell stories about the color of light that would be given to the lineage of the Youth, who sat eagerly willing to listen.

Sophos was the first to start. "Do you see that color? Do you see how beautiful it is?" Sophos said as the flames danced in different colors. "Jah has created this world so that no one should need or rely on these devices again; you will be able to train your talents so that your future will glow with the powers that Jah has given to you and use them for good. You will be able to enjoy and live a fruitful life, the way Jah intended."

"What color do you think I will have?" Athirst inquired.

"Hmmm…..I don't know, let me look in your ears. Yep, I think I see something in there!"

"What is it?"

Sophos, who loved to tease Athirst, took a silver coin and pretended to pull it from behind Athirst's ear. Athirst could not help but giggle.

"Ahhhh," Sophos said, pretending to analyze this discovery. "Your lineage will glow metallic silver, just like this coin, and become some of the greatest leaders of the Third World." Hearing this, all of the other Youth ran to Sophos, asking what was in store for their own future.

When Jabari ran over to join the other Youth, Mediorocris called for him. "Jabari, I need you to help me with this pot of water."

Jabari reluctantly turned around to go help her, wanting to have joined the other children in finding out their destiny.

"Did you need my help?" Jabari asked.

"Oh, yes, well… I didn't realize that I could get it myself."

"Okay!" Jabari said excitedly, attempting to head back off to hear one of Sophos' stories. "Wait, um, can you help me with this?" Mediorcris began looking around for something Jabari could do.

"I was really hoping I could hear one of Sophos' stories. He really seems to understand vision so well and I…I have such a difficult time. Can I go?"

"Fine, I guess you can go. I'll just struggle with bringing all this food over to the table myself," Mediorocris said, trying to gain sympathy.

Jabari, picking up on his Elder's somber demeanor, chose to stay and help her clean up at the end of the festival.

It was important that the Elders meditated with the Youth after all of the Potentiam Libertas festivities were over. They would clear their minds to allow Jah to speak to them. Although the Youth and Elders practiced meditation several times a day, meditation after the Potentiam Libertas was especially important. In this meditation, Jah would give both the Elders and corresponding Youth the same vision. This further enhanced the connection of the Youth to their Elder and allowed the Elders to see how they could best help them. The purpose of these meditations was to reveal the Youth's gifts, and how to properly utilize them to fulfill their calling, but this evening, Athirst seemed distracted.

"Did you see that Sophos? It's like they're twinkling."

"No, I don't see anything. I need you to concentrate, Athirst."

"I'm trying to, but it's like they're trying to tell me something." Athirst continued to gaze up at the stars. "Are you sure you don't see anything different?" Athirst was confused. Sophos was the one who spoke about them being gods, but he couldn't see them move. Maybe there was something special just for him?

"Look." Athirst pointed up. The stars seem to get larger in size, almost as if they were heading toward him, but when he blinked again, they were back to where they started.

"The stars -- are they shining for you? I used to see the same thing when I was younger, but not so much anymore. Get focused."

Sophos and Athirst meditated together in the still of the night. Both received the same vision, and pondered what Jah had shown them.

"So, what did you see?"

"It was really difficult for me to tell. None of it made sense."

"Oh," said Sophos. "Well, tell me what you saw and maybe I can try to figure it out."

"At first I saw a tree. It started off with five branches and from those branches it grew five more branches, and from those, five more. This continued to happen until I couldn't tell how many branches there were in total. As the tree transformed, so did the ground underneath it. The ground became as high as a mountain and the tree rose to the mountain's peak. The mountain was the color of mercury. From where I was on the ground, I could see a small sparkle on the tip of one of the branches. So, I climbed up to see what it was. As I climbed, the sparkle became a brilliant gold light on the tip of the tree. It was a radiant light, like no other light I had ever seen. I couldn't help but want to touch it, but……"

"Then what happened?" Sophos asked.

"Well," Athirst continued, "I couldn't. I couldn't touch it. I couldn't finish the vision. I…"

Athirst looked down with disappointment. He felt ashamed because Sophos had great visions and could retell them with such ease and elaborate detail.

"Why do you look so down? It takes time to develop your skill, Athirst. You must be patient with yourself. Sometimes we don't always have the answers and visions can be quite confusing. Sometimes they are blurry, even for me."

"Well," Athirst asked expectantly, "Was I close? Can you tell me?"

"My son, you are a very special boy, very special indeed. Keep working. You must never stop your desire for vision. You'll get the hang of it eventually. But for now, I cannot give you the answers you seek."

Unlike the other Elders who spent time with their Youth confirming every little detail of their visions, Sophos did not. Every time Athirst shared a vision, Sophos would respond by saying, "You must never stop the desire for your vision. Keep working." He wanted Athirst to be independent and learn for himself.

They headed back to their house. When they got to the door, Sophos patted Athirst on the head. "Don't work too hard on meditation tonight. You've got to wake up for lessons in the morning."

10.
Taming the Beasts

The Youth attended lessons, which were required of every Youth in the community. A group of special Elders called Magisters were to not only take care of their assigned Youth, but to also deliver instruction and impart wisdom to all the Youth through special classes. Lessons were opportunities for them to learn about the history of the First and Second Worlds as they were described in the original sixty-six chapters of the Writ. They read of the prophecies given to the people of the First and Second Worlds, as well the corruption and the fall of the Second World in chapters 67-211. They also learned in chapter 212 how they were to address many aspects of their life, as well as prepare for the things to come. They practiced many skills during lessons, as all Youth were expected to know how to survive without the use of technology. Both guys and girls learned how to hunt, cook, sew, build houses, and use the elements of nature to make medicine. They understood astronomy and used it to determine the time and seasons.

All of the Youth were dedicated to their lessons and took the information taught seriously. They understood the value of knowledge and appreciated the insightful conversations they would have about the Writ.

Today, the Youth found lessons particularly interesting because it focused on the gifts Jah had given to the inhabitants of the Third World and how each village was given different powers and abilities. There were unique things about Eirene, but most unique was their ability to control animals.

"Well, you already know that we have the ability to control things. I see Discernmos control wild animals all the time, so it's no big deal," Thieler said to the rest of the group.

"Really, no big deal? Have you been able to control something yet?" Governess asked pointedly.

"No, but I will and I am sure that I will do it better than the rest of you."

"No way," Athirst responded. "Just because your Elder is able to do something well, doesn't mean that you will be able to do it, too."

"Okay boys, it's not that serious. I don't mind a little competition; let's see who will be able to control their animal the best. Less talking and more doing." Jabari had gotten excited and began rubbing his hands together, waiting for their response.

"Hey, wait a minute. What about us? We want in as well." Nia crossed her arms and looked at Jabari.

"Okay, then we all will all participate," Jabari responded.

"Thank you!" Governess and Nia said at the same time. "So, Governess continued, "What are we going to do?"

Each of them thought for a moment. It was Athirst who came up with the idea. "I've got it, we will race the animals with our minds."

"Okay. I like that idea," Theiler said. "But, to make it even more interesting, we will not be able to choose our own animal. So, let's do this right now. Everyone, come on, take out paper and ink."

Each of the Youth did just that.

"Now," Theiler continued, "Write down the name of an animal that you want to see in the race. I will take all of the pieces of paper and each of you will draw one. That will be the animal that you will race tomorrow."

Each of the Youth secretly wrote their animal on a sheet and handed it to Thieler. "Ladies first. Governess, you pick." Governess reached her hand into the folded bits of paper, grabbed one of the crumbled sheets and opened it. "A rabbit." Governess smiled. "Well, that shouldn't be too hard."

"Your turn Nia."

Nia reached into Theiler's hand and pulled out a sliver of paper. "A deer. I guess I can learn to race a deer. They're quite large animals though, and probably use a lot of power."

Before being told, Jabari reached into the pile and grabbed one of the sheets. "A sloth, what in the name of Jah is a sloth?"

The others burst out laughing. "Who wrote a sloth? That's hilarious!" Athirst said grabbing his stomach as he laughed.

No one fessed up. "Your turn," Theiler said to Athirst. Athirst grabbed his paper feeling confident that nothing could be worse than Jabari's pick.

"A turtle?! You expect me to race a turtle?" Even more howling erupted; this time, Jabari included himself in the hysterics.

"Ha ha ha, so funny. Well, let's see what you have. Come on," Athrist demanded.

Theiler slowly opened his sheet. Before he could even open it, Governess began to laugh. She knew what was on the paper.

"You seem a bit too happy," Theiler said to Governess.

He opened the sheet and didn't say anything for a while.

"Well, out with it!" Athirst prompted.

"A slug," Theiler whispered in dismay.

"What do you have?" Athirst asked, making sure he heard correctly.

"I have to race a slug," Theiler said as he continued to read over the sheet, hoping there was some mistake.

The Youth could not contain themselves. Athirst found himself rolling on the ground and Nia was grabbing at her side.

"Alright. It's not that funny." Theiler kept his composure and tried to get everyone back on track. "Just find your stupid animals and do the best you can to train them tonight. We will meet here tomorrow after lessons."

The next day, each of the Youth came with the animals in tow. Theiler had drawn a start and finish line in the dirt that was about 300 feet apart. They placed their animals at the start: a rabbit, a slug, a sloth, a deer, and a turtle.

"Here are the rules," Theiler proudly announced. "Each animal has to start here and end at the finish. If any animal drifts past those areas..." Theiler pointed to the left and right of the path, "...then they are considered out of bounds and cannot finish the race. They must cross over the finish line to count. The first one completely over the finish line without going out of bounds is the winner."

The Youth made last minute adjustments to each of their animals. "Go ahead and get your animals in your mind. Start placing your hands out to send them a signal."

Each one of them had a different strategy. Athirst, Nia, and Theiler thought it best to go to the finish line so their animals could see them. Jabari and Governess stayed at the start line and stood behind their animals.

"On the count of three, you can begin!" Theiler shouted. "One, two, three!" And with that, the animals took off. Athirst was concentrating and beckoning his animal to come toward him. No one had ever seen a turtle move so quickly. It's little legs looked as if they were spinning in circles to the point where they seemed to float. Governess' rabbit was hopping all over the place. It bounced from one side of the path to the other, eventually heading out of bounds.

Governess decided the best thing to do was to scoop it up and cradle it in her arms. Initially, the sloth didn't appear to be moving at all, but upon closer inspection, Jabari could see that it picked up its long arm and dug its nails into the dirt, sliding its body toward the finish line. The deer gracefully trotted along the path. It continued along but was eventually distracted by seeing a turtle zoom by, followed by a slug that seemed to be speeding up with each passing minute. Jabari, realizing that he was losing, closed his eyes and began to concentrate even harder. He started picturing his sloth at the end of the finish line. He put his hands out and moved them in a way that indicated he was pushing it. As he did this, the sloth started picking up the pace. Its claws reached into the dirt and began picking up speed. The turtle was in the lead, with the slug and sloth close behind. Athirst got so excited about his turtle being in front that he lost concentration for a bit. Before realizing it, all three animals were neck and neck. Nia ran over to Governess, who was still petting her rabbit. "Do you see this?" She asked, exasperated.

"Yes, why is your deer headed toward the village kitchen?" Governess responded.

"Oh no!" Nia ran off to get her deer back on the path.

"Yes!" Athirst shouted. "He did it! My turtle is the winner!"

"No he's not, it was clearly a tie," Theiler said irritably. "Look, my slug was over the line at the same time as your dumb turtle."

"What about my sloth? His fingers were touching the line when Athirst tried to claim his victory."

"I thought you said that their entire body had to be over the line and mine clearly was."

At this time, Governess came over to join them.

"What happened to you?" Theiler asked.

"I didn't want to play in your silly little race. Besides, my sweet puffy wanted to cuddle with me," Governess said.

Nia came over as well, but she was mounted on top of her deer. "I don't think either of you won. I could see everything from up here. Athirst called his victory, but his turtle wasn't quite over the finish line. By that time, both the slug and the sloth managed to catch up. I say it's a tie."

"No way!" Athirst insisted. "My turtle won fair and square."

"I think we'll just have to have a tie breaker," Theiler said slyly.

"Sounds like a fantastic idea," Jabari agreed.

"You both are only saying that because you were clearly the losers, but whatever makes you both happy. I know who the real victor was today."

"The next competition should test our ability to ride the animals," Nia said. "And this time, we get to choose our own animal. Let's all take time to get better with our riding skills and we'll do this again."

"Agreed." All of the Youth walked home, eager to tell their version of the race to their Elders.

11.
Vision

Sophos watched as Athirst grew up right before his eyes. Like many of the Youth in the community, Athirst was growing into a young man. And it was becoming more and more apparent when he started to pay attention to the female Youth. The Elders took notice when they went from innocent play to more flirtatious encounters.

The Elders had to keep a close watch. It was very important that the Youth were united with the one whom Jah approved of. In order for future generations to prosper, the Youth needed to find the correct partner -- one who they could build a close relationship with and who would help them maximize their greatest potential. It was important they find someone who shared similar traits, passions, and desires. A good partner would be one that had the ability to interpret vision in a similar way, so that there would be no division in their household.

The Elders stayed in deep meditation and spent many hours reading The Writ. For the Youth to be assigned to their proper mate, vision had to be interpreted correctly so the Youth could be matched in the most ideal way.

The sun was directly overhead, and everyone was finding ways to make the scorching heat less unbearable. Querulous was sitting under the shade of an oak tree when Mediorocris decided to join her.

"It feels better out here than it does in my house," Mediorocris said as she sat on a wooden bench.

"Yes," Querulous agreed. "I'm not going to do much more today. The more I move, the hotter it feels."

Querulous began to peel the skin off an orange. The sweet juice attracted small flies who were also in desperate need of cool, sweet refreshment.

"I cannot catch a break today," Querulous continued to moan. She waved her hands around to swat at the flying insects.

"Do you know what Jabari asked me today?" Mediorocris turned to Querulous, who continued to wave her arms and fan herself at the same time.

"Something not very bright, I would guess," Querulous responded.

Mediorocris ignored her. She had grown accustomed to Querulous' ornery comments.

"He asked me what I thought about him unifying with Nia."

"Interesting... Nia... she's a lovely girl. She's Vera's girl, right?" Querulous went from irritated to full-on gossip mode. "So how do you feel about that?"

"I don't know how to feel. I didn't realize I would grow so accustomed to having Jabari in my life. It's been just us for so long; it's like we're family. I was so thankful Jah allowed me to have my sweet Jabari, but this is just a reminder that it is not my will but the will of Jah that matters. I just wish I was better at vision, because I don't know if I see Nia when I meditate, but if Jabari sees her, then I guess..." Mediorocris' voice trailed off.

"Jabari is a sweet boy, but he's not much for vision. Just make sure that he is fulfilling the will of Jah. We don't want him straying down the wrong path." Querulous, however, felt a sense of relief that Jabari had his sights set on someone already. She had received vision a while back that her Youth, Governess, was to be united with him, and this troubled her. Personally, she wanted her to be matched with someone whom she thought possessed more intellect.

Querulous watched as Mediorocris' eyes became glossed over. Mediorocris wiped away the tears that were starting to well in the corner of her eye and turned her head away from Querulous. Querulous placed one hand on Mediorocris' back and used the other to continue fanning both of them to ward off the heat.

"Well, I can tell you one good thing. You're going to have a lot more free time on your hands. Jabari eats about 20 pounds of food per day. He has you in the kitchen from sunup to sundown."

Mediorocris and Querulous laughed. "You're right about that. Jah gave me a big boy!"

"He's not a boy anymore. You're going to have to get used to that. We all are. They're all growing up so fast," Querulous said.

Many of the Elders were having similar conversations. Sophos felt a bit relieved, as he had not been sent vision of Athirst's union-mate. He was kind of glad he didn't have to deal with it quite yet, however, he took every opportunity to poke a little fun at the other Elders, who knew the time was coming when their Youth would leave and go off to fulfill their destiny.

Over the next week, the weather was much cooler. Many of the Elders began to venture outside again. Sophos made an extra effort to walk to Mediorocris' home. Querulous could not keep a secret and managed to slip it to Sophos that Jabari had received vision for his union-mate. Mediorocris opened her door but walked away quickly; she had something cooking over the fire and didn't want it to burn.

"Come on in, come on in. I seem to have lost my hunting knife. I'm trying to get the scales off this fish for my boy."

Sophos looked around for a bit. "Did you want to borrow mine?"

"I may have to. So, what brings you by today?"

"I heard Jabari has interest in Nia. He must have grown tired of eating your lentils and is ready to move on to better cuisine."

"Sophos, that's not very nice. Is that why you came by? To insult me? I'm sure Athirst will come to you soon with a union announcement, so don't be so quick to make fun. We'll see who's laughing then when it happens to you next." Mediorocris sighed. "You know, this has been quite difficult for me. I'm going to miss my big boy. I don't want him growing up and not needing me anymore."

"He's not a child anymore. None of them are," Sophos said, but then quickly grew sympathetic when he saw Mediorocris' downcast face. "I will admit though, it is quite scary for many reasons. The familiar disappears. Our Youth grow more strong-willed and independent with each passing day. They carry more responsibility with them, and with that, the ability to make their own choices. All we can do now is trust that we did our best to raise them well." Sophos looked off into the distance. "I'm sure Jah has revealed to you who his union-mate is supposed to be, correct?"

"Of course he did." Mediorocris tried her best to respond with confidence. She didn't want Sophos to know that she was uncertain of who Jabari's mate was supposed to be, nor did she want him to know that she thought Jabari might be wrong.

"Well, I am glad that you and Jabari have received matching visions," Sophos said warily, lifting an eyebrow since he knew that both Mediorocris and Jabari struggled with interpretation of vision. "You know that this is the way things are supposed to be. All of the Youth will eventually…"

Mediorocris interrupted Sophos. "Yes, please don't finish. I know. It could be why I find myself peddling about trying to make sure that everything is in proper order before he's unified, and I depart." She couldn't bear saying what she knew was the inevitable. The Elders knew they served one purpose and it was to guide the Youth in the ways of Jah. Once their Youth was unified, they knew their presence would not be needed much longer. Several scriptures in the Writ spoke about marking time, and typically when some were unified and starting a new life, others died because their job was finished for the time being.

Sophos could see tears welling in her eyes and his tone softened. "You're right. Let's not discuss such things. Let's just enjoy the time that we still have," he replied. Sophos usually had a glimmer to his brown eyes, but the mood of the atmosphere managed to make them appear more of a dull grey. The Elders were old when they arrived in the Third World and looking at their seventeen to eighteen-year-olds was a reminder of how long they had left. Every Elder in the village was at least eighty years old -- some were approaching ninety.

"Well," Sophos continued, "you know I'm not much for solemn conversations. So let's change the subject, shall we?"

"Right. So, I think I'll need to borrow your hunting knife. There are a few fish that I need to descale. I'm going to make Jabari's favorite meal. Feel free to come by later on if you'd like."

"You must've had to catch an awful lot of fish if you have enough for both Jabari and me to eat."

Mediorocris chuckled. Sophos placed a hand on Mediorocris' shoulder before leaving her house. Sophos didn't get to delight in everyone else's sadness for long because a few weeks later, he noticed Athirst had his eye on someone. This made him worry. He began to notice him walk home everyday after lessons with a young lady and would overhear them talking as they got closer to the door. It was pretty easy to overhear conversations in the Third World because none of the windows had glass panes like they did in the Second World.

"So...the lesson today...what'd you think?" Athirst asked Governess eagerly. Sophos listened and watched. He could sense Athirst's nervousness and noticed that Athirst was carrying both his and Governess' Writ.

Governess was of simple beauty, and had a kind heart. She was soft-spoken but had a quick wit, and Athirst admired her for her quiet strength and intellect. She was very patient with everyone, including her Elder Querulous, who had grown even more ornery in her more mature age, if that was humanly possible.

"The lesson today really had me thinking a lot about our futures. What about you?" Governess responded.

"I felt the same way. What about that scripture the Magister read? What'd you think about it?" Athirst inquired.

"I kinda feel like there's a lot of pressure to make sure we do the right thing, especially now. Everyone's talking about their union-mates. If we choose the wrong mate, then we don't fulfill Jah's purpose and we risk facing whatever punishment that comes with that. It's so much to think about. I dislike making those kinds of decisions. Just doesn't seem fair for one thing to have so much impact," Governess replied, distracted.

"I guess you're right," Athirst agreed, struggling to find other questions to ask just to keep Governess from leaving. He seemed so enchanted by her that he ignored her tendency to bore easily.

"So, who do you think your union-mate is going to be?" Athirst asked nervously.

"I'm not sure. I haven't received vision of it yet. Oh, did you hear about Nia and Jabari? And then that question Jabari asked today? I would have been so embarrassed if I were her."

"I didn't think what he asked was that bad. He just wants to make sure he's seeing the right thing when he meditates," Athirst responded.

"I guess, but it's like he's admitting that he's not sure if she's the right one...like he cannot interpret vision for himself. You on the other hand always seem to have the right interpretation." Governess smiled at Athirst.

"Well, not always." Athirst blushed.

By this time, Sophos was not the only one watching their conversation. Querulous was staring out her window, curious as to why it was taking Governess so long to get home.

Querulous began shuffling about in her house and doing what she did best. "If Governess having interest in Athirst is going to make her miss her chores, then Athirst needs to find someone else. There are too many things that need to be done around here. I can't have her being all google-eyed about some boy," Querulous muttered to herself while she picked up around the house.

Querulous' face seemed to match her disposition. There was a reason she seemed so cross all the time. Her life in the Second World wasn't easy. Two of her three children participated in the mass suicides that took place before the end of the Second World. Her husband died of a rare cancer that was caused by the intake of artificial vegetation.

Those circumstances made Querulous grow quite bitter over time, but deep down she had a good heart. Below her wrinkled exterior, Querulous truly loved people and loved Jah. She didn't understand the reason why she was going through so much, but there were so many people hurting that she did not feel alone. In the Second World, she spent her quiet time meditating on the first 66 books and got her joy from reading about the love that was given to those who remained faithful. But as time went on and her family was killed off one by one, she developed a coping mechanism so as to appear unfeeling, unattached, and unhurt. It made her feel like she had control of everything when things were inevitably falling apart.

When Querulous saw Athirst and Governess gazing at each other, she had the last straw. She stopped milling around the house and decided to find her way over to Sophos.

"Well, it seems like you and I will be stuck together forever now. Why has Jah decided to punish me in this New World? I thought this would be a place of peace," Querulous teased, bounding through his door.

"How do you think I feel?" Sophos quipped. "Governess is quite lovely, but her Elder...I'm not so sure. I feel sorry for Athirst. He's going to have quite the interesting in-law on his hands."

Querulous laughed. "I haven't heard the term 'in-law' since the Second World. My mother in-law in the Second World was a nightmare."

"Well then, you and her must have gotten along quite nicely seeing as you both had so much in common."

Querulous nudged Sophos and they both chuckled. As their laughter died down, they could hear Athirst and Governess giggling in the distance.

"I don't have time to watch them be all mushy-gushy. I'm getting Governess and heading home." She turned away and poked her head out the door.

"Hey Governess, I've been waiting for you to get back so you can help me with dinner. You know it takes you a lifetime just to decide what you want to eat."

"Okay, I'm on my way! Give me a little while so I can say bye to him."

"No, I have waited for you to say goodbye for the past thirty minutes!" Querulous said as she rushed toward them, not even bothering to tell Sophos goodbye. "I will do it for you. Bye, Athirst! She has things she needs to do." And with that, Querulous grabbed Governess' arm and started pulling her home.

"Bye, Athirst!" Governess said, looking back and tugging her arm away from her Elder.

"So you no longer need hands I see?" Querulous raised an eyebrow.

"Why do you say that, Querulous?" Governess said, playing the fool. She knew that whenever there was a random comment, she was in for it. She never knew what "it" was, but it was always interesting.

"I asked because I've noticed that Athirst is always holding your Writ for you. Jah might as well have saved the effort of creating one for you since you never seem to hold it in your own hands anymore."

"Seriously Querulous, you come up with the silliest things to say." Governess kissed her Elder on the cheek. Like many things for Governess, her feelings for her Elder seemed to change with each minute. She loved her dearly, but there were many times she wished she had another Elder.

"I guess you want me to die early," Querulous moped.

"Of course not, Querulous, why on earth would I want that to happen? You know I love you."

"Well, I can't tell," Querulous snapped back. "You leave so much of your mess scattered about. I have to pick up behind you all day. My back is starting to give out." She clasped her back dramatically and made an aching motion.

"I'm sorry, Querulous. I will make sure to pick up more." Governess tried as long as she could to maintain a sweet demeanor, but grew more irritated by the minute.

"Don't get me started on how long it takes for you to understand your vision. I stay in the meditative position for so long, my knees lock up."

"My apologies; I will ask Jah to speak to me faster next time." Governess replied sarcastically

Despite her surly nature, Querulous smiled back and said, "Yes, well, I'll let you be the one to tell Jah He needs to work faster."

Both Governess and Querulous smirked at each other.

Before she forgot, Querulous mumbled, "I love you too." Querulous had not said those words since the passing of her husband in the Second World. It felt good.

12.
Governess Writes

Governess quickly dealt with all of the mess Querulous had fussed about and retreated to her room. She had a lot of thoughts in her head. There always seemed to be a lot of things spinning around in her mind. She was so thankful for ink and paper, especially in these times. After her conversations with Athirst and Querulous, she needed to write.

Jah, I am so grateful that you have placed Athirst in my life. It has helped with the bad dreams. I keep seeing bits and pieces of things that don't make sense to me. Red rain falls, but then nothing. I don't know what it's supposed to mean, but when the dreams are over, they leave me with an uneasy feeling. I don't think they are coming from a good place. There is something dark inside of me, but I can't sort it out. What is this thing that is plaguing me? Athirst makes me laugh. He seems to help me focus on the parts of me that are good. I know that I should be more appreciative of being saved from the vanishing, but something is missing. I feel empty. Life here is very difficult and trying to be the perfect Youth is becoming exhausting. I wish I knew my birth mother and father, or if I have a sibling from the Second World located in the village nearby. Maybe they would accept me the way I am. All of me and not just the parts that I am allowed to show -- but I don't even know if that would help.

My Elder, the one that You have given to me -- she means well, but she can be a bit overbearing. I try to smile, but it gets hard especially when she seems so strong. She seems like she can handle anything. So I just go along with it. I never want her to see me down. I think she would lose respect for me. I am grateful that I have a quick wit to jab back when it is necessary. I think it has helped me develop a thicker skin, but I don't want to have a thicker skin. I want to be soft. I want someone to take care of me. Maybe my time is coming soon. Everyone seems to be in the process of finding their union-mate. I hope mine is Athirst. I can really see us having a great union, but I guess I'll just have to wait for Your vision.

"Governess!" Querulous shouted from the front room. "Come help me cut the potatoes."

Governess quickly put the paper and pen inside of her leather sack and hid it under a wool blanket. That was where she kept all of her journal writings. She learned a long time ago that Querulous hated going into a messy room, so she kept things a bit cluttered to make sure Querulous stayed away. This way, Governess could have a space all her own. A place where she could think and keep things private.

Governess joined Querulous and quickly put the pot over the fire and grabbed a knife to help cut the potatoes. Afterwards, Governess grabbed a bucket and went to the wooden barrels by the community kitchen, filling it with water. She wanted to make sure she got enough water for their meal before Querulous had time to fuss about it. Querulous didn't see Governess leave for the water, but was pleased when she returned. Although Querulous appreciated Governess' efforts, she couldn't help but feel that Governess' efficiency stole an opportunity for her to make a comment about something.

"Humph, you sure are learning to set up dinner quickly. Looks like you're practicing to be a wonderful union-mate."

"No, I just didn't want to hear you fuss. So I went to get everything you needed ahead of time."

"Governess, there's no amount of preparation in the world that will keep me from finding something to fuss about."

Querulous nudged her wide hips into Governess, and Governess cracked a smile. Inside, she was growing tired of the constant back and forth.

"So, you and Athirst seem to be spending a lot of time with each other. Have you sought out guidance from Jah?"

"Not yet. I wasn't sure if I was supposed to go to Him or if He was just going to send a vision like He has with so many other things."

"So you have not received vision yet?" Querulous inquired.

"No, not yet. Have you?"

"Maybe, I don't know."

"Oh my goodness Querulous, you have." She swatted at Querulous with a dish rag. Governess could tell that Querulous knew who her union-mate was supposed to be. "So, would Jah approve?" Governess pressed.

"You know that I'm not supposed to tell you until you receive vision for yourself. All I can say is that Athirst is a very intelligent, very handsome Youth. And, I cannot believe I'd ever be saying this, but I would love to have him be the one for you."

"But is he?" Governess couldn't help but feel butterflies in her stomach.

"Let's just see how things go. When you have your vision, then we can discuss this." Querulous continued cutting carrots.

Governess didn't know how to read her this time. She had seen Querulous gossip with Mediorocris for hours. But why was she being so tight-lipped about her union-mate? Governess wondered.

13.
Guidance

On the eve of the eleventh Potentiam Libertas for the year, the familiar smells of the festival filled the air. The flames from the fire blazed in their many colors as piles of technological remnants were sacrificed. Most of the Elders and Youth from the community were gathered around the fire waiting for the feast to begin, but Sophos did not join them. His focus was shifted elsewhere. For several weeks he watched the connection between Athirst and Governess grow stronger, and he knew that things were going to change soon.

In a dark, quiet place, Sophos made close connection with Jah. His knees fell to the ground and his body bent over so that his hands touched the ground. He made a point to make himself humble. He wanted no distractions tonight and felt there was no need to celebrate because, for the first time, he felt fear. He closed his eyes and whispered, "Jah, show me what it is you want me to see."

And then Sophos received a vision. Butterflies were dancing around each other. They moved in beautiful swirls, and as they moved closer and closer to each other, they floated higher in the sky, heading for the sun. When the two butterflies flapped their wings, one butterfly had visible black spots on the underside of its wings; these spots signified that it was male. The other butterfly lacked the spots and was therefore female. They continued to flirtatiously intermingle and move closer to the sun until the female appeared that it could no longer move in the same direction. It flapped its wings but could not get any closer. The male turned around, desiring to go back to help the other, thinking it must have been caught in something; however, as the male began to turn around, a gust of wind separated the two of them and pushed him even closer to the sun. The wind became more turbulent and although it grew more difficult to fly in the direction of the sun, the butterfly continued pushing through until it grew weak. Weak, but still flying, another butterfly, one without spots, came from the north and connected itself to the male. Their unified strength allowed them to reach the surface of the sun. When they reached the surface, the sun exploded into a kaleidoscope of butterflies that filled the air.

When the vision was over, Sophos understood and thanked Jah for his guidance. Sophos stood up and started walking toward the festival. Usually, Sophos would mingle with the other Elders while telling jokes to the Youth. But tonight, he was quiet and simply watched. He watched the colors of the fire as the devices of the Second World were sacrificed. He watched the Elders interacting with each other and the Youth, who were now young adults, dancing and celebrating. He also watched Athirst, who had removed himself from his group of friends to sit near Governess. They would share a few words and smile at each other. Light touches were exchanged between them, and Sophos noticed that they would stare into each other's eyes more intensely with each passing moment.

The next morning after the full moon, Sophos and Athirst sat in a quiet place, meditating. Their heads and hearts were clear, and their minds were open to the words of Jah. As was customary, Sophos asked Athirst about his vision and he responded by telling him of the five tree branches producing five more branches on top of a mercury-colored mountain. Athirst described the vision of the light at the end of the branch and its radiant glow.

"It was the same vision as before. Nothing new. Why is that Sophos?"

"Well," Sophos said, "It may be time for you to interpret your vision."

Athirst was not expecting that response. He was always used to Sophos saying, "never stop your desire for vision."

"I need to interpret my vision?" Athirst asked inquisitively.

"Yes, so let's begin. You dreamed of a tree with five branches. Close your eyes, clear your mind, and tell me what the tree represents."

Athirst thought for a minute. "In the Writ, Jah uses the tree many times to symbolize life. Trees with growing branches symbolize new life. But there were five branches. So there are five new lives?"

"Yes," Sophos responded. "You will bring forth five that will bring forth five more."

"So, I will have five children?" Athirst asked.

"Indeed. You will have five children that will bring forth five children. You may have more that bring forth one child, seven children, or no children at all, or, you may have exactly five children, but what is certain is that five of your children will bring five more children into the world, and from those 25, each will have five more. You are the beginning of a lineage of leaders. The mountain of mercury sitting above everything else...what do you think that means?"

"Mercury is the color of silver. Silver is the color of leadership. Jah has chosen me to be a leader? Can I even be one? I don't know if I have the courage. I don't know if I have what it takes." Athirst was humbled by the interpretation of the vision and for the first time, he doubted his ability to lead.

"You will be a leader, but even better than you, will be those who come from you. Athirst, you will pave the way for great leaders to rise from your lineage. In order to do that, you must remain faithful and disciplined."

Sophos wanted to reveal the vision of the butterflies, but decided against it. It was not the right time. He realized that the vision in particular had to be given to Athirst himself, and Jah would give that vision to him when it was appropriate.

From that day, Sophos no longer said, "never stop your desire for vision." It was evident that Athirst showed great desire. Athirst was hungry for knowledge. He craved the time he spent with Jah and had a thirst for every single new learning experience.

It was on the seventh day of the seventh 28-day cycle when Athirst came to Sophos with a very serious look on his face. The sun was directly overhead and there wasn't a cloud in the sky. Sophos was in the shade of an oak tree reading the Writ when Athirst approached.

"Sophos," Athirst said. "Can I ask you something?"

"Anything my son; what is it that's troubling you?"

"I have great affection for Governess. I guess I'm asking for your blessing in this union."

"Hmmmm, I see... did you ask Jah for the blessing of this particular union?"

"Sophos..." Athirst said with a long, whiny voice -- like a child not getting his way.

"Well, did you?" Sophos snapped.

"I can't see how Jah would disapprove. She's everything. She is so intelligent and beautiful. She'd make for a blessed union."

"I know that's what you feel. I think Governess is quite lovely. So if you're asking for my blessing, well, then my answer is yes, but just remember, I am not Jah."

Athirst, delighted at Sophos' approval, ran across the village of Eirene and found himself in front of the hut where Querulous and Governess resided. Before walking in, Athirst made sure to catch his breath. It usually took a lot more to tire Athirst, but the heat combined with the nerves in his stomach made him weak in the knees.

Whew, what do I say? Athirst thought to himself, realizing that he probably should have thought of the proper words before arriving at their door.

Before Athirst could even knock, the door flew open. Governess had her back turned toward the door. She was bent down, trying to drag a very large pot to the river.

"Ahhhh!" Governess screamed when she abruptly turned around. "Athirst, what are you doing here?"

"I am, well, I am…"

"Who's that at the door?" Athirst could hear Querulous approaching.

"Oh, it's you." Querulous pursed her lips. "What are you doing causing such a commotion? You made me get up and move around in this heat." Querulous walked away to sit back down in her chair. She had a tablet of paper in her hand that she was using as a fan to cool off.

"Good afternoon, Querulous, how are you doing?"

"I'm doing well, given that you interrupted my peace and quiet," Querulous griped.

"Did you need something from me, Athirst?" Governess inquired. "If not," she continued, "I must head down to the river to get some fresh water, or else I'll never hear the end of it."

Governess whispered in Athirst's ear, "I think everytime she complains, Jah purposely makes it hotter in here." Athirst laughed quietly to himself.

Querulous interjected. "I don't know if you came to see Governess right now, but she's about to go to River Aesis and get some cool water for us to drink. I remember in the Second World when we could just turn on a faucet and water would flow out. That is until they became careless with the water. The YSW were selfish."

Querulous would have gone on complaining about the YSW, which was her favorite thing to do, but Athirst interrupted.

"Jah will provide. In fact, I think He's provided an opportunity for us to talk," Athirst said enthusiastically.

Athirst then turned to Governess and said, "I'll catch up with you later. I think this'll be a great opportunity for me and Querulous to spend some time together."

Governess whispered to him again, teasing, "Are you sure you want to spend time with her?"

"I hope you know you aren't a very good whisperer," Querulous snapped.

Governess grabbed the clay pot and carefully placed it on her head, making her way to River Aesis.

"You must want something from me. What is it?" Querulous said suspiciously. *She does seem grumpier in the heat*, Athirst thought to himself.

"Why do you say that?" Athirst's voice squeaked just a little.

"What do you want?" Querulous continued expectantly.

"I really respect Governess." He cleared his throat and started again. "She is such a delight and is very smart and kind. I was wondering if I could receive a blessing for our union."

Querulous grew quiet and looked at the eager Athirst. She saw the love he had for Governess and the respect he had for her. She sighed. She put her paper tablet down. Her wrinkled face smoothed out, and her scowl turned to a small smile. She gave him a kiss on the forehead.

"Yes, Athirst. You have my blessing." Querulous couldn't contain her emotion and felt pure joy at the thought that her Youth would be unified with Athirst. She also felt a bit of relief and began to think that maybe her vision of who Governess was supposed to unite with was incorrect, or at least she hoped that she was wrong. She felt confident that Athirst would make a much better pair for her sweet Governess than the one who she was sent a vision of.

Athirst was so excited that he ran toward the river in search of Governess. When he arrived, Governess was walking back toward the community with the large clay container that had been filled with fresh water. Athirst took the water container from her hands.

"Athirst, what are you doing? I'll never hear the end of it if I don't get this water to Querulous."

"I have something to ask you."

"Well," Governess said as she wrestled the container from Athirst, "What is it you have to ask me? Make it quick."

"I have great affection towards you, and I think of you everyday. Please know this. I cannot imagine life without you and I wanted to know if you would…" Athirst gulped. "…join me in union?"

Governess dropped the container. Her breathing slowed.

"Oh, well…I don't know…I…I think of you often as well…I don't know what to say. How do I tell Querulous? I……"

"She already knows. I spoke to her before I found you. She gave me her blessing. Governess, you are so amazing, and smart, and fun to be around. I can't imagine anyone else giving me such joy."

Governess smiled. She wrapped her arms around Athirst and kissed him. A first for both of them. Athirst was speechless and Governess was giddy. "Of course. I would love to join you in union."

Athirst surely must have received vision. He was one of the wisest Youth in the village, so if Jah had given him vision for this union, then this must be all part of Jah's plan, Governess thought.

For the first time since she could remember, Governess felt whole.

The two of them went back to the center of the community, where Querulous was already gossiping about the news to everyone and planning out the union celebration.

14.
Flaky Feelings

News of the union was all the talk during lessons. The Magisters seemed to drone on today. The Youth felt the topic about 'the power that they possess' was repetitive. As soon as it was time for a break, the Youth rushed to the wooden lunch tables.

"What's that you have there?" Theiler asked Jabari.

Jabari had a mouth full of food that made it difficult for him to answer. "Mediorocris made my favorite meal."

Theiler could not keep his eyes off the green beans, roasted chicken, and little round potatoes.

Jabari took his hand and wiped his mouth and then patted his chest, letting out a huge belch.

"Looks like you have enough to share. Can I have some?" Theiler looked at Jabari's lunch and began to lick his lips.

"Come on," Athirst said as he pulled up a seat at the table. "You know that Jabari would never give up his food for anyone. I don't even know why you bother."

"I would," Jabari protested. "But there just isn't enough."

"So, I hear that someone at this table will be unified soon? Is that correct?" Theiler asked, turning his body toward Athirst and waggling his eyebrows.

"Yes, well. I may be unified soon, but not before Jabari. So, Jabari, how's Nia doing?"

Jabari patted his massive chest again and burped. "Nia's doing well, I suppose. She's nice, but I don't know. I can't seem to figure out from my vision if she's 'the one.'"

"I can help you with that," Theiler said.

"I would really appreciate that. I'm not as good at this stuff as you guys are. But if any of you weaklings need some help carrying an ox back to the village, you let me know," Jabari said playfully as he stuffed another large portion of potatoes in his mouth.

"So," Jabari continued after chewing and swallowing his food, "How did you know Governess was the one? What did you see?"

A silence fell across the table. Many of the male Youth were eager to hear Athirst explain. "Well, I just…kinda…I think that you just know." Athirst mumbled through his response.

Theiler found himself curious as well, and he was not satisfied with this answer. "I know that you kinda know first, but how did Jah confirm it for you? What vision did he send?" Theiler pressed.

"I can't tell you all of that. I would ruin it for you," Athirst replied.

"Hey, whatcha guys talking about?" Nia said as she and Governess approached the table. Athirst was glad the conversation was no longer directed toward him.

"Nia and I were just discussing what type of flowers I should wear in my hair for our union ceremony," Governess said. As she said this, her face became hot, her cheeks flushing a rosy red.

"Look," Theiler pointed. "She's blushing." Theiler laughed and shot Athirst a knowing look. "Isn't that the cutest thing I've ever seen."

"Yeah, so what? I don't see you wooing anyone around here," Athirst retorted. "It's not my fault I'm good with the ladies."

"Ha!" Jabari burst into laughter.

"Okay boys, let's not get full of it." Nia, always the peacemaker, stopped them before they could continue.

"He knows I'm just messing with him." Athirst gave Theiler a slap on the back.

"I don't worry about insults from someone like him. Besides, Jah did in fact give me vision of my future," Theiler said with a smirk on his face.

"Oh really? Has he already revealed the lovely Mrs. Theiler? Well then, who is she?" Athirst inquired.

"It isn't 'who is she,' it's 'who isn't she.' Jah gave me a vision of fish. Many, many fish, and he told me that I could have my pick."

Everyone at the table erupted with laughter.

"So very funny," Governess said, rolling her eyes.

"Thank you, Governess, and you are very beautiful," Theiler said as he picked up her hand and gave it a kiss.

"Okay hold up! Get your own woman. She's already taken," Athirst snapped. Governess couldn't help but feel giddy. She had two of the most desirable gentlemen in the village doting on her.

Seeing all of the attention Governess was receiving, Nia pulled at Governess' dress to move her away from the guys.

"Wow," Nia whispered, "That must be nice. Look at the guy who's interested in me."

At that moment, both Governess and Nia glanced over at Jabari, whose large frame made it difficult for him to remove his legs from underneath the table.

Governess and Nia giggled. "Well, I know that Jabari's a little clumsy and seems to struggle with vision, but he is very kind. Like a gentle giant. He seems like he would protect you with his life," Governess said as she looked at Jabari with empathy. She knew what it was like to feel awkward and out of place.

"You're right; he is very kind. I don't know. He may grow on me yet. I'm still waiting for my vision from Jah. What did Jah show you to let you know that Athirst was the right one for you?"

"I don't know if he sent me anything. I know that Athirst is wise and meditates in the Writ often. I figured that he must have been the one to receive vision for our union. I know that I have affections for him. He makes me laugh and he's such a gentleman. I can see us being together forever. I feel like he's the only thing that makes me feel complete."

"Wow," Nia said in a soft voice.

"What?" Governess inquired.

Nia continued to whisper, "I don't know. Since we were infants, I can remember being told that only Jah could make us feel whole. I just remember the Elders and the Magisters saying that we shouldn't depend on another human to ever complete us. You must really love Athirst to say that."

"It's really difficult for me because everyone here seems so happy; I sometimes feel like something is missing, but Athirst, he..." Governess was interrupted by the loud voices of him and Theiler.

"What are you ladies over here gossiping about?" Athirst asked.

"None of your business," Governess sassed. "I am sure you gentlemen wouldn't be interested anyway."

"I also hope you know that Governess and I watch you guys gossip day in and day out. In fact, we removed ourselves from the table because we're just too mature to participate in such childish conversation," Nia stated.

Both Governess and Nia began to snicker. By this time, Jabari had managed to finally find his way out from under the table. "We're going to have to do something about this. I can't keep sitting on this bench every day."

None of them could contain their laughter. Nia walked over to Jabari and patted him on his back. "You're right Jabari; these seats are just too small."

"Or Jabari's just too big," the other guys joked.

"Thank you Nia. At least someone cares," Jabari shot a look at Theiler and Athirst, who were still laughing.

"I guess it's time to head back to lessons," Governess said before grabbing her Writ and heading back toward the Magisters. Athirst quickly grabbed the books out of Governess' hand and walked with her. Theiler found himself staring at Athirst and Governess as they strolled off. He then glanced at Jabari and Nia, who were side by side. He walked back to lessons alone.

The group casually strolled in not realizing that lessons had already started.

"It is nice for you all to finally join us. Your lunch is twenty-five minutes, not twenty-six," The Magister said sternly, turning around to the large piece of slate that was attached to the wall and continuing his lesson about the power Jah had given them.

"What difference does one minute make?" Theiler whispered to Athirst.

"One minute makes all the difference in the world!" The Magister snapped back.

The other members of the group snickered under their breath and continued listening to the lesson, excited for lessons to be over so they could resume their conversation from lunch.

When lessons were over, the group quickly found each other. "The lesson reminded me of that time we all raced those animals when we were kids," Governess said.

"Racing the animals. You were petting your rabbit like it was a toy," Athirst chuckled.

"Shut up, Athirst." Governess swatted at him.

"Yes, shut up Athirst, Governess was just trying to take care of it," Theiler said slyly. "Besides, you were too busy claiming a fake victory to even notice what Governess was doing." Theiler squeezed Governess' arm.

"Well," Nia chimed in, "we never did the second part of our bet. We never did get around to riding on the animals to see who had the most control."

"That was years ago. We're all much better at controlling them now," Theiler reminded the group.

"You're only saying that because you're afraid that I might beat you," Nia jabbed back.

Hearing this, Jabari gave Nia a high five. "That's my girl."

"You're on! Let's settle this then. Governess, you can watch from the sidelines and tell us who really won this time," Theiler said.

"Absolutely not! I want to ride too. I am pretty good you know."

"It's true," Athirst said. Governess blushed.

"So, what are the rules this time?"

"Okay...let's see. We will pick our own animals and race one lap around the entire village. Beginning at the edge of the village, down along River Aesis and ending right outside the sparring pit," Athirst said.

"Sounds good to me. Count me in," Jabari agreed. "So, when do you think would be the best time?"

"Let's not put it off. I don't want any of you to be intimidated by me and decide not to participate. Let's do it tonight," Thieler said proudly.

"Please! I've got this in the bag," Nia said dismissively.

"I'll gather the Elders, so this time people don't act like there's no winner." Athirst grabbed his leather sack and headed off. The others followed his lead and walked back home.

That evening, the entire village was out, excited to watch the race.

"They're having a lot more fun with the animals than we ever did when we discovered our power," Discernmos said to Sophos.

"It's fantastic isn't it? This should be fun." Vera was so proud of Nia as she watched her mount her deer. Vera remembered Nia's fascination with the animal after the race she participated in many years ago.

Athirst, on the other hand, took a liking to the wolves. They were one of the most difficult animals to tame because of their tendency to be aggressive, but Athirst enjoyed the challenge.

Jabari, scared that he would break the back of any other animal, climbed aboard a rhinoceros. He trotted up to Governess, who managed to find an ostrich.

"Seriously?" Theiler said to Governess. "You're really going to race that thing?"

"Yes I am, and I plan on beating you with it." As she said this, Governess lost a little balance when the large bird adjusted its leg.

Theiler sat proudly on his cheetah, ready for the race.

"Well, this is something you definitely wouldn't have seen in the Second World," Querulous said chuckling. "We only saw these animals in the zoo when we were children. Now they roam around here freely, co-existing with us."

"Yes, it's quite fascinating. Jungle animals, desert animals, woodland creatures...altogether just the way Jah intended," Mediorocris agreed.

"I see why he separated them across different ecosystems in the Second World. This is funny to watch." Querulous chuckled, giving one last look at the ridiculous line up.

Sophos walked over to the Youth who were mounted on their animals. "On your mark, get set, go!"

And with that, they were off. The Youth concentrated on sending their animals messages telepathically and using their body language to give the beasts direction. The ground shook as each animal began running along the East Gardens. Each pounce sounded like thunder.

"Woo-hoo!" Athirst shouted with exhilaration. The wind rippled through his hair. As they rounded the first bend, it was obvious that Governess' ostrich wasn't making turns properly. Governess tried to regain control.

"Come on, straighten up!" She shouted. The bird rocked Governess back and forth.

"Governess, are you alright?" Nia shouted from her deer as they passed.

"I think so!"

"Good." Nia held onto the antlers and crouched down to get more speed and quickly took the lead.

"No you aren't!" Athirst said as he saw Nia making headway. He closed his eyes and concentrated even harder. The wolf seemed as if it were beginning to fly.

Jabari was right next to Governess. He could see that she was having a difficult time. Her bird was flopping clumsily all over the place. Jabari slowed down and hopped off his rhinoceros just in time to catch Governess, who had been thrown off her bird. The ostrich ran off into the woods.

Onlookers who happened to be in that area gasped, thinking that Governess had surely hit the ground. They were relieved to see Governess in Jabari's arms.

"This is so embarrassing. I can't believe I lost again," Governess said as she held onto Jabari.

"Nothing to be embarrassed of." Jabari placed Governess on top of his rhinoceros and hopped on in front of her. "Hold on." He knocked the side of the enormous beast with his foot and took off. As they came around the bend, Jabari could see the others in his view but it was too late. It appeared that Nia made it to the finish line first with Athirst and Theiler tying for second.

"What are you slowing down for?" Governess asked Jabari.

"It's too late." Jabari was disappointed.

"Don't feel bad for one second, Jabari. You saved me and I will never forget that." Governess placed her head on Jabari's back and they rode to the finish line together.

"I see you finally made it, my friend," Theiler teased.

"Yes, well. He would've beaten all of you if he hadn't had to stop and help me."

Athirst jumped off his wolf. "He had to save you? What happened?"

"I don't know. I somehow lost control of that stupid bird and it flung me off its back, but Jabari caught me." Governess bashfully gazed at Jabari.

"I am so sorry Governess. I...I didn't know…" Athirst grabbed her hand and held it up, slightly twirling her around to see if she had any bumps or bruises.

"I'm fine, Athirst. Really. He caught me before I hit the ground."

"Well, I guess we know who the real winner is today." Athirst walked over to Jabari and gave him a hearty pat. Theiler walked over to him and did the same thing.

"On the day that I actually win something, I still get outshined?" Nia said, shaking her head.

"You won fair and square," Athirst said, reassuring her.

"Thank you Athirst, takes a real man to admit when he has lost."

"I'm just glad that someone beat Theiler." Athirst grinned.

The bystanders ran up to the group. Jabari had a small crowd around him retelling what they witnessed.

Vera was beaming from ear to ear. She was immensely proud that Nia came in first place.

Athirst, Theiler, and Governess distanced themselves from the crowd. "This was fun," Theiler said.
"It sure was, my friend," Athirst replied.

Governess was quiet. She was now confused. Just this morning, Athirst seemed perfect, but he wasn't there to save her. Jabari had swooped in and rescued her. All of a sudden, Jabari seemed so dashing and brave.

"Everything alright Governess? You're pretty quiet." Athirst placed his arm around her shoulders.

"Yeah, I'm fine."

"I'm sorry you had to go through that. I can tell you're still shaken up a bit. I should have been the one to be there for you. I'm sorry." Athirst gave her a kiss on the forehead.

"Athirst, I'm fine." Governess laid her head on his shoulder, and just like that, she was back under Athirst's spell.

15.
The Test

A week had passed since the race and the villagers were up to their daily tasks. It was humid and they knew the clouds wouldn't hold out much longer. As night fell, the clouds grew heavy and thunder roared. Most of the villagers were in bed, but many of them couldn't sleep. Their houses shook as loud booms and flashes of lightning filled the air, illuminating people's rooms. Athirst was lying in bed when Jah spoke to him.

"Athirst, you are good. You meditate with me daily, but you let your feelings overshadow your better judgement. You did not seek me when you made your selection for your union. Even when you were advised to seek me, you chose to make a decision without me. I have great things in store for your lineage, but you must be faithful to the Writ and be guided by the vision which I provide to you. You must never lose your desire for vision."

The voice of Jah disappeared and Athirst received the vision of the butterflies that had been given to Sophos several moons ago. Athirst woke up with a heavy heart. He was full of shame and sorrow when he realized that Governess was not the butterfly that helped him reach his destiny.

The sun broke its way through the clouds. The rain ceased but drops of water still rolled off the tips of leaves. The birds, who were silent in last night's thunder, chirped with a song that woke everyone in the village, all except Athirst, who was already awake. He sat on the edge of his bed, his face in his hands, trying to shield himself from the morning light. He knew that eventually he'd have to get up and face what he was dreading to do. He dragged himself out of bed and went down to River Aesis to wash off. He walked down to the portion of the river that moved the slowest because it was most suitable for bathing. He took the time to practice the many ways he would tell Governess that he couldn't go through with their union. Nothing seemed right.

He dressed himself and moped all the way to the center of Eirene, where everyone was getting ready to begin their day. There was a lively energy in the village.

"Congratulations Athirst. You and Governess will make a fine union," one of the Elders called out as they walked past him. It was obvious that Querulous managed to tell every Elder in the village in less than a full cycle of the moon.

"Thank...Thank you..." Athirst could not help the hesitation in his voice.

"There you are, Athirst." Another voice -- but this one was very familiar to him.

"Hey Theiler, how are you?"

"Brother, I know we were discussing your union during lessons, but I had no idea that you both have already picked a date to have your celebration."

"Thanks brother," Athirst responded before fully processing what Theiler just said. "Wait...what did you say? Did you just say we picked a date?"

"Yeah, Querulous let everyone know that you and Governess plan to have your ceremony before our next Potentiam Libertas celebration." Theiler patted Athirst on the back.

"Well, brother..." Athirst cleared his throat before finishing his sentence, "This is news to me."

"You know that Querulous can't keep a secret, but no matter. I wish you the best. I can honestly say that I'm a little envious. Governess is a good mate for any man here. Congratulations, my friend." Theiler gave Athirst another friendly jab, but Athirst found himself at a loss for words.

"Well, I guess I'll see you around." Theiler jogged off in hopes to come across anyone who was cooking salmon and eggs for breakfast.

Athirst continued to walk toward the center of the village with a slouch and a long, solemn face.

Sophos, who had gotten up before the sun rose to catch fish, and made his way into the village where he began trading a portion of his catch for sugar, cocoa, and butter. Sophos was talking to an Atarian. Atar was a nearby village known for their sugars and spices. Sophos had quite the sweet tooth, so it was very difficult to keep those ingredients stocked in the house.

"Ahh...well worth getting up early this morning. You always have the richest cocoa," Sophos said to Malachi, an Elder from Atar who came to make a trade.

"Yes, and we have something else you might be interested in as well." The Atarian took out a small sack tied with ribbon. "Smell this," Malachi offered.

Sophos opened the pouch to see a finely ground up brown powder. He took a whiff. "Goodness, what is that?"

"Another seasoning we found off one of our trees, nutmeg."

"I'll take some of that as well." Sophos handed him some lavender as payment. "Good for sleeping," Sophos said.

Malachi took the lavender and was on his way.

Trading between the villages took place on the morning of the first day of a new moon. Each village seemed to have their own special items and wares that were native to their region. On the mornings right after a new moon, each village would send one individual to villages nearby to see what goods and valuables were up for trade. Although coins of silver and copper were the official currency, trading seemed to be a form of payment villagers liked best.

It was always exciting to see what other villages would bring to Eirene, but Eirene had its own specialties. Eirene was known for having rare flowers in the East Gardens that could heal diseases, and fish that seemed more abundant on their side of the river. Sophos was one of the Elders who traded often. He loved going to the other villages and had made many acquaintances over the years. He never had a bad experience trading with others, but couldn't help but to be overly protective of allowing Athirst to participate, despite Athirst's age.

When Sophos finished getting all of his treats, he walked back toward his house. He could see Athirst in the distance. His posture indicated that he was troubled. Sophos watched Athirst and soon realized that he must have received the vision of the butterflies.

Sophos knew that this day would come. He thought back to the time when he received the vision and remembered that he was to have no interference with Athirst's decision. Athirst was to begin his own legacy and make the decision to do the right thing without guidance from Sophos. Athirst wasn't an infant anymore; he was a young man and Jah had to see if Athirst would follow the commands given to him on his own. Despite Sophos' attempt to tip-toe out of there, he was spotted by Athirst, who began waving him down.

"Sophos! Wait up!" Athirst jogged over to him. "I was wondering where you'd gone earlier this morning. I see you've been trading. How was it?"

"Yes, well, I was able to make some very valuable trades to help the village of Eirene."

"Very valuable trades, huh?" The solemn look on Athirst's face turned into a smirk. "Let me see what you've brought back that is so important."

"I am your Elder; I am the one who's supposed to guide you and show you things. I don't need you to check over me." Sophos withheld his leather sack from Athirst, but he quickly snatched the bag and opened it to see its contents.

"Sugar, butter, and...what is this? Cocoa? Oh yes, I see you've bought some items of great value indeed."

"Yes, yes they are," Sophos scowled. "Now, you were the one waving me down. What'd you need from me?" Sophos took the bag back from Athirst and pulled the brown leather drawstring closed.

"I had a vision last night and I don't know what to do."

Sophos sighed. "Yes, well, I knew this day would come. I see you've interpreted your vision from Jah. The vision of the butterflies?"

Athirst nodded anxiously.

"You'll soon learn that it's better to go to Jah first, but this is part of your journey. So, what do you think you're going to do?"

"I was hoping that you would tell me what it is I need to do." Athirst paused for quite some time before finishing his thought. "I have a great idea. Why don't you tell her for me?" Although Athirst tried to have a jovial tone, he was hoping that there would be some chance Sophos would do the dirty work for him. "Or maybe I can just write her a letter and then move to a far-away land. I can send you all of the cocoa and sugar you want." Athirst knew this second suggestion was a bit out there.

"Well, if we still lived in the Second World, you could send her a digital message. But considering the state of things now, I'm afraid that you'll have to do this one all on your own," Sophos responded with a slight grin on his face. "I know that you'll do the right thing, but you may want to tell her soon before the whole community begins preparing for your union."

"Ugh." Athirst did a facepalm. "What's Querulous going to do? When I asked for Governess' hand, it was the first time she actually seemed pleasant."

Sophos dismissed this with a wave of his hand. "Don't worry about her. Has Jah already revealed what's going to happen to you?"

"You already know, don't you? Tell me, what's my fate?" Athirst's face was downcast.

"Jah revealed to me that we'll have our first death in the community." Sophos couldn't contain his laughter. Although

Athirst knew Sophos was joking, it didn't make him feel any better.

The community was always bustling with people cooking, woodworking, and socializing, but today Athirst didn't join with everyone else. He walked down a grassy path by himself. His palms were sweaty and it felt like everything was moving in slow motion. What was normal chatter and typical glances now seemed like judgy gossip and disapproving looks. As he continued his walk of shame, villagers continued to approach him with pleasant greetings.

"Congratulations Athirst! You and Governess will make a fine couple," an Elder said to him, but Athirst couldn't look him in the eye. Instead, he found a quiet spot in the woods near the edge of the village and began pacing back and forth. Athirst wracked his brain trying to find the right words to say.

"Hi Governess." Athirst pretended that she was standing in front of him. "I'm sure you'd never want to unify with someone like me, considering I'm quite the slob behind closed doors." He tried again.

"Governess, this won't work; I cannot unify with someone who has an Elder as irritating as Querulous." This one made Athirst chuckle.

"This is foolish…none of these are going to work," Athirst sighed.

He took a deep breath and accepted what he knew to be true. He didn't have to have the perfect words; he just had to follow the will of Jah.

Athirst looked up. "Jah, why couldn't you have just stopped me?!" Athirst kicked the base of a nearby tree. *Maybe I shouldn't. How bad can things get if I just don't say anything?* Athirst thought to himself, but he knew better. Athirst dropped to his knees. The voice of Jah came and comforted him. "You must go to her and tell her that the union is not My will. She will be very upset, but she is not part of your future legacy."

"What should I say?" Athirst asked, distraught.

"You will say what is placed on your heart to say. The words will come but you must act first," Jah replied.

Wow, thanks for all the great advice, Jah. All seeing and all knowing...geez...I wonder if He knows that Querulous is going to kill me, Athirst thought to himself.

At that moment, Athirst left the woods where he'd been pacing and headed back toward the center of the village.

It wasn't long before he saw Governess sitting on a wood bench near the fire pit. There was no fire today, only remnants of charred pieces of wood from the last celebration. Very few were gathered around the pit. Most were eating breakfast under the shade of the trees, while others just seemed to be out and about -- crafting, gardening, lugging buckets of water, playing chess. Athirst was relieved that no one was in earshot of them and that he didn't hear anymore "congratulations."

When Governess saw him, her eyes lit up.

"Athirst!" Governess said excitedly. "Where have you been? I haven't seen you all morning."

"I've just had a lot on my mind. I needed to talk to Jah. I needed to mediate."

"Oh...I've been doing a lot of thinking, too. I was talking to Querulous and she had so many ideas about our union celebration. I've never seen her this excited before."

Athirst had butterflies in his stomach. He quickly blurted out, "There won't be a union celebration, Governess! I'm sorry. I asked you to unite with me based on my desire for you, not the will of Jah."

Governess stood still for a minute before she responded. "Not the will of Jah. Well, I never thought you would stoop so low as to blame Jah for deciding to change your mind. You're not man enough to follow through with this, are you?" Her voice broke.

Athirst continued to talk to Governess as if her response did not just pierce him like daggers.

"It isn't up to me! If it were my way, I'd unite with you right now. I think you're an extraordinary person. When I'm near you, I feel joy. You make me smile. I can't tell you how much it pains me to say these words, but Jah will not bless our union. My will is not His."

Governess couldn't contain herself much longer. "You're a coward Athirst! Simply a coward! Every girl in the community has it wrong. They told me I was lucky to have someone like you. They're fools and so are you."

Her tone, initially filled with fury, grew softer, and tears welled in the corners of her eyes. "Our union has been announced to the entire community and you're just gonna break it off? Everyone our age is forming unions! No one has had their union called off. What will everyone think? What do you think they'd think of me? That I'm annoying, insufferable, unintelligent, or not pretty enough? Who am I if the amazing Athirst, Youth of our leader Sophos, best in all the village, doesn't want to join me in unionship?" She made an effort to hold back her sobs.

Her emotion changed again and the tone of her voice shifted. "You know what? It isn't a matter of what they're going to think of me, but what they're going to think of you! Did you ever consider what this would do to you and Sophos? How will anyone respect his vision if he's not able to prevent his Youth from making what's supposedly such a terrible decision?"

Athirst was silent the entire time, knowing that he deserved every word. "I'm sorry. I am so sorry Governess. I cannot imagine the pain and embarrassment I have caused you. I wish I could make it go away. I wish that things could be different and that I could have my way, but I must do what I know is the right thing to do. I must follow Jah." Athirst slowly began to back away.

Governess said nothing as Athirst walked off. She began to look around to see if anyone had noticed the verbal exchange between them. Her eyes followed him as his figure faded off in the distance.

16.
Governess' Vision

Governess knew that she would lose all composure if she heard the villagers utter even one word of congratulations. She felt even worse when she thought about what would happen when they eventually knew the truth. She decided to head to the East Gardens. Governess felt so exposed and wanted to hide away for awhile.

In the middle of the garden, the intoxicating perfume of the flowers calmed her, and the thorns felt more like a form of protection rather than a nuisance. She looked for a clearing where she could settle down and rest. Her petite frame could fit in between the bushes. She took the bottom of her skirt and gathered it together, forming a cushion for her bottom. She knew that no one would come looking for her here. She needed to sort things out. She couldn't figure out what was wrong with her. Why would anyone want to do this to her?

Opening up her Writ, Governess scrambled to find a resolution. She tried looking for the right words or a phrase from the text, hoping something would jump off the page and reveal itself to her. She didn't know why she was saved from the Second World. Was it simply to be humiliated?

She closed her eyes in an attempt to block out the feelings. *Governess*, she thought to herself, *get it together*. She hated that she was like this. No one else in the village seemed to be constantly plagued with toxic thoughts and feelings of worthlessness. Governess felt that this was bigger than the union. Maybe there was something wrong with her? Before she could continue being hard on herself, the spirit of Jah came to calm her and Governess knew He was about to send a vision.

Governess saw a vision of herself walking along a path. It twisted and turned, winding its way through the trees and brush. She felt free and at ease as she journeyed, but before long, the sky turned dark and erupted with thunder. Powerful gusts of wind swirled through the air, almost knocking her off her feet. Governess found herself in need of protection and began looking for shelter from the weather. The path split in two directions and she found herself not knowing what to do. One path would lead her to a rocky, weathered fortress that looked like it had seen better days. But, when Governess looked down the other path, it led to a mansion that was already established. The yard had well-manicured gardens with fountains. Birds were playing in the birdbath that was near the entrance. It was stately and beautiful.

In her vision, she immediately asked Jah for guidance and He shined a light on the path that she was to take. She was supposed to choose the path with the plain fortress. It wasn't flashy or ornate, but it was strong and indestructible. Governess looked back and forth between the path that was illuminated and the path that led to the grand, elegant mansion. In her vision, she toiled over which was the best way. After deliberating, she ran away from the path that was illuminated and traveled down the path that was more pleasing to the eye.

Governess opened the door to the residence and felt satisfied that she had made the right decision. As she walked around to find a place to rest after the journey, she was startled by small bugs and rodents that scurried around her feet. Water leaked through the newly-formed cracks in the ceiling. The wind from the storm shook the shingles off the roof and rattled the walls. She soon realized that the shelter could not protect her from the elements. It was all artifice and no substance. But instead of heading toward the fortress that could protect her, she decided to stay put.

When Governess woke from the vision, she realized that she was supposed to unite with someone who was physically strong and mighty, because he would protect her, care for her, and provide her with the feeling of security that she wanted. She realized that he would protect her and she would help him become a mighty fortress, even if the person in question didn't necessarily appear to be the most dashing or handsome or influential. Governess immediately thanked Jah for the vision and asked Him to help her make the right choice. She laid down in the the prickly thorns and felt safe from the world around her. There, she fell asleep.

Hours had passed and dusk had settled over the Third World like a blanket. Crickets chirped all around and fireflies sparkled here and there. Rustling in the bushes were creatures looking for food, but none of that woke up Governess. It was not until she received another vision that she bolted upright. Another night where she was plagued with a terrible dream. She had a vision of the red rain again. The same one that gave her such a bad feeling. She had written in her journal so many times about the red rain pouring in the street. She was jolted up out of her sleep, gathered her things and began walking home.

Athirst had already made it home where a curious Sophos bombarded him with questions.

"So how did it go?"

"Terrible. She's so mad at me."

"How do you feel?"

"I feel like an idiot. I mean, what harm could it have caused to just stay with her? Who else in the village am I supposed to unify with? I really thought she was the one. Now, all of the other Youth will be unified before me."

"Interesting. Is this a race for you? You wanted to beat everyone else to the finish line? Well, I'll tell you one thing that's constant. Love...love is patient. You can't rush these things. You have to see someone in every season of life. Kristen, my wife, played hard to get for a long time, but she was worth the wait. I am sure, no matter who you are destined to be with, that it will be worth the wait as well."

"I guess you're right. It just hurts right now, and we all have lessons tomorrow. I'm sure everyone will know. I don't even want to show my face."

"Get some rest. I'm sure things won't be as bad as you think." Sophos left Athirst's room.

17.

All Mixed Up

Lessons did not go the way Athirst predicted. The awkward silence could be cut with a knife. He wasn't sure what anyone knew, other than Governess, who appeared to be even more beautiful that morning. Was it a new outfit that she created? Or maybe it was her hair. Either way, seeing her made his stomach feel weak.

"Psst!" Athirst tried to get her attention. "Psssst!" he whispered again, but Governess didn't budge. A few seconds later, she quickly turned around and put a note on the small wooden table in front of him.

Athirst was elated. At least she was acknowledging him. He quickly opened the note that read, "Please stop making noise behind me. I'm trying to concentrate."

It wasn't quite what he expected, but somehow, it still made him feel better. The Magister was at the slate writing about choices. How fitting, Athirst thought.

"I have watched you all from the time you were little learn many lessons from me, but as you get older, your lessons are no longer learned in this room -- they begin to manifest in every choice that you make outside of here. You must be wise and listen to Jah. You must read your Writ daily and make sure nothing is able to sway you."

Athirst watched Governess squirm in front of him.

Theiler raised his hand. "So, let's say someone didn't know who they were supposed to unify with and chose the wrong person; what might happen then?"

Athirst froze. Did Theiler know? Athirst slowly looked back to see Theiler pat Jabari on the shoulder. Across the room, he could see Nia folding her arms.

"Seriously Theiler, you're really going to ask that in front of everyone?" Nia snapped at Theiler.

"It's just a question! I just want to help my friend. Besides, not everyone is as sure as my dear friend Athirst here. Some people need guidance."

Whew, Athirst thought. Theiler seemed as if he didn't know yet.

"Are you going to let me answer the question or is everyone going to keep talking?" The Magister said as she tapped her desk in an effort to quiet everyone. "Unionship is the most important connection you will have other than your connection with Jah. Connecting with the right person can create a partnership that is not only satisfying for the two people involved, but can literally change the world. Unionship with the wrong person, however, can be detrimental."

"So, what if I just want to stay single? No need for someone like me to be all tied down right now anyway." Theiler sat back in his chair in a cocky manner.

"Well, you're all getting old enough for me to ask this question, I guess. Do you plan on ever having a physical relationship?"

The class snickered.

"Well... do you?" The Magister waited.

"I...well...yes, I do?"

"Not without unionship you don't, unless you plan on defying the will of Jah."

A quiet fell over the room.

"I guess I'll unify when the time is right. I just want to check out all my options first is all I'm saying." Theiler's cocky demeanor changed and he quieted down.

When lunchtime arrived, Nia couldn't help but take the opportunity to relive the classroom conversation.

"Did you all see how quickly Theiler was shut down? Serves him right for trying to embarrass me."

"Sorry Nia," Jabari said. "I asked him to help me with a vision. I didn't think he would do it like that."

"No need to apologize. Theiler got what he deserved today."

"I got nothing of the sort. That didn't embarrass me at all. It just let the other gals in the classroom know that I'm still available," Theiler boasted. "I won't be tied down so soon like our friend Athirst."

Athirst looked away.

"Where is the lovely future Mrs. Athirst anyway?"

"I see her, she's over there writing in her journal. I'll talk to you guys later." Nia grabbed her Writ and her leather bag and headed in Governess' direction.

"You've been awfully quiet today. Have a lot on your mind?" Nia asked Governess.

"I just didn't want to hang out with them today," Governess said as she placed her journal in her sack.

"Well, I don't blame you. They can be some real idiots if you ask me."

"Tell me about it."

"Seriously, are you sure you're alright? You just seem really down today. I want you to know that whatever it is, I am here. I know that trying to do the right thing all of the time can be a lot of pressure. I feel the same way. Today, when Theiler was asking about what happens if we don't unify with the right person, this huge knot formed in my stomach. Everyone assumes that Jabari and I are supposed to be together, but the truth of the matter is, he and I are good friends. I was probably one of the few people that treated him nicely and I think that made him develop a crush on me, but neither of us have had anything confirmed yet. In the meantime, he is nice, and it doesn't hurt that he can help carry my books." Nia nudged Governess and chuckled a bit.

Governess smiled back. "I guess you're right. Thanks Nia."

"No problem. Hey, it's about time to head back."

A few days had passed and the village didn't seem to know about the broken union. Athirst was even more shocked when Querulous greeted him with that same cheesy grin she had when he asked for Governess to unify with him.

"Hi Athirst, haven't seen you around in a while. Getting ready for the big day? I understand. Nerves. Well, I'll talk to you later." Querulous would walk away so quickly that he never even had a chance to respond.

Later that evening, Athirst walked over to see Governess.

"Hey. How are you?"

"I'm fine and you?" Governess was in her yard on top of her ostrich.

"You still trying to tame her?" Athirst asked.

"I think I've have mastered that, just trying to see if I can get her to fly with me on her back." Governess hoped down. "Let's talk somewhere else. I don't want Querulous to hear." Governess grabbed Athirst's arm and pulled him away from the window openings.

"Governess, why does Querulous think we're still going to unify?"

"I just haven't found the right time, okay? Besides, I've been thinking, maybe we should just go through with it. Everything is already set," she responded eagerly.

"You know that's not a good idea. Did you not hear the Magister?" Athirst asked. "Breaking off our union was one of the most difficult things I have ever had to do. I thought it was all taken care of. I prepared myself for the entire village to whisper about it for weeks, but this could be worse. People are still congratulating me, and you for that matter, on a union that will never happen."

"You really don't want to go through with it? You know what, it doesn't matter anyway. Jah already sent me vision for my real union-mate, and you are correct, it is not you!"

"You had your vision? Then who is it?" Athirst immediately became jealous.

"It doesn't matter does it?" Just then, Governess shouted for Querulous to come outside. "Querulous, can you come here please!"

"What do you want now?"

"Just come here please!"

"Oh, hi Athirst. So, what is this all about?"

"Athirst has something he wants to tell you."

"You do? What is it, boy? I was just about to take a nap." Athirst felt as if Querulous' eyes were burning a hole in his face.

"I, um, I can't unify with Governess. I broke it off nearly two weeks ago. I thought you knew."

No snappy comeback. Just silence and her eyes still piercing the side of Athirst's face. Athirst quickly left and headed home.

When Athirst had departed, Querulous grabbed Governess and pulled her close. "You okay?"

"I just need some time to myself. I think I'm going to head down to the river."

Governess thought she had found a quiet place near the river when she saw a large figure headed her way. *Great*, she thought to herself. *Why is he here?* She found a rock and sat down, trying to hide. She was doing her best to not be seen. She had her journal with her and kept her head down. All she wanted to do was write. She needed to let all of her feelings out on paper.

"Hi, Governess. I didn't think I would see you here."

"Yes, I know the feeling. How are you Jabari?"

"I don't really know. I came out here to think."

"Really? So did I. What's on your mind these days?"

"I don't think you want to know," Jabari said bashfully.

"Well, maybe it can help me not focus on my problems so much."

"I'm sure a girl like you doesn't have any problems."

Governess looked away. She could feel tears welling up.

"You okay?"

"Yes, I'm fine. So --" she said wiping away her tears, "-- what has you out here?"

"You," Jabari responded.

"Me?" Governess replied, puzzled. "Why?"

"It started a while back. The day you fell off the ostrich. Something in that moment had me question what I was doing. Then, last night, I received a vision. Jah showed me my union-mate."

"Nia, I assume."

"If it were Nia, do you think I would feel conflicted? No, it was definitely you... Governess, I know that I am nothing like Athirst. He is so wise and well-respected and I know that people don't see me in the same way, but I just wanted to know if you ever think you could give someone like me a chance?"

"What happened with Nia?" Governess deflected.

"Well, Nia and I kept asking Jah if our relationship was right. If we were supposed to unify. He never gave us a clear picture. I liked her because she was the only one in the village that didn't seem to be intimidated by my size, and she doesn't laugh at me when I always seem to be knocking into things. You on the other hand have done it on countless occasions." He glanced at her knowingly. "So I wondered if you could ever picture yourself with someone like me, or would it be too embarrassing?"

"Would you even be able to tell if it were me in the vision or..." Her voice drifted off.

"You don't think I'm smart enough to know if I see you in the vision, huh? Believe it or not Governess, I have seen you. I just didn't know what to do or say because Athirst had affections for you. It made me feel like maybe I was wrong. That maybe I was really, really terrible at interpreting vision. How could I go up to Athirst, one of the wisest Youth in Eirene, and tell him that I thought he had it all wrong?" Jabari couldn't quite read Governess' expression, but something told him that she had her reservations about him as a potential union-mate.

"Jabari, all I'm saying is that I don't know if anyone sees me in their vision. How do you know if you really saw me? How can you tell?"

"Governess, I had a vision that I found the most beautiful, rare flower. It was red and speckled with morning dew. It grew in between two rocks where all the other flowers seemed to grow in a field together. It was alone. It drew me in but as I got closer, someone else was reaching for the flower. During the vision, I had this overwhelming feeling that if someone else touched the flower, it would wilt, so I ran over to it as quickly…" Jabari paused before finishing. "Governess, I know that you're that flower. Jah showed me what each part of the vision meant. He showed me that you grew in between the two rocks because you felt stuck there. You feel torn between two choices. You were willing to give yourself to the first passerby who came along because you didn't want to grow alone, but he wasn't the one for you. I was the one for you."

Governess' face softened.

"Thank you for your kindness, Jabari." Governess moved her dark brown hair out of her face and looked up at him. His face was plain. On the outside, he didn't seem like anything special. But the depth of his heart was unmatched.

"Do you mind if I walk you back home?" Jabari asked shyly.

"Of course not," Governess replied. Jabari held her hand and they walked back to the center of the village together.

The sun was going down and many of the villagers had already gone inside. Only a few remained, sitting and chatting at a nearby picnic table. Governess, afraid of any wandering eyes, pulled her hand away from Jabari.

Theiler happened to be mulling about and spotted them instantly. "What are you two doing coming from the woods together?" He said as he ran up to them.

"Nothing," Governess said quickly. "I was feeling a bit down and Jabari was there to listen."

"You were feeling a bit down? Well, I hope it wasn't because of our dear friend Athirst. He's an idiot for not unifying with someone like you. Querulous just told me. Well, she nearly told the entire village a few minutes ago," Theiler said, cupping her face in his hands and moving a strand of her hair behind her ears.

Jabari looked uncomfortable.

"Oh really, someone like me. What does someone like me mean?" Governess asked playfully.

"Oh you know, someone beautiful, someone witty, someone intelligent...someone who'd make an ideal mate."

Governess blushed.

"I love Athirst and usually I'd say he's pretty smart, but I have to admit -- not unifying with you was a very foolish decision."

Governess playfully swatted at Theiler. "You're just saying that?" She giggled and gazed back at him. His eyes were blue-green -- the color of a calm sea. His hair was light and wavy. He was extremely handsome and confident. Everything Jabari was not.

Jabari didn't laugh at Theiler's comment. He found himself growing quite frustrated with the scene altogether.

"I'll see you both later," Jabari said as he walked away, leaving Governess and Theiler alone.

"Yes brother, I'll see you later! Tomorrow I'll help you work on that vision you were having trouble with. I'm sure we'll figure out who the flower between the rocks is!" Theiler shouted after him.

Jabari took one last look at Governess. She felt bad and wanted to tear herself away, but Theiler still had his arm around her.

"How about I walk you home, eh?" Theiler suggested. Governess nodded, but not before looking back at Jabari, whose figure was slowly shrinking in the distance.

18.
Torn

Jabari felt very confused and sought out his Elder for guidance, but when he arrived, Mediorocris was sound asleep.

"Mediorocris," Jabari whispered.

At the sound of his voice, Mediorocris grunted and rolled on her side, still very much asleep. "Mediorocris!" Jabari whispered louder this time.

"Huh?" Mediorocris slowly turned over to see Jabari standing at the foot of her bed. "Yes Jabari, what is it?"

Jabari sat by her bed and told her the vision of the flower between the rocks and his recent encounter with Governess.

"Oh, I see. So you finally received confirmation from Jah? It wasn't Nia you were to unify with, but rather, Governess?"

"I believe so, and I think she may have felt the same way. She even held my hand as we began walking back home, but then…"

"Then what?" Mediorocris inquired.

"Then we ran into Theiler and she let go of my hand. He started telling her how beautiful she was and how much of a fool Athirst was to break off the union with her."

"What did she say?"

"It wasn't what she said; it was the fact that she said nothing at all. She didn't even seem to be bothered by the fact that I left."

"Do you think Theiler knows that you're the one who belongs with her?"

"I don't think so," Jabari replied with his head down. He's still trying to help me interpret my vision, but he has no idea."

"Do you really believe that Governess is the one for you?" Mediorocris questioned. "Do you? You just seemed so sure that Nia was the right fit for you that I never even considered that you would be a fit for someone like Governess," Mediorocris replied before she realized the impact of her words.

"I should've known better than to talk to you about this."

"Why would you say that to me, Jabari?"

"This entire time, I've been made fun of for not being able to interpret vision as well as everyone else, but I can only be as good as my Elder. I have to seek out others to help guide me in my interpretation because my Elder lacks the skill necessary to provide me with clarity, and when I finally believe I have something right, she questions me. I should've had an Elder like Sophos."

Mediorocris slapped Jabari across his face. She instantly regretted it.

"Jabari! I'm so sorry; I didn't mean to do that, really I…"

Jabari got up and left.

Surprisingly, Sophos was still up. He was in his kitchen mixing some butter, sugar, and spices together to cure his late night sweet craving when he heard an urgent knock on the door. "Good evening, Jabari," Sophos whispered, surprised.

"I'm sorry this is such short notice, but I needed to speak with you. I need your help."

"Of course, but you must do me a favor as well," Sophos said quietly, putting the evidence of his late night snack away. "I need you to keep this little snack a secret. I told Athirst I would try to do better. So, how can I help you?"

"Well, I believe that I've interpreted my vision correctly, but things keep happening to make me think otherwise."

Jabari found himself explaining his vision yet again. He also explained the awkward encounter between himself, Governess, and Theiler. Jabari ended the story with the conversation he had with Mediorocris.

"All of this happened tonight?" Sophos asked.

"Yeah," Jabari replied. "Do you think my vision is wrong?"

"Well, I'm not entirely sure. I know that Athirst is not supposed to be with Governess and I knew it when he asked for my blessing."

"You did? Then why did you let him ask Governess for unionship?"

"Well, I also knew the day would come where Athirst would find out she was not designed for him. I was given strict instructions from Jah to allow him to choose his own path, so I did as I was told."

"Everyone in Eirene thinks I'm foolish."

Sophos didn't respond with words. He grabbed Jabari's hand and made him kneel down. Sophos kneeled down next to him, and then began to meditate. He asked Jah to send him some confirmation that Jabari was correct, although Sophos knew that he wasn't going to receive Jabari's full vision since he wasn't his Elder.

Jabari eyed Sophos skeptically.

It wasn't long before Sophos received a vision of a dove. It was a sign of confirmation.

Sophos opened his eyes and looked at Jabari.

"You have done well with your interpretation of vision."

"So what does that mean?"

"It means you'll be okay. Just keep trusting Jah."

When Jabari walked back home, Mediorocris was up waiting for him.

"Jabari! Oh thank goodness! Are you okay? Where'd you go? I --"

"I went to see Sophos." Jabari kissed her on the cheek and said no more, retreating to his room.

Mediorocris looked out into the night, distraught.

19.
Led Astray

The Magisters were teaching from the old books today, but Jabari couldn't concentrate. His focus was on Governess. She loved lessons; it was one area where she really excelled. She was excellent at debating matters of injustice, and was adept at being able to look at things from multiple points of view; maybe because she spent so much time defending her actions to Querulous.

Jabari hadn't worked up the courage to revisit their conversation from the previous day, but he hoped he'd have a chance soon.

"Pssst." Theiler threw a small wad of paper at Jabari to get his attention.

Athirst, sitting next to Theiler, tried not to pay any attention to all of the commotion. He desperately wanted to fade into the background so that Governess wouldn't notice his presence. Jabari turned around to see Theiler throw the note in his direction.

The note read, *I think I've figured out what your vision was about Jabari.*

Instead of writing back, Jabari asked aloud, "What do you think it means?"

"I think Jah may have sent you a vision for your union-mate, my friend," Theiler whispered.

"I was thinking the same thing." Jabari was so relieved. After seeing the interaction between Theiler and Governess last night, he feared that Theiler might try to move in on Governess and steal her away.

"You're getting much better, my friend. You are. Do you think you know who it is?" Theiler asked.

"Yes, but, I believe that Jah would like me to keep that to myself." For once, Jabari felt proud of himself.

They both went back to focusing on the lesson.

Nia was sitting next to Governess and noticed that she seemed overly engaged with the lesson.

"Trying to show him what he missed?" Nia whispered.

Governess looked back at Athirst, then rolled her eyes. "Yes."

"I think he already knows." Nia tried to comfort her friend.

"How are you doing?" Nia asked.

"I guess I'm doing as well as one can expect. I was feeling really embarrassed before, but someone helped me feel better." Governess looked in Jabari's direction and smiled. "We can talk more about it during our break or at lunch. Right now, I'm just trying to make him miss me."

"Sure. Lunch."

When lunchtime arrived, Governess approached Nia first.

"So, how are things going for you and Jabari? Were you two supposed to unify?" Governess couldn't help herself; she wanted to know if what Jabari had told her was true.

"Well, I thought we were, but he and I both kept asking Jah and we didn't get a clear picture. I guess it's for the best, though."

"Why do you say that?"

"I mean, Jabari is nice and all, but really, who would want to be with a guy like him? He's so big and clumsy. He's not that smart either. Besides, I think Jah may have sent me a vision of another guy."

"Who do you think it is? Spill!"

"I'm not allowed to say."

"Can you at least give me a hint?"

"All I can say is I'm glad he's not Jabari." She looked over in his direction.

Governess looked in that direction as well.

The conversation between Governess and Nia died down. Nia joined Athirst and Theiler, who were in debate yet again over which of them was the best at something. Governess made her way over to Jabari, who was reading The Writ under a tree.

"Hi Jabari. How are you doing?"

Jabari began to smile from ear to ear. "I'm doing well. How are you?"

"Holding up, considering," Governess said. "Yes, well, I came over here because I never got the chance to thank you for the other day. Your words were so kind."

"Don't worry about it."

"So," Governess said in an attempt to change the conversation, "What are you up to?"

"Yes, well, I don't know. I feel like I'm getting a little better with understanding the Writ and interpreting vision. You know, the Writ says that if I do in fact study, then I will gain more understanding."

"Yes, it does say that. So, you feel pretty sure about your vision of…us?" Governess asked.

"I do. I've been going to Theiler to help me with my vision and he confirmed that it was about my union-mate."

"You didn't tell Theiler it was me, did you?" Governess suddenly changed her demeanor, and her tone was sharp.

"No, I didn't. But if I did, why would it bother you so much?"

Governess became defensive. "It wouldn't bother me, it's just that typically you're supposed to keep that kind of thing to yourself."

"Well yeah, but people will have to find out one day. Have you received vision concerning me?"

"Uhhh...well...um...I don't think so?" Governess stumbled through her answer. She did receive a vision. The vision of the plain fort -- she just didn't want it to be true.

"You don't think so? Are you sure?"

"I may have seen something, but I don't know anymore. I don't know what any of it means or what I'm supposed to do."

"It's okay. Everything will happen the way it's supposed to." Jabari gave Governess a hug.

Theiler came walking over to them. "This is the second time I've seen you two alone together."

Governess felt herself pull away from Jabari again.

"We're just friends, Theiler. Nothing more to tell."

"A friend? Well, that's good... I can be a good friend as well," Theiler said with a wicked smile.

"Oh great. He's coming," Governess said as Athirst approached the three of them. "I'll see you both later."

"What are you guys talking about?" Athirst inquired.

"Nothing," Jabari said quickly, grabbing his Writ and heading back to lessons.

When the second lesson was over, Athirst tried to approach Governess.

"Look, I know that you're mad at me, but it doesn't have to be like this. I said I was sorry. I tried to make you understand."

Governess kept walking. "Looks like she doesn't have anything to say to you, brother," Theiler said. He quickly went over to Governess, grabbed the Writ from her hand, and walked her home.

"What's going on with them?" Athirst asked.

"I guess Theiler is just trying to be a good friend since you..." Jabari stopped before finishing his sentence.

"Okay, I know. I messed up and I feel terrible. I don't know if she'll ever forgive me but I want her to know we're still friends."

"Well, the way I see it, there are other females in the village besides Governess," Nia scoffed as she joined in on the conversation. "The world doesn't revolve around her. It's ridiculous to see all three of you working so hard to make sure Governess' feelings aren't hurt. I'm happy you're all so attentive to her needs, but Governess can handle a little heartbreak. No one is rushing up to me to make sure that I am okay," Nia said bitterly.

Athirst and Jabari grinned and shook their heads, and began walking home.

20.
The News Goes Viral

Over the next few days, news of the broken union spread across the entire community. Awkward silence filled the air and people gave both Athirst and Sophos looks of doubt and disbelief. Governess was right. Rumors about their credibility and the authenticity of their visions began to spread. Those who once revered Sophos as a respected leader and friend now shut him out and whispered behind his back.

"There he is, everyone -- Sophos the visionary. What did you hear from Jah today?" Mediorocris jabbed.

"Well," Sophos responded, "I did see a vision of you getting younger and better looking, but, like so many of my recent visions, it was clearly inaccurate," Sophos retorted.

"I know that Jabari came to you the other night. I'm guessing he told you about his vision."

"He told me a few things, but I cannot clearly interpret anything since he is not my own Youth. I did however ask Jah to give Jabari confirmation of his vision, and he sent the symbol of the dove." Sophos sighed. "Unfortunately, that is all I can give. You should be able to fill in the rest, but..."

"What is that supposed to mean? Are you insinuating that I'm not a good enough Elder for Jabari because he had to go to you for vision? From what it seems, you aren't too good at interpreting vision either." Mediorocris' eyes narrowed.

"I didn't mean to offend. Is everything okay?" Sophos realized that the playful banter was over.

"No, everything is not okay! You are going behind my back and filling my Youth's head with ideas of a union between him and someone like Governess. You are the one getting his hopes up. We all know that Jabari struggles with vision! He spent the past few moons telling me that Nia was his union-mate! Now all of a sudden he believes Jah sent him vision for Governess and instead of telling Jabari that he's not right for her, you decided to allow him to be led astray just so you can be considered the wisest of us all."

"Maybe you're right. Maybe I'm not as wise as you all have made me out to be, but I do know this, Jabari is an amazing Youth. He's hungry for knowledge and possesses determination, but how can that ever be nurtured when his Elder doesn't even discipline herself to read and meditate?"

"You do think you're smarter and better than everyone else! All you've ever done is *share your knowledge and wisdom* in the name of helping others, when really you just think we can't do a good enough job on our own. And so you try to steal away our Youth, one by one."

"I hate to tell you this Mediorocris, but he does not belong to you specifically. He was saved from the vanishing by Jah. Your only role is to guide him so that he can live out his potential. Elders are more than welcome to help other Youth find their way. You seem to have lost sight of that."

"No, brother, I think I see perfectly clear and I will not have you take him away from me." Mediorocris was so filled with rage that her hands shook. She then stormed off, huffing and puffing. Discernmos soon joined Sophos at the table. It didn't take long for him to notice the tension that hung in the air.

"Jah has sent another beautiful day," Discernmos stated in a lame attempt to diffuse the situation.

"Yes it is, brother," Sophos responded, wanting rather to make small talk than to indulge in more drama.

Others joined the table and soon the tension gave way to Querulous' typical commentary.

"I need you all to move over. I've been up half the night taking apart bouquets that I made for a union that is clearly not going to happen," Querulous said, giving Sophos the side eye.

Discernmos snorted.

Sophos no longer felt like being around the other Elders. He got up from the table and walked home.

The whispers and jabs continued on for quite some time, but Sophos carried on. He remained an ever-present help for the Youth, while respecting Mediorocris' wishes for him to stay away from Jabari.

Over time, however, the community's respect for Sophos and his visions eventually returned. Things seemed to be back to normal. More and more of the Youth were paired with each other as well.

Initially, the news of upcoming unions bothered Athirst, but like so many things in life, time seemed to soften the blow. To keep his mind preoccupied, Athirst focused more on his studies, the Writ, and meditation.

Nearly five months had passed since Athirst told Querulous the ceremony was off. He was up early one morning reading when he heard Sophos sneaking around the kitchen.

"Hey, what are you doing?"

Sophos appeared to jump out of his skin.

"Are you trying to kill me? You nearly scared me half to death."

"You wouldn't feel like that if you weren't trying to sneak around and eat sweets."

"Well, I need my energy today. I'm going to some of the villages north of here to do some trading, do you want to come?"

"Of course! You've never asked me to go with you before."

"Well, I think it's about time you join me."

Both of them gathered their belongings and made their way out of the house before the sun was up. Sophos hopped on

Cuddles, his giant grizzly bear, and Athirst joined his side with his trusty grey wolf and they rode off heading to the villages north of Eirene.

"My goodness, that smell," Athirst said. "It literally smells like chocolate and cinnamon."

"Yes, we're heading to Atar. Look." Sophos pointed.

Atar was one of the most unique villages Athirst had ever seen. It looked dry and dusty, a stark difference from Eirene. The paws of their animals left marks in the ground that quickly blew away like sand. The barren landscape, however, was offset by the decadent fragrance that permeated the air.

"Let's stop here." Sophos nudged Cuddles' side and they came to a stop. Athirst followed suit.

"Why are we stopping?"

"I want you to do something for me. Scrape off that bark from the tree and eat it."

"Sophos, have you lost your mind?"

"No, just do it."

Athirst was a little apprehensive, but did as he was told. His face was scrunched up, waiting for something terrible to happen. Then his expression changed.

"So, what do you think?"

"It's delicious! Like chocolate."

"Yes, it is! It's abundant here. Taste this." Sophos pulled a round object that looked like a nut off a nearby tree and began to crush it in his palms. "Try this."

"Smells fantastic." Athirst held it up to his nose. "Is this nutmeg?"

"Yes, and now you can see why this is one of my favorite villages."

The men hopped back on their animals and rode toward the center of Eirene. As they traveled, Athirst took the opportunity to sample every delicacy Atar had to offer.

"There she is," Sophos said, gesturing to a woman up ahead. She was tall and slim, with rich, dark skin that glowed under the sun's light.

"Sophos! Good to see you. I have more of your favorites." They paused for a moment to make their trades. "Is this your Elder?" The woman asked, directing her attention towards Athirst. Athirst found himself speechless. He had never seen someone so exotic. She was stunning.

"Pick your jaw up off the ground," Sophos said after noticing that Athirst was awestruck.

"Oh yes, sorry. He's my Elder. Excuse me for my rudeness, I've just never seen…"

"Oh, I see. It's your first time to our village. Well, it's nice to meet you. My name is Alexis. I have two Youth of my own."

"You're an Elder." Athirst was stunned again. He couldn't believe that she could possibly be one, given that she looked so beautiful and young.

"Yes, I am 73 years old," Alexis replied.

"I know," Sophos whispered to Athirst. "Can you believe it?"

"Sophos, we're looking forward to the next trade day. Please bring us back some of that salmon."

"Sure thing."

Athirst and Sophos waved bye and hopped back on their animals.

"Do all the woman in Atar look like that?"

"Not bad huh?"

"They're beautiful. And the men…are they using spears?"

Athirst looked in the distance and saw two men sparring.

"Yes, they are not able to tame animals like us. So they have learned to use spears to hunt. They practice sparring with them as well, but never to harm each other."

Athirst continued to watch everything around him as they headed out of Atar. The sweet smell of cocoa faded away as they left the village.

When the scenery changed, Athirst asked, "Where to next?"

"We're heading to Siomon next. Just started visiting here not too long ago. One of the villagers here gave me some healing sand. I was skeptical at first, but it worked, so I'm headed back."

"This is nice, Sopohos. Just you and me traveling."

"It is," Sophos said, smiling. "So, I've seen you in the Writ a lot more, any questions? Thoughts?"

"The Gold One. Such a mystery to me."

"The Gold One is a mystery to everyone. At one time, I thought you would be the Gold One."

"I was hoping the same thing."

"Nah, you wouldn't want that much pressure."

"So, who do you think it is now?"

"I don't think it's any one of you. The way you all are rushing around, jumping into relationships, not seeking Jah's guidance first, I'd be distraught if it was one of you."

"Yeah, I guess you're right."

"The Gold One has to be pure and humble, willing to sacrifice themselves to help others. I'm not sure if any of you are able to do that."

Athirst's feelings would've been hurt, but he knew Sophos was right.

"Sophos, look at the ground."

As they left Atar, they could still see Mount Boreal in the distance.

"It is so hot here, but looks like it is freezing up there. Is that ice on top of the mountain?" Athirst inquired.

"It is snow, and yes, it's very cold. We will not be heading that way for trades." Sophos chuckled.

"Do you think anyone lives up there?"

"I am sure someone does, but it's not for me."

As they entered Siomon territory, the vegetation grew even sparser and the dirt beneath their feet began to sparkle, almost like someone took the stars of the sky and sprinkled them into bits on the ground. The way it glinted in the sunlight was almost blinding. The few trees that dotted the terrain had leaves that appeared to be made of gold and silver. As Athirst passed by, he pulled one of the leaves off the trees and examined it. Its surface was so shiny that he could see his reflection in it.

"How is this possible?" Athirst asked.

"Siomon's landscape is carpeted with beautiful minerals and gems. The ground here has so many rare healing elements, but one of the villagers found out they are enhanced to their maximum potential when mixed with our flowers. So we started trading."

Athirst could tell they were approaching the center of the village. Unlike Atar, where all the people had the same very distinct features, this village had people similar to Eirene. It was a melting pot of people of all races, ethnicities, shapes, and sizes.

Sophos and Athirst left their beasts just outside the center of the village and Sophos went to find an alchemist named Hanndonfield.

"I should be right back. Stay here and watch the animals."

Athirst commanded the beasts to rest so he could roam the village freely.

Athirst bent down and grabbed a handful of soil. He let the shiny dust fall through his fingers.

"I've never seen you here before. Coming to trade?"

Athirst looked up to see a woman with sunkissed, golden-brown skin and thick, curly black hair that fell over her shoulders. She was shapely, with full lips and bright brown eyes.

"Not me. My Elder." Athirst pointed in the direction of Sophos, who was wandering the village in search of the alchemist.

"Yes, we've seen him here a few times. Pretty funny guy. Here." The woman handed him a bag. "Why don't you take some with you? We're all still trying to find its many different uses. Experiment by mixing it with some things in your village. I expect a full report when you make some new discoveries." She smiled.

"What's your name?"

"Cearney. And you?"

"Athirst."

"Well, I guess I'll see you later, Athirst. It was nice to meet you. I'll be waiting for that report." She flashed another radiant smile and walked away.

Athirst ran up to Sophos.

"Are you kidding me? You mean to tell me that there are villages out there with women that look like this and you're just now bringing me?"

"Well, I didn't think about it. Truth be told, you shouldn't, either! I happen to like the Athirst that keeps his head in the Writ and stays focused on Jah. Not the Athirst that has his head in the clouds."

Athirst looked offended.

"Anyway...I found Hanndonfield, the woman I was looking for. I gave her some of the flowers from the East Gardens and she gave me some of their element-rich soil and a few other crystals that should help this old body feel new again."

"I have a bag as well," Athirst boasted. "A woman gave it to me. I think she was flirting with me."

"With you? I would stay away from her, then. Flirting with you proves she has bad taste."

Athirst jabbed Sophos in the arm and Sophos returned the favor.

The men went back to the edge of the village, got on their animals, and headed back to Eirene.

It was the middle of the day and Eirene was bustling.

Sophos and Athirst got home and unloaded their items. Athirst stayed inside but Sophos headed out. It wasn't long before he overheard Querulous' loud mouth.

"Yes, such a fine young man," Querulous said. "He and Governess will make a beautiful union."

Then, Sophos overheard a name and went back home to tell Athirst.

"Theiler?" Athirst asked incredulously. "Theiler, who I see during lessons every day? That Theiler? She can do so much better than him. What does she want with someone like him anyway? He's arrogant, conceited, and too overtly flirtatious to be focused on Jah's purpose."

"Athirst, it is the way it should be," Sophos said in an attempt to comfort him.

Athirst looked dejected.

"Listen," Sophos continued, "You're strong. You are going to be fine. Jah has much bigger plans for you than a union with Governess -- plans that you will surely find more satisfaction in."

Sophos cared very much for Athirst. He wanted to take his hurt away, but Sophos knew he couldn't protect him from everything. "Jah reveals many things to me. We have a beautiful life here, Athirst. Do not disrespect Jah by coveting after things that aren't meant for you. It's not pleasing to Him. That envy will cause you to fall. Your day will come. Just be patient."

"You're right."

Sophos nodded.

"I just have one question," Athirst continued.

Sophos raised an eyebrow expectantly.

"Is she beautiful -- my future union-mate?"

Sophos rolled his eyes. "My, you boys sure move on quickly."

"What?" Athirst asked unashamedly.

"You need not worry about your own union. You need to find something to wear to Theiler and Governess' celebration, after all," Sophos said, chuckling as he left the room. Athirst couldn't help but smile.

21.
Growing Up as Theiler

It was written that one brother grew jealous of the other, and desired the attention from Jah. Instead of doing His will, he took away the will of his brother. Through him sin entered the world. *Desiring another man's place will lead to destruction. Seek what is yours, and you will reap abundantly. Seek what belongs to another, and you will perish, never satisfying your desires or the desires that Jah has for you.* (Writ 212:13-15)

Many considered Theiler to be one of the wisest Youth, despite his self-importance and penchant for wooing young ladies. His birth parents, who died in the vanishing, were very wealthy and attractive people and he mirrored them in every way. Many of the female Youth were enamored with him and it was surprising that Theiler actually wanted to commit to someone. People assumed he must've received instruction from Jah. Theiler's Elder was very respected, but unlike Sophos, Discernmos was much more stern. He put a lot of pressure on Theiler to be the best. And although he appreciated the friendship he shared with Sophos, he often felt that Sophos took much of the Writ too lightly and that his many jokes could be misread as disrespectful to Jah. Discernmos knew that it was his own actions that caused the end of the Second World. He felt incredibly grateful to be chosen as an Elder in the New World, and in a way felt like he could make up for his past by being as devoted as he could to Jah's cause.

Discernmos noticed many of Theiler's gifts early on and made sure that he spent ample time harnessing his abilities. Theiler appeared to be great at most things. His quick wit allowed him the ability to participate in debate with Athirst during lessons. Other Youth wouldn't dare argue with Athirst, but Theiler enjoyed the challenge.

Theiler's gifts were not just intellectual, but physical as well. He could spar with any Youth. His favorite 'rival' was Jabari, who was considered the strongest of them all. Theiler enjoyed the challenge that Jabari gave him. And although he was a tough opponent, Theiler was persistent in continuously challenging his own strength. Jabari appreciated Theiler's desire to spar with him and this created a close bond between the two of them.

Sparring match days were highly anticipated in the community. It not only allowed Theiler and Jabari a chance to show off their talents, but also allowed the Elders to make evaluations based on their performance. It also might have given them something to do to escape boredom.

Even though Jabari had brute strength and the power to pulverize anyone who came his way, his massive size made him slow and he tired quickly. This gave Theiler an advantage. His muscular yet slim build allowed him to move fast, and paired with his intellect and ability to strategize, it made him an equally formidable opponent.

A Youth could sign up to spar for either one or three rounds. Many Youth would typically only sign up for one, but Jabari would beg Theiler to sign up for three. Theiler didn't mind signing up for multiple rounds. In fact, as he got better with sparring, he found more rounds to be beneficial in his training. He also respected Jabari, and wanted him to have many chances to show off his skills.

Sparring was one of the few areas where Jabari felt confident. He was not as bright as the other Youth and was often uncomfortable dabbling in conversations about the Writ. And as pompous as Theiler appeared, it bothered him when people made fun of Jabari. He would often defend him. He would have never asked Governess to be his union-mate if he had known the person in Jabari's vision was her. Theiler had no need to compete against or feel jealous of him, as he cherished their friendship.

Initially, Theiler also enjoyed sparring against Athirst, but for a different reason. Athirst was highly intelligent and extremely strategic in his sparring. Both men had a similar build and mindset. Their slim, muscular frames were agile and strong. Many of the villagers compared them and over time, those comparisons to see who was better changed their attitudes toward one another. They became prideful and both wanted to determine who was the strongest, fastest, wisest, and most desirable. Theiler especially wanted to prove his superiority at the time when Athirst and Governess were together. One fight in particular would push his jealousy and determination to the edge.

On this night, Theiler showed up to their usual meeting place in the woods; only this time, he brought daggers with him. Daggers were forbidden to use unless faced with an enemy, but Theiler didn't care. When Athirst saw them, he was shocked.

"Don't worry, Athirst, I brought you one as well so the fight's fair." Theiler tossed the dagger to Athirst, who struggled to keep from grabbing the blade's edge.

"This seems wrong, Theiler. I can't fight like this in good conscience. I won't stop you from using one, but for me I just can't."

"Suit yourself." Theiler positioned himself to fight.

They circled each other for what seemed like forever. Athirst made the first move, throwing a punch and hitting Theiler squarely in the jaw. Theiler was quick to return the favor.

Eventually, Theiler took out his blade, which glinted under the moonlight that came through the trees. Athirst saw this and strategized a way to get the dagger out of his hand and pin him to the ground. When he had the opportunity, Athirst lunged forward and grabbed Theiler's wrist, grabbing the blade with his other hand and tossing it into a nearby bush. Athirst threw him on the ground, and after catching his breath, reached out to lend a hand to Theiler.

Theiler was enraged. He brushed Athirst's hand away and left the woods, scowling.

Ever since then, Theiler wanted to find a way to best him. So when he heard that Athirst and Governess' union celebration had been called off, he took no time trying to arrange a union of his own. He made every effort to attract Governess and eventually his plan became a reality. Only then did Theiler feel satisfied, as he felt like he was back in the lead. So after seeing Athirst for the first time since the announcement, he felt a little less hostile.

"I didn't see you during community dinner the other night. How have you been?" Theiler asked with a spring in his step.

"I've been good. You?" Athirst replied.

"Things have been going well for me, too. I'm sure that you heard about the union between me and Governess. I never thought I'd find myself with someone like her but when you feel it's right, you just have to go with it."

Athirst didn't know how to feel about this statement. "So," Athirst said, "What did it sound like when Jah told you she was the one you were to unify with?"

"Well, friend, I really didn't hear much of anything until you asked for unionship with Governess. After that, I began to feel this really overwhelming sensation that she was supposed to be with me instead. It was literally giving me stomach pains when I saw you two together. I never had Jah speak to me in that way before, but it was such a strong feeling that I just had to listen."

"So, you knew Governess was the one when you grew sick to your stomach? If that's what a union feels like, I'm not sure if it's for me."

The joke seemed to ease the awkwardness between them and they both laughed.

Athirst tried to get his bearings. "Theiler, if you think she's the one for you, then you have my blessing."

"Thank you friend. I truly appreciate it."

22.
Athirst Watches the Union

Union celebrations were very different from the Potentiam Libertas, where there was lively chatter, lots of laughter, and the telling of stories. It was considered a very sacred tradition in which Jah spoke to the couple about His expectations of their future together.

Theiler and Governess' union ceremony took place in the lush gardens along the border of River Aesis. The air was fragrant with the scent of jasmine, roses, calla lilies, and vanilla, among other beautiful flowers.

Discernmos led the ceremony, which began with reading passages from the Writ:

"Wisdom, love, respect, grace, and discipline are all virtues necessary for a union in which Jah approves. You both are joining to carry out plans that are greater than yourselves. You are not unifying for the pleasures of self; you are combining spirits to develop your talents which will be used in order to fill the world with good. (Writ 212: 1-2)."

Theiler and Governess wore traditional unification clothing. Theiler's earth-toned garment was adorned with beads of rose petals that draped around his neck. Governess wore soft curls, pinned back behind her ears with a white rose. Her garment was dyed using red and orange flowers, which gave her dress a soft peach hue. Their apparel fit in perfectly with the surrounding nature. Similar to the wedding ceremonies of the Second World, each person of the union made vows, but the difference was that they did not direct the vows toward each other. In the New Age, vows were made directly to Jah so there was a clear understanding that marriage was not for self, but for the creator.

Sophos and Athirst watched the ceremony from their wooden stools. At this point, the village had performed many unification celebrations and there were just a few of the Youth left without a mate. Despite Athirst's initial feelings about the union, he was happy to see both Governess and Theiler working toward the path that was set before them.

It was during the reciting of vows where Athirst could see a very strange look grow over Theiler's face -- a look of fear, coupled with sadness. Then Theiler looked up to the sky and closed his eyes, mouthing words that no one could make out. It occurred for a brief moment, and then, realizing that people were watching, Theiler dropped his head and carried on reading his vows.

Athirst looked over at Sophos to see if he noticed. He then whispered to him, "Writ 212:14-15." Athirst knew the Writ inside and out. He couldn't help but recite the scripture in his head: *Desiring another man's place will lead to destruction. Seek what is yours, and you will reap abundantly. Seek what belongs to another, and you will perish never satisfying your desires or the desires that Jah has for you.*

"There's nothing you can do about it now. It's the way that it should be," Sophos whispered to him. It was apparent that Sophos noticed the same thing.

As much as it pained Athirst to see Theiler go into a union that was not blessed by Jah, he knew Sophos was right. It was written long before today's ceremony. Jah tested Theiler in the same way that he tested Athirst. Jah wanted to see if Theiler could be faithful to him despite the desires of his flesh and feelings of jealousy. But it looked like Theiler had chosen wrong.

After the ceremony came the celebration with lots of food and festivities. Many of the Youth and Elders played music or engaged in loud conversation. The newly unified couple mingled with other couples.

"Do you mind if a single guy joins you?" Athirst asked, walking over.

"Hey Athirst! Come on over! We're just chatting." Theiler patted him on the back.

Athirst's feeling of awkwardness quickly subsided. They're the same friends as before; no need to feel any different, Athirst thought to himself. Soon, he found himself laughing with all of the couples, truly enjoying the conversation. He felt as if he were soaking up all of the secrets to success.

The crowd was loud and the sound of woodwind instruments and drums did not help. The group found themselves struggling to speak over the noise. Athirst was mid-laugh when he noticed that Theiler gave him a sideways glance and motioned for him to step aside. Theiler's demeanor was very strange. He started looking around to see if anyone else had noticed his lack of enthusiasm. "Something's not right." Theiler did his best to whisper through the noise, but his attempt failed.

"What did you say, brother?" Athrist shouted, attempting to drown out the noise of the drums.

"Something's not right," Theiler repeated again.

"What do you mean?"

"I saw how much you wanted her and I wanted her for myself. All I can do now is ask that you forgive me." Theiler looked remorseful.

"I forgive you, but what do you mean?" Athirst already knew what Theiler was suggesting. Athirst felt for Theiler because he could only imagine what lay ahead.

Athirst could hear the fear in Theiler's voice. From the time they were young, they were warned about the wrath of Jah and what He would do to those who were disobedient. All of the Youth knew of Jah's power, so Athirst understood Theiler's worry.

"During our vows," Theiler continued, "I heard Jah. The writings from the Writ kept playing in my head and I knew that I was making a mistake, but instead of stopping the ceremony, I allowed it to continue on. I made a commitment before Jah that was not what He intended. You know which verse came to mind?"

Before Athirst could respond, Theiler answered his own question.

"Chapter 212, verses 14-15."

Athirst could not help but play along and ask, "Are you sure you made a mistake? I thought you told me that you knew she was the one for you. Since you're so good at receiving vision, how could this be? How come Discernmos didn't stop the ceremony? Surely he received vision as well."

"I have always looked to you as a friend, Athirst, but I realized I made a grave mistake. Every time I saw you with Governess, it made me jealous. I competed with you to improve myself at first, but after we sparred with the dagger and you won, I began competing against you. Governess felt like a way for me to redeem myself. I spoke to Discernmos about it and he told me that he didn't see me with Governess, but that it was up to me and I had to make my own decision. Discernmos and I meditated together and my unionmate was revealed to me. And it wasn't Governess -- it was Nia."

"You were supposed to unify with Nia? So why are you here with Governess?"

"I don't know," Theiler replied. He hung his head in shame. "I really don't know; everyone seemed to be coupled off and I was okay, but when you and Governess got together, it bothered me. I need you to forgive me, brother."

"I forgive you," Athirst reassured him. "I don't know how to tell you this, but I believe that Jabari knew that Governess was to be his union-mate. Sophos told me that Jabari had a talk with him," Athirst told Theiler.

Theiler was overwhelmed. He grabbed Athirst's arm and pulled him even further away from the crowd.

"Brother, Jabari was asking me to help him with vision. I was the one that told him his vision was about his union-mate, but I had no idea. I had no idea it was Governess." Theiler covered his face with his hands, massaged his temples, and then glided his fingers through his blonde hair. "This entire thing began just because I let my envy get the best of me. I hope that you can forgive me."

"I forgave you when you asked me the first time." Athirst appreciated Theiler's sincerity and wanted to make things better for him. "Maybe this is that nervous feeling you get when you become one with another person. Jah talks about the power of union; maybe that's what you're feeling. Sophos told me what it felt like when he became one with his wife in the Second World. He said he was so nervous he couldn't eat anything for days, but he said it was the best decision he ever made."

"Maybe you're right, Athirst. Maybe you're right." Theiler's voice trailed off and he looked over at all the other couples. He observed the look of joy and happiness on their faces and reluctantly went over to join Governess, who appeared to be looking for him. He put his arm around her and gave her a kiss on the forehead. She smiled and they blended in with all the other happy couples. Despite his initial feelings, Theiler went home and sealed his bond with Governess that evening.

The morning after the union ceremony, Athirst got up early to hunt for devices. He wanted to find as many items as he could to make a pleasing sacrifice to Jah. He found himself near where the woods and the edge of River Aesis met. He noticed a hump on the ground covered with lots of grass. As Athirst reached down to see what it was, he noticed small pebbles near the hump begin to shake. Athirst looked behind him to see Jabari approaching.

"Hey brother, how are you?" Athirst called out.

Jabari, not noticing Athirst at first, was startled when he heard his voice. Jabari jumped, making the earth beneath him tremble once more.

"Oh, I guess I'm doing okay," Jabari sighed.

"Tell me. What's going on?"

"I came to the woods to get away from the center of the village. I really didn't expect to run into anyone this early," Jabari explained.

"Oh, I see. Well, I guess I'll leave you to it then." Athirst was about to walk away when he heard Jabari call out to him.

"Since you're already here, let me ask you something."

"Sure brother, what is it?"

"The union ceremony between Theiler and Governess -- what did you think about it?"

"It was a beautiful ceremony. Similar to all the other ceremonies that we've had. Why do you ask?" Athirst knew why Jabari was asking, but hoped his vague response would mask what he knew.

"Oh, well, I guess I just wanted to know what you thought," Jabari said.

"It's got to be more than that. What is it? You seem troubled."

"I guess it doesn't matter if I tell you now because it already happened. Governess was the one I was supposed to unify with," Jabari said.

Athirst continued to play ignorant. "Are you sure?"

"Yes, I'm sure. She was the one that Jah sent to me in my vision."

"You know that you're not..." Athirst managed to catch himself before finishing his sentence.

"What? Say it! I know what you're thinking." Jabari's voice got really tense. "I have worked very hard over the last few years to grow my connection with Jah but no one gives me any credit for that! Unlike both you and Theiler, I may be the only one who actually interpreted his vision the right way."

"I'm sorry Jabari, you're right. I shouldn't have said that. I guess what I mean is, are you sure that it was Governess and not Nia? I mean, I thought maybe you and Nia would make an ideal match."

"For the last time! We never received absolution! And now, there has never been a vision that was more clear to me."

There was a long pause. Jabari's shoulders began to slump. "Maybe I am just as terrible at interpreting vision as everyone says I am."

"Don't say that, Jabari. I believe your vision. I think it's worth mentioning that even us gifted people are not perfect at interpreting everything," Athirst joked. "This whole thing, life in the Third World -- the signs and clues in the Writ, the dreams and the visions -- it's all so difficult to know exactly what is the right thing to do all the time. All we can do is hope that we make the best decisions for ourselves and hope that we are doing the will of Jah." Athirst gave Jabari a pat on the back.

"I guess the only choice I have is to be happy for the new couple and hope that Theiler followed the will of Jah... and that I misinterpreted my vision," Jabari said reluctantly.

"Believe it or not Jabari, I feel the same way."

Athirst bent down to unearth the mysterious object that was hidden under the mound of grass, and placed it in his leather sack.

"I feel like I mess everything up," Jabari mumbled under his breath.

"Jabari, stop. We went over this; you are not..." Jabari walked away before Athirst could finish his sentence. Athirst sighed and finished gathering devices. He collected 42 in all, and hoped that some of them were made with Lithorium energy so he could see the brilliant glow in the flames during the next Potentiam Libertas festival.

When he arrived back home, Sophos was sleeping. Athirst decided not to wake him and instead went to his room and meditated to Jah. He not only asked Jah for guidance for himself, but on this night, he asked for guidance and healing for everyone in the village. Athirst realized that one decision not aligned to the will of Jah would have repercussions that affected many. All Athirst could think about was the last words in chapter 211 that foreshadowed grave things to come.

23.
The Butterfly

As the months passed by, Jabari found a new way to divert his attention. He took to practicing controlling the animals, specifically birds.

"Good girl." Jabari stuck out his hand, and a large brown and black eagle with green eyes flew to him, its large talons grasping his arm.

"Tell me what you saw today," Jabari asked the bird. The bird started squawking and Jabari listened intently. "I see, yes, very interesting. You did very well today, Cecile." Jabari moved his forearm, signaling for the bird to fly. It took off and headed toward River Aesis in search of food.

"Bye Mediorocris! I think I'm going to head out. Maybe help Athirst!" Jabari shouted through the glassless window.

"Okay, well don't stay gone too long. Lunch will be ready soon."

Jabari left and immediately found Athirst, who was near the edge of the river struggling to roll the massive tree he just chopped down. Athirst was hunched over, too distracted to notice Jabari standing there.

"I heard that you might have needed help," Jabari called out. "So, I came to see what I could do."

"Who told you that?" Athirst struggled to catch his breath. I'm actually working on a secret project. Nothing that I've shared with anyone," Athirst replied, looking a bit confused.

"Cecile told me."

"That bird you've been taming. That's pretty cool. So, I guess you're doing well with that huh?"

"Yep. I would say so. Got me here to help you. So, a secret project? Can I know about it?"

"Not yet my friend. Soon, but not just yet. I could use your help, though. If you can help me roll the tree here, I can cut it into smaller sized pieces."

"Come on, I promise I won't tell anyone. Besides, keeping a secret won't matter much anyway. I'll just send Cecile to spy on you. She'd let me know."

"Alright, fine. But I promise if I hear it from anyone..."

"Your secret is safe with me," Jabari said, rubbing his hands together.

"I'm..." Athirst struggled to get it out. He didn't want people to think he was crazy. "I'm building a house for my future family."

"Really?"

"That's it? That's all you have to say?" Athirst was puzzled.

"Well, it doesn't sound like a bad idea to me. It's bound to happen soon, right?"

"That's exactly what I was thinking. I'm not sure who my future mate will be or when I'll meet her, but Jah showed me that I'm going to have a big family, so I think I need to prepare now."

Athirst and Jabari worked together to cut the log down into twelve-foot-long pieces. They rolled each one to a pile where several other pieces were already stacked.

"Have you been working on this for a long time?" Jabari asked.

"Not too long, shortly after Theiler and Governess' union."

"Yes, well. I think both of us are finding ways to busy ourselves. Everyone else seems to be working on their families."

After working for a while, Jabari and Athirst sat down.

"I think I'm gonna head back."

"Where are you headed?" Athirst inquired.

"Back home. Mediorocris is cooking. You?"

"I don't know. I think I'm going to stay out here for a little while. Maybe do some fishing. Thanks for the help; I'll see you later."

"No problem."

Athirst had gone past the village borders in search of Chinook Salmon. The fish were always appreciated by the Elders, but especially Sophos. Athirst could almost hear what he'd say -- "Too lazy to get up before the sun and go fishing." He placed a small herring fish on the end of his pole and cast it into the water, hoping that Sophos' theory about waking up early was wrong.

The waters at this part of River Aesis rushed over large, jagged rocks and it took great skill to catch anything. Athirst, however, was determined to bring some succulent pink fish back home. He soon realized Sophos was correct. He only managed to catch two fish after hours in the river. He started gathering his belongings to make his way back when he noticed her. She began as a shadow. But slowly, the shadow took the form of a beautiful, voluptuous woman. She had glowing, sunkissed skin. Her brown eyes were bright and full of life, and her rosy lips were full. She had thick, dark, wavy hair that cascaded over her shoulders. She looked so familiar to him. He soon realized that she was from Siomon.

Athirst couldn't help but to call out, "I haven't seen you here around these parts. Are you lost?"

"No," she replied. "I'm looking for a special flower, Crossandra orange; do you know of it?"

"There are some that grow in my village...in the gardens east of the river. Why?"

"I need it to make a special herbal remedy for my Elder who's sick. How do I get there?" she asked.

"I'm actually heading back in that direction. You are more than welcome to follow me, but I'm afraid that we're about 12 miles north of there."

"Yes, well, I have traveled quite some way from my own village. I would hate to travel much further."

Athirst thought for a minute and then said, "For a woman as beautiful as you, let me gather the flower and bring it to you. I'm sure I can have it to you by tomorrow. You should go back and comfort your Elder."

Athirst's offer drew a warm smile across her face.

"Thank you. I live seven miles north of here in a village called Siomon. I'm Cearney. My Elder's name is Iris. And forgive me, what is your name again?"

"I remember you! You're the girl I met when I went with my Elder to trade! I'm Athirst. You already know my Elder, Sophos. I live south of here in Eirene."

"Ahh yes, I remember now." She grinned. "Do you like living in Eirene?"

"I do. And you? How do you like Siomon?"

"It's beautiful there. So, what ever happened with the task I gave you? I believe I wanted a full report."

She remembered, Athirst thought to himself. "Well, to be honest, I haven't really taken much time to look at it. Besides, everyone in my village is healthy."

"Oh really? That's your excuse?"

Athirst was captivated by Cearney's beauty and soon realized he'd gotten lost in thought as she was talking. An awkward silence filled the air. Athirst scrambled to find words to keep the conversation going. "Well," Athirst could hear his voice break the silence. "I guess I'll see you soon... I mean, I'll bring the flower to you before the next moon, or if you want it sooner, I can find time..." His voice faded and Athirst realized that he was beginning to ramble.

"I hope you're better at keeping promises than you are at doing assignments."

An uneasy laugh came from Athirst.

Cearney chuckled. "Yes, well, I guess I will see you tomorrow before the moon is hanging in the sky. I hope you're a man of your word."

"Oh, trust me, I am." Athirst puffed out his chest.

"Well, it has been a pleasure meeting you again, Athirst."

Cearney turned around and began her journey home. Athirst tried to wave bye, but he forgot that he had so much in his hand that he fumbled and dropped the fish from his catch. He quickly gathered them up in hopes Cearney did not see, and began walking home toward Eirene.

Athirst never looked at the East Gardens in the way that he had today. He wanted to pick the most lovely and perfect flowers for the beautiful woman from Siomon. He pushed through the brilliantly bold colors, inspecting each flower carefully. He plucked ones with little to no flaws and carefully wrapped them in a soft cloth. The next morning when he woke up, he reviewed his choices once more, giving them his final approval before heading out the door.

"Bye Sophos!"

"Where are you headed off to?"

"Siomon."

"Siomon, interesting. Why are you headed there?"

"I...I need to make a trade."

"A trade...Okay, I guess I will see you later then." Sophos smirked. "I'll be interested in seeing what you come back with."

Athirst didn't let Sophos continue. He headed out the door and debated on how he should travel to Siomon. He greatly improved his beast riding ability, but didn't want to scare Cearney off. He decided it best to walk. Athirst couldn't help but notice how dramatically his surroundings changed. The plush woods thinned out, leaving sparse, barren trees and evergreens sprinkled here and there. The magical shimmer on both the leaves and the ground became more apparent as he got closer to Siomon.

He wandered the village for a little while in search for Cearney. Besides the lack of foliage, Siomon reminded him a lot of Eirene. He looked through the various window openings and noticed a heavy-set woman cooking that reminded him of Mediorocris. He also saw an athletically built, olive-skinned older man with gray hair that could have passed for Sophos. The man was whittling a piece of wood. It looked like he was making a musical instrument of some sort. What set Siomon apart from other villages was all of the small trade markets that specialized in a variety of elements designed to heal ailments of the body. The trade markets were nothing more than several little wooden stalls that could only fit a person or two. The posts that held up the cowhide roof were connected with wooden shelves that held little clay bottles of medicines made from the special, glittering dirt native to their region. A sign on the front of each stall showed what healing quality they specialized in.

"Fever," Athirst read the sign as he passed by.

A few feet away there was one that said, "Cold". He kept walking past them until he got to one with a woman who had thick, black wavy hair.

"Cearney?"

"Athirst! How lovely to see you! You made it. I guess you are a man of your word." She smiled.

"I'm always so fascinated when I come here. Is this your stand?" Athirst glanced at the bottles that were on the wooden shelves.

"No, not mine. I'm still honing my craft. This is my Elder, Iris' stand. She's not doing very well and can't operate the place like she used to. I'm hoping to find a way to cure her."

Athirst picked up one of the clay bottles and poured the contents in his hand. A glittery purple sand emptied into his palm.

"Don't waste it!" Cearney swatted at him.

Athirst cupped his hand and carefully attempted to get the powder back inside the bottle.

"How does it all work?"

"Not sure what that one does, but I have some that I've been working on." Cearney grabbed the bottle out of his hand and placed it carefully back on the shelf. "Did you happen to bring the flower?"

"Oh yes, of course." Athirst fumbled around, looking for it in his leather sack. He was proud to pull out a perfect Crossandra orange and a wide range of other flowers he thought she would find useful.

"The flowers in Eirene are beautiful." Cearney took the flowers and examined their leaves. She held it up to her nose and sniffed its delicate fragrance. "It's quite beautiful in Siomon, but it's terrible ground for growing plants and flowers. That's why I traveled south. I needed this plant to help with Iris' arthritis."

Cearney suddenly grabbed Athirst's hand. "Let's go. I can show you what I've been working on."

They walked about a hundred feet to a small house that was surrounded by a fence. At the back of the fence was a little wooden shed that looked like a small workshop. Like the ones in the center of Siomon, it had several clay bottles that were labeled with different ingredients and the ailments they helped alleviate.

"Which ones are these?" Athirst could not help his curiosity. He started reading through the different labels, some saying 'Headache,' some saying 'Bruises,' others saying 'Cough.'

"Well, that sparkling sand that you're infatuated with has a way of bringing out the healing qualities of things in nature when they are mixed together. So I'm trying to see what would work best to help my Elder. I have mixed it with all kinds of herbs and liquids to try and find the best remedy." Cearney took an empty clay bottle and placed it on the table in front of her. She bent down and grabbed a handful of shimmering dirt and slowly poured it in a bowl. Cearney took the flower Athirst brought and ripped it into little pieces, sprinkling it on top of the dirt. Then she took a smooth rock that was nearby and used it to mix the flower into the dirt.

Athirst felt a little crushed after seeing how quickly she shredded the perfect flower that he picked for her. Nonetheless, he was fascinated by the process.

"Now, can I see your canister? I know you must have one, considering you've traveled quite a long way." Athirst searched inside his leather bag for his water canister. After seeing how carelessly she ripped the flower, he was a little hesitant to give his container over to her. He didn't have it in his hand for long before Cearney grabbed it from him and poured the water on top of the powder, turning the powder into paste.

"We're supposed to be natural healers. We run a large apothecary here and specialize in creating medicines for various things. Most everyone here has created some kind of unique and inventive remedy. I'm still working on finding my 'thing'."

"Well, I'm sure you'll find it. You have so many different bottles here; at least one of them must work. Besides, I've brought you a wide range of flowers to experiment with. You'll probably be able to concoct some of the best medicines in the village soon."

"Why thank you, Athirst. That was very sweet of you to do." Cearney looked at the flowers again and Athirst couldn't help but feel proud of himself.

"We're also responsible for distributing a lot of our supply to local villages nearby… in fact, that is how we know of Sophos."

"Who doesn't know Sophos?" Athirst chuckled. "So, where is this Elder of yours that I keep hearing about?"

They collected the medicine and headed to Cearney's house. Her Elder had to be at least ten years older than Sophos, if not more. Her face and hands were worn and wrinkled. Her long, white hair was pulled into a ponytail, and she squinted her eyes as if it were difficult for her to see.

"I have something for you, Iris." Cearney held up the small clay container with the paste mixture.

Athirst wasn't certain if Iris could see him, but nonetheless, she must have sensed his presence.

"Cearney, who is that?" Iris pointed a long, frail finger in Athirst's direction.

"Iris, this is Athirst. He's from Eirene. He's the one who brought the flower that we needed."

"Come here and let me get a good look at you," Iris said.

Iris grabbed his face and pulled Athirst so close that their noses were practically touching. "You are a nice looking young man. I can tell...you'd be a good fit for my Cearney," Iris said as she ran her hands through Athirst's hair.

"Iris, you can stop examining him. I'm not interested in any unionship right now. I have to take care of you and Jendahi."

"Who's Jendahi?" Athirst asked.

Iris was instructed to save two girls from two different families of the Second World and raise them as sisters. Only those with the most unselfish of hearts received more than one child. Jendahi had a slim, very petite figure. She was extremely fair with freckles that dotted the bridge of her nose, and her crisp blue-green eyes were the color of the ocean. Her hair was the color of honey. Both women were beautiful despite looking nothing like sisters. Even though they came from two different families, the bond they shared was strong.

"Here she is now!" A small, petite girl walked in, eyeing Athirst suspiciously. Cearney made an attempt to introduce them, but it did not go over well.

"What do you want with my sister?" Jendahi demanded.

"I...uhh...I was just trying to help your Elder." Athirst couldn't believe this pint-sized person had the ability to intimidate him.

"Well that's good," Jendahi said, walking off.

"She's friendly," Athirst commented.

"She actually is once you get to know her."

Cearney scooped some of the paste mixture with her hand.

"Iris, let me see if this will make you feel any better." Cearny rubbed the paste on Iris' hands, massaging it in around her knuckles.

"I'm trying it with a flower that Athirst brought for you. The Crossandra orange you told me so much about." Cearney continued to rub the mixture onto her Elder's hand.

"This flower was one of my Elder's favorites. She spoke of it all the time."

Athirst could see the lumps around Iris' knuckles begin to shrink. Her fingers appeared to straighten up right before his very eyes.

"My goodness." Athirst was astonished. "This is one of the most amazing things that I've ever seen."

Cearney seemed just as surprised. "You were right. It really is working. How do you feel?"

Iris started flexing her fingers back and forth. "It's not completely gone, but the majority of the pain has subsided immensely," Iris said in her soft, raspy voice. "I knew there was something special about you, Athirst. Thank you for bringing that flower to me." Iris continued to wiggle her fingers around. Cearney, overcome with joy, gave Athirst a kiss on the cheek but quickly withdrew after realizing what she had done. A blushing grin stretched across Athirst's face.

"Well, thank you for bringing the flowers and staying to meet my family." Cearney began walking Athirst toward the door.

Athirst lingered for a few more minutes. "So, when do you think I could see you again?" Athirst asked, praying that it would not be his last encounter.

"You were quite nice to come all the way here and your flower did help my Elder. I guess we can see each other again," Cearney replied slyly.

"Really? Okay, well...I guess I can come again in a few days."

"How about I come to your village? I may need to gather more flowers."

"It's quite a long walk. I don't think you should walk that far."

"Athirst! I will be fine." Cearney patted his shoulder.

"How about this...How about I come pick you up?"

"Pick me up?"

"Yes...just trust me."

He then shouted bye down the hallway in the direction he saw Jendahi head earlier before going back to Eirene.

He thought about Cearney on the way back to Eirene. As he entered the village, the first thing he saw was Cecile flying about.

"Cecile!" Jabari shouted, proceeding to whistle. The bird came swooping down and rested on Jabari's shoulder.

"What have you been up to? Cecile tells me that you left the village today."

"Cecile told you? You two are becoming quite the nosey pair." Athirst looked at Cecile. "Don't tell him everything. I've got to keep some secrets." Athirst smiled at the bird.

Cecile squawked.

"It's just that, after the union ceremony, I haven't seen much of anyone these days. So, just wanted to know what you were up to and if you may have wanted to spar or something. You know, like the good ol' days before everyone was coupled off." Jabari looked at Athirst, waiting for a response.

"Yes, well, I would love to, but..." Athirst struggled to find the words.

"Don't tell me you too?" Jabari groaned.

"What?"

"You're sneaking off because of a woman?"

"No, of course not."

"All right, then, where were you?"

"Just making a few trades. That's all." Athirst looked away.

"On a non-trading day. Well, good luck with whoever she is." Jabari chuckled and walked away.

Despite feeling guilty about Jabari, Athirst was still feeling euphoric from his encounter with Cearney. Sophos was asleep when Athirst got home, passed out in a chair near the fireplace. *Good*, Athirst thought. He didn't want to be bombarded with any more questions about his visit today. He headed to his room and placed his bag down before going back outside.

"Look," Athirst said to Swift and Nimble, his pet grey wolves. "In a few days we're going to pick up a friend. But she's never been on a wolf before, so you two must be gentle."

The wolves looked up at Athirst curiously.

"Yes, I want you to be gentle and you need to be chivalrous. Maybe bow when you meet her. So, let's see what you've got."

Athirst concentrated and sent a signal to both wolves, who then stood up. Athirst took his hands and did a down motion. Swift and Nimble made an attempt to bow.

"No, no, no! Not like that." Seeing that they would need a little more instruction, Athirst got down on all fours and showed them what he wanted them to do. "Okay, now it's your turn." Athirst motioned with his hands again. "Great job Nimble. Swift, what was that?" Swift looked away and Nimble stood up proudly. "Nimble, you'll carry Cearney. Be gentle with her. Swift, I'll ride with you. In the meantime, both of you continue to practice. I want to make sure you're both on your best behavior."

The next morning Sophos was up, ready to see how Athirst's visit went. "So, you're not going to say anything?"

"What is there to say?"

"How did your visit go?"

"It went well. I was able to bring a flower that seemed to help one of the Elders in Siomon. In fact, I will be headed there tomorrow morning to make sure that she's still feeling well."

"Ha, is that what you are telling yourself? Well, that is certainly kind of you to go back and check." Sophos was shaking his head. He had a playful grin on his face.

"Come on, I'm just trying to be nice." Athirst playfully jabbed at Sophos and left to work on his daily chores.

The next morning, Athirst got up early, packed a few items in his leather sack, mounted Swift, and was off to Siomon. Nimble was running alongside them, excited that he was the one chosen to carry this new acquaintance. When Athirst arrived at Cearney's door with the large beasts, Cearney was nearly speechless.

"Oh my! Is that a --"

"Wolf, yes. And I brought one for you as well," Athirst said, smiling.

"Brought one for me. What would I want with one of those?" Cearney clung to Athirst, trying to hide from the beast.

"In your village you can make medicine, but in our village, we can tame beasts. Don't worry...I'm strong enough now that I can control him for you. See, watch this." Athirst concentrated and then bent his wrist. Both of the wolves bent down as if they were bowing to Cearney.

"How are you doing that?" Cearney could not believe what she had just seen.

"Climb aboard," Athirst commanded.

"Have you lost your mind? I will not risk getting eaten alive by that wild animal." Cearney crossed her arms.

"Do you want to get more flowers or not? If we walk, it will take most of the day. On him, maybe 20 minutes."

"Athirst, I will not get on top of that wolf."

"Okay, I guess we'll have to do this the hard way, then." With that, Athirst gave the wolf a command. The wolf went behind Cearney and flipped her with his nose so that she tumbled onto his back.

"Hold on," Athirst said. Before Cearney had a chance to think, they were off.

The wolves seemed to move at the speed of light. The trees were a blur as they whizzed past. Dirt kicked up behind them in dusty clouds with each stride. Cearney held on to the wolf like her life depended on it. Both her arms were gripped around his neck.

"You may want to loosen your grip on his neck. He needs to be able to breathe!" Athirst shouted.

Cearney looked at him incredulously.

"I really think if you just relax, you might actually enjoy it. I promise. I will not let you fall off. Trust me."

"Why should I trust you?"

"You're quite stubborn, aren't you? I've proven trustworthy enough to take care of Iris, am I wrong?"

Cearney slowly loosened her grip from around Nimble's neck and sat up a little higher.

"I told you I wouldn't let you fall. Now, just take it all in."

Cearney tried to relax.

"We are going to head to the East Gardens. You will find some of the most beautiful flowers there."

The wolves made a right turn and ended up near the gardens. They lowered their bodies to the ground and Athirst hopped off, walked over to Cearney, grabbed her hand, and she jumped off as well.

"Stay here," Athirst told Nimble and Swift. The wolves bowed to him, walked off and began playfully wrestling with each other.

"So, how was your ride?"

"It was frightening at first, but I must say... it was one of the most exhilarating experiences of my life." Cearney looked relieved to be standing on the ground. Her full head of thick hair was windblown. She ran her hands through her hair and adjusted her clothes before entering the East Gardens.

When they entered, wild animals of all kinds were hanging from branches or prowling around. Cearney grabbed Athirst's arm. "Are we safe here? They won't eat us, will they?"

"They would, but you have to control them in order to prevent that," Athirst replied.

"So you're controlling them right now?" Cearney dug her nails into his forearm.

"Yes, watch this." Athirst pointed up to a colorful, large bird that was perched on a branch. He quickly moved his finger to another tree and the bird flew across to its new location and landed there.

"How are you doing that?"

"Jah gave us the ability to do so many wonderful things. Right now, I'm letting all of the animals know to give us a little space and to not come toward us."

"Wow." Cearney was still in disbelief.

"Sophos is still fascinated with all that Jah as allowed us to do in this new world. He tells me that we've always had the ability to do mighty things but the people of the Second World became so reliant on technology, that over time, their gifts went away."

"My Elder told me the same things. Do you think they had animals like this in the Second World?"

"They did, but Sophos said they didn't live together like this. He said that most of these animals were locked in cages for people to look at, but didn't roam freely."

"It's difficult to imagine isn't it?" Cearney said, finally loosening the grip on Athirst's arm. She continued to look around in amazement. It was so different from her village. "I've never seen anything so lush in all my life." Cearney circled around, looking at all of the exotic flowers before picking a few she had never seen before and putting them in her leather sack. They stayed in the East Gardens until dark.

When they arrived back in Siomon, Jendahi was waiting for her sister at the door.

"Where have you been?"

"I was with Athirst. We were getting more flowers for Iris."

Jendahi looked Athirst up and down. "I think it's time for you to say bye."

"She's right. Jendahi, could you please give us a moment?"

Jendahi still stood in the doorway.

"Jendahi, give us a few minutes," Cearney said, giving her sister the side-eye.

"I don't know why he needs a few more minutes. He spent most of the day with you," Jendahi mumbled as she walked away from the door.

They gazed at each other for a moment. Then Athirst said, "I probably shouldn't have let you pick so many flowers; you'll have no need to come back to Eirene and I may never see you again. It also looks like you have a lot to do around here, so...I guess this is goodbye."

"I do have a lot to do around here. Iris and my sister need me..."

"I see."

"...but, you may have given me a new reason to visit. I might just sign up for wolf riding lessons."

"So, you did enjoy that, eh?" Athirst grinned.

"Yes, it was fun. Thanks."

"Until next time Cearney."

"Bye, Athirst." Cearney gazed back at him as she closed the door.

Over the next few months, visits between the two of them became quite frequent. Even Jendahi began to like Athirst, but she didn't miss an opportunity to give him a hard time.

"Do you have to go with him? Why can't you stay here with me and Iris?" Jendahi asked.

"I kinda like him," Cearney responded.

"Did you ask Jah about him? Don't you think it's strange that he comes from another village?" Jendahi continued to recite a list of questions, in hopes that Cearney would reconsider leaving with Athirst.

"You do know that I'm standing right here? I can still hear you!" Athirst shot back.

Cearney giggled.

"You're right, Jendahi, he is rather strange, isn't he?" Cearney teased, glancing at Athirst.

"Goodness, quit with the flirting already! Just stay here, Cearney!" Jendahi begged.

"I think it's time for me to visit him again. He's come here so many times. It's time for me to meet some of the people in Eirene." She hugged Jendahi, kissing her forehead.

"I promise I will bring her back safe," Athirst interjected, hoping that his promise of Cearney's safety would win Jendahi's favor.

Nimble and Swift carried them to Eirene.

"I've only met Sophos. Do you not want me to meet your other friends?"

"I didn't think you would be interested. I guess we can visit a few people today."

Their first stop was Jabari's house. Mediorocris answered the door. "Is Jabari here? I wanted to introduce him to a friend." Mediorocris was in the kitchen as usual. She wiped her hands on the bottom of her skirt to clean off the fish scales that were sprinkled on them.

"Nice to meet you. You're the girl from Siomon, correct? Athirst has told me so many wonderful things about the people there...well, make yourself comfortable." Then she shouted, "Jabari, Athirst and a new friend are here to see you!"

As Jabari walked down the hallway, Cearney could see items on the countertops begin to tremble.

"Hi Jabari, this is Cearney, she lives in..."

"The woman from Siomon. Yes, it's so nice to meet you." Jabari stuck out his massive hand to give Cearney a shake. Cearney grabbed two fingers and shook them while looking Jabari up and down.

"Jabari is a big fellow, but don't be intimidated."

"Nothing to be scared of here," Jabari said to Ceareny.

"He's a big one but he's a good man," Mediorocris said to Cearney. Then she turned to Jabari, whispering, "You may need to visit Siomon as well; you might find your union-mate there."

"You know that Nia and I have started talking again, right?"

"This is news to me, when did this all happen?" Athirst was curious.

"You've been gone most days. Visiting her I assume, but yes, Nia and I figured that we're the only two left in Eirene not unified yet, well, with the exception of you. So, it just seemed to make sense."

"Have you talked to Jah about this? You don't want to make the same mistake..." Before Athirst could finish, Jabari said, "Like you did?" and started chuckling.

"What does he mean, 'like you did?'" Cearney inquired.

"Nothing," Athirst responded and quickly changed the subject. Athirst continued, "Both of you are so good at taming animals."

"That reminds me...come, let me show you a few new things Cecile can do!"

Jabari took them to see Cecile, who was perched in a tree near Jabari's house. He showed how the bird could fly at his command. He showed them how she would look over the village and bring back news of the goings on and he amazed them when Cecile began to say a few words.

"Pretty girl," Cecile said, looking at Cearney.

"You're a pretty girl, too," Cearney said back to the bird. "Jabari, were you really able to train her to do all this?"

"Yeah, I've been working on it for quite some time, but she's learning more new words everyday."

"That's so fascinating. You'll have to teach me how to do that someday," Athirst said.

"No problem brother, come by any time."

Both Athirst and Cearney said their goodbyes to Jabari and resumed their tour.

As they walked through the village, they ran into Querulous.

"Hi Querulous, how are things going?"

"How does it look like it's going? They moved out of the house and she left a whole bunch of her junk here," Querulous said as she continued tossing small items into a bag to take to Theiler and Governess' new home. "Who is this?" Querulous pointed to Cearney.

"She's from Siomon. Her name is Cearney."

"Ahh, so this is the young woman Sophos has been telling us about. Well, she is pretty, but no more beautiful than my Governess."

Querulous continued to drag items from her house out to the yard. "Whew, my back ain't what it used to be." Querulous was slightly bent over, rubbing her back.

"I may be able to help you with that." Cearney began digging around in her leather sack. She had so many random items in there that it was difficult to find what she was looking for.

"Ah, here it is." Cearney pulled out her mixture of soil and Crossandra orange and handed the small container to Querulous. "Try some of this. You'll need to rub it where you feel the pain."

Querulous sniffed the contents of the tube. "What is it?" Then she turned to Athirst. "This little mixture that your friend made better not do anything to me." She poured the glittering mixture into her hand.

"It helps if you make it into a paste. Athirst, let me use your water again." Cearney poured a little water on top of the mixture that was in Querulous' hand. "Mix it together and apply it to the area where your back hurts."

Querulous hesitantly rubbed the paste on the sore spot on her back. "Well, I don't feel anything."

"Just give it a few seconds." Athirst said.

"Oh, alright...wait...I...I can feel the pain going away! What is this? Thank you, what was your name again?"

"Cearney."

"Goodness, well, thank you Cearney. Glad you came to visit."

"Yes, well...see you later Querulous."

As they walked away, Cearney kept thinking about the female name Querulous spoke about. "Who is Governess?"

"Governess? Well, that's Querulous' Youth. She unified with a good friend of mine several months ago. Querulous loves to complain about everything, but you'll grow to love her over time."

"She reminds me of a few women in Siomon," Cearney chuckled.

"It's getting pretty late. I think I need to get you back before Jendahi has my head."

"I really enjoyed spending time with you today." Cearney gave him a kiss on the cheek. Athirst felt butterflies in his stomach.

As the visits continued, Athirst could see that even Sophos would light up when she was around, but wanted to make sure Athirst had not gotten too distracted by his new friend to do the right thing. After eight months of seeing Cearney in Eirene, Sophos began to ask questions.

"You sure have been spending quite a lot of time with Cearney. Have you meditated on this?" Sophos inquired.

"Would it be wrong if I told you that part of me is afraid? What if He doesn't approve?" Athirst responded quietly. He didn't even want to know the answer.

"Then, it is best you cut your relationship off now before your affections for her grow stronger. I think it may be best to not see her until you know whether she's the one for you," Sophos responded.

That night, Athirst got down on his knees and asked Jah for guidance. In the peaceful stillness of his mind, surrounded by a blanket of darkness, the vision of the butterflies came to him again. But this time, the vision began when the female butterfly from the north came to join the male butterfly. The butterflies circled each other and headed toward the sun, eventually bursting into a kaleidoscope of butterflies of all different colors. He now understood that he (the male butterfly) needed Cearney to help him reach his destiny. Athirst woke from his vision and his heart was warm. He was elated that he had received confirmation from Jah.

After receiving the vision, Athirst didn't wait. He traveled to Siomon and immediately asked Iris for her blessing.

Iris motioned for Athirst to come over. She wrapped both of her hands around his face and pulled him in closer. Iris' voice was nothing more than a raspy whisper. "I was wondering what was taking you so long. Of course, Athirst." Athirst watched as a tear rolled down her face. His eyes followed the tear around the lines of her mouth, which formed a smile. "I am so happy. Jah has blessed me to see this day."

Athirst thought receiving Iris' blessing was all he needed, but Jendahi, overhearing the conversation, came into the room. She raised an eyebrow. "Were you even planning on asking me if you could unify with my sister?" She tapped her foot.

"Of course. I was headed to you next," Athirst quickly responded.

"I bet you were." Jendahi rolled her eyes but then smiled. She opened her arms and gave Athirst a hug.

"Where is Cearney?" Athirst asked, feeling relieved.

"She's out back mixing up another concoction. Now that she's found a cure for arthritis, she's determined to find a cure for something else."

Athirst went outside to find Cearney mixing some of the flowers she picked from her many visits to Eirene with special sand.

"My goodness, you scared me Athirst! What are you doing here? I wasn't expecting to see you today." Athirst turned to Cearney and grabbed both of her hands, squeezing them lightly before taking a breath. "Cearney, you are what Jah has intended for me. I had to be patient, but I am so grateful that Jah has seen fit for me to unify with someone who is so strong and beautiful. I cherish the time I've gotten to spend getting to know you. I hope that you've received vision for me as well. I love you, Cearney." Athirst was nervous. He paused for quite some time, hoping to hear Cearney say something. He continued. "I...I was afraid that Jah's vision would not be of you, so I didn't meditate to him until last night." Athirst didn't want to lose the moment by mentioning his failed attempt of a previous proposal. "Will you unify with me?"

"Of course I will, Athirst."

Cearney and Athirst embraced for a while, taking in the moment. Then Cearney walked back into the house and immediately went to Jendahi, who was grinning from ear to ear.

"So did he ask you anything special?" Jendahi playfully asked.

"Yes, and now it's going to be up to you to look after Iris."

"I know. I am going to miss you." A small tear rolled down Jendahi's face. "Please make sure you write. I want to know everything that's going on in Eirene."

"Of course I will."

"I will come back in a few days, my love. I'm going to head to Eirene to prepare everyone for the union ceremony. There is much to do!"

While Athirst was in Eirene telling everyone about the upcoming ceremony, he told Sophos everything that happened. Sophos had some news for him as well.

"You aren't the only one who is to be unified. Querulous told me that Jabari asked Vera to unify with Nia."

"Really? He told me they were back together, but I didn't know he was serious."

"Well, you've been too preoccupied to notice for several months now. You really haven't paid much attention to anyone. I hope that after you and Cearney are officially unified, then you'll be back to your disciplined self."

"When is Jabari's ceremony?"

"He and Nia wanted something simple. Not much in the way of flowers and extras, just good food for Jabari; Nia wants to ride away from the ceremony on her deer. Their ceremony will be the day after tomorrow."

Most everyone at the ceremony knew that this union was a result of mixed-up unions that occurred before, which somehow seemed to excuse them all from receiving confirmation from Jah. The union between Nia and Jabari was quite possibly one of the most festive of all the unions since the pressure was off. Immediately after the union, Athirst went off to Siomon.

Cearney was all packed up when he arrived. On the day she was to leave for Eirene, she walked over to Iris. "I love you.

Thank you for taking such good care of me. You are the best Elder I could have ever asked for. I'll send you a letter to let you know when the union ceremony will take place."

Iris' soft raspy voice responded, "I am looking forward to it. Being your Elder was the best thing that happened to me, but I knew this day would come. Athirst is the one that Jah sent for you. You both will have a wonderful legacy together." Cearney bent down to give Iris a hug. Jendahi came over and hugged her as well.

24.
The Butterflies Unite

The day of the union ceremony, Cearney couldn't have been more beautiful. As promised, she sent a letter and several Elders from Siomon made the journey to Eirene in order to witness the union celebration.

In Eirene, the females wore bright colors to match the flowers of the East Gardens, but in Siomon, females who were going to unify wore plain white. Cearney's dress clung to her curvy figure and contrasted beautifully against her sun-kissed skin. She had a wide range of colorful flowers in her hair. In her hand, she carried Crossandra orange.

Iris was too old and frail to make the journey to Eirene. Jendahi, on the other hand, was front and center.

Sophos was the one who performed the union ceremony. He managed to refrain from making jokes and read straight from the script:

"Wisdom, love, respect, grace, and discipline are all virtues necessary for a union in which Jah approves, for you are both joining to carry out plans that are greater than you. You are not unifying for pleasures of self; you are combining spirits to develop your talents, which will be used in order to fill the world with good (Writ 212: 1-2)."

After the ceremony, the entire village danced to music and celebrated with food. The Elders had made dishes that were native to both Siomon and Eirene. Athirst and Cearney were surrounded by people from both villages, and as usual, the couple was bombarded with questions. Despite this, Athirst maintained a smile on his face during what felt like an inquisition.

"You just had to be different, brother....going off to find a girl far away from here. Was it because the woman you asked to unify with the first time decided to go with a real man instead?" Theiler said, squeezing Governess' arm and pulling her closer to him.

Cearney was sitting right next to Athirst. Her eyes narrowed. Athirst realized that he may have skipped telling Cearney that he had asked another woman to unify with him before. She grabbed his upper thigh under the table and gave it a hard squeeze. "You asked another woman to unify with you?" She whispered through her teeth.

Athirst tried to ignore her, responding instead to Theiler.

"Is that what you're calling yourself? A real man? Well, I've always heard that if you have to announce to everyone that you're a real man, then, you're probably not." Athirst let out a loud chuckle and Jabari, who was sitting nearby, joined in the laughter.

At that moment, Theiler got up and wedged himself between Athirst and Cearney. He placed his arms on both of their shoulders and drew them to him.

"This man is like a brother to me," he said to Cearney. "No need to be mad at him, I just thought he might've told you already." Theiler continued to relish in the discomfort that he was obviously causing.

"Athirst is the wisest man I know," Cearney said to Theiler sweetly, making sure to not give him the satisfaction of being the one to cause discord. "If he felt the need to wait to tell me something, then I trust his decision."

"Wow, Athirst, you've got yourself a good one here," Theiler said, giving him a slap on the back.

Governess rolled her eyes at Cearney's remark.

"Athirst, I'm gonna get some water, would you like something as well?" Cearney asked in an effort to remove herself from the conversation.

Theiler then turned to Governess. "Can you get me some water as well, darling?"

Governess begrudgingly got up and headed toward the community kitchen.

"Now that the women are gone, how are things? Cearney seems lovely," Theiler stated with mock interest.

"Things are going well. I'm grateful that I was obedient to Jah."

"I see. It appears that she is trained well. Are all women in Siomon like her? I may have to take a stroll there myself."

"First of all, brother, I don't appreciate the manner in which you decided to announce my previous engagement. Secondly, she's not trained well. She just knows how to respond when surrounded by fools and she deserves much more respect than you're giving her. And thirdly, you have no reason to visit Siomon. You have Governess."

"As perfect as she seems, you must admit that she has pretty bad judgment if she settled for you." Theiler playfully jabbed Athirst in the arm, hoping to remove the look of frustration from his face.

"Don't start getting jealous, my friend," Athirst quickly responded.

"What do I have to be jealous of?" Theiler asked.

"I think the question is what is there not to be jealous of," Athirst retorted.

"Ha," a slight chuckle escaped Theiler's mouth before he gazed off in the distance. After a few seconds of silence, Athirst asked, "Are you okay, brother?"

Theiler looked around before answering, "I thought being unified with someone would feel different. I thought it would give me a different feeling, but…"

"Governess is a wonderful woman. What's the problem?"

"She is wonderful. But I don't know. I guess I just expected more from unionship. It's not her, it's the entire thing.

Quite boring if you ask me. I think I would've much rather stayed single, but everytime I said that, people acted as if I'd sinned against Jah. She and I don't seem to have much in common. We try our best to be cordial, but that seems strange to do when you're full-on unified. We should have more of a close bond, but we just don't."

Athirst didn't know what to say to Theiler, so he remained silent. He began to look around, trying to see what was taking Cearney so long to get back. He noticed her and Governess in the distance. He could see their mouths moving and could only assume they were talking about him. Athirst immediately began to feel uncomfortable.

In the community kitchen, Governess and Cearney were getting water. "I heard your response to Theiler. You really are the perfect woman, aren't you?" Governess said with a smirk.

"Well, what would you have done? Seeing as you have all the answers," Cearney snapped.

"If I'd been embarrassed in front of everyone like that, I'm not sure if I would've been able to keep my composure."

"I don't like what happened, but I'm not going to let a few comments from a jealous man affect my relationship."

Cearney's comment was aggravating to Governess. "You do realize that I'm the one that he asked to unify with before you came along?"

"Yes, I inferred that," Cearney gave her an icy glare. There was a long pause before Cearney continued. "We've been over here for quite some time. I'm going to head back." Cearney grabbed the goblet and walked back over to Athirst.

When Cearney arrived back to the table, she placed the goblet in front of Athirst and began rubbing his back. "Is there anything else you'd like, my love?" Cearney gazed at Governess as she continued to rub his back.

"I saw you both talking; is everything okay?" Athirst whispered in her ear.

"Of course, my darling Athirst, what could possibly go wrong with your new union partner and your former love having to mingle in the same place?" Cearney whispered to him as she removed her hand from his back and pinched his thigh. Athirst jumped slightly.

Cearney turned her head to rejoin the group conversation, relieved that the discussion had moved on to other topics.

"I love you, Cearney," Athirst whispered in her ear.

"Well, you should. I make you look good."

25.
A New Era Begins

Several months had passed and many of the Youth were focused on building their new families. It was an exciting time for them, but they also knew that their Elders would not be around much longer. Chapter 212 of the Writ insinuated that many of the Elders from the Second World would leave once they had completed their task of raising the Youth. With every happy moment, or birth of a new baby, the Youth grew more nervous that eventually the Elders would vanish.

Sophos was following his nose to the sweet breads that were baking in the community kitchen. Discernmos was already there helping divide up the wild hog they were to eat for the Potentiam Libertas festival.

"Can you give me a hand?" Discernmos struggled to turn the massive hog over.

"No problem." Sophos quickly assisted.

"I remember when I didn't have to ask you to help me with much of anything."

"Yes, well, we're a lot more frail than we used to be," Sophos responded.

"We are. It won't be much longer now," Mediorocris said sadly. "Are you scared?"

"I don't know," Sophos said. "I try not to think about it too much. I just hope that I've done what Jah wanted me to do and I pray that He will accept me into the heavens. You know, I used to want Jah to make me one of the gods of the night sky."

"Why? Aren't they cursed?" Querulous said as she and Sophos continued to cut the meat for the feast. "When I was younger--" She glanced up from chopping the meat. "--I was told they were warriors that people praised so much that they were lifted above all others, but Jah saw that people praised them more than Him and they were prideful. Jah saw how people exalted them, and therefore he trapped them in the sky."

"I just always thought it was pretty cool to be a great warrior on earth and be given the opportunity to look over everything that was going on."

"I guess. But for me, I just want to go in my sleep. I've worried so much in the Second World and I worry now about whether I did the right thing by Jah," Querulous said. "I don't wanna have to worry about anything anymore."

"Me too," Mediorocris agreed. "I feel as if I've done my best." She looked over at Sophos, expecting him to make some backhanded remark about her lack of vision or the fact that Jabari's union was misguided, or about the time she asked him not to speak to Jabari about vision again, but she was wrong. He remained quiet.

"I think we've all done the best we could, but they make up their own minds and create their own path," Sophos stated.

"They do. I think that has been the biggest lesson I've learned. We can lay the foundation and clear a path for them, but inevitably, they all make their own choices," Discernmos replied.

"I am reminded everyday that the time is drawing nearer. I've seen Athirst working on the house he wants to build for his family."

"Jabari is doing the same thing. He's nearly finished. His size and strength came in handy. It's a beautiful house," Mediorocris beamed.

"Athirst is being so secretive about it. Like he doesn't want me to see it until it's complete. I think he's unaware of how much time I have left. I'm not sure of the exact number of days, but if he doesn't finish soon, I may not be around to see it."

"Enough of all this talk," Mediorocris said, wiping tears from her eyes. "Yes, tonight we celebrate. We're all here to enjoy each other's company," Sophos said.

"If you all can stop running your mouths, maybe I'd enjoy your company more," Querulous told the group.

The Elders enjoyed the ceremony that evening, but, by the next festival, they were one Elder short.

The first to leave was Querulous. After receiving vision from Jah, she went to sleep at night and didn't wake up. Her body laid there just long enough to provide a visual reminder to all that their time was temporary. She vanished shortly after Governess discovered her. Everyone in Eirene gathered together to discuss their favorite memories of her.

"Despite what many people think, Querulous was truly my best friend. She and I had a lot more in common than people would guess. In the Second World, our spouses died in the same way and we both lost our children, but we found comfort in each other. We were able to make a family in both the Second and Third World. I...I will miss her dearly, and I pray to Jah that I will see her again." Sophos could not hold back the tears. Everyone around was crying. Each person in the village took flowers from the East Gardens and walked to River Aesis. They placed them in the water and watched them float downstream.

"I'll miss you, Querulous," Governess said with tears in her eyes. She placed her head on Theiler's shoulder and cried. He cradled her in his arms. Several villagers were embracing each other and trying to console those who were crying. They all watched as the flowers moved down the river, and once they were out of sight, everyone headed back home.

Several weeks later, a letter came from Siomon. Iris appeared to be in critical condition. Athirst and Cearney left for Siomon just in time to see Iris before she passed.

"I think this is it, Cearney. She's been sick for a long time, but I can tell she's not gonna bounce back," Jendahi said. They both stayed by Iris' side and it was only a few hours later that she closed her eyes and vanished. Athirst and Cearney stayed in Siomon for a few days. Cearney organized all of the Elders of Siomon together to recognize Iris.

"She was a woman of great wisdom and very kind. She was given many gifts that we all have benefited from. Most of you learned how to create medicine from Iris. Some of you went to her for healing. It may seem that she's far away, but I know that she's watching from the heavens smiling down on everyone."

Although it was a sad occasion, Cearney enjoyed her time with Jendahi. It had been several months since they last saw each other. The women ducked off into a back room of the house to catch up. Athirst remained in the center of the village collecting all of the items from Iris' small medicine market and worked to take care of other things so Cearney could spend time with her sister.

"So how is it? You know, being unified," Jendahi asked.

"Athirst is a good man. I'm happy, but he's far from perfect. Did you know that he asked another person to unify with him before me?"

"No! Seriously Cearney? Did you get to meet her?"

"Have I? She made sure to let me know that she was his first love."

"What did you do?"

"Nothing needed to be done. She's unified with a man named Theiler. He's a very nice looking man, but he's also quite cocky. Takes his looks down a bit if you ask me."

"Who else is interesting?"

"They have a giant in their village named Jabari. He's actually one of the first people I met in Eirene. He's very kind and so is his union-mate, Nia. They may be the best in the village at taming animals."

"Are you able to tame animals yet?"

"Not yet; Athirst is helping me learn, but I'm not that good at it."

Athirst returned to the house with all of the medicine jars he collected from Iris' shop. "I think we need to take these with us. We may be able to use them for something." We'll need to head back tomorrow."

Cearney made sure she was able to catch up Jendahi on all the drama before they had to leave.

When they arrived back in Eirene, Athirst found himself looking at Sophos and wondering when he would no longer see him. He could tell that Sophos wondered the same thing. In typical Sophos fashion, he would make jokes about his departure, but over time it became difficult for Athirst to laugh. Sophos' once broad shoulders curved in towards themselves, which created a slight hump on his back. His movements grew slower and Sophos soon found more comfort being in bed than being out socializing with the community.

Three Potentiam Libertas festivals were spent with Sophos sitting around looking depressed, and Athirst couldn't take it anymore. "Are you going to finally head out today, old man?"

"No, I think I'll stay here tonight and talk to Jah. By the way, when are you and Cearney going to finish building your house?"

"We're hoping that it will be done soon. I'm trying to get some of the others to help me finish it up. Jabari was helping me get logs cut down to size, but he got busy working on his own home."

"You need help putting it together? I would've had it done by now." Sophos smiled.

"I know you would have, Sophos. You never needed help with anything."

"I wish I could say that now. Every time I look in the mirror I can see a new wrinkle, or when I move I feel a new pain.

Every time I look at you, I can tell that you need me less and less and I instead rely on you more and more," Sophos solemnly stated.

Athirst didn't know how to handle his sadness. "Why are you trying to get us out so soon, anyway? If Cearney and I were not here to bother you, you would be bored out of your mind," Athirst teased.

"You're right about that. But hey, when you go out this evening, make sure to bring me back something to eat, especially if Mediorocris is cooking."

"I will, but you know Mediorocris doesn't cook as much anymore," Athirst replied.

Sophos was in his house reflecting over all that he had done in the New World and he felt unaccomplished. Athirst was a good son, but he hadn't shown his colors yet. Sophos wondered if he had done what Jah wanted -- if there was more to be done, and how much time he had left. He asked Jah to keep him around a little longer, but when there was no answer, Sophos made a decision to enjoy what was left of his life. Sophos headed to the Athirst's up-and-coming house, took out his knife, and carved in one of the logs: Never forget your desire for vision.

After leaving Sophos that morning, Athirst spent most of the day hunting for devices. He shook his leather bag up and down in order to feel the weight of his sacrifice to Jah. Athirst found himself fascinated by the amount of technology that the YSW used. He had been hunting for devices since he was little and there were still plenty yet to be found.

Athirst opened his sack to look at the multitude of electronic gadgets he possessed. Most of the devices were marked with bitten fruit. Athirst found it strange that the YSW would use a bitten piece of fruit as the symbol on their devices; to Athirst, it seemed like a sign to mock Jah.

Later that evening, Athirst threw all of the devices into the fire, watching it spark.

"Athirst, there you are." Cearney ran over to him.

"Hello love." Athirst embraced his union-mate. "What have you been doing most of the day?"

"You would know if you had allowed me to come on your little hunting adventure today."

"I didn't think I should bring you out on an adventure considering your current condition." Athirst put his hand on Cearney's belly. Cearney lightly swatted Athirst, "Don't make it obvious. I don't want anyone to know until we make our announcement."

"I am going to tell everyone today, so what does it matter if someone sees me?" Athirst replied.

"Okay," Cearney laughed. "Anyway, are you hungry?"

Athirst smiled. "Not really, I was just about to look around to see what I could bring back to Sophos."

"Oh, well, I don't think you'll have to do that. I saw him wandering around looking pitiful and I made him come join in on the festivities." Cearney pointed over to Sophos, who was sitting on the opposite side of the fire.

Athirst was shocked to see Sophos outside. He took in the moment and was thankful that his Elder was still around to participate in the festivities. Cearney walked over to the community kitchen and quickly came back to greet Sophos with a plate of food. She gave him a gentle rub on the shoulder before turning back to the village kitchen.

The villagers seemed to prefer the community kitchen over the ones in their homes. Home kitchens were very small, and it was much easier to cook in the village kitchen since it had a huge wood-burning stove, several stone ovens, large areas for pots and pans, and multiple fire pits. More room meant people could cook more efficiently for larger groups of people. Lots of fruits, vegetables, eggs, and spices were held in wooden bins within the village kitchen for everyone to use, and two large water barrels sat next to them; one was meant for cleaning while the other was meant for drinking. The kitchen was constantly bustling with people, each cooking their own recipes in their own way or working together to provide for a feast.

Sophos lingered about to see what other delicacies were being created. Athirst was about to talk to Sophos about all he had done that day, but before he knew it, Sophos had made his way to fix another plate.

Despite the passing of many Elders, there was still much to be celebrated in the community. As the Youth were starting families of their own, sounds of infants crying, laughing, and playing filled the atmosphere. Sophos watched with joy as he saw a new generation rise up, being raised in the traditions of the Elders. Sophos returned to the fire pit with another plate that was heaped with food.

"I must say Athirst, you did very well with Cearney. This chocolate sweetbread could be the best thing I have ever tasted. She could give Mediorocris a few pointers."

"Hey, get your own woman to cook food for you."

"Are you jealous that she brought me a plate and left you to fetch one on your own?" Sophos couldn't help the laugh that barreled out from his chest. Eventually he grew quiet. "I'm glad I came out this evening," Sophos said softly.

"I am too, Sophos. I see that Mediorocris decided to cook after all," Athirst pointed out, gesturing toward the fish on Sophos' plate. "Mediorocris stopped bringing you food a long time ago -- whatever happened with you and her? You seem like you're still cordial."

"You're very observant. Well, things changed after she told me to stop helping Jabari with his visions. Jabari was a lot brighter than many people gave him credit for. He worked so hard to prove to everyone that he was intelligent. I was really impressed with his efforts, but Mediorocris grew jealous of our connection and requested that I stop working with him. So, I did. I think it is the worst thing I've ever done. Mediorocris' love for Jabari was more like an obsession. She forgot that her mission was to teach him the ways of Jah."

Athirst knew that Sophos was right -- Jabari had worked very hard and he had gotten his vision right when so many others, including Athirst himself, had not. "I need to apologize to him. I feel bad. He was right all along and I was wrong, but I never let him know it. It was easier to continue to see Jabari the way we labeled him instead of the young man he was working to become."

Athirst continued to reflect on what Sophos said before noticing that Sophos' plate was completely devoured.

"You know, Athirst, something about today feels right. I didn't want to lay in my house and continue to watch life pass me by. I know I don't have much longer, but I'm going to push these old bones as long as Jah allows me to."

"Well, that's good news. It's nice to see you out of the house. I have some good news as well." Athirst grinned. Then he stood up to share his news with everyone.

"Attention, everyone!" Athrist shouted so that those near the roaring blaze of the fire could hear him. People continued with their chatter.

"People! Everyone! Listen up!" Athrist shouted louder. Eventually the crowd quieted down and people turned their attention towards him with curious expressions.

"I have great news! Cearney and I are expecting a baby."

Cheers and excitement erupted from around the fire. "Aye, brother, that's great!" Jabari gave him a hard pat on the back.

"That's great, brother!" Theiler exclaimed.
Hearing his announcement, Cearney joined Athirst's side.

Soon Governess walked over and congratulated the couple as well.

"Congratulations, Athirst." Governess' soft voice floated through the air. "I am…" She started looking down at her belly, but her statement was interrupted by Theiler. "Attention everyone," Theiler shouted to the crowd. "I would like to give a toast to my dear friend, who's been like a brother to me." The crowd cheered again. Cearney gave Athirst a hug and he returned her affections with a kiss.

"This is truly a great day!" Theiler continued to shout to the crowd. "In fact, Governess and I are also expecting a little one soon!" Even more cheers and celebrations filled the air from the people who were nearby.

"You just had to do one better than me and steal my moment. Is she even expecting or is this one of your little tricks you pull to get under my skin?" Athirst said to Theiler, giving him a playful pat on the back.

"It's my lot in life to try and outdo you, my friend," Theiler responded. "But yes, she is very much expecting."

As they were talking more villagers approached and Athirst was taken aback at the overwhelming response from them. They continued to receive congratulations and words of encouragement.

"Remember when we were Youth and and we'd sit by the fire listening to the Elders' stories? That'll be us soon. We'll have to tell them everything we can about the Second World, Jah, and the Writ. I really want to make Jah proud. I want to raise my Youth with great power so that my future generations will glow in their true colors," Theiler said.

"That's what it's all about, my friend."

It could have been all of the joyful announcements, or the smells of Athirst's favorite foods filling the air, or maybe because he was looking at his Elder dance a jig to the tune of the woodwinds, but this night felt very special. The energy in the atmosphere was exciting. Sophos was clapping his hands and dancing when he decided to make his way over to congratulate both Athirst and Theiler.

"Theiler, I know your Elder departed a little while ago, but I can assure you that he's so pleased with the man you've become," Sophos said, gripping Theiler's shoulder.

"I know that I haven't always done what I was supposed to, but Jah has still seen fit to bless me. I'm grateful. I also appreciate Athirst here. He's found it in his heart to forgive me for the things that I've done in the past, and I know that he learned that from you, Sophos." Theiler looked at Athirst and Sophos with a smile of gratitude.

"Everything happened exactly as it should. Who am I to hold a grudge?" Athirst replied.

Jabari interrupted the conversation. "Come on men, let's spar like we used to during our lessons." Jabari took position and began to circle around Theiler, holding up his fists.

"Game on, brother," Theiler grinned. He squared off with Jabari, throwing kicks and punches in the air with mock effort. Eventually Theiler managed to put him in a choke hold, scruffing up Jabari's hair as he went. It was like they were kids again. Suddenly, the bells rang from the community kitchen.

"Let's eat!" Many who had gathered round Theiler and Jabari left at the announcement of the feast. "You heard them!" Jabari bounded towards the community table, the ground trembling in his wake. Athirst followed. "Jabari, wait up!"

Jabari turned around and looked at him expectantly, eager to fill his plate before all the food had gone.

"Just wanted to say sorry. For everything. You're a good man and, you were right about a lot of things. We didn't give you any credit for it."

"Ah, no worries. I understand, but thanks. I appreciate you telling me. Now, let's get to the food."

Athirst waited on Cearney, who was just a few steps behind. He grabbed her hand and they walked toward the table together.

"Well Nia, I guess it's just you and me," Governess sighed. They walked together, arms linked, without their union-mates.

The laughter and festivities continued as the villagers had dinner. Athirst and Cearney found themselves sitting across from Theiler and Governess. Every now and then, Athirst would look up and see Governess trying to get his attention. Curious as to what she wanted, Athirst made eye contact and excused himself from the table.

Governess then got up and made her way to a quiet corner where they could talk. "Is everything okay, Governess?"

"Do you have to do that?" Governess asked sharply.

"Do what?" Athirst was confused.

"Be all lovey-dovey and perfect?"

"I honestly don't even know what you're talking about."

"You know what, never mind." Her demeanor quickly changed. How have you been, Athirst? I feel like I haven't spoken to you in such a long time."

"I'm doing well. Are you sure you're okay?" Athirst was still baffled.

"I'm not sure. I feel like I should be happy, but I don't know what I feel," Governess shrugged.

"Well, everything seems to be going right for you. I can see you've made Theiler a happy man."

"I'm glad one of us thinks so. I don't. He doesn't seem to pay much attention to me." Governess looked sad.

"What are you talking about? He just told the entire village that you're about to have a baby. Aren't you excited about that?"

Cearney sat at the table, her eyes searching for Athirst. Despite the lively conversation around her, Cearney was too distracted to participate, especially when she noticed that Governess was also missing. Cearney excused herself.

Athirst and Governess were still whispering quietly in the corner. "Every time I see you and Cearney, you both look like you're in love. I want that. I want to know what that feels like." Governess looked directly into Athirst's eyes.

"I am." Athirst felt awkward sharing his feelings for his union-mate to Governess. "And I'm a lucky one. The love she has for me, and the love I have for her...it's a nice feeling to have."

"You do realize that Cearney has my life? You gave her the life that I was supposed to have. You were supposed to love me like that," Governess whispered.

Cearney finally spotted Athirst and started walking toward him. As she got closer, she also saw Governess standing there. Cearney could tell they were having a private conversation. It made her uneasy.

"Governess, I have long since moved on from this! Our union was not blessed by Jah! You know this! We're supposed to follow his will -- that's our main goal. So I've tried to move forward in the best way I know how and you're stuck here living in the past."

Governess opened her mouth to say something, but held her tongue. She then spotted Cearney heading straight toward them. Governess quickly left and headed back to the table.

Cearney was furious. "What were you doing over here with her?" Cearney asked.

"Nothing. She kept signaling to me at the table like she wanted to speak with me, so I got up to talk to her. I'm sorry. I realize that I shouldn't have done that."

"Listen to me, Athirst, I don't care that you and Governess use to have a thing for each other, but I find it very disrespectful that you would leave me at the table by myself to talk to another man's union-mate. Ever since I moved to Eirene, I've been compared to her. I have done my absolute best to make you look good. I've done my best to love and honor you and remain faithful; I try to not let your previous relationship bother me, but I will not allow you to disrespect me again."

Athirst knew that she was right. "I'm sorry Cearney. I didn't consider what that must look like to you and how that made you feel. It won't happen again."

Athirst was quiet for a moment. "But I can tell you this -- you are quite beautiful when you're angry." Athirst leaned in for a kiss, hoping to end the argument, but Cearney brushed him aside. "I don't think so," Cearney said as she pushed him away. Athirst watched as she walked back to the table. He followed closely behind her.

When they arrived to the table, Theiler and Sophos were in a heated debate about different aspects of the Writ. Governess did her best to not make eye contact with Cearney. Although Cearney was still upset with Athirst, she laid her head on his shoulder and grabbed hold of his arm to look like nothing happened. When Governess saw this, she grabbed her plate and excused herself from the table. Theiler didn't notice her leave. He continued his debate about the Writ with Sophos.

In all of Athirst's studying of the Writ, he knew that certain people stood out among the rest, and he wanted to be one of exemplary character -- a person he could truly be proud of.

26.
A Mark in Time

To Athirst, Sophos was another man whose legacy deserved to live on in books. Athirst spent as much time with Sophos as he could before his passing. He was elated to see that Sophos lived through most of Cearney's pregnancy. He hoped that Sophos would be there to see the birth of his baby, but when a vision was sent eluding to Sophos' passing, Athirst knew he would not be so lucky. Sophos was the last living Elder in the village, and his death marked the end of one generation and the beginning of another. Sophos died at 11:59 PM and Athirst's son, Ugo Primis Athirst, was born minutes later at 12:01 AM on the first new moon of a new year.

Sophos took his last breaths just minutes before Ugo Primis was born. Sophos kept a quick wit and a sharp sense of humor until his very last breath. He left the world just as only he would -- with a joke. "I hope Ugo gets his looks from his mom. Tell Ugo all about me." Athirst and Sophos both laughed. "I am glad you were able to finish the house in time. You did well Athirst. Very well." Sophos closed his eyes. A tear rolled down Athirst's face as he watched Sophos depart from this life. "Until we meet again, old man." With his exit came the cries of a newborn baby. Athirst and Cearney gave their son the name Ugo Primis. They chose Primis because he was born on the first day of a new year. Sophos suggested the name Ugo, which signified intelligence.

The Youth who were saved from the vanishing of the Second World had no last name. Jah didn't want any of them to have an attachment to the Second World, as their last names served as connections to their old families. But now, they were able to create a legacy of their own. And for Athrist, it began with his son.

Ugo was a beautiful baby. He was Athirst's joy and he filled his heart with a feeling never felt before. In him, Athirst saw the future. Upon his birth, both Cearney and Athrist meditated and spoke words of life into Ugo, whispering to him in the tongues of a language that only he could understand. This was a power given to them by Jah explained in the Writ:

Fathers and mothers must speak into their children the direction for which Jah has intended -- in tongues specific to his talent, so that no man can interfere with the plans Jah has for him. In doing this, each child becomes a child of Jah, sent to fulfill their destiny and develop their talents according to His will (Writ 212: 24-25)."

It was only fitting that after speaking into Ugo's future, that Cearney discovered the carved message in Ugo's room.

"Athirst, come here."

Athirst rushed in to see what was going on.

"Look." Cearney pointed to the message engraved on the wall. "When do you think he had time to do this?" Cearney wondered.

"I don't know, but...Sophos always managed to find a way." Athirst grabbed baby Ugo and traced his little fingers over the message.

By the next Potentiam Libertas, Theiler and Governess were expecting the arrival of their own son. He was born under the first blood moon Eirene ever had. He was named Cadmael Theiler. The night Cadmael Theiler was born, the entire village received the same vision -- a warning sent from Jah. The vision was of a man carrying the Writ in his hands. The man held up the book and split it in half, the words from the Writ falling off the pages and breaking as they hit the ground.

Athirst woke up in the middle of the night and called out to Jah. He prayed and read the Writ for the remainder of the night.

27.
New Age – The Second Era

The community was filled with new life. However, with all the excitement came much responsibility. At night, the unified couples would take time to receive vision for the way in which their Youth were to be raised. They also kept up with traditions that were established by the Elders. They found themselves around the same fires, participating in the same festivals, and telling the same stories.

It would not be long before Ugo was joined by siblings. Each of Athirst and Cearney's children were beautiful, and each of them had their own gifts. Athirst was curious as to what color each of those gifts would shine. His son, Triston, was born after Ugo. Triston Athirst was a rambunctious child with a quick wit. He was brave and always willing to fight for what he believed in. He was passionate and bold, but could be reckless at times.

Athirst's oldest daughter, Anah, was every bit like her mother. She was beautiful, patient, kind, and a little sassy when she needed to be. In her lessons, she won countless debates with her cunning and intelligence. She was always thinking; always processing and observing. Anah could see the patterns of nature and make predictions about things to come.

Romilda was their fourth child. She was quiet and obedient. Most people didn't even know she was around, as she rarely spoke and seemed to stay in her own thoughts. Lastly, the baby of the family was Illiana. She was the chubbiest of all Athirst's babies, weighing in at over ten pounds at birth. Cearney and Athirst spoiled her, since they decided that she would be their last.

Athirst loved all of his children, but there was a special bond between him and Ugo. Ugo hung onto his father's every word. Athirst would often tell him about Sophos and many times, Athirst could feel Sophos' presence as he shared his memories of him. Although he never quite mastered Sophos' storytelling abilities, he nonetheless tried to emulate them for his son's sake, and taught Ugo the same nuggets of wisdom that Sophos had shared with him long ago.

Athirst told Ugo stories about the Youth of the Second World, how he never met his biological parents, and about the vanishing. He told him about the vision of the butterflies and how he was about to unite with Governess, but how it wasn't in Jah's plan. Ugo loved listening to the story of how Athirst met his mother.

Ugo looked a lot like Cearney. He had the same sun-kissed skin and thick, dark hair. His eyes were big, round, and bright. From his father, he acquired a unique gift for vision and meditation at a very early age, and if Athirst thought he himself was dedicated to interpretation as a child, Ugo was even more so. The combination of Athirst's love for Jah and his strength and wisdom, combined with his mother's heart, patience, and determination, made Ugo a very special child.

By the time Ugo was five, he knew the history of the old chapters of the Writ front-to-back and knew many verses in chapter 212 by heart. However, he too, like many other little boys, just wanted to play and rough-house. Ugo also did a much better job of learning how to control beasts than Athrist did as a child. Ugo also seemed to have that same level of friendly competition with Cadmael, Theiler's first born son. Athirst liked the friendship he saw developing between the two boys, but could not shake the dream he had over five years ago, the night Cadmael was born. He often wondered if he should be more wary of his son's friendship with Cadmael.

"Ugo, tomorrow will be your first day of lessons. I want you to make sure to focus. They're going to teach you some really important things. What are you excited about most?"

"I will get to be around my friends."

"Who are your friends?"

"Well, I like Stultus and Fortis, but my best friend is Cadmael."

"They are all very nice. But you need to remember, no matter what anyone tells you, Jah and the Writ always come first." Athirst paused and then asked, "What would you do if one of your friends tried to make you believe the Writ is not true? Would you still be their friend?"

"Yes. That doesn't mean they are a bad person."

"But what do you do?"

"I don't know. I guess I will try to show them the good things about Jah and the Writ."

"Very good. There is only one truth Ugo. The truth is in the words of the Writ. No one, not even a friend, should make you feel any different."

As Athrist was talking to Ugo, Cearney walked in.

"Go on off to bed so you will be ready for lessons in the morning." Athirst patted Ugo on the head and sent him off.

"That was a pretty serious conversation for a five-year-old. What's going on?"

"It's just...a long time ago, I received this dream. It happened the very night Cadmael was born."

"The torn Writ and the words falling out?" Cearney asked, concerned. "I remember that vision. It made me feel very uneasy, but do you really think we need to be concerned with Cadmael? He seems like such a good boy."

"I don't know Cearney. But we must make sure that Ugo is strong. We need to prepare all of our children to make sure that nothing takes them away from the true words of Jah."

That night, Athirst and Cearney meditated together. The vision from five years ago returned. They prayed and asked Jah for guidance before going to bed. The next morning, they gathered all of their children together and thanked Jah for everything He had done for them. "And promise you will always obey the Writ," Cearney added to the end of their conversation. All of the children promised, nodding their heads in agreement. Illiana made babbling noises. "Yes, I guess that counts as well," Cearney said, kissing her little one on the forehead.

"Ugo, I know you're excited, but hold on. I'll walk with you." Athirst could see that Ugo was headed out the door, ready to begin his first day of lessons.

"Remember, you must never stop your desire for vision. Do you understand?"

"Yes, father," Ugo said as he looked in his leather sack to see what his mother packed for lunch.

"Okay." Athirst realized he was just a boy, and decided against overloading him with such heavy, serious topics. When they arrived at the wooden benches where lessons took place, Athirst bent down and gave his son a pat on the head. Ugo gave him a hug. "Bye father, see you later."

"Bye, son. Have a great first day."

28.
Ugo and Cadmael

Athirst's initial concern died down after several years of a budding friendship between the boys. The boys were now eleven years old and seemed to be the best of friends. Athirst was out early one morning, bringing in his catch for the day to the village kitchen. The morning breeze was gentle and felt like kisses against his cheek. It was a relief from the humidity that typically accompanied this time of year. He glanced up and saw Cearney with their youngest, Illiana. Illiana was spoiled and seemed to take her 'tantrums' well past the terrible twos. She was nearly five years old but, to Ugo, she demanded more attention than any of his other siblings.

"I see that face. What's wrong?" Athirst said as he walked over to him.

"Will she ever shut up? None of my other siblings are remotely as annoying as her. You barely hear a peep from Romilda and Anah!"

"They're a little older and plus, they adore you, especially after the gift you gave them." Ugo was taking a woodworking class and managed to whittle them some dolls.

"Why don't you go play?" Athirst said. Ugo then ran off to find Cadmael.

Athirst looked over to see Cearney's eyes closed. She was sitting with her head resting on the outer clay walls of their house. Her face was peaceful, as if she were silently meditating. She was humming quietly, rocking back and forth lightly in an attempt to put Illiana to sleep. Athirst looked off in the distance to see Ugo sparring with Cadmael.

Cadmael and Ugo were tall, skinny boys. Cadmael was very fair with deep blue eyes. Ugo had light brown skin with dark hair and dark eyes. They both had sticks in their hands pretending they were swords. The boys quickly jumped off hills, rolling onto the ground. Each one tried to overpower the other. Despite the cool of the evening, they were covered in sweat and it didn't look like their 'battle' was going to end any time soon. They possessed a lot of energy and a competitive spirit that kept each of them from surrendering to the other. When Athirst saw Ugo pin Cadmael down and call out his victory, he felt a sense of pride. Theiler was in the distance watching them spar as well, but did not pay much attention to the victor of the match.

Theiler walked toward Athirst. "Can you believe it, brother? Not too long ago, we were just skinny boys just like them, running around the Potentiam Libertas fires." Theiler beamed as he looked at his son, who seemed to be growing up right before his eyes.

"You may have been a skinny boy running around the fires, but I was always built like a warrior," Athirst declared confidently.

"Is that what you tell yourself? I wonder if Jah is pleased with the lies that are coming from your mouth."

Both men laughed.

Theiler continued, "Honestly, brother, I did not know what type of father I would be; I wasn't sure if I was going to be able to do this. You know, I think a lot about our biological parents, and I wonder what happened to them. What they were really like. What kind of father and mother I had. I wonder if they would be proud of me..."

Athirst stopped Theiler before he could finish his thought. "I wonder the same thing. What was so special about us that we were saved, and they weren't?"

"There was nothing special about us, we were just too young to have messed up yet," Theiler responded. "I can't take any credit for being here."

"Well," Athirst sighed. "That is true." There was a pause in their conversation before Theiler changed the subject.

"How is Cearney doing?"

"She's doing well."

Both Theiler and Athirst looked over in her direction. "I guess she is using this time to sneak in a nap."

The men looked back at each other and chuckled.

"And Governess?" Athirst asked.

"I don't know," Theiler responded.

"I know that at one time you were worried you hadn't made the right decision."

"There are times when I still feel like that, but Jah has seemed to bless our union, so I can only assume everything worked out for the best," Theiler shrugged. "But you know what I found? Governess' journal. She tried to hide it under her pillow, but I found it and every day when she goes out, I read a few pages."

"Are you sure you should do that?" Athirst asked.

"I'm her husband now. She really shouldn't be keeping anything from me."

"I know, but I remember when she use to write in her journal. It was a way for her to get everything out. Governess seems to have a lot of complex feelings. You have to tread lightly and give her privacy," Athirst suggested.

"You don't think I know her better than you? I know you have to tread lightly and that's exactly why I haven't told her about it."

"So...did you find anything?"

"I know she realizes that she was never supposed to be with me. After Cadmael was born, she received the vision of the fort. She finally accepted that Jabari was the one meant for her.

She also keeps writing about this recurring dream with red rain. I can't help her figure it out because she would know that I've been reading her journal, but I wish she would ask me. I want to help her and comfort her. Anyway, I guess I can't really do anything about it now."

They both looked over at their boys, who were still going at it. This time the boys were by the edge of the village near the woods. It was Governess' call for Cadmael to come for dinner that ended the sparring match.

"Well, brother, I guess that means it's time to head back." Theiler ran off chasing his son, and Ugo ran toward his father.

"Father, did you see that?" Ugo ran to Athirst. He was excited to share his victory.

"Yes, I did. You did well son. You're still not as good as me, though," Athirst joked.

Ugo balled up his fist and took a few jabs at his father's stomach. "Okay, let's see what you have, then."

Athirst lovingly placed his arm around Ugo's neck and with the other hand, ruffled Ugo's hair. They began to walk home. Athirst tapped Cearney on the knee and she quickly woke up, startled. "Athirst," she protested. Ugo grabbed Illiana and walked into the house.

"I was afraid that you were going to let Illiana slide right off your lap."

"You know I'd never let that happen." Cearney playfully pushed Athirst on their way inside, laughing.

29.
New Knowledge

The entire village prepared for the Potentiam Libertas by collecting technology to burn in the fire later that evening. Cearney was cooking a maple-glazed duck with roasted potatoes and carrots -- a specialty from Siomon. The smell of food wafted throughout the village. Athirst watched his other son, Triston, play woodwind instruments. Athirst realized that he took a liking to music early on. Triston started playing at five years old, but had perfected his craft over time and eventually became one of the best woodwind players in all of Eirene.

People sat around the fire chatting and eating, while others tossed devices into the blaze. Afterwards, each adult took their Youth to share in meditation. Athirst walked with Ugo and went to their quiet place near the East Gardens.

"Father?" The tone in Ugo's voice made Athirst slow down. "What is it?" Athirst replied.

"Earlier today, I could have sworn I saw Cadmael gather devices for the fire, but I didn't see him throw anything in! We usually throw things in together and look at all the colors, but tonight, I couldn't find him."

"Are you sure that you saw him with technology for the fire?"

"Yes," Ugo responded and then looked down nervously.

"Did you see what he was carrying specifically?"

Ugo remained quiet for several seconds before continuing. "Cadmael and I went to the north end of River Aesis, near mother's village. Very few people look for technology there, so I figured there would be plenty of devices in the forest. I didn't expect to find what we did."

"What was it?" Athirst's tone was urgent.

"Well, there was a cave located in the thick of the forest. I walked in and found a few devices and quickly put them in my sack. Then I saw Cadmael begin to run toward the corner of the cave and I noticed an unnatural light that was coming from behind some rocks and brush. I quickly ran over to join him to see what he found. It was a time piece. The writing on it said THE THIRD EYE and it had a symbol of a bitten fruit on it. I've seen time pieces before and have read about them in the Writ, but this one was different."

"How?" Athirst was curious.

Ugo looked up at Athirst. Ugo's usually bright eyes were filled with worry.

"It was still working. I've never seen any of the devices that we collected still function. I thought that it would make a magnificent glow once we got it to the fire. I suspected that it had to be running on Lithorium. You've told me about how powerful its energy was to those in the Second World. Cadmael and I talked about how amazing it would glow all the way home, but..."

"...but you never saw it go into the fire," Athirst finished, rubbing his temple.

Ugo shook his head glumly.

"I see. I appreciate you telling me this, but I'm afraid this means trouble. Now, let's do what we came here to do."

Ugo and Athirst got down on their knees and just listened. In the silence, Athirst could hear Ugo's whispers to Jah. Ugo asked for guidance. He asked for wisdom and strength.

After their meditation, Athirst went to Cearney. "Ugo will be tested soon and we cannot interfere. I know you love your children, but this will not be a time to baby him. He must prove himself. That dream, the one that you and I had of the broken words of the Writ -- Ugo received that vision tonight."

"This is it, isn't it? This is the great divide that the Writ speaks of -- where some will follow the light of the Ambers, and others will develop their light for Jah."

"I believe so."

"Do you know what's going to happen?" Cearney asked.

"No, but I do realize that Ugo somehow plays a major part. We have to make sure he knows how serious this is."

"He's just a boy," Cearney said, concerned.

"He's not a little boy anymore. He's growing up. More disciplined and wise than both of us at his age."

Cearney was quiet for a while and then spoke. "I'm even more nervous for the village. All we have is the word of Jah; if someone does anything to take that away from us, we're all doomed."

Cearney went into the children's room. Ugo had his eyes closed but he was not able to sleep. He had too much on his mind. He had received a vision that made him uneasy and he knew that he would have to confront Cadmael tomorrow. Cearney sat on the end of his bed. "You are strong, Ugo. Never stop your desire for vision and always protect the words of Jah." She gave him a kiss and left the room quietly.

30.
Ugo's Test

The noise of Ugo's siblings at sunrise did not help an already restless night. Ugo got dressed and went into the main room. Illiana was having her usual tantrum, Triston was playing music, and Romilda was singing a song. Anah was helping their mother cut up fruit for breakfast. The sound of the knife hitting the wooden counter seemed to be louder than normal.

"Ugo," his mother said. "You must eat before going to lessons."

He looked at his father, who responded for him.

"Well, he looks healthy enough to me. I don't think missing breakfast is going to hurt him."

He knew Ugo's stomach was unsettled. He knew that he was nervous and what he had to do. He knew what the result was going to be. It was confirmed last night after meditation. Last night was the first night where they did not discuss their shared vision. Last night they walked home in silence.

Athirst looked at him and mouthed, "You can do this; trust Jah." And with that, Ugo walked out the door.

As usual, Cadmael and Ugo sat right next to each other during lessons and with every pause in instruction, Ugo tried to work up the courage to ask Cadmael what happened to him during the festival. He wanted to know where the device went.

Although Ugo was nervous, he couldn't wait for their break between lessons. *Maybe he was there and I just didn't see him*, Ugo tried to tell himself. When their break came, Cadmael rushed out. Ugo quickly gathered his belongings and chased after him. During break, many of the other Youth were talking or picking fruit off the trees to snack on. Someone picked up an apple and bit into it. Ugo was then reminded of the time piece. He looked around the lunch tables before spotting Cadmael, who had removed himself from the others. Ugo walked up to him with hesitation.

Ugo cleared his throat. "Hey, Cadmael. Do you by any chance still have the device in your possession?" His voice squeaked and Ugo didn't know if it were from nerves or if it was because his voice was changing due to puberty. Either way, he asked again, "Well, do you?"

"I do. I came over here because I didn't want anyone else to know about it." Cadmael reached into his leather sack and showed Ugo a small part of the device. The glow emanating from it illuminated the contents of his bag. Its light was alluring. Ugo had the desire to reach in and touch it, but quickly remembered to not be tempted. He cleared the lump in his throat. "You were supposed to throw it into the fire."

"I can't throw this into the fire. Ugo, it still works! I thought Jah stripped the power from everything, and I thought he never wanted us to know the powers of the Second World, but it still works. It's unbelievable!"

"Cadmael, keeping it violates the Writ. It goes against all our teaching," Ugo warned.

"How? Every scripture I've ever read refers to the technologies of the Second World as if they are old relics incapable of working. This one works and seems like it could be useful for something."

"The Writ never makes a distinction about whether it is working or not; we are to sacrifice all devices to Jah. Is this not a device?"

"It's better than a device; it's a working device! All the secrets of the Second World are possessed in this time piece. All the mysteries, all the stories we've heard, everything is right here. Imagine what we could do with it!"

"You have got to sacrifice it, Cadmael. You can't hold on to that kind of power. I know it looks cool, but it's forbidden."

Cadmael grew quiet and paused for a moment. He opened the sack and looked around to make sure no one else was watching before pulling it completely out of the bag to sneak one last glimpse of it.

"Look, I just need to see…" Cadmael didn't get to finish his thought before the call that break was over was announced. The nagging feeling Ugo had stayed with him throughout the duration of lessons, so after they were over he rushed to catch up to Cadmael once again.

"Cadmael, I think you need to at least tell your father. I'm sure he'll understand and do the right thing."

"I never said that I was going to keep this a secret. I just want to hold on to it for a little while and see what it does. Aren't you curious?" Cadmael sounded annoyed.

"It doesn't matter if I'm curious. I know what the Writ says. I know that we're supposed to sacrifice the devices of the Second World. I know that Jah has given you an opportunity to make the biggest sacrifice to Him, and you have chosen to keep it for yourself. What do you plan on doing with it?"

"I want to know what the big mystery is all about. Maybe it is not as bad as everyone thinks. At one time, devices had to be good for something right? Maybe, I'll be the one to bring back devices in a positive way."

"We are not supposed to do that. Cadmael, just get rid of it."

"I think I have a way to settle this." Cadmael responded. Both of them didn't notice that their conversation caught the attention of other children nearby. Cadmael pulled him away from the crowd.

"Tomorrow we spar," Cadmael said. "If you win the sparring match, then I will tell my father and throw the device in the next Potentiam Libertas fire. But if I win, then I'll hear nothing else about this."

Cadmael ran off. Ugo walked home with his head down. Athirst greeted him at the door.

"So, how'd it go?" Athirst's square jaw, broad shoulders, and muscular build made his presence intimidating to many. However, despite his outward appearance, his tone was gentle.

Ugo looked at his father. "I tried. I tried to reason with him, but he's being very unreasonable, father."

Athirst's soft expression changed as Ugo explained what happened. "Then that means you didn't try hard enough. You need to try again."

"I don't think you really understand. I did try." Ugo pleaded with his father to believe him.

"Then tell me what happened?"

Ugo took a breath. "I asked Cadmael to tell his father about the device and throw the time piece into the next fire. He refused and challenged me to a sparring match. He said that if I won, then he would tell his father and throw the device in the fire."

"So," Athirst interjected, "What happens if he wins?"
"He would keep the device and I was not to tell anyone."
"So, is that what you agreed to?" Athirst tried hard to mask his concern, but it still showed.

"I never agreed to anything. He ran off before I could answer."

"Then, tomorrow we must go."

"Go where?"

"We must go to Theiler and let him know. Theiler is wise. He and I have been friends since our Youth. He will do what is honorable."

31.
Unnatural

That night, the visions warning them of things to come continued. Both Ugo and Athirst found themselves receiving dark images that left both of them feeling uneasy. It began with a ram feeding on grass. As the ram kept eating, its head began to split until there were two heads on its one body. One of the heads continued to feed on grass and plants, while the other head wanted to feast on mice, lizards, snakes, and other animals. The body of a ram was not designed to do this, so the ram who was feeding on plants had to tear itself away. Both rams, now missing a part of themselves, began eating again to make themselves whole. The ram who ate plants was lean and fit; the ram who ate other animals was large and strong. The ram that fed on grass then began charging at the ram who fed on animals, because its unnatural tendency disgusted him. The ram who fed on animals charged back. He thought only feeding on plants made the other ram weak. Both wanted to prove who was superior.

At the point of impact, Athirst and Ugo were awakened from their dream. Ugo panicked, shaking and taking deep breaths. Athirst was deeply troubled.

The next morning, the chaos that typically filled Ugo's house was nonexistent. Ugo got ready for lessons and went into the living room, where the rest of his family was already present. The quiet was uncomfortable. It was almost as if they knew. One by one they removed themselves from the room, leaving him and his father alone.

"Son come here."

Ugo walked over to his father. He still had the images of the dream stuck in his head.

"Yes, sir."

"Jah is trying to tell us that there will be a great divide in our community," Athirst said sadly. "It will leave us completely torn apart. I don't know how we'll come back from this. I do know, however, that you will play a role in the events to come."

"What do you think is going to happen? You think it's related to the device that Cadmael found?"

"Probably. I don't know for sure." Athirst grabbed his son's arm and looked him in the eye. "I don't know what'll come of your friendship with Cadmael, but I want you to remember that nothing should ever remove anyone from the words of Jah. His word is what gives us life."

"I understand." Ugo said quietly.

"When you finish eating breakfast, we need to head to Theiler's house."

"I think I would rather get it over with. I don't have much of an appetite right now."

Athirst left the house with Ugo trailing behind. Ugo's mind was racing.

"Theiler!" Athirst called his name loudly, knocking on the door at the same time. Theiler came to the door with a smile on his face.

"Hello, Brother! How are you? I wasn't expecting you. Please, come in."

Theiler had a jovial tone to his voice, excited to be in good company. His grin quickly disappeared when he saw that his guests' body language suggested more than just a casual meet up.

"Brother," Theiler continued. "You seem troubled, what's going on? Something I can help you with?"

"I'm not sure. My son told me that Cadmael may have a device that he needs to throw into the fire. He's currently keeping it for himself."

"There are devices everywhere; I'm sure if he didn't throw it into the fire this time, he'll throw it in at the next

Potentiam Libertas. Is that what you came over here for?" Theiler didn't seem to be concerned with what they had just told him.

"But sir, you see, the thing is…"

It was then that they saw Cadmael emerge from the back room. He briefly looked at Ugo before turning around and retreating down the hallway. Ugo felt his stomach drop. Theiler's demeanor changed. His casual dismissal turned into a look of concern.

"What is it, Ugo?"

"Well, we found a device from the Second World that still works. It was a time piece with the title 'The Third Eye'-- the ones made with Lithorium energy -- and it still works." Ugo stopped to catch his breath. "I thought that Cadmael was going to throw it into the fire, but I never saw him do it. He still has it."

"If you're sure," Theiler said, furrowing his brow. His body grew stiff, his smile fading away.

"Cadmael!" He called out.

Cadmael slowly emerged from the hallway. Instead of looking ashamed, he actually looked quite satisfied with himself. "Yes, father?" Cadmael calmly replied.

"Athirst and Ugo tell me that you have a working device from the Second World."

"I did, but it's gone now. I was curious and couldn't help myself. I wanted to learn about it, but Ugo was right. The Writ speaks of the evils of such devices. I destroyed it when I came home today."

Cadmael pulled out a cloth bundle and opened it up, revealing metal remnants scattered about.

"I will burn the remaining pieces in the next fire." Cadmael looked up at his father, then Theiler glanced at Athirst.

"Well, brother, crisis averted. Was there anything else?" He quickly dismissed them, slamming the door as they walked out. On the way home, Athirst mumbled under his breath.

"Humph, crisis averted. I don't believe him for one minute" Athirst grumbled all the way back home.

32.
Sparring

"Do you want me to walk to lessons with you?" Athirst asked his son.

"No, I can handle it." Deep inside Ugo desperately wanted his father to go, but knew that was not the best idea.

The lesson focused on tailoring meditation to bring forth the things from Jah that would lead to success, prosperity, and expression of light. The Youth learned that light came from the spirit and that spirit was all around -- in the air, the ground, the plants, and the animals. The Magisters taught that Jah gave everyone the ability to harness spirit, and that they must be careful of where they received the source of their energy.

The Magister heading the lesson was named Illilumus. He had straight, dark black hair, pale skin, and green eyes. He opened the Writ and read the following verse:

"Many will ask why Jah would create evil. He did not create evil. Evil is, just as He is, for both evil and good are energy. Spirit and energy cannot be created or destroyed. It can only be expressed, transferred, or contained (Writ 212: 73-75). So, can someone tell me what you think that means?"

Ugo glanced across the room to see his classmates eager to answer. He found himself lacking the desire to participate in the lesson today. He knew what the scripture meant. As Ugo looked around the room, he wondered how many of them would truly be able to resist the draw of evil. *If it were me who found the device, what would I have done?* He thought to himself.

After break, it was time for sparring matches. Each of the Youth who signed up to spar found a partner and went over to the pit. It was a large, squarish field of dirt that sloped inward, and it had enough space for several matches to occur simultaneously. Cadmael was already there practicing.

"Well, brother, are you ready?" Cadmael grinned and continued moving about, throwing jabs, punches, and kicks in the air.

"You two are sparring today? This should be good." Stultus was Jabari's daughter. She was joined by her fraternal twin brother, Fortis, who came over to watch the sparring match. They did not sign up today. Like their father, they were often left without partners since very few were a match for their physical strength.

Stultus was decently attractive. She was tall and stocky but had a round, pale face with full, rosy cheeks and brown eyes. She was fortunate to have enough of Nia's features to soften the masculine ones she inherited from Jabari. Fortis, on the other hand, was a spitting image of him. He was extremely large and, at times, it proved to be more of a detriment than an asset. He would often flop about clumsily and knock into things. If only someone would spar with him once in awhile, he might be able to refine his skills with more agility and grace.

"We'll just keep score," Fortis said. Both Fortis and Stultus sat down on a bench nearby. Scores were kept in the dirt. Each time someone was knocked to the ground, they would get a point. If someone was down with their back on the ground for more than ten seconds, a point was given. The person with their back to the ground could call for a break and they would get five seconds to catch their breath. If they were able to catch their breath at the end of five seconds, they would be allowed to continue to spar; however, if they failed to get up, they lost the round. One also had the option of giving the win to their opponent if they felt too tired to continue. Although sparring was competitive, it was not done with malicious intent. It was done for fun and for exercise. It kept the Youth sharp, agile, and quick.

Today, however, Cadmael's attitude suggested an unfriendly battle. Ugo placed his leather sack on the bench, and before he could turn around, BAM! Cadmael swung and hit him, knocking Ugo down on his knees.

The other students watching were shocked. The beginning of the matches had not officially been called yet.

"Get up, Ugo! Get up and fight!" Cadmael shouted.

Ugo charged at Cadmael with everything he had and before he knew it, they were both on the ground punching and hitting each other recklessly.

"This is going to be a difficult one to keep score," Stultus observed.

"Yeah, let's just watch," Her brother responded.

Cadmael managed to get to his feet and Ugo quickly followed. It was clear that they weren't playfully sparring to test their level of agility. "The wise and noble Ugo!" Cadmael shouted. He spun around, lifted his leg and kicked Ugo, who managed to move out of the way and return with a punch to Cadmael's gut. He seemed unfazed, charging at Ugo again. This time he picked up his left hand and swung it at the right side of Ugo's face, hitting his jaw. Cadmael was enraged. The whites of his eyes were red with anger. It was clear that Cadmael must have dabbled with the secrets of the device. He appeared to have the same anger the YSW had. Or at least that's what Ugo thought after hearing the stories passed down from Sophos to his father.

Cadmael appeared as if he was possessed. He wasn't himself. "I never thought you would be the one to betray me!"

"I did not betray you. I did what was right in the eyes of Jah. Your father had to know!" They were both breathing hard. They continued to circle each other, throwing quick punches when they saw an opening.

"You were jealous that I found it first! You have always been jealous of me and now I have something that you don't!"

Ugo was angry now. "I am not jealous! I haven't done anything to you to warrant this much hatred!" He forged his way toward Cadmael, but he was faster. He managed to avoid Ugo and flipped him over on his back, causing him to land face-up. It knocked the wind from Ugo's lungs.

"One, two, three, four..." Stultus counted to see if Ugo would get up before the end of the five seconds. Ugo could feel his legs swirling around, his feet trying to find the ground. His back ached. He didn't know if he could stand. But Cadmael did not wait for Stultus to get to five. He grabbed his leather sack and ran off. Ugo felt dizzy. He could see people in a blurry haze, playfully mimicking the moves of the fight. He was humiliated. Fortis finished sparring with his sister before reaching down to help him up.

"Pretty good battle, but it looks like you've lost this one," Fortis said. He grabbed Ugo's hand and hoisted his aching body up on his feet. "It's alright, though; you'll get 'em next time. You usually do," he said, smiling at Ugo. Fortis and Stultus had few friends, but they were good people with kind hearts. They were often misunderstood because of their awkwardness and intimidating strength, but Ugo liked them.

"Yeah, next time," Ugo responded.

"You will," Stultus reassured him. "I've seen you spar with Cadmael dozens of times. You just seemed off today. I noticed in class you were drifting. I even answered a few questions today and noticed you weren't chiming in to make my answers better."

Fortis began to chuckle to himself.

"What?" Stultus asked.

"I didn't realize how much you paid attention to Ugo. I think you like Ugo!" Fortis said teasing his sister. "Stultus likes Ugo. Stultus likes Ugo."

"I do not!" Stultus began chasing her brother around.

"Who cares if she does?" Ugo sheepishly asked, rushing to her defense.

"Thanks, Ugo." Stultus shot him a grateful look, although her cheeks were bright red. "Well, I guess I'll see you later!" she shouted. She ran off chasing her brother, who was still chanting.

When Ugo got home, his younger siblings were running around, Athirst chasing them from behind. Cearney was in the back garden, picking vegetables for dinner.

Ugo wanted to slip through the door quietly and hide, not wanting to be noticed. As he took another step, his mother spotted him. "Ugo, what's wrong? What happened to you?" Cearney stopped what she was doing and ran over to her son, sizing him up and down.

"Cadmael and I sparred today. He won." Ugo looked at the bruises on his arms, which had changed from their initial bright red color to a deep bluish-purple.

"I'm sure I can find something here that'll help," Cearney said, digging around in a sack she had tied to her waist. She pulled out a bottle that said, 'Cuts and Scrapes' and another that said 'Bruises', popping open the lids and applying the bottles' contents onto the affected areas. "Ugo, you're strong. I did not give birth to weakness. All of Jah's power lives in you and you better not forget it. When you were born, I whispered promises and hope into your sweet little ears. I whispered your future to you, and I whispered the future of your legacy. I know that you feel defeated today, but you will be victorious." She grinned. Her smile was filled with softness and strength.

"Thank you, mother."

Ugo felt the pressure of the fate of the entire village on his shoulders. He left to clear his head and fell asleep in the lush grass of the East Gardens.

33.
The Storm

The villagers of Eirene knew a storm was coming. They all had an innate ability to sense changes in their environment. The humidity made the air uncomfortably sticky. The rain then hit the ground, soft and melodic at first. But it wasn't long before the villagers witnessed the storm's fury. The clouds covered the sky like a thick blanket and cast a dark shadow over the entire village. Lightning flashed and thunder roared. The storm raged for four full moon cycles.

For many in the village, this was a time to connect; it was a time to think, a time to meditate, and a time to read. They all studied the Writ and took time to pray to Jah, all but one.

Cadmael hibernated in his room for many moons. He called out to the "Third Eye" that he kept hidden from his family. The device soon took the place of his time Jah. The storm provided the perfect opportunity for Cadmael to tamper with the gadget and unlock the secrets of the Second World without anyone noticing. He asked all the questions that came to his mind, and the device answered. With each answer, Cadmael took ink to the Writ and slowly began changing the words of Jah.

He entered a world where knowledge of the Writ and knowledge of the Second World became one in the same, where truth and fiction danced, and where the spirit of Jah and the spirit of the Earth mingled together. He found that place between Heaven and Earth where all understanding lied and wrote down everything he learned, hoping that he would be able to share his findings. He wanted to give the people of Eirene a choice as to what they wanted to believe. He wanted to give the people freedom.

It was on the third full moon of the rainstorm and Cadmael was meditating in his new understanding. An evening like this would have been filled with the lively sounds of community, but tonight was different. The heavy rains kept people indoors. In Cadmael's room, the glow of the device illuminated the words of his Writ that now contained messages in Cadmael's handwriting.

On this night, Theiler, who was quite the social butterfly, grew bored of the isolation the rain caused and decided to join his son in meditation. When he walked into his room, he saw something he had never seen before. A tiny device was casting images onto the wall. They displayed people not of their world. They were all using technology. They were wearing the same pieces of metal and plastic that Theiler had spent so much time throwing into the fire, but in the scene that was cast on the wall, the devices worked. Not realizing his father was in the room, Cadmael spoke to the device. "Show me a war."

"As you wish, Cadmael," the device responded. "Which war would you like to see?"

"A war where people fight for the right to believe what they want to believe."

"There are over one million wars where people fight over what they believe. I will show you a few and you can make your selection." The timepiece then showed a scene where planes were dropping bombs on another country, killing off its citizens. Theiler could not believe his eyes. He was in utter shock.

"So they were right."

Cadmael jumped. "How long have you been standing there?"

"Long enough." Theiler's face was filled with dread. He was finally seeing everything he once ignored and feared most come to pass. As he walked closer, that light, the eerie glow from the Second World, also illuminated the new additions to Cadmael's Writ. Theiler grew disheartened. No one had ever written over the words of Jah. It was considered disrespectful, but

Theiler could no longer deny seeing his son's book covered in scribbles and notes.

"Son, what have you done?" Theiler said quietly.

Cadmael paused his meditation, making way for awkward silence. Theiler and his son exchanged glances for several minutes before the silence was broken.

"Father, I..."

Cadmael had many feelings swarm through his body. "I am alive father! I understand more than you could have ever taught me; not because you are not a noble and wise man, but because you did not have all of the pieces. The Writ is just a small piece of something that is much greater. Jah has only given us a tiny piece of the truth, but there is so much more and you all have been blinded and deceived from the very beginning!"

Theiler struck his son across the face. "What has happened to you?" Theiler yelled.

Cadmael grabbed his Writ and showed it to his father. "All the questions, all the things I have ever wondered about -- I know and understand now. It all makes sense to me. There is a power that lives in me that I've never felt before. I want you to have it, too. As wise as you are, your wisdom is nothing compared to what I now know and understand."

Theiler snatched the book from Cadmael's hands. He flipped through the book to find that every page now contained notes, pictures, symbols, and writings that were not part of the original text.

"See father?" Cadmael said. "It's all here. I figured it all out."

"You have done nothing more than bring dishonor to Jah. You are foolish!" Theiler threw Cadmael's Writ on the ground and spit on it. "This is no longer a book sent by Jah. This is blasphemous!"

Theiler quickly went over to the source of the glow. He grabbed the device and gazed at it, examining all of the words that were engraved on it. He saw the words "Third Eye" and "Everlasting Life" imprinted on the glass face. He looked at the symbol of the bitten fruit. Theiler then took the device and bashed it on the ground, stomping on it. The Lithorium slowly oozed its way out onto the floor and quickly solidified. The glow of the device was no more.

"It's too late. I know what I know. I've seen things that no one else in this world has seen and you will never take that away from me. Both the spirit of Jah and the spirit of this world live in me!"

"You cannot have both the spirit of Jah and the spirit of the World live in you, Cadmael! Good and evil cannot exist in one body!" Theiler responded angrily.

"These worlds do not have to live separately," Cadmael said. He looked at his father, who no longer looked angry, but concerned. "Don't you see father? There's no need to worry! This is a good thing."

"Sit down, Cadmael!" Theiler's voice was stern.

Cadmael didn't sit. He was too busy explaining his feeling of enlightenment to hear what his father was saying.

Theiler grabbed his son's arm, pulling him down on the edge of the bed with him.

"I don't know if I ever told you about me and your mother. Athirst and I were the best of friends, probably since we were so much alike. So many of the Elders compared us. Our strength and wisdom, our interpretation of vision, and our intellect were constantly being compared. We sparred together because we found each other to be worthy opponents. His Elder, Sophos, was like a father to me as well. But I began to notice that over time, Athirst found less enjoyment in our friendship and more enjoyment in the company of Governess, your mother. I grew jealous. Athirst proposed to Governess, but didn't follow through with union because he was told by Jah that he wasn't supposed to be with her. When I saw that he'd broken it off with her, I decided that I wanted her for myself. I did not seek Jah first and unified with her anyway.

"During the ceremony, Jah gave me vision and showed me that I wasn't unified with the right person. The vision scared me. It showed me a pair of hands sowing seed into the ground. The seeds grew to make a strong, beautiful tree that bore succulent fruit. The fruit was very appealing to the eye and everyone desired it. One day, a piece of fruit fell from the tree and opened up. But the inside of the fruit was filled with disease."

"What does any of this have to do with what I'm telling you?" Cadmael said, lacking interest.

"For so long, I've had difficulty interpreting this vision. Governess and I seemed to be doing well. Jah had blessed me with so many other things. Our lives were good, but nothing compared to the moment I saw you. You were so magnificent, talented, and smart. It was not until today that I realized the consequences of my actions have fallen upon you. Cadmael, I don't know when or how your story will end, but I was disobedient to Jah once; I will not do it again. I would advise you to never go against the will of Jah, but I realize that you must go your own path. In the end, I cannot force you to do anything."

Theiler got up and walked away from Cadmael. Governess, who was standing nearby, overheard bits and pieces of the conversation.

"What was that all about?" Governess inquired, playing the fool to mask how horrified she was.

"Nothing. I've taken care of it." Theiler walked past Governess, accidentally nudging her shoulder on his way out. A tear rolled down her face. Her heart was heavy.

34.
Red Rain

The rain had persisted over Eirene for so long that it soon became an afterthought. Everyone accepted it as part of their daily routine and began to find comfort in its melodic pitter-patter. Governess was broken-hearted after overhearing the conversation. She could sense that things had not been going well for some time. She noticed her son spending all of his time alone and could see how withdrawn he'd become. She didn't know what to do. And whether it was her instincts or a feeling given to her from Jah, Governess felt that things between her and Theiler had changed. She soon began to realize that this all might've been happening because she was never meant to be with Theiler in the first place. She left the comfort of her home and walked in the rain. She found herself in front of Athirst's house.

The soft knock on the door could have easily been mistaken for the rustling of branches that seemed to hit the house with the gusts of wind and rain, but when the sound of the knocking became louder, Athirst answered the door. "What are you doing out in the rain? Please, come in."

"Thank you," Governess said softly.

Cearney came into the room. "Goodness Governess, the weather is so terrible! What brings you by?" Cearney quickly went to find something to help Governess dry off.

Governess grew quiet and just looked over at Athirst. Athirst could tell that she needed to speak to him privately.

"Cearney, it's been so long since I have spoken to my friend. Give me a few minutes, my love."

Cearney could sense that something was troubling Governess and understood that she needed a moment alone.

Athirst had grown to be a man that many in the village sought after for sound advice and guidance. It was evident to Cearney that Governess needed to have that time; besides, the tension that she and Governess had before had long gone. Cearney decided to let the past be the past, and trust both her and Athirst.

"Let me know if you need anything," Cearney said as she left the room.

Governess began to speak. "Athirst, we used to be the best of friends, remember?"

"I do. I remember everything. Is that why you came by?"

"Athirst, I need you to be my friend, a confidant. Can I talk to you? I…" a tear rolled down Governess' cheek, and she paused to compose herself.

"What is it? What's wrong?" Athirst felt genuine concern for Governess. He could sense she was not in a good place.

"It's Theiler and Cadmael. Something is wrong. I overheard a conversation they had and it scared me. I kept hearing Theiler yell at Cadmael and eventually I heard him say that unifying with me was a mistake. Was there not anyone in the village that I was supposed to make union with? Was I everyone's mistake? Why was I everyone's mistake?"

Athirst watched as tears rolled down from her eyes. She was trembling. His heart was broken for his old friend, and he reached over to console her. "Have you meditated to Jah? Has he told you anything?"

"I tried, but I don't think I'm interpreting vision the right way," Governess said carefully. Truthfully, Governess had not meditated in quite some time. She spent much of her time trying to figure out what was wrong with the things in her life, without seeking Jah for guidance. She tried to figure out everything on her own.

"You're smart, Governess. You can interpret vision," Athirst reassured her.

"Thank you, Athirst. You always know how to say the right thing... except when you're breaking off a union." Governess tried to smile as if it were a joke, but it was clear there was still pain behind her words.

"Governess, if it were up to me, you know things would've been different, but I have to follow Jah's divine purpose."

"I see...well, I'm happy for you, but I could've loved you, Athirst. I did love you. I don't love Theiler! We barely speak to each other. I couldn't understand it at first; I could not figure out why our connection seemed to grow stagnant. In the beginning, everything seemed okay. We were bonding, growing together... but now, there is nothing left. He looks at me and there is nothing. So many times I have watched the other unionmates in the village. They giggle and laugh with each other. They have this thing, this connection that I personally don't feel with my partner."

She walked closer to Athirst and rested her head on his chest.

"I know that I'm not interpreting vision the right way, because when I do have vision, I envision you; I envision someone that would love me like I thought you would. Theiler doesn't love me. I've always known that, and today just solidified my feelings. But you! You loved me at one point in time, Athirst. I miss that feeling."

Governess lifted her head off Athirst's chest and inched her lips toward his. She delicately moved her fingers around on his chest and walked them up to his chin. Her index finger nudged his lips toward hers.

"You don't want to do that Governess; this isn't you. This isn't the will of Jah."

"The will of Jah. Humph." Governess backed away from him.

"Do you know what it feels like to live and breathe the Writ, to meditate to Jah, and know that, because I have the unfortunate curse of being in union with someone who made a mistake, that my lineage is cursed? You're correct, Athirst; I do receive vision. I see that the fall of mankind has been brought upon us because of me. Through me, Athirst! Do you know what that feels like? It feels like death!" Governess shouted, her anger giving way to sobs.

"Governess, I'm so sorry. I don't...I don't know what to…"

Governess interrupted him. "It's okay. You don't know what to say or do. You can't make it better, Athirst. Jah sees and knows all, right? So I was saved from the Second World just to bring sin and destruction into this one? Some life! It doesn't make sense. None of this makes sense to me!"

Governess broke down on the floor, crying.

Athirst began rubbing her back to calm her uncontrollable shaking.

"Athirst, I just wanted you to know that I truly valued your friendship. I'm sorry for coming over here and disturbing you. I appreciate you listening. Tell Cearney that I'm sorry for everything. She's the perfect woman for you."

Governess got up and walked to the door.

"Do you need me to walk home with you? We're still friends, Governess. Please know that." Athirst knew he needed to be there for her in some way, but he didn't want to be overbearing or intrusive. Athirst quickly tried to determine the right move and the right words to say in his head. "Let me walk home with you."

"No, no thank you."

Governess walked through the rain and headed in the direction of her home alone. On the way, she passed the community kitchen, where she noticed a knife lying on the countertop. She was full of sorrow. She examined the sharp silver blade and pricked her finger with the tip of it. She felt an odd release from seeing the blood trickle down to the palm of her hand. She was filled with sadness and wanted to be free.

That night Governess did not return home. Red rain flowed through the village of Eirene. When his mother didn't come back, Cadmael went looking for her. It didn't take long before he found her body. His screams rang out through the entire village, piercing the air and leaving a permanent scar.

35.
The Word Spreads

The rain finally lifted, but the atmosphere of the next Potentiam Libertas festival was heavy. Governess' death wasn't foreseen in anyone's visions since her death was not the will of Jah. The villagers were speechless and felt numb. They carried out their rituals as usual, but this was the first time that it felt like a chore. The fire roared and begged for them to feed it, and as usual, they threw in devices from the Second World. However, it didn't elicit the same excitement that it once did.

Cadmael then stood up and addressed the community gathered around the fire.

"Listen up, everyone!" His voice commanded attention. He looked so different, like life itself no longer resided in him. His face was pale. His forehead held beads of sweat and there were dark shadows under his eyes. It was easy to tell that Cadmael hadn't slept in days.

Everyone looked to see him holding up his copy of the Writ. Theiler looked up to see what everyone was paying attention to. Theiler's face wore so many emotions that it became difficult to read. He looked like a man who was mourning, ashamed, depressed, but stern all at the same time.

He walked over to his son. "Cadmael, what are you doing? Sit down!"

"I am not sitting down. I just lost my mother so I think that gives me the right to speak. I have things I need to say." Cadmael quickly turned away from his father.

"Listen up, everyone. I know you're all mourning the death of my mother; as am I. It's maddening to know that Jah didn't make any of us aware of her departure, or warn us of the signs of her sorrow. I cannot express in words how hurt and confused I am with Jah."

Cadmael paced back and forth.

"I have studied the Writ since I was a young child. I've dedicated myself to meditation and vision. I've done everything that I was supposed to do, and yet, here I am, motherless. Jah has let me down. I was told that everything I needed to know was in this book!"

Cadmael held up an original Writ he had taken from where lessons took place. He held it up high for all to see.

"We've all blindly followed every single word in this book since the vanishing of the Second World, and now look where it's gotten us! It has led us astray. Jah has led us astray. How could he keep something like this from us? How could he not tell us about this unexpected death? There are questions that this book alone cannot answer. There are situations that the all-knowing Jah doesn't reveal. This book is not the answer!"

Cadmael took the Writ and threw it into the fire. Loud gasps came from several people in the crowd. Children started crying. The Writ was sacred, and their guide since the beginning of the Third World. Seeing someone throw it in the fire was unimaginable.

Ugo looked at his father. Athirst's expression of shock mimicked how everyone else was feeling. The crowd responded with a mix of gasps, screams, questions,cries, and before long, silence. But in human nature, the villagers could not turn away. They stood still, anticipating what Cadmael would say next.

Cadmael continued pacing back and forth. "I've figured out why Jah placed in us a desire to burn the devices of the Second World. He knew that if we found devices that could still reveal the secrets of the Second World, we would have access to exorbitant amounts of knowledge. We would know more about the world than we've been previously allowed. Well, I found one of those devices. The device still showed its glowing face. Anything I asked, it answered. All the places in the Writ that caused confusion -- all the visions where I asked Jah for clarity because they were extremely complex and took many moons to understand -- they were answered in seconds. And yes, brothers and sisters, the device has since been destroyed by my father." He cast an accusing look at Theiler.

Theiler looked away. Athirst began walking towards him, but Theiler was in no mood to talk. He felt that he had not only lost a wife, but a son as well.

Cadmael continued to address the crowd. "Isn't that right, father? You knew about the working time piece for three new moons before you destroyed it!"

"Sit down, Cadmael! You are making a fool of yourself!" Theiler was livid.

"The wise Theiler chose to ignore all the signs because deep down, my noble father wanted to feel its power as well, but like many of you, he couldn't handle it. He destroyed the device because he could not handle knowing the truth. But fear not! I've managed to take all of the valuable secrets from the device and write them down." Cadmael kept speaking as if his father's voice was inaudible.

It was then that Cadmael held up his version of the Writ, with markings and symbols that covered the original title. "It's here! This is the Book of Veritas! It's a book of truth. This book now holds all of the secrets that the Writ never answered. It contains all the additional information and knowledge we need to survive."

It was then that Cearney rushed over to Theiler. "Theiler, I understand that Cadmael is going through a lot right now, but you must put this to an end! He's going against the will of Jah, he is disrespecting the Potentiam Libertas, and his actions are insulting to both you and Governess. His words are blasphemous!"

"He is no son of mine." Theiler coldly walked away from the fire and headed toward his home, his figure fading into the distance.

Cadmael seemed unfazed by his father's departure. "Yes the Writ is our foundation, and there is so much truth within its pages, but there's so much more that we weren't told. There are answers to questions that haven't yet been asked because we knew not to ask them. But I'm here to tell you that we now have answers. I have found answers. Unlike the Youth of the Second World who found no use for the Writ, I have found that the Writ and information from the Second World can coexist! They..."

"Cadmael!" Ugo shouted, interrupting him. Ugo couldn't take this much longer. Athirst got up amidst his son's protests, but Cearney sat him back down.

Ugo grew enraged with Cadmael's level of disrespect to Jah. He couldn't stand how Cadmael was using his mother's death to spread his new agenda. "Does the Writ not speak of a day and time where there will be confusion? Does it not say that we must remain focused on the true words of Jah? Have you not learned about the wrath that will be placed on those who stand against His will? You are one of the most well-versed in the Writ and yet, you try to find fault in its teachings! Do you not feel ashamed? The Writ (212:93–95) says, 'there will be a time where all will hear the words of Jah, but few will understand, and when that day comes, those who remain in His favor will delight in treasures too great to be contained by the boundaries of the Earth.'"

Ugo looked around at the faces of those who gathered by the fire. Several of the adults nodded their head in agreement.

"I too can quote scripts from the Writ," Cadmael boasted. "The Writ (212:62–67) says that, 'there will be one who will come. No one will know his talents, but he will come to act as a light for all those who are lost, all those who do not know the truth.' The Writ (212:46–51) says, 'those who lack the ability to interpret vision and only rely on the Writ, and those who understand vision but do not heed the word will be lost. Only those who understand the fullness of the Writ, who seek to find answers to questions unknown, and who spend time with Him daily will truly know all that is given to them.'"

"Now," Cadmael continued, "We can continue this battle of wits, but I am afraid that you will lose this fight, just like you lost the fight before."

Ugo's blood boiled. He could feel rage consume his body. His fists clenched. Ugo was able to knock Cadmael to the ground quickly, but it was not long before Cadmael got his bearings and retaliated. Athirst tore through the kicking and swinging of arms and legs. The young boys were no match for Athirst's strength, and they were definitely no match for Jabari, who came running to help settle the feud.

Athirst addressed the crowd as Jabari kept Ugo and Cadmael separated. "You must understand that this young man has had a tragic loss and is speaking from a place of pain; however, my son is correct! Cadmael's words do not align with the will of Jah and should not be listened to. Jah has told us many times that we must treat each one of our brothers and sisters with grace and kindness. We must love him through this tragedy. He is speaking from a place that none of us know. I hope we all leave here today with a new wisdom and understanding of the type of support Cadmael needs. Now, the show is over!"

Jabari released both Cadmael and Ugo from his monstrous grip and they walked in separate directions, huffing and puffing. Ugo joined his father, and Cadmael began his walk home, alone. Athirst grabbed a large pail filled with water and threw it on the fire. As the smoke from the fire rose, the crowd dispersed.

"Brother!" Jabari shouted to Athirst. "I think I'm going to make sure Cadmael gets home safely. You're there for your son, but no one is there for him."

"Good idea, brother. We all need to come together and support him right now." Athrist gave Jabari a pat on the back. Jabari left to catch up with Cadmael.

"I'm proud of you for defending the Writ, son." He affectionately grabbed his son around his neck and they walked home.

Hearing that brought a smile to Ugo's face. But as much as Ugo wanted to feel proud of himself, he still felt a lingering worry for Cadmael.

36.
Jabari's Walk

Jabari caught up with Cadmael and put his arm around Cadmael's shoulder. "It's going to be alright. The closest thing that I felt to what you're going through was when Mediorocris departed, but you're right, I knew that it was coming because it was in Jah's time. I never thought anything like this would happen in Eirene. It would've made sense to be aware of Governess' pain. We're all so dedicated; I wonder how we ever missed it."

Cadmael dismissed Jabari's attempt to comfort him.

"Alright brother," Jabari continued. "I'll stop talking; let's just walk home."

The short distance from the center of the village to Cadmael's house seemed to be marked by birds humming and crickets chirping. They all seemed oblivious to the unfolding chaos.

"Thanks for looking after me. All the others had their mother and father with them tonight, but things are different for me now, so I appreciate it." Cadmael went to close the door, but Jabari's hand stopped it.

"I wanted to walk home with you to make sure you were alright, but I also wanted to ask a few questions. Do you mind if I come in?"

Cadmael widened the opening of the front door and let Jabari in. The house was dark, with the exception of the light coming from the fireplace that gave the room an orange glow.

"What'd you want to ask?" Cadmael tried to remove the angst from his voice. The adrenaline from everything that occurred earlier was beginning to fade away. He tenderly rubbed his arms, which were sore from fighting.

"You know I have great respect for your family. When your father and I were younger, he was the only one that would take the time to spar with me. I understand that my size can be quite intimidating and not many people had the courage to fight me during our sparring lessons. Theiler was not only bold and brave, but he was also well-versed in the Writ. When I struggled with understanding vision, he was the one that would help me interpret what Jah was trying to tell me. He never made me feel ashamed about not interpreting vision the right way. Tonight, I listened to you and what you said made sense to me. What if the reason why I wasn't interpreting vision correctly was because I didn't have all of the pieces? I was born in the Second World; it only makes sense to me that I need to understand the Second World if I'm to do the will of Jah in the New Age."

Cadmael's posture changed and his weakened demeanor seemed to shift as he heard Jabari speak.

"Maybe," Jabari continued, "You could let me read what you've written. Maybe it'll help me understand my purpose here. I want my children to be better than I am at interpretation. If I can read your Writ, maybe it'll help me understand all of my unanswered questions."

"Brother, I appreciate you sharing this with me, however, I will not allow you to read from my Book of Veritas."

"Oh, okay. I'm sorry, I…I understand," Jabari muttered, turning back toward the door.

"Stop, Jabari. I don't want you to leave. I'll make you one of your own so you won't have to read from my copy. Since my father destroyed the device, I'll have to study my book, but I will share everything I've learned about the Second World with you. I'll teach anyone who's willing to listen. I know that Jah is pleased with you. You are wiser than you give yourself credit for. Bring your Writ to me after the sun begins to peak its head over the horizon. I'll fill your Writ with all the answers to questions unknown by the next new moon. Your Writ will be marked with its new name."

Jabari brought his Writ to Theiler's house early the next morning just as Cadmael asked. Cadmael was preparing a meal for his younger siblings, a chore he took up after his mother passed away. Theiler, hearing Cadmael and Jabari's voices in the house, woke up and walked in their direction.

"Good morning, Jabari! What brings you by, old friend?"

"I stopped by to bring something to Cadmael."

"Oh really? Well, I appreciate anything you can do to make him feel better. That was quite a show he put on the other night. But I think that, with all of the support you and the others in the village are showing us, we'll be alright. This has been really tough for everyone..."

Jabari stopped Theiler before he could continue.

"Theiler, I know the Potentiam Libertas wasn't what you expected, but I don't want you to be upset with Cadmael. Not only does he need all of us right now, but I think he's really on to something."

Jabari handed his Writ over to Cadmael, who had just finished preparing breakfast for everyone.

"What's going on? Why are you giving him your Writ?" Theiler asked suspiciously.

"Look, brother," Jabari's voice was low, as if he were trying not to disturb the younger ones eating. "Your son is such a blessing. He's very wise, Theiler. I heard a lot of truth in what he said and I want to know more; I need to know more."

Jabari turned to Cadmael.

"Thank you for helping me, brother," Jabari said as he walked out the door. He didn't wait to see Theiler's reaction.

When Jabari returned home, Nia was waiting for him.

"The situation with Cadmael broke my heart for Governess. She would've been so upset to see Cadmael making a show like that."

"It is really sad. I can't believe she's gone, but...I must admit that Cadmael made some pretty interesting points."

"No he did not! He looked as if he were going mad. It was all gibberish. Besides, it doesn't matter what he has to say; none of it was aligned with the word of Jah."

"True, but what if there is more than just the Writ?"

"If there was more than the Writ, then Jah would have given it to us. Don't tell me that you actually believe what he was saying?" Nia said, concerned.

"I just think maybe we shouldn't rule out the possibility of there being a new way. A better way," Jabari said.

"Well, speak for yourself. I am perfectly content with what Jah has given me." Nia looked around for a bit before finding her shoes. "All of this has been a lot for me. I miss my friend and she's never coming back..." She struggled to hold back tears. "I need to clear my head. I'm going to go for a ride."

"I understand." Jabari gave Nia a kiss before she left.

He walked outside. "Cecile! Cecile, come here!" Jabari shouted. She swooped down and perched on Jabari's shoulder. "You're the only one that seems to understand me." Jabari picked up a small piece of fish and fed it to her.

"I don't know what's going to happen, but just promise that you'll stay with me."

Cecile let out a squawk.

37.
Serpent's Tongue

F*or the mouth of man without the wisdom of Jah is like a serpent's tongue. It was created in truth, yet sows contradictions and false wisdom, separating man from his true purpose and life with Jah* (Writ 212: 97-99).

A year had passed since Theiler's encounter with Cadmael. Things were a little tense for a while, but both Cadmael and Theiler had much more to do now that Governess was gone. They seemed to bury whatever tension was between them and move on, until a young villager named Damion approached Theiler while he was in town.

"Hi sir, are you Cadmael's father?"

"Yes...how are you?"

"I'm doing fine. I know you probably don't know who I am. My name's Damion."

"Well hello, Damion. I think I've seen you around."

"Yes, well. I hate to bother you. I wanted to tell Cadmael in person, but he's so busy now that I haven't seen him much, so tell him thank you on my behalf. He really helped me understand things in a completely different way, thanks to his Book of Veritas."

Theiler was taken aback. He didn't realize that his son was still showing others that foolishness. Theiler thanked the young man for telling him and then headed home.

"Cadmael, come here. I need to speak to you."

Cadmael walked to meet his father.

"I just met with a young man named Damion who said you were sharing your book with him. Why are you doing this again? Why are you spreading these lies?"

"They are not lies!" Cadmael snapped. "How can you call something lies when you never even read the words that have been revealed to me?"

"The only book I need to read is the Writ, and I forbid you from continuing to spread your foolishness."

"Father," Cadmael's voice softened. "I understand how you feel. I understand that you see me as someone who has fallen away from Jah. What I'm trying to tell you is that I still meditate to Him. I humble myself before Him as I always have. I read the Writ daily and understand that there is a power greater than my own. I've submitted to powers that are far beyond my own physical body. The Writ itself even speaks of spirit that is all around. I just choose to not limit myself to one source. I use both the spirit of the earth and the spirit of the heavens."

"Cadmael, you are my first-born. You are such a blessing. I look at you and see how intelligent you are, how strong you are, how determined you are... but I also see that you have so many lessons to learn."

"Father, I'm afraid that it's you who has a lot to learn." Cadmael picked up his Writ and handed it to Theiler. "Since you're so strong in your faith and so discerning with vision, reading the Book of Veritas shouldn't have any effect on your relationship with Jah. Why don't you give it a chance? At least entertain a son who just lost his mother."

Theiler raised an eyebrow.

Cadmael continued to hold the book out to his father. "Take your time with it. I've already begun to transcribe my words into several other books, so you don't have to rush. See if anything I've written or learned makes sense. I would appreciate the insight from you, father."

Cadmael walked out of the room and left his father alone with his copy of the Writ. Other than the change in title, the leather cover looked similar to the ones that all the Elders were sent to look for after the vanishing. The smell of the leather was the same as well. It wasn't until the book was opened that Theiler could see, in a handwriting all too familiar to him, words that filled in all of the empty spaces of the original Writ.

Theiler sat down on the edge of his son's bed and began reading the new verses that were added. He was immediately intrigued by the new philosophies. He found that many of the mysteries of the Writ had been answered, and he began to see things in a way that he had never understood before. He stayed in that room for seven days and read the Book of Veritas cover to cover. When he turned the last page, all knowledge and the forbidden secrets of the Second World were now made clear. He became enlightened just as his son had. The desire of learning from the Writ was replaced with a hunger for the words from this new and improved version.

Theiler went to his quiet place to talk to Jah. He approached Jah with sadness, confusion, and frustration. "Why have you not told us so many things? Why did we have to find out using forbidden devices? Why did you want to hide our true abilities from us?"

When all of his questions were asked, Jah responded by showing him a vision.

38.
The River

In his vision, Theiler was led to a clear river. It ran freely and was safe to drink from. The river was a source of life for the village. One day, a man came, and seeing there was plant and animal life in the river, he decided that it was not suitable for humans to drink. So the man went out and told people the water wasn't safe, since it was supposedly contaminated. He decided to find ways to remove the plant and animal life so there would be nothing in the river except the fresh water.

In the beginning, he was successful. He removed all source of life from the water. The villagers celebrated his accomplishments and began drinking the water from the river. They also found the plants and animals that were removed from the river suitable to eat, so they joined the man in his efforts. They delighted in all the work they had accomplished. They drank from the water and feasted on the wildlife. But soon, the water became murky and filled with bacteria and disease. People didn't realize that the plants and animals were placed there to filter the water and make it clean for them. Without them, the river became contaminated and undrinkable. Overtime, everyone in the village became sick and many died.

The man in the vision saw that people were suffering. He then began experimenting with plants to create medicine to help those in the village who were sick. The medicine helped ease the pain and the villagers were grateful, but the disease did not go away. The man kept giving them the medicine and the villagers became dependent on its pain relieving qualities, and at the end of the vision, hundreds of men, women, and children were lined up at the man's door to receive treatment. He spent the rest of his life giving them something they would've never needed if he hadn't told them the water was unclean and made unnatural changes that disrupted the balance of the ecosystem.

When the vision was finished, Theiler got up from his place of meditation. Knowing the Writ, but being enlightened with words from the Book of Veritas, he misunderstood what Jah was trying to tell him. He went to find Cadmael and he shared his vision of the river with him. This allowed the two of them to grow closer.

"When people read the Writ, they're drinking unclean water and they will be filled with sickness. The Book of Veritas is the medicine that'll make them well." Theiler felt good about his interpretation. He and Cadmael stayed up until dawn discussing how they could spread the Book of Veritas in a way where the village would listen. Jah watched over Theiler and grew disheartened.

It was midday when Theiler was near River Aesis gathering water for his family when he spotted Fortis.

"Greetings, Theiler," Fortis said. "I miss my friend at lessons. He doesn't attend much anymore. How is he?"

"Things were a bit rough at first, but they're getting better now. Thank you for asking," Theiler responded.

"I'm glad to hear it. I hope he'll be back soon. I can imagine he has a lot more to do to help out with the family now," Fortis said.

"Yes, things are quite a bit different now, but Cadmael is doing a great job of helping take care of everything." Theiler finished filling the container with water and was turning to walk back toward the center of town when Fortis stopped him.

"Hey, could you tell Cadmael thank you? I never seem to be able to catch him but I wanted to thank him for what he offered to do."

"What did he offer to do?" Theiler inquired.

"He promised to give my father one of his books. He's looking forward to gaining new insight. He has always admired you and your family. I think this book will make him feel just as wise as you."

"I will let Cadmael know," Theiler said, feeling like a proud father.

39.
Like a Wildfire

When Theiler returned home he saw Cadmael and gave him the message from Fortis. Cadmael was pleased. "Father, I've been giving the vision you shared with me much thought and I agree that it may be time for us to share the Book of Veritas with others outside Eirene." Theiler agreed and they decided they would begin to travel from village to village.

"I want to show you something," Cadmael said suddenly.

"What is it?"

"Just come along." Cadmael grabbed his father's arm and pulled him to his room.

"I didn't want to show you this at first because you weren't enlightened, but now that we both see things the same way, I can finally show you."

Cadmael went under his bed and pulled out a wooden container with hundreds of flat, wooden tablets with carvings on them.

"What is this, son?"

"I wanted to find a way to spread the word. I knew this day would come. I asked the device to show me how to spread my message quickly. It played an image of a man who created a printing press that was able to create multiple copies of the same thing. I don't have all the tools he had, but I was able to chisel words into these thin pieces of wood."

"Oh my. How long did this take?"

"Several months, maybe. I didn't keep count. I just kept working. I knew that somehow the device may get destroyed and wouldn't be able to help me anymore, so I worked for as many hours as I could to do this."

"Son, you are brilliant."

Over the next year, Theiler and Cadmael laid low, spending most of their time working to make copies of the books. They made sure to go out into the village just enough so that people wouldn't get too worried.

Many villagers would ask each other if they'd seen or heard from Theiler and his family. The response was always something like, "I saw him not too long ago, but I'm sure they're just trying to get things back on track," or "leave them alone, they're going through a lot. I'm sure they'll join in the festivities when the time is right."

Eventually, people stopped looking and soon, Theiler and Cadmael were free to travel from village to village with the Book of Veritas in tow.

Theiler and Cadmael packed up food for the younger children, as well as their leather bags for travel. The first stop for Theiler and Cadmael was Jabari's house. Theiler left his younger children with him and asked him to take care of them while they traveled. As they walked out the door, Cadmael gave him two copies of The Book of Veritas.

"One for you and one for Nia," Theiler said as he shook Jabari's hand.

"Thanks brother." Jabari pulled him in and gave him a hearty pat on the back. "I will make sure your children are looked after." Jabari was honored to take care of Theiler's children and humbly accepted his role as caretaker.

"Nia!" Jabari shouted down the hallway.

"What?!"

"I've got to tell you something."

Nia walked down the hallway. "What is it?" As she came into the room, she saw Theiler's youngest girls, Grayson and Tabbatha, standing there with their possessions. Grayson was one year younger than her brother Cadmael. She was thirteen years old and Tabbatha was eleven.

"Hi girls, how are you doing?"

"Fine," both girls said at the same time.

"Where is your father?" Nia asked. Before the girls could answer the question, Jabari interrupted, "Um...that's what I wanted to speak with you about. Girls, Fortis and Stultus are in the back. Why don't you take your things back there and see if they can find some space for you?"

The girls took their bags and headed down the short hallway to the back of the house.

Jabari turned to Nia. "Dear, I don't want you to be mad and I need you to whisper. I don't want them to hear what we're talking about."

"Goodness Jabari, what have you done this time?" Nia whispered.

"I promised Theiler that I would watch his girls for him while he goes to spread The Book of Veritas to neighboring villages."

"Are you crazy? You can't seriously be helping him spread this foolishness to other villages! Come on Jabari, I thought you were a better man than that. Don't you see what's going on here? This is exactly what the Writ always warned about. Once we fall away from the word of Jah, we're doomed."

"Nia, I hardly think we'll be doomed for trying to learn more about where we've come from and how to use technologies to help us understand Jah better."

"You're right! You hardly think!" Nia snapped.

"I can't believe you would say that to me. You know I don't appreciate when people make me sound stupid. Here -- " Jabari grabbed the copy that Theiler left him and passed it to Nia. " -- this one's for you."

"Jabari, I love you, I do, but I won't do this with you."

Nia placed the book down on the kitchen counter and walked back to where Jabari was standing. "I think you have some decisions to make. Now, as far as the girls, we will take care of them because I would never leave children to fend for themselves, but you need to figure out the path you want to take. Will it be with Jah or will you follow in the footsteps of a hurt son and his misguided father?"

"Theiler is far from misguided. You, Governess, our classmates... all of you used to hang on his every word. I think you're just jealous that I might be more knowledgeable once I read this book."

"Do you hear yourself right now? I never hung onto Theiler's every word. You and I both know that I was supposed to unify with Theiler until that cocky little man chose someone else because he didn't listen to Jah. I chose to be around you, to support you when everyone else was laughing at you. I chose to unify with you despite what we both knew. You know why I chose to do that?"

"You got stuck with me because there was no one left."

"No! Because I thought you were a good man who desired to have a connection with Jah. You pushed yourself to learn more even when others were making fun of you. But now, I see that it has never truly been about Jah, but about you wanting to be accepted by that...that man. Believe me Jabari, I have no problem being by myself. You better figure out what it is that you want." Nia left the room and went outside to clear her head. She hopped on her beloved deer, Nova, and headed toward River Aesis to think.

Cadmael and Thieler also rode their animals to travel from village to village. Cadmael rode on the back of a white tiger while Theiler rode on his trusty cheetah.

"Where to now?" Cadmael asked.

They both looked up. "Mount Boreal?" The mountain had never been traveled by anyone in Eirene. They did not know what to expect. The animals slowed their speedy pace as they traveled higher and higher up a mountain. The wind grew more brisk, and they noticed little white puffs falling from the sky.

"What is this?" Theiler inquired.

"We don't have it in Eirene, but I believe its snow. The device showed it to me."

"I'm sorry about destroying the device. It seems to have taught you so much."

"It's okay. I'm sure we'll find more one day."

"You think so?"

"I know so. But right now, I think we need to figure out a way to stay warm."

Both of the men hopped off their animals and searched their leather bags for blankets to wrap up in before continuing their journey. The wind was blistery and the snow began falling harder. They continued to go until they saw a cluster of houses made from large blocks of ice. Each house was a translucent, light blue color. Blurry figures could be seen moving throughout them. It was difficult to make out any real features.

Theiler reached out his hands and touched the exterior wall of one of the buildings. "How do they stay warm? It's freezing."

"Hey, you two aren't from around here, are you?" A strange voice yelled out to them.

Theiler quickly removed his hand and both he and Cadmael turned around to see a large, extremely hairy man standing in front of them. He had to be at least a foot taller than Jabari. He had a long, thick, dirty brown beard with tiny icicles hanging off the end.

"Can I help you with something?" The strange man asked again.

"Yes, actually," Theiler said, trying to show no fear. Cadmael stood beside his father, speechless. "We're looking for some place warm for the night. We are visitors from Eirene. My name is Theiler and this is my son, Cadmael." Theiler stuck out his hand and the giant stranger grabbed it, giving it a firm shake. "My name is Hiemal. Welcome to Inber. So, why are you here?" Hiemal asked. "We don't get very many visitors. Most cannot stand the cold."

"We're here because my son found out some interesting things and we wanted to share it with the neighboring villages. I see why you don't get many visitors; it's freezing. How do you do it?"

"Well, for us, this is normal. Watch this." Hiemal stretched his hands out and streams of water ejected from his fingertips, immediately turning into ice. Within seconds he constructed a large, frozen block. "This is how we build practically everything here. I suspect Jah gave us this gift in exchange for living in these conditions." Hiemal chuckled.

"I guess I meant how do you stay warm?" Theiler laughed.

"Ah, that's what the beard is for, my friend. But since I'm sure that you won't be growing a beard overnight, we do have accommodations for visitors." Hiemal took the men to his house. Inside there was a long gathering table made of wood, surrounded by twenty wooden chairs. In the living room there were three couches the size of most beds in Eirene.

"Please, have a seat," Hiemal said.

Theiler and Cadmael were still shivering, but sat down on the large comfortable couch. There was a fireplace, which were also made of ice blocks. Both Theiler and Cadmael looked at this quizzically.

"Most visitors are amazed that the fire doesn't melt the ice. 'Another phenomenon from Jah' is what I tell them."

Hiemal put a few more logs on the fire and then called for his union-mate. "Cantus!" He shouted. She came down the crystalized ice staircase. She was strikingly beautiful, but vastly different from any woman that lived in Eirene. She was extremely pale with thick, long white hair that cascaded down her back. Her eyes were a striking pale blue, and her nails were fashioned in the shape of long, sharp icicles. As she walked down the stairs, she glided her fingernails down the banister and the friction of her nails on ice made a slight 'ting' noise. "Ah, I see we have some guests." Her voice was like a song. As she walked past them, the smell of mint wafted through the air.

"They came from Eirene," Hiemal said.

"Eirene! You've traveled quite a long way, then." Cantus brought the men some warm tea. "Why are you so far from home?"

Cadmael sipped his tea, then put it down. "I found a working device from the Second World."

As soon as Cadmael said this, Hiemal and Cantus froze. "A working device," Cantus gasped.

"It let me see that at one time, technology was a wonderful thing. It showed me that we can have both technology and a relationship with Jah," Cadmael continued.

"So where is this device now?" Hiemal asked.

"It's been destroyed," Cadmael said as he looked at his father.

"I hardly doubt there is anything better than Jah's word. The Writ warns about anything that goes against it." Hiemal looked suspiciously at Cadmael and Theiler.

"I used to think the same thing. But the Writ takes much dedication and a high level of skill to interpret. I have many friends in my village who have feared misinterpreting the Writ. When I found the device, I went to all of the concepts in the book that we struggled with and asked the device for clarity. I wrote down everything I learned in this book." Cadmael took his leather sack and pulled out the Book of Veritas.

"Don't look much different than the Writ, does it?" Hiemal said to Cantus. They examined the outside of the book before opening it and flipping through the pages. "Ah ...now I see.

Looks like you've put a lot of work into this," Cantus said in her melodic voice.

"Yes, and I would love to leave one here with you as a gift for your hospitality," Cadmael said.

"Well, I guess we can give it a look. We already know the entire Writ front to back. Might be nice to have something else to read. In the meantime, why don't you all get some sleep?" Hiemal told his guests. "You two may want to stay down here near the fire. Too hot for me; I'm headed upstairs."

Cantus and Hiemal headed up the massive staircase. Cadmael and Theiler quickly fell asleep.

The next morning, Cadmael and Theiler woke up shivering. The fire had gone out. Both of the men decided to pack up, and prepared to head to another village. Noise from the kitchen let Theiler and Cadmael know that someone was up. Theiler headed in the direction of the noise to see both Hiemal and Cantus up making something to drink. She put her hands out and quickly formed a drinking glass from ice. Then she squeezed the juice of an orange into the glass. "Would you like some?" She offered.

"No, but I wouldn't mind filling up my canister with a little bit of water," Theiler said.

Hiemal took the canister and pointed his index finger inside the container, filling it with ice cold water. He did the same for Cadmael. "That should hold you for a little while."

"Thanks," Cadmael responded.

"I will make sure to read the book. It was nice to have visitors." Heimal walked them out.

Cadmael and Theiler climbed aboard their animals. Icicles were hanging off their fur. It was evident they were ready to leave because as soon as Cadmael and Theiler mounted them, they both took off like the speed of light.

"Nice trip don't you think?" Theiler shouted over the noise of the swirling wind.

"It was a nice trip, but not what I expected! I really don't feel as if we truly convinced them. We've got to be more aggressive in the way we deliver our message!" Cadmael shouted back.

"Well, it was our first stop. I'm sure we will reach more people in the next village," Theiler reassured his son.

"I hope so. I feel like it's my mission to help others find the real truth."

Cadmael and Theiler traveled to many villages over the next few months and were more persistent with their message. They spoke to all of those who had difficulty interpreting the Writ. The teachings caught on like wildfire and instantly Theiler and Cadmael had a large following. But despite the instant popularity, there were those who did not agree with the teachings and found the Book of Veritas to be blasphemous. Those who stayed true to the Writ were angry at Theiler and Cadmael for coming to their village and teaching against the original word, but Theiler and Cadmael pressed on.

A waning gibbous was hanging in the sky. Despite the fact that the sun had gone down a long time ago, the air was still warm and humid. Gnats were swarming around the sweet fruit that hung from the trees. Theiler and Cadmael decided to rest, and set up a tent on the outskirts of the village of Atar. They had gone to many of the Atarians earlier in the day and shared the Book of Veritas. The book found its way to Logicist, an Atarian who was a wise and dedicated follower of Jah. When he opened the book and saw that someone had altered the original text, he decided to search for the people who had brought it into his village.

"Where are you going Logicist?" Xar-Ann, Logicist's wife asked.

"I need to find them. I need to stop this."

"Well then I am going with you." Xar-Ann gathered stones and put them in ther leather sack to protect herself from the unexpected.

Logicist gathered three other male Atarians and headed in the direction he was told he could find the outsiders. When they arrived at the tent, Cadmael and Theiler were sleeping.

"Wake up!" Logicist commanded. His voice seemed to shake the ground when he spoke. Theiler and Cadmael woke up immediately, startled. Theiler and Logicist stood eye to eye. They had a similar build and height. Logicist had dark, smooth skin. The surface of his bald head gleamed under the light of the moon. All of the Atarian males shaved their heads. It was a tradition passed down by their Elders. The female Atarians wore their hair in neat braids that were flush to their head and flowed down to the middle of their back. They too had dark complexions and tall, athletic frames. The Atarians wore minimal clothing, most likely due to the hot, humid temperatures of Atar. Theiler, on the other hand, had a fairer, olive-toned complexion, as well as a full head of blonde hair. He looked out of place with his long cotton garb on. The Atarian men stood on either side of Logicist, with swords at their hips. Xar-Ann stood behind the men gripping her leather sack that was filled with stones.

"I am a man of Jah, so I will not harm you, but I'll only say this once. You must leave this place immediately." Logicist gazed at Theiler, looking at him directly in the eye. Logicist had no fear. His demand was quite clear.

"I will not be scared off by an Atarian! I too am a man of Jah. I haven't come to do anything besides guide those who desire a deeper connection with Him," Theiler proclaimed.

"You haven't come to help, but to turn the people of Atar away from Jah. We don't need you to help us. Jah has given each of us the ability to interpret vision and understand the Writ on our own -- the right way. You must go."

Cadmael moved to stand in front of his father. He looked directly into Logicist's eyes and said, "You are foolish to believe that there is nothing more than the words of the Writ. There is so much more, and I've uncovered the secrets of the Second World and found where they fit into the Writ."

"Your son is the one who's a fool! He dares to find fault in the words of Jah! He will find himself burning in hell's fires."

Theiler moved to defend his son. "I will not have you say such insolent things to my son."

Immediately the men surrounding Theiler and Cadmael drew their swords, and Xar-Ann opened her sack, placing her hand on a stone.

Logicist gestured to his fellow Atarians. "Tarin, Malachi, Atamin, no swords! I'm sure they are reasonable and will leave," Logicist said as he looked at Theiler and Cadmael, hoping they would take him up on his offer.

When they did not budge, Logicist grew irritated. "I will ask you only once more to take your things and leave this place. You and your false teachings are not welcome here."

It was then that Cadmael closed his eyes and began to meditate right in front of them. He got on bended knee and placed his hands on the ground. With his eyes closed, he said, "It is not by my will, but the will of all that is within the Earth. All that has come and all that will come -- fill me so that others may see my light!"

With those words, Cadmael's skin began to emit a dim glow and the whites of his eyes shined. He was manifesting his beliefs through a visual expression of light. It was too soon to tell the color of light he was emitting, but nonetheless Cadmael was the first in all of the villages to express his spirit through illumination. When Tarin and Malachi saw the power that he possessed, they were frightened and got down on their knees to ask him for forgiveness. Cadmael touched the men on their heads and said, "Now, you are enlightened. You see the way." The two of them looked up at Cadmael, trembling. "If you wish to be further enlightened as I have, you must study the words of the Book of Veritas and learn the secrets that Jah has kept hidden from all of us." Cadmael handed each of them a book. Tarin and Malachi took the books from his hands. "Yes, of course, sir."

Logicist grew furious. "You're the one the Writ sent warning about!" Xar-Ann removed a stone from her bag and was gripping it tightly ready to attack. Atamin picked up his sword and headed toward Theiler. Cadmael, seeing him charge toward his father, used the spirit of the Earth that he summoned into himself. He gathered all of the power he had inside and rushed to stand as a barrier between the tip of the sword and his father. The tip of the sword pricked Cadmael's skin, leaving a small cut. And then, almost immediately after, his flesh began to transform, hardening like stone and causing the knife to bend. It was evident that Cadmael now had more power than any of them would have imagined.

Logicist stood there boldly in the center of the chaos, unfazed by the show displayed before him. Cadmael grabbed the end of Atamin's blade and continued to bend it until the sword was of no use. "Father!" Cadmael glanced at Theiler. "Let's not waste our time with these men. We've converted some in this village already. Our mission here is done."

"Yes, go. Your words are poison! I will not stand idly by as you pervert the sacred writings of Jah. Go now before I decide to gather an army and wage war against your kind."

"We'll leave, but just know that your men and women have been awakened to my teachings already. My mission has proven successful. Once they see the truth, they will never go back." Cadmael flashed a devilish grin at the Atarian.

"There will be many that fall away, but those who stay true to the will of Jah will prosper," Logicist declared, quoting a verse from the Writ.

"Ah yes, I am all too familiar with the Writ. That's Chapter 212, verse 51, correct?" Cadmael responded sarcastically.

"You better watch yourself, boy. Your treachery will not prevail. I'll make sure of that." Logicist briskly walked away.

"I think it is best that we leave now. We've done what we needed to do here. We've stirred up enough trouble already," Theiler said.

Because Cadmael was in spirit he was only slightly wounded from the sword that pierced him. Cadmael touched his cut and was amazed that it did not inflict more damage. He couldn't help but revel in his newfound abilities. He vowed to keep refining his powers so that he might one day become invincible.

The two of them left the outskirts of Atar and traveled for several days. At night, they rested and studied the Book of Veritas, but Theiler was troubled with dreams and couldn't sleep. He saw demons and evil spirits circling all around him and it made him wake up in a panic. He looked over at his son, but Cadmael was resting peacefully. Theiler stayed awake until sunrise.

When they began walking again, Cadmael could tell his father was troubled.

"Father, what's wrong?"

"You are the first to show your light. It was incredible to witness. I don't know what to think or feel. How were you able to do it?"

"Father, you've grown up to believe that you can only get your power from Jah. But after I found the device, I learned so much. There is power and life in everything. You can acquire energy from any tangible thing or life source that has been created by Him. It's still Him."

It was evident that Theiler had his reservations about this sentiment. "Yes, the Writ does tell us that there's energy and light in everything, but it warns us about how exactly we should gain that energy and light because so much of it has been tainted. I just want to make sure we're doing the right thing. I know so many who are dedicated to Jah and who meditate to him often, but they have not displayed the type of immense power that you just did."

Cadmael responded in disbelief. "I can't believe what I'm hearing. I thought we were both enlightened. I thought we both understood that there is something bigger and greater than what we have been blindly following since the creation of the New Age. Do you not believe in the work that we're trying to accomplish?"

Cadmael came to a halt, waiting for his father to answer.

"Of course, I believe we should let as many people know about the goodness and wonder of Jah, but is that what we're actually doing? Have I lost my way? You're growing more powerful by the day, but could it be that you aren't actually wiser, and instead tapping into something forbidden? Something sinister? I must take some time to meditate. I must take some time away to think."

Both of them were silent the rest of the journey.

They soon arrived in Siomon. While there, Theiler and Cadmael began going from door to door to see all who lacked the ability to interpret clear vision or had difficulty with the Writ. On their second day there, they unknowingly arrived at the house where Cearney had grown up.

Upon their knock, Jendahi answered the door. She immediately recognized the men as villagers from Eirene. Jendahi had heard rumors of men traveling from village to village with a new word and heard that many people were enlightened. She was curious as to what it entailed and how it was different from the Writ.

"Greetings, my name is Theiler, and this is my son, Cadmael. We wondered if you had a moment to hear us out."

"Of course. Wait, did you say Theiler?"

"Yes, Theiler, and my son's name is Cadmael."

"Do you know a man named Athirst? He's my sister's husband."

"Of course; Athirst and I are very good friends. We grew up together in Eirene."

"He's a really good man. I didn't get to spend much time with him before he unified with my sister, but my Elder Iris spoke so kindly of him."

"It is truly a small world," Theiler said, smiling.

"Yes, it is. Well, this is quite a delightful surprise. So, what is it that you wanted to show me?" Jendahi asked.

Theiler and Cadmael then proceeded to share the Book of Veritas with her. When they left, she felt troubled and her heart felt heavy. Although she had not sent a letter in quite some time, Jendahi felt compelled to send word to her sister. After writing the letter, Jendahi asked one of the men who trade with Eirene to take it to her sister.

It had been months since either one of them had communicated, so when the tradesman brought the letter to Cearney, she was surprised.

Cearney,

I hope this letter finds you well. I know that it has been some time since you've been back home. The village often asks about you and Athirst. They all grew quite fond of him when he would come visit. They saw wisdom in his words and thought he was quite the gentleman. I'm writing because we were visited by two men from Eirene who are spreading a new word called The Book of Veritas. Their names were familiar to me, although the names have left me now, but they seemed to know of you and Athirst. Many people here are confused and are looking to you and your family for guidance. We know that Athirst is one of the best interpreters of Jah's word and we are hoping you can tell us whether The Book of Veritas has any truth. Several of the younger Siomonites have begun reading the text and have found it to be rather enlightening. I haven't read it myself. I've only heard about it from the two visitors. Many of the adults have chosen to only read the Writ, but we're concerned that it may cause discord within the community.

We hope to hear from you soon.

Jendahi

"Athirst!" Cearney called to her husband. "Athirst, I received a letter from Siomon." She handed him the letter and Athirst read it carefully. As he scanned the page, his expression changed from one of excitement to unease. Cearney sat near her husband and began rubbing his shoulders.

When Athirst finished reading the letter, he was filled with questions. "How is the Book of Veritas in Siomon? What other villages do you think they've gone to already? What do you think this all means?"

Athirst didn't want to admit what he already knew. He got up and immediately took the letter to his quiet place. He meditated and paced back and forth. He knew that Cadmael had lost his way, but the letter said two men from Eirene. Who was this other man? Who from Eirene had also fallen away from the words of Jah?

It was difficult to wait on vision from Jah. Athirst was hurt, furious, and embarrassed that two from his village could speak against Jah in this way. In his meditation, he asked Jah for strength and for a calm spirit, and it was given to him. Athirst went to Cearney and let her know that he and Ugo needed to leave for Siomon at once. Cearney reluctantly agreed.

The path was all too familiar. He remembered when he met Cearney for the first time and how he searched for the special flower that she wanted for Iris. He remembered being scared to feel anything for her because he was nervous that Jah wouldn't approve. Athirst shared his stories with Ugo throughout their journey. In the silent moments of the walk, he remembered to thank Jah for the family that he had.

They soon arrived at the house where Jendahi still lived. She answered the door. "Athirst, I'm so glad you're here! And this must be Ugo! You've grown to be quite a young man! How old are you now?"

"I'm sixteen, about to be seventeen soon," Ugo said.

"I bet there's a lot of young ladies in Eirene who have got their eye on you," she teased.

"I don't know about all that, but thank you," Ugo said shyly.

Jendahi motioned for them to come in. The long trip left them famished, and the savory-sweet smell wafting from the kitchen wasn't helping.

"I'd know that smell anywhere. It's one of my favorite things that your sister makes."

"My father will do almost anything for maple-glazed duck," Ugo said, shaking his head.

"Well brother, you have great timing. I was just about to eat."

Athirst made a beeline for the kitchen.

"I am sure you know why I'm here," Athirst said through a mouthful of duck.

"Yes, I am assuming that you received my letter." Jendahi did not look up as she spoke. She scooped glazed carrots onto everyone's plate. The smell of Jendahi's cooking found its way into the village and soon there were a few others who came to eat. They were younger Siomonites who had Elders that were not as gifted in the cooking department.

"Do you remember the men's names? What did they look like?" Athirst inquired. As much as he was trying to stay on topic, Ugo could see that his mind was preoccupied with stuffing his face with food.

"Well," Jendahi said, "I'm not the best at remembering names. Something like Cad…"

"Cadmael?" Ugo interrupted. Ugo glanced at his father, who was now paying attention.

"Yes, something like that. The other one was The...The... I am sorry brother; I can't really remember."

"Was his name Theiler?" Athirst said anxiously.

"You're good! Yes, I think that was it. He mentioned you two were friends."

"We are, or were, good friends," Athirst responded.

"Should I be concerned? Is there trouble?"

"There's no need for you to worry. I'm sure that everything will be alright. I just need to see them. Do you happen to know what direction they were headed when they left here?" Both Ugo and Athirst had finished their meal. There was not a crumb of food left on either plate.

"Hmmm... let me think of the best way to find them. If you head north, you'll come to a place where the path splits. You will need to veer to the left. You will know you're headed in the right direction because you'll see a tree that we refer to as a tri-tree, because it is so large that it looks like three trees have grown together. It is the only tree of that size that will grow in our soil, so it will stand out. Last I heard, they were there under its shade."

Athirst and Ugo set off in the direction they were told. When they got to the tri-tree they saw Theiler at its base, preparing to rest.

"Theiler?"

Theiler was laying wool blankets on the ground to set up camp. When he turned around, he saw Athirst standing there with Ugo at his side. Cadmael was off in the distance gathering wood, but began to walk back toward the tri-tree when he saw people standing by his father.

Theiler was surprised to hear a familiar voice. "My goodness, brother! What are you doing here? It's so good to see you." Theiler went over to Athirst and immediately greeted him with a hug.

Athirst's demeanor was cold. "What are you doing here?"

"We're on a mission for Jah. He sent me great vision and I must fulfill his request. We're taking those who struggle with understanding the Writ and introducing them to a new way."

"You are defiling the word of Jah," Athirst said testily.

"Brother, you don't understand. I too once believed that Cadmael was misguided, but I read his book and I see the truth now. We can never live in our fullness and understand spirit until we know and understand where we came from. You and I were rescued from the Second World. Don't you think it's strange that we aren't allowed to know its secrets? We've spent our entire lives burning the very devices that hold all of the information of the Second World, but I know that there is a better way and my son has found it! We can use the same things that destroyed the Second World to help us grow and connect with the current one in a way that is unimaginable. We'll be able to enhance our relationship with Jah as well. You see, it wasn't that the technology was wrong, it was that the people of the Second World used it in the wrong way."

"I can't believe what I'm hearing. I can't believe that you have fallen so far from Jah. You don't see that what you're doing is exactly what the Writ warned us about."

"I haven't fallen away, my friend. In fact, I am more connected than I've ever been."

"You must leave this place. You must come back to Eirene and put these ridiculous theories to bed!" Athirst pleaded.

By this time, Cadmael had walked up. "We will leave when our job is done," Cadmael said coolly.

Suddenly, a figure emerged in the distance. Athirst and Theiler seemed too preoccupied to notice, but as the figure got closer and closer, Ugo's eyes lit up. "Jendahi!"

Her hair was tangled, and her cheeks were ruddy as she ran up to the group of men. "Look at all of you arguing amongst yourselves! Jah's word never stirred up this kind of trouble!"

Cadmael was quick to respond. "You're all fools. You wouldn't know Jah's will if it was right in front of you. You don't know what it's like to be truly connected to everything around you. You all are weak and narrow-minded! Why squabble about power when you can just take it?" Cadmael closed his eyes and dropped down on one knee. He pressed both hands to the ground and began meditating to himself. Everyone could hear the whispers of a scripture that sounded vaguely familiar, like one from the Writ, but it was different somehow.

"And he who believes has been given the power to manifest spirit from the Earth, and bring into themselves power that will surpass the limits of one's physical body. They shall connect with the spiritual world (Book of Veritas)."

It was at that moment everyone saw Cadmael's expression of light. The power surging through his body sent a shockwave that rippled across the landscape, knocking everyone backward. The color his glow emitted left them all in shock. What was once a blinding white light now settled into a deep, ominous orange. The light transmitting from the glow swirled and lapped, almost mimicking flames. His expression of light was Amber.

Athirst turned to Ugo. "It's time to go. We must prepare the others. An Amber has shown himself. There is not much time."

Athirst then turned to Theiler. "Brother, I know you love your son, but you know this is not the way! This is something far beyond what I dreamed!"

Theiler seemed to be in shock.

"Brother, I implore you! You are my best friend, but now isn't the time to concern yourself with trivial feelings. This power poses much danger to us all. If you won't join me, then I must warn the other villages without you." Athirst waited for a moment, hoping that Theiler would be reasonable, but when he saw that Theiler wouldn't budge, he grabbed Ugo by the arm and they headed back to Eirene with a sense of urgency. Jendahi ran home to warn those in Siomon.

40.
The Amber Glow

Cadmael's glow eventually faded. Theiler looked at his son in disbelief. He watched as Cadmael's skin reverted back to its normal flesh tone. Theiler could sense that his son's power was growing with each passing moon, and that he would soon be in the spirit of the Amber permanently, with no definite physical form. This scared Theiler.

He had many thoughts rush through his mind. He couldn't figure out how he ended up this way. He was once considered so close to Jah, and now he had found himself in the company of an Amber. He was the first to be deceived and had helped spread this new word -- this new way of thinking, the way that twisted the Writ and the true word of Jah. He realized he was filling people's heads with false wisdom.

Theiler played the words of his son's meditation in his head and compared it to the words of the original Writ:

"And he who has faith in Jah has been given the power to manifest spirit from the gifts given to us by Him, and brings into themselves power that will surpass the limits of the physical body. You shall surely connect with the spiritual world (Writ 212: 201 – 202)."

In the Book of Veritas, there was no mention of Jah. "Son?" Theiler asked. "You believe in everything you found out from the device?"

"Yes, the device and the Writ." There was a long pause before Cadmael continued, "I'm beginning to grow a little frustrated with those who don't understand that it takes both the Writ and the knowledge of the device to manifest your full powers. It should be evident that I've tapped into something amazing. I have fulfilled what those who have studied the Writ for years could not. You and I have been helping others do the same thing, but yet, it appears that you continue to question our work."

"Your words...where did they come from? How did the device guide you to them?" Theiler's curiosity flooded his mind with questions he was dying to know the answer to. They were questions he now realized he should've asked a long time ago.

Cadmael was frustrated. He made every attempt to be respectful to his father, but it was growing difficult. Cadmael grabbed the wood he collected earlier and started piling it to make a fire. His response was sharp. "I asked the device to tell me how I could have power. The images I saw were so real that I had no doubt I was experiencing the truth of the Second World. I asked the device to show me the way and it displayed images of people who worshipped the Earth, celebrated the trees, and brought forth the spirits that live in nature. I saw people elevated and idolized by other people and they were lifted up high. They achieved great levels of success in the Second World. They had great influence and I knew I wanted that same power. The more I asked the device things, the more it told me, and I realized then that knowledge is power. The reason why Jah is respected is because He holds all the knowledge. But I want to put the power back in the hands of the people!"

Although Cadmael sounded convincing, Theiler knew in his heart that what his son was saying was wrong. Theiler continued to listen as Cadmael spoke.

"What do you think we've been doing all this time?"

Theiler was speechless. Cadmael continued. "Jah wants you to believe it's by His might alone, but it's about more than just Him. That is what the Book of Veritas is all about."

After several moments of silence, Theiler finally spoke. "We have unknowingly started a war between those who believe the words of The Writ and those who believe the Book of Veritas."

Cadmael stopped throwing around firewood and walked over to his father, placed his arm around him, and whispered, "Then they need to be prepared to fight." Cadmael grabbed the blankets that were on the ground, turned around, and began to set up their sleeping arrangements. Theiler grew deeply concerned for both him and his son.

As nightfall rolled in, the light of the fire kept them warm but Theiler was restless. Theiler meditated and waited to receive vision. He asked Jah for something, anything that would let him know what to do. Jah did not respond. Theiler, once one of the wisest visionaries of his village, received nothing.

He meditated to Jah in hopes that He'd validate what he was doing, instead of meditating for direction and guidance. He wanted to be told that what he was doing was okay instead of doing what was just and right by Jah. Jah had no sympathy for Theiler's outpouring of emotion, as He could see that Theiler wasn't repenting, nor desiring forgiveness. The spirit of Jah had been with Theiler since he was a boy. Theiler knew right from wrong but chose to turn away. Like a father, Jah knew that He could not step in and answer every cry from him. This was a lesson that Theiler would have to learn on his own, so Jah remained silent.

41.
Stop

When morning came, Theiler hesitantly joined his son and continued their mission. He didn't know why he had decided to continue. Was it because Jah was silent and so disappointed with his actions that what he did no longer seemed to concern him, or did he feel the pressure of helping his son? Regardless, Theiler and Cadmael went back to Siomon to recruit more followers.

Jendahi made it to as many houses as she could before morning. She went door to door warning Siomonites about the visitors from Eirene. Theiler and Cadmael, with the Book of Veritas in hand, began knocking on doors as well. They came to a house located a few doors down from Jendahi's. A man answered the door and immediately told them to leave, quoting scriptures from the Writ. They moved on to the next house. They were dismissed there as well. Each door they knocked on gave the same scripture: "Those who are deceived by the light of the Ambers will take pleasure in the riches of the Earth. But when the end comes, they will be stripped of their Earthly riches and pulled down into the fires of hell (Writ 212:112)."

Hearing that scripture for the second time convicted Theiler. He grabbed his son's arm and tugged.

"Cadmael, my son, we cannot continue to do this. We're not fulfilling the will of Jah. Last night, I meditated to Jah and He didn't respond. This was the first time in my life where He didn't send me vision. I realize now it's because I'm no longer connected to Him. You are no longer connected to Him. You've removed Jah from the word and have filled it with desires to glorify yourself. You've exalted the power of the Earth above Him."

Cadmael and Theiler didn't realize they were making a scene in the middle of the street. A few onlookers were standing by. Jendahi, who was in her house, could hear the commotion and came outside.

"You know what, father? I've had enough of your insolence!"

Theiler watched as Cadmael began to glow in his Amber light. It grew more vibrant and the shape of his body became blurred.

"We must stop and repent now, Cadmael! You heard the scripture. We will burn in hell's fires if we don't!"

Cadmael could not contain his rage any longer. He charged at his father. His Amber glow intensified his strength. He reached for a barrel of water that was nearby and hurled it at his father, knocking him unconscious.

Many people stood around, but were too afraid to intervene. They watched as Theiler opened one eye and rolled over on his back, grunting. He dizzly sat up, struggling to get his bearings.

Cadmael wasted no time. He grabbed a particularly sharp piece of firewood from nearby and thrust it violently into his father's chest. Theiler gasped and looked up at his son in shock and utter disbelief. He coughed up blood, struggling for his last breath before falling to the ground.

Everything from that point seemed to happen in slow motion. Jendahi screamed. She felt a loss of what to do next, as the shock from what just happened left her feeling paralyzed. She was eventually able to make it to her house to send word to Athirst and Cearney about the tragedy.

Meanwhile, the village was chaos. People fled the scene in a panic, bolting their doors and drawing their curtains. The town was a wreck.

Cadmael, realizing what he had done, changed back into human form. He fled, fearing that the people of Siomon would find and kill him.

Cadmael decided to take refuge in the forests miles away from Simon and Eirene. He removed himself from civilization and stayed among the trees for a year. During that time, he feed himself off of wildberries which caused hallucinations and he became a madman. He read the Book of Veritas by the daylight in a feeble attempt to comfort himself, and he meditated to the powers of all that were in the Earth. At night he practiced rituals that he learned from the device and became one with the world.

42.
One Year of Peace (Athirst and Cearney)

During the year that Cadmael went into hiding, the village of Eirene was notified of what happened in Siomon. Cearney was the first to get word. Her sister had written a letter warning her about the evil that she had witnessed. News of all that happened in Siomon quickly found its way to the neighboring villages. People had mixed responses in regard to what happened. When some of them heard the news that Cadmael was able to show his light before any of the other villagers, they put down the Writ and began reading from the Book of Veritas, completely disregarding the fact that Cadmael murdered his own father. They were envious and wanted Cadmael's same ability. Their minds were opened to the secrets that the device had given to Cadmael and they fell away from Jah.

Others, however, immediately began to meditate and read the Writ more intensely. They desired more strength and wisdom from Jah because they knew that war was imminent. Athirst tried to buckle down and focus on the Writ, but Theiler's death rattled him. "First Governess, now Theiler!" Athirst cried out to Jah. "How did it come to this?" He could not believe that his friend was gone. He was even more shocked that his life was taken by his own son. Flashbacks of them as children constantly ran through his mind. It was clear that a dark force was now present in the Third World and he knew that he must put it to an end.

"Athirst, are you okay? You haven't come out of here for nearly two days," Cearney said as she walked into their bedroom. The room was dark and filled with an eerie silence.

"Cearney, I can't believe that two people I grew up with are now gone. This can't go on. I feel like I need to do something."

"But what can we do?" She sat next to him and rubbed his back.

"I don't know, but this is much bigger than a hurt boy trying to get people to understand him. He murdered his own father! It seems like whatever he learned from the device has unleashed something evil, and now he's spreading the information he learned to everyone he comes into contact with. He has to be stopped."

"I agree, but how do you plan on doing that? I've heard that he went into hiding. We may not have anything to worry about anymore."

"I wish that were true, but he's reached a lot of people. Something's telling me that we need to prepare for war."

Athirst thought it best to leave Ugo to watch over the other children so that he and Cearney could travel from village to village to help others strengthen their connection to Jah. His goal was to create a group of allies in case of battle. Jah kept sending Athirst visions of a spirit war, but he wasn't sure when it would occur.

"Ugo, we need to speak with you!" Cearney called out to Ugo, who had just woken up.

"Yes mother?" Ugo replied. He rubbed his eyes to focus on his mother.

"As you know, your father and I have done a lot of work here in Eirene making sure the word of Jah isn't lost, but now Jah had demanded more of us. We need to travel to other villages to rally allies. Your father and I keep seeing visions of war."

"I've foreseen them, too," Ugo responded.

"So, then you know how serious this is. We must go." She paused for a moment.

"It's up to you to look after your siblings. Anah, Triston, and Romilda are old enough to help out with a lot of the work here..." Cearney looked around and began to whisper. "...Ilianna is a bit...difficult...so you may need to make sure that she makes it to lessons in time."

"You would've never let me get away with half the things she does when I was her age."

"I'm serious, Ugo. You're in charge now."

"Okay, mother! I'll do whatever you need me to do."

"We plan on leaving in a few days. I will speak to your brother and sisters to let them know they need to help you out around the house and in the village. In the meantime, I really want you to make sure that you pray, meditate, and read the Writ." Cearney gave him a kiss on the forehead.

Three days later, Ugo rose early to make sure he saw his parents off. He tried to remain hopeful that they'd be successful in their mission.

During their travels, Athirst and Cearney could see the effects of The Book of Veritas' influence. Cadmael's words took root in the hearts of all who read it. When Athirst and Cearney arrived to the villages of those who had been exposed, they discovered that many had abandoned all they knew of the Writ.

Athirst and Cearney traveled up a mountain on the backs of Swift and Nimble. As they went up the mountain, it grew cold and blistery. Eventually they reached Inber. They witnessed a sparring match taking place in the town square. Two men were fighting with spears made of ice. Athirst and Cearney slowed down to watch the match before being approached by a local.

"You two aren't from around here. My name's Shalum." Shalum stuck a large, hairy hand out to greet the visitors. He had a beard that nearly reached his thick, brown leather belt that was holding up his black pants. Athirst had to look up to make eye contact with him.

"Nice to meet you. My name's Athirst. This is my union-mate, Cearney. You all spar as well, I see. We do something similar in Eirene, but we don't have those fierce-looking ice spears."

"Did you say Eirene?"

"Yes," Athrist replied. He could see Shalum's warm greeting turn just as cold as the weather.

"You're the reason why everyone's divided. Your village brought a book that has torn our entire village apart."

"I promise we didn't do this. We're here to help." Athirst got nervous when he heard the giant man call out to one of the men who was sparring. "Hiemal, stop what you're doing! Here's the man that has doomed us all! He's the one you should be fighting." Immediately Hiemal began charging toward Athirst. Cearney screamed and Athirst put his hand up and motioned for the man to calm down. "Wait, please!"

Hiemal paused mid-stride, eager to pummel the man before him.

"It wasn't me! I promise. I'm a man of Jah. I have not come to cause discord," Athirst pleaded.

"Then why are you here?" Hiemal boomed.

"A...a man named Theiler and his son may have visited you and showed you a book that contradicts the Writ. We have come to get things back on track."

Hiemal held his ice spear close. "It's too late. Nothing can get us back on track. That book tore my family apart. Cantus, my mate, read the book before I got the chance to. When I saw her change, I asked her to put the book down and return to Jah, but she did not. She continued to read the book night and day. Then, one morning, she said she didn't have anything in common with me anymore. She had given the book to another man--that man," Hiemal said, pointing to the man he was sparring with.

"And now --" Hiemal continued, "-- she's left me for him! This falls on the shoulders of the people of Eirene." Hiemal pointed the spear in Athirst's direction.

Cearney stepped forward. "Put your spear down. It does not fall on the shoulders of our people and most certainly does not fall on the shoulders of my husband! It is the fault of one misguided boy and his father. We've come to make peace and to rally people to fight in the name of our God, Jah."

Hiemal saw truth in Cearney's eyes and put his spear down. "It is best if you leave. Our village has been torn apart because of this book; it might be too late to make amends with my people now. You won't find many allies here."

Athirst and Cearney left disheartened. They wanted to turn those who were lost back to Jah, but they were met with indifference. They meditated to Jah and he told them to avoid certain villages because they would most certainly be killed.

Jah protected Athirst and Cearney and gave them guidance as to what villages they were to visit. Many of them were introduced to the Book of Veritas, but it had not yet been meditated on. They were able to convert those hearts back to Jah.

When Athirst and Cearney arrived at the village of Atar, it was clear that Cadmael had already been there. From the looks of it, the village was divided.

"I remember coming here with Sophos a few times," Athirst told Cearney. As he spoke, a beautiful Atarian woman walked past. "I see why you made an effort to join him during his travels," Cearney smiled slyly.

Athirst blushed, scrambling to find the right words to say. "You know I only have eyes for you, my love."

Just as they were beginning to feel comfortable enough to find a place for the night, they heard someone yelling.

"Seriously, you're charging for cinnamon now?" A young Atarian was standing near a trade post. "You've never charged for spices before."

"Yes, well, I need your money or you won't be able to take this with you," another villager replied.

As Athirst and Cearney kept walking, they saw a series of large fires. They gradually drew closer to the flames to see what was happening.

"What's going on here?" Cearney asked a bystander.

"A few of the teen Youths set fire to the house of their magisters because they were making them learn verses from the Writ!"

"Why on earth would they do such a thing?"

"They believe the Writ is limiting their powers. They have chosen to study from the Book of Veritas," The Atarian replied. "My name is Xar-Ann." She shook Cearney's hand. "And who are you?"

"My name is Cearney, and this is Athirst, my union-mate. Nice to meet you. We were afraid that we wouldn't be greeted so warmly."

A tall, dark man with a bald head came to join them. "Here is my mate, Logicist," Xar-Ann gestured toward him.

"Greetings, friend. We're from Eirene," Athirst said as he approached Logicist, who was clearly a man of great physical strength. Athirst reached out to shake his hand, but his display of kindness was not returned.

"Eirene. It is your people who caused this division in our village. You must leave now. You are not welcome here."

"I understand your distrust of us, but please don't take the actions of a few and associate them with the entire village. The people of Eirene respect the Writ and the words of Jah. We have come to support your efforts to bring people back to the Writ. I have been here before with my Elder, Sophos." Athirst put his hand out once more.

"Sophos was your Elder? I knew him from when he'd come to trade with us all the time. He's a good man."

"He taught me not to stray from the Writ. He made me who I am."

Logicist gave him a doubtful look, but eventually returned the handshake with a firm, strong grip. He eventually turned his attention toward Cearney. "Please forgive me for my rudeness; I've been fighting battles ever since the visitors from Eirene left.

A few of the younger Atarians got hold of the Book of Veritas and they've revolted against the teachings from the Magisters."

The four of them gazed at the fires. "This is terrible. What are you going to do?"

"We cannot collect enough water to put out all of the fires," Xar-Ann said worriedly.

"Right now, we're housing the Magisters with us until we can figure out the next steps," Logicist said, scratching his head.

"Well, we're here to help, whatever you need. Hopefully we can reverse at least some of the damage," Cearney offered.

"Unless you have an unlimited source of water, I'm not sure you can do much," Logicist said. "They will burn down every house of those who follow Jah within the next few days if we don't figure something out."

Cearney turned to Athirst, "I think I know how we may be able to help." She pulled Athirst's sleeve. "Excuse us." Cearney pulled Athirst to the side and spoke to him quietly. "Inber. Let's see if we can get someone from there to help us!"

"Did you see how that man wanted to stab me with the ice spear? I don't think we're welcome there, and I especially don't think they'll be receptive to our plea for help."

"You may think that way, but the people there are just hurt and scared. Let me go -- maybe I can try to convince them." Cearney gazed intently at Athirst.

"I cannot let you go alone."

"Athirst, it will be fine. I trust that Jah will protect me. If..."

"What if she is not alone?" Xar-Ann asked suddenly, overhearing their conversation. "What if she goes with me?"

All four of them were quiet for a minute. "Logicist, we need their help. We cannot afford any more of our village to be burned down," Xar-Ann reminded him.

Logicist sighed. "I guess we don't really have a choice."

The four of them came together and prayed for protection over the two women. When they finished, Cearney and Xar-Ann prepared for their journey.

"It'll be bitterly cold when we make the journey up the mountain...you might have to wear something different," Cearney said. Xar-Ann looked down at her outfit, which barely covered her body. "So, this won't work?" The women laughed. Before leaving, Athirst trained Xar-Ann to ride his wolf and Cearney found clothing for her traveling companion. The women set off, heading up the mountain.

They traveled most of the night. "You were right. It is freezing," Xar-Ann said, shivering.

Eventually they arrived at the center of the village of Inber. "My goodness. These are the most peculiar houses I've seen. They're made of ice?" Xar-Ann was mesmerized by all of the buildings and sculptures that surrounded them. "Where is the man you said can help us?"

"I don't know. Look for an extremely large man with a thick, dirty brown beard."

Xar-Ann and Cearney looked around. "There he is. Look." Cearney pointed to a man who was creating ice spears by pointing his hands out. Water ejected from his palms, and within seconds he had created several weapons.

"Hiemal!" Cearney waved to get his attention. "It's Cearney, from Eirene. My husband and I visited here. Do you remember me?"

"Yes, why are you here?" He said without turning around.

"We've come because we need your help."

Hiemal never responded. He kept working to shape his spears. Xar-Ann got off the wolf and walked up to Hiemal. "Look, we're desperate. In my village, the Youth are burning down the houses of anyone who teaches or reads the Writ. They're trying to get everyone to follow the Book of Veritas."

Hiemal stopped working on his spear and looked at Xar-Ann and Cearney.

"So this is happening in your village as well? I'm sorry, but I'm afraid I don't know how I'm supposed to help."

"Well," Cearney said, glancing at the ice spears, "we were hoping you could use your powers of manipulating water and ice to put out the fires."

"I'm desperate!" Xar-Ann pleaded. "We are desperate. This is not just about our village. This is about protecting the word of Jah."

"Well..." Hiemal paused for several seconds before responding. He sighed and scratched his head. "...there's nothing left for me here anyway. So, I guess I can help you."

"You'll go?" Cearney asked.

"I saw the truth in your eyes when I first met you. I was just too disheartened to do anything." Hiemal then turned to Xar-Ann and said, "I can hear the desperation in your voice. I can tell that your desire to protect the word of Jah is strong. It would be an honor to fight alongside you."

Hiemal packed nothing. He followed the two ladies all the way to the village of Atar. He traveled by shooting ice from the palms of his hands and gliding on top of the ice path he created.

They made it to the village as fast as they could. "Our house is this way." Xar-Ann took them to her home, where Athirst was sleeping on the couch in the living room. Hiemal had to duck down to fit through the door. The sounds of his footsteps woke Athirst, who sat up, startled at the large man looming over him.

Heimal looked at Athirst. "I am sorry that I nearly killed you earlier, but is there anyway that you can scoot over so I can have a seat?"

Athirst ran over to Cearney. "I can't believe it! You actually did it."

Hearing all of the commotion, Logicist came into the room. "What is all of the noise about?"

"We got help," Xar-Ann said triumphantly. "Now we can put out all the fires."

Logicist, who was used to being the largest person in the village, looked Hiemal up and down. "You weren't lying. He is a giant." Logicist then looked at all of them. Well what are we all sitting around for? Let's put his gifts to the test!"

Logicist, Hiemal, and the others and headed to the side of the village where most of the houses were located. They were just in time. Five more houses were ablaze. A group of young Atarians were taking a long wooden branch with hay and dried leaves on top and lighting it on fire. They were headed toward the last standing Magister's house.

"Stop!" Logicist commanded.

"Or what?" One of the Youths yelled back.

Heimal put his hands out, spraying water on all of the young Atarians, which then froze them into place. Athirst and Cearney's animals guarded the frozen figures while the rest of them moved from house to house.

Heimal then turned toward the burning houses, using his powers to control the blaze. After the fires had died down a bit, the group paired off and went into different houses to find any survivors in need of help.

They were able to rescue several people from the flames, but with every person they rescued a body was found as well.

The group took the rescued Atarians back to the house of Logicist. Many of them were injured or had difficulty breathing. Cearney whipped out various bottles and ointments and began providing aid to all of the hurt men and women.

It was a long night for them. Although lives were lost, they were able to sleep a little easier knowing that they had rescued several people. After tending to the wounded, they along with other Atarians helped honor the dead and gave them proper burials.

The next morning, each of them checked on the wounded Atarians. "Cearney, look." Athirst pulled the coverings off one person's scars. They were virtually nonexistent.

"Simply amazing!" Xar-Ann commented in awe.

They all looked at each other. "We make a pretty good team," Logicist said, cracking a small smile.

"You all rest here. We saved you from the fire, but there is more work to be done," Athirst said to the villagers.

Athirst, Logicist, Hiemal, Cearney, and Xar-Ann prayed and meditated together before heading out to begin their mission work.

The group went from door to door in Atar and were able to convert many hearts back to Jah. On the next full moon, they made sure that all who were committed to Jah sacrificed devices. The Potentiam Libertas celebrations in Atar were extremely similar to the festivals held in Eirene. The feelings of joy and devotion were the same, but the smells were slightly different. As opposed to Eirene, where villagers typically feasted on Chinook Salmon, Atar instead preferred roast pig, rubbed in all sorts of savory, exotic spices. Instead of woodwind instruments, the Atarians seemed to prefer percussion. They danced around the fire, banging drums and tambourines.

"It's good to see so many here sacrificing devices tonight. I truly appreciate you and Cearney coming to help guide so many back to Jah. I thank you." Logicist shook Athirst's hand.

Hiemal joined in the conversation. "Seeing the work done here has inspired me to keep persevering in Inber. I will go back there tomorrow and see who I can rally together. I am sorry I misjudged your intentions," Heimel said, mainly directing his words toward Athirst.

"If it wasn't for you, none of this would have even been possible," Logicist said to Heimal, patting his back.

"Agreed. I know we got off to a rough start, but what's important is that we figured staying true to Jah was our primary goal." Athirst tried to pat Heimal on the back, but decided to settle for a handshake. "I really hate that Cearney and I will have to leave soon."

"Yes, well, I think I can take it from here. Besides, there's many other villages in need of your support," Logicist said.

Cearney and Athirst rested for one last night in Atar before heading north. They mounted Swift and Nimble, who carried them for many days before eventually growing tired and taking refuge in the village of Divinity. Athirst and Cearney both went to a quiet place and meditated. They fell on their knees and asked Jah for strength to complete the task given to them.

Jah looked at them with love and was pleased with their work. That night while meditating, they both received their colors. It wasn't long before Athirst noticed a gentle, teal-blue glow radiating from Cearney. The color teal represented peace, protection, and healing. The light emitting from his own body was the color of silver. He immediately remembered the vision he received as a young boy with the mercury-colored tree and the five branches. He was consumed with joy and elated that Jah had rewarded his obedience with the color that signified a natural-born leader.

A euphoric zeal consumed them as they looked at each other's glow. The form of their bodies seemed to dissipate and transform into a weightless, floating spirit. Athirst was overcome with love for his mate and she felt the same toward him. Their love resulted in the first child ever conceived in spirit. Cearney and Athirst remained in Divinity until Aurum was born since it was safe for them there. Cearney had desperately wanted to go back to Eirene so Aurum could be born there, but Athirst received a vision.

"Why can't we go back now?" Cearney begged. She was due any day now and wanted to see her other children.

"Jah sent me a vision letting me know that if we leave now, we will lose Divinity to the Book of Veritas. His book is far reaching, and we cannot afford to lose any allies."

Cearney reluctantly agreed.

43.
One Year of Peace (Ugo)

Ugo and his siblings received several letters letting them know of their parents' accomplishments in the different villages.

Other letters gave the exact number of people that were reconnected to Jah. Each time they sent a letter with those numbers Ugo would keep track. By the end of the year, Athirst and Ceareny were able to reinforce unbreakable connections with 444,000 individuals from the villages they visited, a total of seven villages in all. Ugo was happy that his mother and father were able to do such great work for Jah, but felt that he wasn't making the same amount of progress in Eirene.

It was late in the evening. The only audible sound you could hear was crickets chirping somewhere in the distance. Ugo was troubled. It was then that Jah sent him a vision. The land was bare until the rains came. Then, all of the seeds planted in the ground began to grow. They sprouted up quickly and covered the bare land with grass and other low-lying vegetation, but one seed did not grow. It hadn't found the right soil.

Other dirt tried to sustain it, but the desire for proper soil did not go away. The wind blew the seed around. Rain eventually carried it away, and it found itself on rough patches of grass or gravel.

It was when all of the low-lying vegetation began to die and return to the Earth that the soil became rich enough for the seed to take root. The seed then grew to be a giant Sequoia that provided shade to all that lived underneath its branches. It also dropped many more seeds of its kind, and soon there was a forest.

When Ugo awoke from the vision, he understood that it was foreshadowing his potential. He realized that he needed to be placed in the proper circumstances to show the fullness of his gifts, and until that time, he needed to be patient.

The next morning, Ugo worked to remove the sadness from his heart. He walked out of the small house and into the sunlight, closing his eyes and directing his face towards the sun to feel its warmth. He could hear the rustling of small animals that were scurrying around, looking for food. The sounds of the birds chirping seemed to center him, and a peace came over him as images from the vision replayed in his head.

One day, as Ugo walked toward River Aesis, he saw Jabari with Fortis and Stultus as well as Theiler's daughters. It made him remember Governess' death, the night that Cadmael gave his speech at the Potentiam Libertas celebration, the events in Atar, and how Cadmael killed Theiler. Ugo felt for Jabari and Nia, who ended up being the permanent caretakers of Theiler's other children.

"Hello brother, I haven't seen you in a while." Ugo realized how good it felt to see Jabari. Jabari quickly returned the greeting.

"How have things been with you?" Jabari asked in a manner that let Ugo know he wanted to move past formalities to discuss something else.

"I'm not going to lie; it's been really difficult with my mother and father going to villages to help others with vision." Ugo hoped his response would allow Jabari to see that they still had something in common.

"I understand," Jabari responded. "I've had quite a tough time myself. I thought I would be watching Theiler's youngest girls for just a short while, but now…"

"It's so hard for me to believe that Cadmael could…" Ugo cut his sentence short, knowing Jabari and Theiler's family had a close bond.

"I know. I heard that he went mad eating wild berries. Do you think that's what made him kill Theiler?" Jabari's efforts to blame Cadmael's actions on anything other than his new beliefs frustrated Ugo.

"No. I think we both know what happened," Ugo responded, rolling his eyes. He wasn't shocked that Jabari would try to make excuses for Cadmael. After Jabari was introduced to the Book of Veritas, he practically worshiped the ground that Cadmael walked on.

"Besides," Ugo continued, "I heard he didn't start eating the wild berries until after his father's death. Maybe that was his way of coping with what he did."

"Well Ugo, all I know is that they treated me and my family well."

"I don't doubt it. I miss my friend, though. I don't know what happened to Cadmael. It's like he became a different person after he found the device and wrote his book."

Jabari interrupted him. "I know you don't believe in the Book of Veritas, but he makes so many good points."

Jabari continued, "The Writ seemed so difficult for me to understand, but his book -- it seemed to bridge the gap between the world I was taken from and the Third World, where we are now. I've been able to read it every day and gain new understanding about things that I didn't know or understand before. Fortis and Stultus even began reading it and Fortis was able to show an expression of light. It was a dim light and it was difficult to tell his color, but it was light nonetheless. I have to be honest; I know that I am not the wisest person in the village. I know that my children are not, either. What we have is our physical strength. But to see that Fortis was able to connect to the Earth in a way that brought forth a visual sign of spirit... it made me proud."

"Jabari, aren't you concerned that they may be learning how to connect to a spirit they shouldn't connect to? The Elders spoke of the false glow of the Ambers and yet there are so many that still choose to follow in their ways."

"I'm offended that you're suggesting we're following the light of the Ambers. I thought you would be happy for me. All I wanted to do was make Theiler proud. I wanted to let him know that I was carrying out his plan in spite of his passing, and here you are dismissing my efforts."

Jabari took Theiler's children home. Fortis followed, but Stultus stayed behind and waited until everyone was out of earshot. She walked over to Ugo and whispered, "Do you mind if we meet tomorrow at sunrise by the portion of River Aesis where we gather our drinking water?"

"Of course not," Ugo responded. Stultus smiled and quickly ran off to catch up with her family.

The next morning, Stultus met Ugo by the river at sunrise and they discussed the meaning of the Writ. It was clear that Stultus was committed to chase after the power of Jah, and Ugo helped her become better at interpreting vision.

"I'm afraid, Ugo. I'm afraid that I would be going against Jah if I continue to study from the Book of Veritas. Something just feels wrong about it to me, but I don't know what else to do."

"It's okay. I understand. We'll just take this one step at a time. You're already in the right place and Jah knows your heart."

It seemed as if Ugo was noticing Stultus for the very first time. Her vulnerability in wanting to know Jah more was endearing. When Stultus and Ugo used to take lessons together, she just seemed like one of the guys. She was rough like her twin brother and Ugo constantly saw them wrestle and jump on each other.

Stultus was built similar to her father. She still had broad shoulders and a much more angular body than many of the other women in Eirene, but from the time since they were kids she lost a lot of her baby fat and her striking features were more accentuated. Her face resembled Nia's delicate beauty, in a way.

Nonetheless, it was often hidden by her wild, stringy locks that she apparently still refused to brush.

Ugo felt comfortable around her. Stultus made him feel like he had some value; some worth. He was grateful to Jah for it.

"I hope I'm not bothering you. I don't want to take up all of your time as I know that you have a lot more to take care of now," Stultus said.

"No, it's fine. It's actually a nice distraction from all of the mundane chores of running a family. I mean, my siblings help out a lot, but there is still much to do."

"Well, I'm not much for helping around the house, but I am a great hunter," Stultus said, perking up.

"Oh really? I don't believe I've ever seen you go hunting for anything more than devices."

"As big as my family is, don't you think we all know how to fend for ourselves?"

"I guess that's true. I haven't had much time to hunt these days. I typically get food from whoever is cooking in the community kitchen."

Stultus chuckled.

"Why is that so funny?"

"My father told me a lot of stories about his growing up. He told me about Sophos and how he was always hanging around the community kitchen trying to sneak food. Just found it funny that he passed on that trait to you."

"I hadn't thought about it like that." Ugo had a smile on his face. Stultus' comment made him feel more connected to Sophos in some way.

"Remember the time that your brother was chanting that song?" Ugo laughed as he reminisced.

"Oh my goodness, that seems like forever ago. I was so irritated with him."

"Nothing wrong with it if you ask me."

"My brother always finds a way to embarrass me, but I love him. I love him and my father, but I'm really afraid for them."

"What about your mother?" Ugo asked.

"She believes they are doing the wrong thing as well. She hasn't touched the Book of Veritas, but my father keeps pressuring her to read it. To be honest, this is the most I have ever seen them fight."

"I am sorry Stultus. It is like the knowledge from the device and Cadmael's book has changed everyone that comes in contact with it." Ugo could see that Stultus was a little upset. He opened his arms to give her a hug. She returned his hug with a strong squeeze that nearly pushed all the wind out of his lungs. That is when he remembered that she was much larger than him.

"Thanks for listening to me Ugo. Same time tomorrow?"

"Yep, same time tomorrow." They looked at each other for a few seconds, feeling awkward.

"Well, I guess it's time for me to go. I don't want my family to get suspicious and think I actually like hanging around you," Stultus said, blushing. Ugo watched as she ran off.

With each passing day, Ugo grew more excited to see her. He was thankful that she was willing to forsake the Book of Veritas and was humbled by the power that Jah had given him to bring at least one back to the original Writ.

Ugo's gratefulness and humility was very pleasing to Jah and Jah rewarded him. One early morning, before the sun was fully over the horizon, Ugo went to his quiet place in the East Gardens to meditate. Suddenly, his physical body transformed into spirit and he began to glow in the color of jade, since Jah saw his gift for teaching.

Ugo and Stultus continued to meet by River Aesis for many moons. In fact, on mornings when they didn't meet, Ugo felt things were amiss. He hadn't realized that the innocent bond between the two of them had shifted into something more.

Ugo, the son of the great Athirst and Stultus, the daughter of the unwise Jabari seemed to be an unlikely pairing. When he was younger, Ugo would have never picked someone like Stultus. Now, Ugo no longer saw her as the daughter of Jabari or the sister of Fortis; he saw her as her own person.

It wouldn't be long before Ugo received vision confirming his desire to unify with Stultus, but the time for him to proclaim his love had not yet come. He had to wait until she displayed her light, and only then could he know if she was truly the one.

44.
Stultus Displays Her Light

Stultus was on her way out of the house early one morning when she saw her father and Fortis reading the Book of Veritas.

"Where are you going?" Jabari demanded. He had his suspicions about her whereabouts for quite some time, but between the arguments with Nia and his desire to learn the Book of Veritas, he chose not to make a big deal out of her absence.

"She's probably going to see Ugo. I always knew she liked him," Fortis said with a grin on his face.

"You sure go visit with him a lot. Is there something that you want me to know?" Jabari asked.

Fortis started laughing.

"Shut up, Fortis," Stultus said, rolling her eyes. "Besides, what's so wrong if I visit with him a lot?"

"I think Ugo is nice, but he has different beliefs than we do now," Jabari pointed out.

"No, father! His beliefs have always been the same. It is you who has strayed. I've stayed true to the Writ. That is why I've been seeing Ugo. He's helping me understand the Writ and I get it. I'm learning more every day. I can help you, too."

"I don't need any help, Stultus." Jabari was offended. Fortis stopped laughing and grew silent when he noticed the tension in the room.

"Yes you do, father. I'm scared that if you don't turn back to Jah, something terrible will happen!" Stultus cried.

Before Jabari could even think, he lifted his hand and wacked Stultus across the face. "If you want to dishonor me, then you can go!"

"But father!" Stultus pleaded, crying.

"Leave now!" Jabari demanded.

Stultus had never seen her father like this before. Nia, overhearing the argument, walked into the room and stood between them, shielding her daughter.

"Jabari, that is enough! It's one thing for you and I to have our disagreements, but it's another for you to put your hands on my child for doing what is right in the eyes of Jah!"

Stultus was in the background still sobbing while Nia had gotten nearly inches away from Jabari's face. "Is that what you wanted to do to me? You think you can control me through violence and sheer force just because I don't obey you every time you ask me to read this stupid book? You are nothing more than a coward!"

Jabari lifted his hand. His eyes were full of anger and his body trembled. He lowered his hand. "Go, both of you! Get out of here and don't come back!"

Cecile flew around Nia and Stultus as they walked out the door, almost as if to shame or mock them. "Don't come back, Don't come back, Squawk"

Stultus and Nia left the house with nothing more than the clothes on their backs. Nia hopped on Nova. They trotted beside Stultus, who was on foot and heading to the river to meet Ugo.

Ugo was sitting on a rock waiting for his usual meet-up with Stultus. When he saw her, his face lit up, but his smile slowly faded as he saw both Stultus and Nia approach.

"What's wrong?"

Stultus' eyes were bloodshot and puffy. She tried to gain her composure, but could not stop crying.

"What happened?" Ugo asked gently.

"I'll tell you what happened, Ugo. Whatever is in that book has made Jabari lose his mind," Nia said as she jumped off her deer. "I knew that he and I were having our issues, but I never thought that he would turn on Stultus the way he did. I don't think we can stay there any longer."

"My father hit me. He put us out of the house for continuing to learn the Writ." Stultus tried to muffle her sobs.

"You've got to be kidding me! I can't imagine Jabari putting you out of the house for something as innocent as that!" Ugo was astonished.

Stultus rested her head on Ugo's shoulder. Tears soaked his sleeve. Nia came behind her and embraced her daughter.

"Why don't you both stay with me until my mother and father return?" Ugo suggested.

"Thank you so much Ugo. That is very kind of you," Nia replied. "Well, I'm sure you were not expecting me, so I'll give you two a little time alone. I need to clear my head anyway." Nia whistled for Nova, who was nibbling on wildflowers. She came running over. Nia hopped on her back and they trotted away.

"You know what you need to do right?" Ugo asked Stultus who was still whimpering.

"I don't know what to do right now. It feels like everything is falling apart."

"Stultus, I know that it feels bad right now, but Jah knew this day would come. It's going to get better.""

Stultus wiped her tears away. "Do you really think so?"

"I know so. What should you do in a situation like this? What does the Writ tell us to do?"

"It tells us to meditate." Stultus gathered her composure, took a few deep breaths, and wiped the tears from her eyes. "I am going to thank Jah for giving me the strength to walk away." Stultus got into meditative position with Ugo following suit. They sat face down for several minutes before something disrupted Ugo's concentration. When he opened his eyes he saw Stultus glowing with a brilliant blue light, but she was too focused on meditation to notice.

"Stultus, look!" Ugo nudged her.

She opened her eyes and then glanced down at her body. She was ecstatic. She finally received confirmation from Jah about her purpose.

Ugo gazed at her magnificence and without a second thought, he immediately asked her to unify with him.

When she heard this, she lost concentration and reverted to her human form. Nearly breathless and overcome with emotion, Stultus asked, "What did you just say?"

"Will you unify with me?" Ugo repeated.

Stultus, still trying to calm herself, beamed. "Of course I will Ugo." She ran off excitedly in search of her mother, leaving Ugo standing there alone. Ugo could do nothing but chuckle.

When Athirst and Cearney received a letter from Ugo about his union with Stultus, they returned to Eirene with baby Aurum. Ugo and his siblings were elated to see them.

"My goodness, it feels like it has been forever."

Romilda and Anah ran up to their mother. Then Anah grabbed baby Aurum out of their mother's hand.

"He's so cute!"

"Let me hold him," Romilda said to her mother.

Triston and Illiana ran up to Athirst. "I thought I was supposed to be your last baby," Illiana said, crossing her arms.

"You will always be my baby." Athirst gave his now thirteen year old daughter a kiss on her forehead.

"How was your trip? What did you see? How are the other villages?" Cearney and Athirst were bombarded with questions. Meanwhile, Nia and Stultus came from around the corner.

"Nia, Stultus!" Cearney ran over them and gave them hugs. "How are you doing?"

"We are doing alright, considering... I'm sure Ugo has filled you in on what happened with Jabari. But Ugo and the rest of the children have been wonderful to let us stay here," Nia replied.

They all sat down in the living room and spent most of the night catching up. Before going to bed, they discussed the union ceremony. Stultus blushed as they discussed the details. Nia and Cearney couldn't help but get excited about possible dress colors and flowers. Ugo and his father discussed the task of building a house for them to live in after the ceremony.

The union ceremony between Ugo and Stultus was one of the most memorable events in Eirene. They unified by River Aesis since they had spent so much time there together. They were also the first couple to unify in the colors of their light. Their glow illuminated the evening sky and reflected off the gentle ripples of the river as they read the sacred scriptures of the Writ. Those who witnessed the ceremony were so moved by seeing Ugo and Stultus in their colors, that they too displayed their light. Stultus was so happy that she didn't pay much attention to her father's absence.

45.
Colors

Eventually, more and more people had began to display their light, each wondering when the mysterious Gold One would emerge. Many of them practiced displaying their colors during meditation and vision. During the Potentiam Libertas celebrations, most of the men and women decided to join the festivities in their spirit colors, and it was a beautiful sight to see. Swirls of color danced around the fire, contrasting against the dark velvet backdrop of the night sky, almost mimicking the Northern Lights.

As more and more people began displaying their colors, it became obvious that the talents they possessed in human form were only magnified in spirit form. The people of Eirene began to take note of all the many different colors of light associated with their gifts. They kept a record of their observations, which they nailed to a wide tree located near the center of the village. They deduced the following:

Human Talents	Spiritual Color
Teachers, Philosophers, and Healers	Shades of Green
Priests, Prophets, Leaders	Silver
Bakers, Butlers, Cooks	Shades of Orange

Hunters, Farmers, Gatherers	Shades of Blue
Scribes, Storytellers, Writers	Shades of Red
Singers, Songwriters, Musicians, Dancers	Shades of Purple
Inventors, Engineers, Craftsmen	Shades of Yellow
Unknown	The GOLD ONE

During the day, most did their work and chores in human form. But in some cases, when tasks called for a lot of physical strength, they would immediately activate the powers of their spirit form. The goal of anyone in the village was to eventually display their spirit and channel it on command and one day, remain completely in their new form.

Sparring matches were some of the most exciting events to watch when the opponents fought in spirit form. Color and light would slam against the ground, putting divots and holes in the dirt. Light would flash quickly from one side of the pit to the other in a great energy exchange. If one were standing near a sparring match in human form, they would be able to feel intense vibrations travel throughout their body, causing the hair on their head and arms to stand up straight. The Youth often surrounded the pit intentionally, trying to get as close as possible to experience that euphoric and sometimes shocking feeling. They laughed every time they'd see their friends' hair stick straight up.

Because matches were nothing more than an exchange of energy, the winner was determined based on the one who was able to transfer the energy from their opponent into themselves. In friendly battles, no one ever completely extinguished the other's light and at the end of the match, it was expected for you to give back the energy you took.

As the villagers became more comfortable with their spiritual powers, they began to test the boundaries and push the limits to see exactly how much power Jah had given to them. Their biggest discovery was the strength of their powers unified. When they joined together, they seemed to be an unbreakable force.

After realizing that the villagers could connect their spirit to one another, Athirst decided to recruit the villagers who had the most faith to help create a force field over the entire village. He told the villagers that they would test it out to protect the town during the next storm. So, one day when Athirst heard the sound of thunder approaching, he gathered the villagers who were strong in faith and comfortable with their spiritual abilities. They formed a brilliant, multi-colored dome of light and they sheltered the entire village from the thunder, lightning, and rain.

They managed to stay connected and protect the entire village that whole time. However, there was a downside to using so much of their strength. This exertion of power left villagers spiritually, mentally, and physically drained afterward. It took them several weeks to regain their energy. Athirst took note of the benefits and effects of unifying their light. He watched the villagers as they sparred and paid close attention to how they fought. He paid attention to their level of endurance and their mannerisms, because he needed to know who was ready for war. He wanted to test the fullness of their individual powers, as well as their powers unified so that he knew exactly how to engage in battle with the Ambers. After observing the powers of those in Eirene, Athirst sent for followers of Jah in all the seven other villages that he and Cearney visited during their travels.

Athirst expressed gratitude towards the villages for responding to their call for aid, and told them about the impending battle. They all soon fell under Athirst's leadership, and therefore came to be known as the Athirites.

46.
Exodus

There were still those in Eirene who swore their life on the Book of Veritas. Realizing they were outnumbered, they traveled to the villages where Cadmael's influence dominated.

Jabari was one of those people. He realized that his thoughts no longer aligned with the Athirites' values. He packed up his belongings and began to search for Cadmael, who he heard was hiding in the wilderness.

"Cecile!" Jabari shouted. He whistled and Cecile came swooping down, landing on his shoulder. "I have a special job for you. You must go and find Cadmael, then come back and let me know where he is." The bird took off in search of Cadmael. Jabari, Fortis, and Theiler's children packed up bags and waited until Cecile came back. Three days later, Cecile returned with news of Cadmael's location. "Squawk! A madman! A madman! Squawk! Follow me!"

Jabari, Fortis, Grayson, and Tabbitha left Eirene with Cecile leading the way. The bird flew for several miles, stopping every now and then to allow the humans to rest before circling around in the air again. "Madman! Squawk! Madman!"

"Shush, Cecile!" The group was growing tired of the bird's incessant outbursts.

A dense fog had settled over their path. Eventually they stumbled upon a thicket of overgrown, thorny bushes and the squawking resumed, growing louder and louder. There was a bit of movement coming from behind the entanglement of vines and branches.

"Stay back," Jabari told the others. He quietly waded through the brush, not wanting to cause alarm to whatever was there. Jabari moved leaves and limbs aside and watched. He saw a man that looked like he hadn't bathed in years. His hair was matted together and his skin was covered with dirt. He was eating wild berries and dancing around. The Book of Veritas was open on the stump of a tree. The wild man abruptly stopped dancing and fell to his knees. He began to meditate. While he was meditating, he took the dirt of the Earth and rubbed it on his face and body. As he did this, he began to glow with an Amber light so magnificent that it nearly blinded Jabari. Jabari instantly recognized him as Cadmael.

"Cadmael?" Jabari asked.

The Amber glow of the wild man stopped moving and slowly converted back to human form.

"I have not been called by my name in over a year." He twitched, scratching all over his body. "Who are you?"

"Brother, it's me, Jabari! And your sisters... girls, come over here."

Tabbitha and Grayson were fearful. This was not the brother they grew up with.

"Don't be afraid, girls; it's your brother." Jabari reassured them and nudged them toward Cadmael.

Cadmael smelled sour and his entire body was tinged a dull brown. He lifted his hands to touch his sisters' faces. His nails were caked with dirt. Tabbitha recoiled, but Grayson did not. "It's me, brother. Grayson. Do you remember me?"

Cadmael examined his sisters' faces, his eyes wide. "It is you. It's all of you. Seeing you here..." Cadmael broke down crying. "I can't believe it. I haven't seen you in so long." Cadmael reached out to embrace them. "So, does this mean it is safe for me to go out into the world again?"

Only Jabari and Grayson returned his embrace; the others were stand-offish, driven away by his smell.

"I would say so. You have no idea what your book has done, do you?" Jabari said.

"What do you mean?"

"There are a lot of people looking for you," Jabari said.

"Why, because they want to hurt me for what happened in Siomon?"

"No, because they want you to be their leader. So many of us are leaving the villages where they only read the Writ in hopes to develop a new village were we can be free to read the Book of Veritas without persecution. Athirst has assumed leadership over everyone who reads the Writ. They're calling themselves Athirites."

"So, the Athirites want to punish you for reading the Book of Veritas?"

"They saw how passionate you were about protecting the knowledge of the Second World that they are now training for battle. Thousands of us have left our villages. I'm just happy Cecile was able to find you. We need a leader."

Cadmael was quiet for a minute and then let out a tremendous scream of excitement. He was elated to see familiar faces and even more pleased to hear that his book had such an impact. He wasted no time giving his visitors wine made from the wild berries and teaching them how to harness the powers of the Earth. Seeing how quickly Jabari's family took to his instructions and teachings made him miss going from village to village spreading his message.

After a week of being in the wilderness with Jabari and his family and training them to develop the powers of the Earth, Cadmael came out of hiding.

"You and Cecile go find as many followers of the Book of Veritas as possible. Gather them all in one place. If the Athirites want to fight, it's a fight they'll get!"

It took Jabari and Cecile four full moon cycles to rally followers. People numbered in the hundreds of thousands, coming from all different villages in the land. Once they had all assembled at Cadmael's hideout, Cadmael immediately channeled his spirit, glowing in his sinister Amber light.

"I have heard that you all remained faithful to my teachings while I was away."

Cheers erupted from the crowd.

"I've also heard that you all are more enlightened and more powerful than any of the readers of The Writ."

With that statement, hundreds from the crowd grew so excited that they reverted to their spirit form. Bursts of Amber light glittered throughout the massive crowd.

"Not only am I proud of all that you've done, but I'm also proud to call myself your leader. Today, you are not just strangers defined and divided by your different villages. Today, you are Cadmaelites!" The crowd responded with shouts and thunderous applause.

"You must study and read The Book of Veritas. Tap into the power of the Earth and the things of the Second World. We will need our energy if we're to win this fight."

The Cadmaelites did as they were told. They harnessed the spirit of the Earth, and manifested the power of every act of treachery and evil deed imaginable. They celebrated the presence of their new leader. When Cadmael saw their level of zeal and dedication, he marked the current day as a holiday, calling it the Day of New Freedom.

47.
The Feast of New Freedom

And Jah, seeing and knowing all, watched as they danced, sang, and partied in the streets. The air filled with the light of the Ambers. The Cadmaelites' voices were like thunder as they celebrated the Feast of New Freedom.

As part of their celebration, they created fires and tossed the Writ into the flames. They delighted in the burning of the sacred book and they mocked its words, laughing at its wisdom.

After drinking the wine from the wild berries, Jabari was intoxicated. He looked around and noticed that his light wasn't shining with the same intensity as those around him. He grew jealous. The only other person that seemed to be burdened with this same affliction was his son Fortis, who struggled with manifesting spirit as well. As everyone continued to celebrate, Jabari went over to him.

"Why aren't you out there celebrating?" Jabari asked.

"Father, look at them! And look at me." Fortis looked down at his body, disappointed. "I'm barely glowing." Fortis took another sip of the wine.

"I understand. I lack the luminous glow as well. I can't figure out why we were cursed to never be as good as anyone else at discernment or channeling spirit. I'm tired of this; I've tried my entire life to be good at something and improve myself and look! Cadmael, someone who's half my age, glows with a blinding light with little to no effort.

"You can get spirit from anything, right?" Jabari asked his son.

"Of course; that's what they've done," Fortis said, slurring his speech. "Look at them, it's as if they're rubbing it in our faces." He gestured toward the people reveling in their light.

Both of the men were not in their right mind when they came up with a plan. "Well, I do know of one way we can gain the power and respect we deserve," Jabari said suddenly.

"Seriously, father? What is it?"

Jabari eyed Cecile, who was sleeping in a tree, her head burrowed in the shelter of her wings.

"The beasts."

Upon the utterance of those words, both Jabari and Fortis devised a plan over the next several months to create and train a new breed of animal that was both powerful and intelligent, in an effort to assume some sort of power. Jabari especially felt that since his only talent was connecting with animals, he could somehow use it to his advantage. He wanted to develop a beast formidable enough to challenge even the deadliest opponent. He hoped that through this, he could finally feel like he fulfilled his purpose and have some semblance of control. He was tired of feeling second-rate to everyone.

The Cadmaelites had been celebrating for twelve months before the screams of beasts filled the air.

Cadmael, overhearing the commotion, went to investigate. Jabari and Fortis were standing nearby, astonished at what they created.

"What have you done?!" Cadmael demanded.

"I wanted to prove that my powers and talents could surpass even yours, Cadmael," Jabari said coldly.

Cadmael angrily motioned for them to step aside.

Jabari and Fortis moved to reveal animals no one had ever seen before. They were daunting at best, combining the bodies of both human and animal to create bizarre, horse-like creatures. Cadmael was in disbelief. He observed the new creations. "My, what are these?"

It was not long before he realized, upon examination, that the creatures' muscular physiques might prove useful for the war.

"Simply amazing creatures. How on earth did you manage this?" Cadmael ran his hands over one of the massive animals, which was nearly the size of an elephant. The six-legged creatures had long horns that adorned their heads. Their rough, scaly skin produced a slightly amber glow. Some had tusks while others were covered with armour made from bone.

"You know what?" Cadmael said suddenly, clasping his hands. "I'm not mad. These creatures will be perfect additions to my army. I think I'll call them 'Voltaurs.' Has a nice, scary ring to it, don't you think?"

Jabari was furious that Cadmael managed to take the creatures as his own and use them for his own devious purposes. "From day one you have done nothing but undermine my capabilities, despite the fact that I've stuck with and supported you since day one! This is my chance to have something of my own!"

Cadmael just laughed. He was too far gone and no longer cared about the person he once called a friend. "You are just a means to an end to me. You should feel grateful that I don't kill you where you stand for your utter disrespect for my authority."

"We are sorry, Cadmael! Please allow us to stay. We promise to never stray or challenge your power again," Fortis said, quickly bowing to Cadmael.

"Your turn Jabari," Cadmael said with a wicked grin. "If you wish to avoid incurring my wrath, you must bow down to me." Jabari's stare could have burned a hole into Cadmael.

"I'm waiting."

Jabari hesitated before reluctantly bowing to him.

"See, that wasn't so bad. Now you know better than to try and challenge me." Cadmael continued to gaze at the beasts in awe before returning to the festivities. "Oh, yes, and..." Cadmael turned around. "Make sure you breed a few hundred more of these, in whatever inhumane, forbidden way you've chosen to use before. They may make a difference in the outcome of the war."

48.
The Signs

After the Cadmaelites' celebrations died down, they began focusing on strategies for war and during that time, the Athirites continued to be faithful to Jah. As a reward for their loyalty, Jah revealed a series of signs to the Athirites letting them know an approximate time the Cadmaelites would make their move. In the meantime, they were to prepare and strengthen their spirit for the upcoming battle.

Some villagers were more suspicious than others and thought that everything in nature was a sign. It soon became quite comical to hear all of the conspiracy theories about the things to come.

"Hey brother, did you notice that the birds are beginning to fly east instead of west? Do you think it's a sign that we need to leave here as well?"

"Last night, did the moon seem bigger to you? Do you think it's a sign?"

"I was coughing really bad this morning; do you think a plague has been unleashed upon us by the enemy?"

The questions came flooding in and Athirst would often chuckle and, after he eased the villagers' fears, he would meditate and thank Jah for the guidance and wisdom given to him. While some of their worries were quite laughable, others seemed to be legitimate concerns. But no matter what Athirst was presented with, he remained sure of himself and waited for the signs.

"It's been nearly a year. Do you think Jah has forgotten about us?" Illiana asked her father.

"Jah would never forget about us," Athirst responded.

"It just seems as if it's taking forever to hear from Him. It's hard for me to sleep at night. I keep waiting for something to happen -- for some sort of direction or guidance -- but nothing," Ilianna said anxiously.

"I agree," Cearney said. "Athirst, not knowing what's to come or being able to predict the foreseeable future and worrying endlessly is much worse than actually knowing what's to come."

"I know that both of you would like to believe I can do something to control the time or force answers out of Jah, but unfortunately I cannot."

"Can't we just attack them first?" Illiana asked.

"I've thought about that, believe me, but I don't think it would be right for us to jump into things just yet. We must be patient," Athirst responded.

Three months after that conversation, they received the first sign, which came in the form of a blood moon. The only other time any of the villagers witnessed a blood moon was on the day Cadmael was born. Despite the range in their ability to interpret vision, the villagers all knew this must be the first of the three signs.

"Ugo, join me in meditation," Athirst said.

"What's going on?" Ugo asked. He had been too preoccupied to take notice of the first sign.

"Look." Athrist pointed up at the sky.

"Goodness." Ugo was astonished. "I've never seen anything like it."

"I have, but only once before. You would've been too young to remember. The first blood moon occurred on the night Cadmael was born," Athirst said.

"So Jah knew he would eventually fall away from the Writ?" Ugo's head was filled with so many thoughts and questions.

"All the stories of our Elders -- all the stories Sophos told me -- they were preparing us for this. The Writ warned us of the

Ambers, but none of us thought their leader would come from Eirene."

"He was my best friend," Ugo said sadly. "I was with Cadmael when he found the device. It could have easily been me instead."

"But it's not. You actively made the choice to do the right thing. You were being tested just like he was. You could have easily ignored what happened, or even encouraged it. What matters is that you did not. I'm proud of you, son."

"Thanks father."

They walked to the East Gardens and found a particularly lush spot to meditate. They could hear the wind rustling between the leaves and the scampering sounds of little ground squirrels looking for food. For the first time in a long time, there was a real fear that hung in the air. Finally, Jah sent them a vision:

A circle lay inside a second circle, that was inside yet another circle. A set of three. The outer circle was bright and shined like the light of the sun. As the light of the outer circle grew more dim, the outer circle receded, and the middle circle grew larger so that it replaced the outer circle. The circle in the very center never left. It stayed protected at all times. Each time the outermost circle would fade, it traded places with the middle circle and its light was restored. The two circles continued to switch places, while the center circle stayed fixed and constant. When Ugo and Athirst looked up from the vision, Ugo looked into the sky. The stars appeared to have gotten brighter. Ugo blinked, trying to make sure he wasn't seeing things.

"Father, did you see that?" Ugo pointed up. The blood moon still hung in the sky, covering the earth below in an ominous red glow.

Athirst looked up at the stars. They were moving and twinkling, almost as if they wanted to speak to them. He remembered when he saw this phenomenon as a young boy. "Sophos always told me that stars were gods trapped in the sky."

"I remember you telling me that. Do you think it's true?" Ugo asked.

"Maybe."

Athirst stopped stargazing and took time to determine the meaning of the vision. They came to the conclusion that it was the way in which the people would be positioned during battle. He and Ugo discussed who should be in the center circle, constantly protected by the rings on the outside. Athirst thought it best to make sure the Youth -- those weak in spirit -- and one person of each spirit color stay in the very center of the circle. The ones who would go to battle first and form the outer circle would be those who possessed the strongest and most magnificent light. Those in the middle circle would be visionaries and meditators, who would act as a support and reinforcement.

Once they were clear on those dynamics, Athirst requested to meet with all the leaders of each village who fell under his leadership and discussed strategies for war.

"You've been up most of the night," Cearney observed one day. "Come to bed. You need your energy."

"We just need to figure a few more things out. Besides, we haven't received the other signs yet. There's still time."

"You're right, but I can't help but worry." Cearney's skirt was being tugged at by little hands. She looked down at Aurum, who was now four years old.

"Don't worry," Aurum said to her.

Cearney bent down and gave Aurum a kiss. "I will try my best not to, just for you."

Despite the appearance of the first sign, all seemed well, but nine moon cycles later and the second sign appeared. It began when villagers noticed the leaves falling off the trees earlier than usual and the birds squawking restlessly. The jars of spices in the community kitchen started trembling up and down. At every disturbance, the water in the community barrels would produce ripples. The entire village shook, almost like giant beasts were drumming their feet on the surface of the earth.

"What is that?" Cearney was in the back of the house working in the garden with Aurum when the fruit began falling off the trees.

Ugo, Stultus, and Nia ran to Athirst and Cearney's house.

"Is everyone okay?" Nia asked.

"I think so," Triston, Anah, and Romilda said.

"What's happening?" Illiana asked. She was clinging onto Ugo's arm.

"Everyone here is okay," Athirst said, reassuring all of them. "But I think your mother and I are going to go out into the village to check on others. Ugo, stay here with them."

"I'll go with you." Nia ran to get Nova. Athirst and Cearney got on Swift and Nimble. They all rode together toward the center of the village.

Romilda grabbed Aurum. "Are you scared?"

"Nah, I'm not scared," Aurum said, shaking his head.

"I hope father will be alright," Anah said.

"I am sure he will be. Father is strong," Romilda reassured her.

They stayed together as the house shook. Eirene and the surrounding villages had never experienced this before. They had only read about it in the earlier chapters of the Writ. Until now, the earth was peaceful and still, but today it shook violently. The episodes of shaking would last for two to three minutes and then stop suddenly, repeating several times. Just when people began to feel comfortable enough to stand on their own two feet, it would begin again.

Several months of the shaking passed and the villagers had grown irritated.

"When will this all be over?" Cearney thought aloud. "This is ridiculous. I can't keep anything in this house from breaking."

"I don't know." Athirst hated to admit that he was growing frustrated with Jah.

"I guess I'm confused as to why we're the ones who are suffering when they were the ones that decided to turn their back on Jah." Cearney threw up her hands in frustration.

"They have the power of the Earth. They're getting stronger. Jah is using these signs to show us how much power they have," Athirst responded.

"If they're this powerful, then I'm scared for all of us."

Athirst sat down on a wooden chair in the kitchen and put his face in his hands. The table jolted up and down, making Athirst rub his temples and sigh loudly. Little Aurum came over to him. "It will be okay," he said.

"Thank you, son." Athirst grabbed Aurum and squeezed him tight.

The tension in the community was high but the Athirites continued to prepare for battle. The Youth of the village practiced sparring and crafted weapons while the adults and Elders meditated constantly and worked diligently to express their light.

Time went on and everyone tried to find a sense of normalcy. Cearney was thankful that she didn't have an infant. Aurum was calm and he kept to himself a lot of the time. He didn't seem to be too concerned with the violent shaking of the ground, and somehow, amidst all the craziness, he managed to comfort Athirst and Cearney when they felt like they should be doing that for him.

When Ugo came over, he watched his brother with curiosity. Every now and then, Ugo would see Aurum with Youth younger than he was, consoling them when they felt fear. In moments of peace, when other children squeezed in time to play, Aurum was always reading, meditating, or playing in his mother's garden.

One morning, while Ugo and Stultus were visiting his mother and father's house, he could hear his mother calling his father from outside. It sounded urgent.

Athirst ran out to see what was going on. Her voice made him nervous and he immediately thought that she had witnessed the third sign of things to come.

"Look!" Cearney pointed at a vine of plump red tomatoes.

"Yes, love, tomatoes. What's so special about tomatoes?"

"Do you not see how full and ripe they are today?" Cearney said.

"Well, how do you suppose they got that way?" Athirst said with a lack of enthusiasm.

"Well, they were shriveled and dying before. They only thing different about yesterday was that I asked Aurum to help me, and then later that evening when I was in the house, I noticed that Aurum was still outside. I looked and saw him place his hands on each one of the shriveled plants. I didn't think much of it -- maybe that he was playing or pretending or something, but when I came out today, they were full and red again."

Ugo called out to his brother. "Aurum, come here!"

"Yes, brother?" He emerged from the house, a cheerful smile on his face.

"What did you do to get the tomatoes to look like this?"

"I asked Jah to heal them."

"Yesterday, the tomatoes were practically dead and today they are full of life," Cearney said, still astonished.

"Huh, interesting," Athirst said as he watched Aurum walk away.

49.

The Third Sign

Gardening, cooking, playing, reading, and meditating in between the violent shaking became a way of life. Everyone learned to pause with every violent quake without feeling startled or afraid; instead they saw it as normal and took it as a reminder that it was time to meditate. Jah in turn gave them a feeling of peace.

Then one day, the quakes just stopped. It took awhile for the Athirites to find comfort in the quiet, as they had grown used to the rumbles in the earth and being knocked around once in awhile. But soon life returned to normal.

Most of the village was asleep, but some enjoyed listening to the melodic sound of the rain. It was the kind of rain that seemed to quench the dry heat of the day and provide relief. The rain slowly made its way down branches, gently hitting the ground with a constant, soft thud.

Ugo was up because he decided to go fishing near the north end of River Aesis. Before leaving his house, he gave Stultus a kiss. She was still in bed sleeping soundly. Ugo grabbed his leather bag and headed to meet his father in the center of the village. Athirst was the best at catching Chinook Salmon, but it was only because he knew that the secret to catching the best fish was waking up extremely early since fish would congregate in one place to feed -- a secret he learned from Sophos.

The sun hadn't yet peaked its head over the horizon, but the orange and yellow rays began to stain the night's sky. The moon was still visible, but would soon be outshined by the brilliant light of the sun. The misty rain had left behind a low fog that hovered over the ground.

Athirst was sitting on a tree stump near the fire pit used for the Potentiam Libertas celebrations when Ugo walked over.

"You're late," he said as Ugo approached. He wasted no time grabbing his fishing pole and a jar of insects to use as bait. They began walking toward River Aesis. Athirst knew that Ugo wasn't the best fisherman, but he enjoyed spending time with his son. As they walked, the rain picked up again. The rhythmic sound provided a calming ambiance as they journeyed toward the north end of the river.

"Was mother awake when you left?" Ugo asked.

"Your mother always wakes up early to send me off. She seems to need something to do now that most of you are out of the house. I think it's good that Aurum is still there keeping her company. She seems to miss all the chaos that Triston and your sisters would stir up," Athirst said.

Ugo was surprised. "I didn't think that she would miss it. We were such a noisy bunch. Besides, all of us see each other every day, several times a day."

Athirst chuckled. "Yes, but your mother will always be your mother. She loves you all so dearly and seeing everyone grow up is a good thing, but it can be hard to let go. What about Stultus? Was she up when you left the house?"

Ugo didn't say a word. He just looked at his father, and Athirst looked back at him, the two of them bursting with laughter.

They continued to walk, looking down to watch out for large puddles when Ugo noticed something strange. The rain had stopped, not in its normal fashion. This time, it was different. It appeared the rain was frozen in midair, as if gravity itself no longer had an effect on it. A drop of rain headed toward a puddle was hovering over the pool of water but never made it in. Ugo stuck out his finger to touch the raindrop that stood still before him.

"Ugo, run back to the village and wake everyone. This is the third sign! There's no time to waste!" Athirst shouted, urging him to move quickly. Ugo did as he was told. Athirst dropped down to his knees and meditated before making his way back to the village.

Ugo ran to the center of the village and grabbed a pot and a wooden spoon from the community kitchen.

"Everyone, it's time! Wake up! Wake up now!" He continued to bang on the pot with the spoon obnoxiously. The loud clangs woke people from their slumber, and they too saw the mysterious rain frozen in space. Several people rubbed their eyes in disbelief.

Athirst joined his son, signaling for people to wake up. "Tonight, we will make final preparations for war! We must be ready!"

Several men and women who were not native to Eirene immediately went back to their home village to warn others. Those people packed their belongings and headed to Eirene. Leaders from every village that read the Writ gathered together, bringing others with them.

By sunrise the next morning, a massive crowd of over 700,000 came to support the war effort. Eirene, along with Siomon from the north, Atar from the east, portions of the mountains of Inber, the village of Divinity, and three other villages came together.

Athirst converted to spirit and elevated himself over the crowd that assembled on the outskirts of Eirene.

"The outer circle will fight, the middle circle will take over when the outer circle tires, and the inner circle will pray, meditate, and stay protected. This plan only works if we stay connected to Jah throughout the entire battle. Through Him, victory will be ours!"

The massive crowd roared. After the plan was understood, people went to make final preparations. Cearney approached him. "Good work, my love. The people seem united."

Athirst retured to human form. "Thank you. Cearney, Look." Athirst pointed and Cearney turned around to see familiar faces approaching.

"Logicist, is that you?" Athirst asked.

Cearney, seeing Xar-Ann, ran up to her and gave her a hug. "It is so good to see you again!"

A giant Hiemal turned around and picked Athirst up. "Good to see you."

"Good to see you as well," Athirst managed to say, his voice muffled under the weight of Hiemal's enormous arms.

While Cearney and Athirst were mingling with both old friends and new visitors, Ugo was working with groups of warriors to make sure they were prepared for battle.

Ugo, in his glowing shade of green, commanded, "Athirites, show your colors!"

With that, all of the Athirites changed to spirit form. Ugo's spirit roamed over them, dividing the crowd into those who would fight in the outer circle, middle circle and the innermost circle. He was careful to have at least one person of each color as part of the inner circle in order to protect them and preserve the skills that Jah had given them. The strongest of each color were placed on the outside first, giving the ones who were weaker in spirit time to train and develop their light.

Ugo elevated himself above the mass of multicolored light. "Cearney, Nia, Stultus, Anah, and Romilda will be the leaders of the inside circles. You will go to them when you need encouragement, prayer, food, water, or if you are injured during battle! You will report to them!" Ugo shouted over the crowd. "Athirst is the leader of the outer circle. He will call the commands on the front lines. He has been given vision by Jah and we must follow."

The crowd roared in agreement. Their bold colors of light radiated and bounced with anxious excitement.

Athirst finished conversing with his friends and elevated himself; making his way over to Ugo. "Ugo, you have done an excellent job working with everyone. Do you think they are all ready?"

"Yes, father."

Athirst turned to the crowd. "You've prepared well and have sparred long enough! Now it is time to rest! Sleep well tonight, for tomorrow will show us no mercy!"

The next morning, thousands of warriors were ready to take their positions. As Athirst walked out into the center of Eirene, Logicist, Xar-Ann, and Hiemal ran up to him.

"Is there anything you need? Hiemal asked.

"Nothing I can think of right now," Athirst replied. "How are you feeling?"

"My mate, or former union-mate, Cantus, is fighting for the other side. That weasle of a man she left me for is there as well. I think it may be difficult to see her like that."

"I didn't think about how uncomfortable that would be, fighting against your mate," Xar-Ann said to Hiemal. She turned and looked at Logicist, taking his hand in hers.

"It is going to be hard for all of us. These people, they were part of our lives. Cadmael was my son's best friend. I went to lessons with Jabari, but none of that matters now," Athirst replied, trying to mask his sadness by focusing on the task set before them.

"You're right, Athirst. We've got to protect the word of Jah. That is our priority." Logicist gave Athirst a pat on the back.

"So, are we ready for the battle?" Athirst asked.

"We made a good team before; I'm sure we can do it again," Hiemal said.

They all continued to talk together when suddenly a young Siomonite male approached them.

"I didn't know if I would get a chance to speak to you before the battle. There have been so many people around you clambering for your attention that I didn't want to bother you."

"You're not bothering us at all. Speak, my friend." Athirst and Logicist showed great compassion for the young man.

"Please excuse me for sounding like I have a lack of faith, but I must ask, if Jah is all seeing and all knowing, and if He has all power in his hands, then why are we going into battle? Why would Jah not just convert everyone's heart back to Him?"

"You do not have a lack of faith; you're just inquisitive, just as I was as a Youth," Athirst said.

The young man breathed a sigh of relief. "I feel so terrible for having these thoughts. I'm so grateful to you for steering me back to Jah, but I can't help but wonder if I'm doing the right thing."

"We've all questioned it at times," Logicist added. "We wouldn't be men of such great faith if we did not continually ask Jah for guidance."

"Jah's spirit lives in His word and His word is true, but there has always been another force luring us away from Him and Jah gives us the gift of free will so that we can choose who we want to follow. We want Jah to be the one to hold our hand and walk us through every decision we make and then be rewarded for our faithfulness to Him, but it doesn't work that way. He has provided instruction in the Writ, but it's up to us to follow the words given to us. So, I will ask you, are you with us? Are you choosing today to fight for Jah?"

There was a glimmer of hope in the young Siomonite's eyes. "Yes...yes, I think so. Thank you so much. Thank you for your time." The young man walked away and found a quiet place to meditate. Afterwards, he received his color and showed a brilliant green light.

Suddenly Cearney ran up to them. "Athirst, I haven't seen my sister. All of Siomon is here, but I haven't been able to find her."

"Okay...let's see if we can find her." Athirst turned to his companions. "I'm going to look for Jendahi; you all get ready. I'm going to need you on the outer circle with me."

Athirst and Cearney transformed into spirit in order to survey the crowd more quickly. Their gaze spanned miles, but still no sign of her. "I don't see her anywhere," Cearney said, her voice trembling.

"I'm sure we will find her," Athirst reassured her.

"I don't think she's here. I know that you have to get back. I will keep looking for her alone."

"Are you sure?" Athirst asked.

"Yes, you head back. Besides, you need your energy for battle." Cearney made her way to Siomon, Nimble carrying her as fast as he could. She was desperate to find her sister. Something told Cearney to check their childhood home.

When Cearney finally made it there, she barged through the door of her old home. Jendahi was sitting in Iris' old room, shaking like a leaf.

"Jendahi, why are you still here?"

Jendahi ran over to her sister and gave Cearney a hug. "I can't do this Cearney. I saw what that man is capable of and I can't do it. I'm scared."

Cearney moved her sister's straw colored hair out of her face. "We are all scared. All we can do is trust Jah."

"What is going to happen to us?"

"I don't know, but what I do know is that I will do what I've always done. I will protect you with everything I have. But I can't protect you if you stay here; I need you to come with me. And you need to come with me now." Cearney did not give Jendahi much time to think. She grabbed Jendahi's arm.

Nimble was outside, whimpering. He seemed to sense everyone's feeling of impending doom.

"Wait, Cearney, no, no..."

Before Jendahi could protest any further, Cearney hoisted her up onto Nimble's back.

"Yahh!" Cearney gently tapped into the side of her beast. "Hold on tight," she said, grinning at her sister. The women sped off to Eirene.

When they returned, Cearney could tell that the villages had begun forming their circles. Athirst saw them approach. "I'm so glad you found her!" Athirst said, giving his sister-in-law a hug. "Jendahi, we need you in the center circle."

There was nothing left to do. The Athirites got into position, waiting in anticipation for the inevitable chaos that was to follow.

50.
The Battle Begins

Athirst could hear the sound of the Cadmaelites coming. It was so unlike anything he had ever imagined. The high-pitched numbing noise of the approaching army sounded like a thousand nails scratching against slate. When he turned his head to look in the direction of the noise, he could see a light forming on the horizon. The Amber glow broke through the darkness of the early morning.

The birds of the air began to chirp and squawk uncontrollably. They flew in the direction of the sound. The creeping and moving things of the Earth began to head in that direction as well. Athirst felt the winds blow more briskly and the leaves of the trees swirled all around. The Cadmaelites were channeling the powers of the Earth.

"Athirites, show your colors!" Athirst's spirit shined boldly. His silver color radiated for all to see. He had been born for this moment. He and the others assumed their positions, doing just as their visions had instructed them. Ugo, Hiemal, Logicist, and Xar-Ann connected to Athirst, creating a strong outer circle. Cearney, Romilda, and Anah took their place as the leaders of the middle circle. Nia, Stultus, and Jendahi protected the innermost circle.

Cearney's voice yelled over the chirping of the birds and the sound of the wind to encourage the men and women around her. "It will be your faith that wins this war! It will be your unrelenting devotion to Jah and dedication to the meditation of His word that will give us strength! No matter what lies ahead, no matter how bad it looks, we must never stop our desire for vision and meditation!"

The Athirites could see the Amber glow steadily become bigger and bigger. Cadmael's light was brilliant and it stood out over even the most magnificent of his soldiers. Mixed in with the Cadmaelites' brilliant colors were Jabari and Fortis with their army of beasts. They both sat atop their abominations of beast, human, and spirit. The Voltaurs came ready to wage war. They charged toward the outer circle, where Athirites waited behind their impenetrable dome.

As the Voltaurs charged, they tried to force their way in to the inner-circle where they could find those weak in spirit and attack.

"Do not waste your time on them!" Athirst shouted to the warriors. "They will tire soon." His voice echoed like thunder for all of the Athirites to hear.

Cadmael snickered at this sentiment and pointed to the vast army behind him.

"Ugo, I see you are still under your father's wing. Step away and fight! Come out and prove you're not the weakling everyone thinks you are!" Cadmael taunted.

Ugo subconsciously disconnected for a split second, causing a small break in the circle. Athirst tried to reassure him. "Ugo, do not listen. We must stick together. Leaving me is what he wants you to do. You must be strong!"

"Yes, father!" Ugo responded, quickly reconnecting.

Ugo wasn't the only one being tempted.

"Oh Darling!" Cantus' melodic voice immediately had Hiemal gazing in her direction. "You want to get me? Here I am!"

Hiemal looked sad for a moment, but eventually snapped out of it.

"Focus! Do not break the circle!" Athirst shouted. They banded close together, leaving no gaps. It took a lot of energy to expand light to connect to each other and form a barrier with other spirits so there were no spaces for the Cadmaelites to enter.

The war of spirit was much different than wars from the First and Second Worlds. They did not involve weapons of metal and chemicals. There were no bombs, no guns, and no bullets. They had swords and daggers in the New Age, but only those in human form or those weak in spirit carried them. Fighting in spirit reminded Ugo of a time when he was a boy during lessons.

The Magisters would put them through various tests and use them as analogies of their faith. Ugo remembered when his instructor gave all of them a seemingly simple task. The instructor took them outside and walked the entire class over to a rock that stood about six feet tall and seven feet in diameter. He told all of the Youth to try and keep at least one finger from the same hand on the rock for as long as possible. The Magister never gave them an exact time, he just said to keep at least one finger on the rock. They were allowed to switch fingers, but could not switch arms. Then he drew a circle around the entire diameter of the rock with a branch from a tree and told the class that they had to stand behind the circle that he just drew. This put them about an arm's length away from the rock. Ugo remembered his classmates snickering because the task seemed so simple. But it was about ten minutes into the exercise when people began to grow tired of holding their finger to the rock. About twenty minutes in, and several Youth had quit the exercise. Thirty minutes in and there were only five left out of a total of forty-two students. At forty-five minutes, there were four still remaining, but they were struggling. Their arms were tired and everyone wanted to quit. In fact, each time the instructor turned his back, Ugo and his classmates would whisper, trying to make a truce to drop their fingers all at the same time, but they were all scared that someone wouldn't follow through, so no one surrendered. At fifty minutes the instructor told all of the remaining students that they could remove their hands off the rock. Everyone was exhausted. When they were finished, the Magister said, 'holding on to this rock is like having faith. You did not know when I was going to give you a break; all you knew was that you had to hold on to the rock no matter what. You were not allowed to do anything else but hold on to the rock and if you did that, then you were going to be victorious. Ugo remembered looking around at the remaining four classmates. They all had smirks on their faces since they had accomplished something that the others could not. Ugo remembered Cadmael being one of them.

Ugo knew that this was going to be quite the battle. Cadmael continued taunting Ugo. He beckoned Ugo to break the circle and fight one-on-one.

"Prove to me that you are not as weak as I think you are! I know that your desire is to win over me, so do it! Come and fight!" It was when Cadmael shouted this to Ugo that he used the power of the Earth to cause powerful winds. They ripped through the circle, creating a small gap.

The Voltaurs took advantage of this and six beasts were able to fit through the dome. Jabari and Fortis charged toward the circle and attacked, targeting the innermost circle. The Athirites lost thirteen men before those in the middle circle slaughtered the six Voltaurs, leaving Jabari and Fortis no choice but to retreat.

Jabari thought about what to do. He took advantage of his physical strength and charged after two Athrite men who were in human form. He quickly snapped their necks, killing them. You could hear the screams of pain over the swirling winds. Athirites on the outer circle knew what was happening on the inside. It was difficult for them to stay focused. It was even more difficult for Hiemal, who was struggling to ignore the verbal attacks Cantus threw at him.

"I know you want me back sweetie, just come here. Join me." Her song rang through the air, drawing him in. It was her voice that had always attracted him. Right before he was about to let go of his connection with the outer circle, the man Cantus left him for appeared next to her. She turned to her new love. "I bet you miss when I use to do this." Hiemal watched as Cantus turned to the man and kissed him.

"Athirst, cover me."

"No! You must stay connected. Do not let your feelings cloud your judgment!"

"Cover me!" Hiemal broke away and the other Athirites quickly filled in the gap. Hiemal charged toward Cantus, creating a shield of ice in front of him with one hand while forming daggers of ice with the other. He charged toward the Cadmaelites. As he approached, his shield of ice melted, and his daggers turned to water.

"Come back now!" Athirst shouted.

Hiemal realized it was useless. He tried to make his way back over to the Athirite's outer circle but was surrounded by Cadmaelite soldiers. Their amber light engulfed his large figure.

"Do not leave the circle until I tell you so!" Athirst screamed. He was disappointed at the loss of his new friend. He was also disheartened by the noise from the inner circle.

Jabari was a mad man. He wanted to prove that he was a commander; a leader in his own right and did not need to bow down to Cadmael anymore. As Jabari slaughtered countless Athirites who were weak in spirit, Stultus turned around.

Stultus saw the viciousness her father displayed. She saw how far he had strayed from Jah and as much as he hurt her, she didn't want to see him like this. Jabari saw her as well and for a moment, Stultus saw a softness in his eyes that reminded her of how he used to be.

Her expression changed and Jabari saw the look of love she had for him turn into panic. Stultus watched as an Athirite pummeled Jabari with a piece of granite that had broken off from the previous attack. The Athirite continued to bash it into his head. Jabari turned and began to fight back before realizing he already had a critical wound to his skull. Stultus turned away, screaming. Nia, hearing her daughter's cries, ran toward her and embraced her. As Jabari began to grow weaker, two other Athirites joined in the attack, taking him down. Jabari's body laid there. He gasped for his last breath, coughing up blood. The scream from Stultus was piercing.

The fight continued, but the Athirites of the inner circle were much more prepared now. They sparred and fought with all their might. The soldiers riding atop the Voltaurs put up a strong fight as well. Their goal was to make it toward the children, who were being protected by their mothers in the very center of the circle, but Cearney refused to let that happen. She was not weak in spirit.

"If you have any ability to fight in the spirit, now is the time to do so! They are all in human form; they cannot beat even the weakest of us if we work together!" She shouted.

The men of the inner circle began fighting viciously against the remaining Cadmaelites. The women of the inner circle formed a protective hedge around the children. Cearney joined the men in battle. The ground was littered with the bodies of Cadmaelites, Athirites, and Voltaurs. It wasn't long before birds of prey slipped through whatever cracks there were in the dome, picking at the flesh of the dead bodies.

The winds continued to tear through the village. Cadmael tried to use the wind to rip through the Athirites' circle once more, but the Athirites held on.

"They have the power of the Earth, but that is all they have. Do not be discouraged! We have the power of the heavens! We have the power of the word and if we have the power of the word, then we have the power of Jah!" Athirst shouted over the winds.

In that moment, Athirst transmitted images to the Cadmaelite warriors. He tapped into their spirit and showed them images of their Youth. He reminded them of their innocence and then showed them the wrath that would come for their disobedience. These images confused many of the Cadmaelites.

Their power faded and the winds slowed down for a moment. They began to quarrel amongst each other. The Athirites saw the light of thousands begin to dim.

In that moment, Athirst instructed a portion of the circle to break free and attack those with dim light, depleting even more of Cadmael's army.

Seeing this, Cadmael became infuriated and vicious. He used his gifts of the Earth and sent swarms of flying creatures to charge and break through the inner circles.

Wasps, bees, birds, and all manner of winged predators came down, fighting their way through small openings in the outer circle. They drilled holes through the dome of protection and began gnawing their way to the center. The outer circle was strong, but focused on making sure the Cadmaelites themselves didn't get through. Many of the small creatures managed to squeeze their way into the circle. They swarmed around, gnashing, pecking, buzzing, stinging, and biting. Birds came and snatched infants out of the arms of mothers, carrying them off and dropping them into River Aesis. The inner circle meditated relentlessly. They did their best to stay focused. Those in charge of protecting the inner circle worked diligently to make sure the warriors who needed to rest had the ability to rest and meditate, while also tending to those who were wounded.

"Athirites, stand strong!" Again, Athirst's voice boomed. "Be patient! It is not time to give up; just hold them off!"

Cadmael, hearing Athirst's plea to his warriors, taunted them. "Why do you all continue to listen to a man who has let so many of your comrades die? Who didn't stop your children from being slaughtered? You are all fools!"

Those words dimmed the light of many Athirites. Xar-Ann shouted, "That's what he wants you to hear! He's trying to make us lose faith! Don't give him the satisfaction!"

"We will not! We must wait!" Athirst commanded. His plan was to see everything the enemy was capable of before attacking. He knew that Cadmael wasn't humble. He would reveal his hand in time.

Athirst wanted to fulfill the will of Jah by not breaking out of the circle until it was the right time, but many lost faith in his ability to lead. Athirst had to be strategic. He traded Athirites who were losing hope with those who were meditating in the middle circle.

"On the count of three, switch!" Athirst called out the names of warriors on the outside to switch with those who were ready to join in the battle.

When the weary ones entered, Stultus and Nia gathered food and water for them. They gave them words of encouragement to replenish their energy.

This exchange went on for several days. The Athirites endured the fullness of Cadmael's abilities. Cadmael used what was left of his power to cause earthquakes and storms to ravage the terrain. He used animals of prey to sneak in and devour children who did not have time to develop their light. He caused famine in the lands and contaminated the waters that ran through the villages. Cearney did the best she could to collect seeds from plants and trees as they fell to the ground.

"Mother, I am going to collect as much water from the rain as possible," Triston said to her.

"Yes, excellent idea son." She was protecting him in the inner circle since he wasn't as strong in spirit as Ugo. "Aurum!" Cearney shouted over the noise. "Here, take these." Cearney handed Aurum a handful of seeds. "Put them in a safe place."

Athirst noticed that Cadmael and his army had begun to tire. On the 41st day of the battle, the Athirites broke the outer circle, charging toward the Cadmaelites. The enemy was caught off guard. Until now, the Cadmaelites were usually the ones charging. But the Athirites wasted no time. They waged war like none that the heavens and the Earth had never seen before. Shock waves reverberated throughout the landscape as they disconnected from each other. All of them, Cadmaelites and Athirites, were an entanglement of energy, power, and light when they struck each other.

Despite his weakening army, Cadmael was still strong. Seeing so many of his warriors' bodies lying before him only seemed to intensify his anger and it magnified his strength. He decided to turn his attention toward Ugo. "Ugo, you still hide behind your father's shadow! You think defeating a few Cadmaelites will change your fate and make you a hero? You are delusional! If you want to prove to me that you can beat me, come and fight!"

Ugo then transmitted an image of his mother to Cadmael. This reminded Cadmael of how everything began and for a minute caused his spirit to weaken. He then shook his head and quickly turned his attention towards Athirst, who was locked in combat.

"You want to know the pain of losing a parent? I'll show you!" Cadmael commanded several of his soldiers to attack Athirst. Athirst could feel the intense amount of energy heading in his direction. He was not prepared for the horde charging toward him. Ugo quickly rushed to join his father's side. He lifted boulders and trees, hurling them toward the Cadmaelites. Other Athirites joined in to help. Ugo continued to make his way to his father. But by the time he reached him, he saw something that made his stomach drop. His father was in human form. Athirst turned around for a split second, a dagger protruding from his chest. He wavered a bit before falling to his knees, eventually collapsing. Almost immediately, he vanished.

At that moment, all the Athirites knew what had happened. The fall of their leader took a hit to their confidence. They still fought, but they didn't know whom they would receive direction from now. They had only seen Ugo in the shadow of his father. They had little confidence in Ugo's ability to lead.

Cearney tried to process what had happened. She could sense that Athirst was gone, but she didn't have time to break down now. She did what she could to comfort everyone else.

"Ugo!" She shouted. "You must take your father's place! I did not give birth to weakness. You will be victorious!" Her words made it over the chaos of the war and into his ears. Ugo saw his mother's strength.

There was so much going on around him that there was no time to mourn. He had no other choice but to rely on Jah for everything and be obedient to His word. Jah revealed once more the vision of the seed that rolled around looking for the right soil. Ugo now understood that this was the right time. He was in the right soil.

Over the cries of pain, Ugo could hear Jah. He sent a vision to him in the middle of the battle of a warrior who learned from those who came before him.

When the vision of the warrior was finished, Ugo looked up at the heavens and was about to pray when he noticed the stars moving and shining brighter than ever. That's when he realized. That's what I'm supposed to do! Ugo thought to himself. I need to call on the warriors who came before me. Ugo remembered his father telling stories about the gods of the stars. He said they were fearless and brave, possessing extraordinary strength and ability, but when they were idolized for their amazing talents and exalted above men they became prideful. Now they are trapped in the sky looking over the inhabitants of earth. Waiting for Jah to give them the opportunity to be warriors again.

Ugo looked up at the stars again. They continued to twinkle and shine. "Jah, you have given the Athirites the power of the heavens. And now, I ask that you release the gods of the stars." Ugo looked up and prayed to Jah.

Cadmael taunted Ugo. "There would've been no need for all this bloodshed had you submitted to me. You would have been filled with the knowledge of the Earth and all that exists in it."

"I don't want the powers of the Earth!" Ugo exclaimed. "I prefer the powers of the heavens." And with that, Jah released the gods of the sky.

The Earth shook violently. The stars dotting the sky came down like bolts of lightning, striking the ground so fiercely that it made cracks in the surface of the Earth. Many sky warriors came down with bolts of lightning in their hands, striking the Cadmaelites and extinguishing the light of thousands. Stars fell into the oceans causing waves to crash into the shore and send water surging through the land.

The stars continued to fall from the sky, splitting the Earth open. The Earth's surface was split apart; exposing the fiery world below. Some of the water from the ocean spilled down into the cracks, causing steam to rise through. Smoke and fire filled the air. Looking down, everyone could see tormented souls beneath the Earth.

Theiler, killed by Cadmael before he could repent, looked up through the crack in the Earth's surface and saw his son. He could see the evil that lived within him and the power that consumed him. Tormented since the day of his death, Theiler desperately wanted relief from his anguish. He wanted Jah to forgive him.

The hands of all things evil reached up through the cracks in the ground, snatching what belonged to them and pulling people and beasts down into the fiery depths below.

Cadmael still pressed forward. With every warrior he lost, his rage intensified. His father, still trapped in the fires of hell below the Earth's surface, fought his way through the hands that were trying to pull him back down. With every hand that grabbed at him, Theiler recited words from the Writ.

Theiler continued to fight, catching glimpses of the earth and sky above, trying to follow his son's path. He finally found his way to the earth's surface and made it to Cadmael.

"Cadmael, look at all that you have done."

Cadmael turned around, shocked to see his father.

"No, father! Look at what you've helped me do. Unless you are coming back to fight with me, you can go back to hell for all I care!" Cadmael shouted back at his father.

With those words, the spirit of Theiler rushed toward Cadmael like a lion chasing its prey. He charged at his firstborn son with all his might.

Seeing what was happening, the star warriors and the Athirites also began charging toward Cadmael. Cadmael fought to get all of them off, but he was quickly overpowered.

Theiler grabbed onto his son and held onto him with all his might. The gods of the stars then used their power to widen the gap in the surface of the Earth directly underneath them. Theiler jumped into the gap, pulling his son down with him into the fires below.

The impact of Theiler and Cadmael's spirit was so mighty that it caused a great explosion. The vibration sent waves of energy rebounding throughout the atmosphere. Suddenly, the ground started to collapse inward, acting as a vacuum and sucking all the evil things down below. The gods of the stars quickly sealed the hole. The star warriors began to celebrate boasting about their victory. They missed the feeling of fighting battles and begged Jah to let them stay on earth. They promised to protect His people, but Jah could see they were already full of themselves. He placed them back in the sky before they grew too vain.

All the commotion, then, complete silence. The battle was over. The Athirites were exhausted. Many of them were too tired to maintain spirit form and quickly returned to their human bodies. They immediately began searching for family members to see who was still alive.

Ugo ran over to his mother and siblings. "I--I tried. I couldn't get to father in time," Ugo cried, placing his head in his hands.

"It's okay Ugo...It's okay. It's over now." Cearney was sobbing. She hugged her son and began looking for her sister. Cearney was overwhelmed with emotion. "Jendahi!" she screamed, scanning her surroundings.

"She's over there!" Ugo pointed. She was in the distance, offering water to a wounded villager. Cearney ran to hug her sister. The two women embraced and broke down crying.

Ugo called out to Stultus. He could see her in the distance. She had picked up Aurum and was bringing him over to the rest of the family. When she got near them, Anah grabbed Aurum out of her arms and began kissing him all over. "You're tough, aren't you Aurum?" Romilda and Triston also gathered round, relieved to see most of their family still intact.

Stultus and Ugo embraced. "I pray to Jah that we never have to go through anything like this again." She paused for a minute. Her eyes were wide. "I saw him, Ugo. I saw my father. He was part of all this. He was filled with so much rage; I couldn't bear to look at him."

Nia joined in, comforting her daughter. She held her close and stroked her hair. "Shhh… it's alright now. There's nothing we could've done. You're okay now; you did so well."

They all continued to embrace, crying into each other's shoulders and hugging. Xar-Ann and Logicist approached the group. "I am sorry that you lost Athirst," Logicist said with regret in his voice. "He was a good man; Sophos raised him well."

"Thank you," Ugo said. "You too are a good man. What are you going to do now that everything is over?"

"Xar-Ann and I will probably head back to Atar and see what damage has been done. And...I guess try to rebuild the village. You?"

"The same, most likely."

"Look at our village." Triston pointed out to all the destruction. They were quiet as they looked at the barren land. But the land could wait. Too exhausted to do much else, the group laid on the ground and rested their bodies.

As they lay there, Ugo felt so disappointed with himself for not being there for his father. His body began to tremble as he worked to hold back tears. Aurum gave Ugo a hug. "Don't cry, brother," he said, cupping Ugo's cheek with his tiny palm. "Thank you for protecting me." Ugo returned his hug, squeezing him tightly. Tears continued to roll down his face.

"Thanks, little brother. You know exactly what to say, don't you? Go ahead...get some rest. We've got a lot of work to do in the morning."

Ugo found himself tossing and turning that night. He kept his eyes closed because he thought that opening them would be admitting that he'd given up on sleep. Just as he was finally dozing off, a sliver of light caught his attention. It felt strange because he knew it was too early for the sun to be rising.

When he opened his eyes, it still felt like he was dreaming. In his haze, he could see the illuminated figure of a little boy. The boy was holding seeds in his hands. He dug up some soil, placing them in the ground. He placed his hands over the earth.

Ugo rubbed his eyes to see if he could focus in on the small, slim figure encased in brilliant light. The light flickered in and out. Ugo immediately recognized him. His little brother Aurum had uncovered the seeds given to him during the battle and was now planting them in the ground. Ugo watched Aurum as he looked up to Jah and quoted scriptures from the Writ before kneeling into a meditative position.

Ugo immediately got up to go wake his family.

Meanwhile, Aurum walked away from the pile of seeds, and within seconds, new life started sprouting from the ground, roots and vines and leaves shooting up out of the dirt. Slowly, lush green grass began to carpet the bare, scorched landscape. Large, established trees seemed to pop up out of nowhere. People who were resting nearby woke up, curious as to what was disturbing their sleep.

Ugo nudged his family, who were all still asleep. "Look."

They gasped when he pointed to Aurum, whose outline glowed against the still dark sky of the early morning. Only then could they finally make out his color. Aurum was the Gold One.

THE END

CPSIA information can be obtained
at www.ICGtesting.com
Printed in the USA
BVHW032144130220
572376BV00001B/4/J